"Ass[illegible] rewarding theme anthology requires a lot of skill on the part of its editors. Getting the mix just right is a delicate balancing act. Greenberg and Helfers pull off this delicate trick here. Variety and consanguinity are in harmony. There's something for every taste in this thoughtfully complied examination of the warrior spirit."

—*Realms of Fantasy*, for WARRIOR FANTASTIC

"Another great idea from Greenberg and his crew for an anthology of original stories. As usual, Greenberg and his collaborators are to be congratulated for helping preserve the great tradition of the short story."

—*SF Site*, for VILLIANS VICTORIOUS

"This neat little theme anthology contains a satisfying mixture of old hands' and newcomers' stories. Despite, or possibly as a result of, a literally limited topic, these stories cover a lot of ground while providing entertaining reading." —*Booklist*, for SPACE STATIONS

"There are some very strong stories in this collection . . . With stories tackling evil in the real world and in fantasy worlds, it's a strong collection that really takes advantage of the theme to tell some daring, and thoughtful tales. It's worth checking out."

—*Chronicle*, for IN THE SHADOW OF EVIL

SLIPSTREAMS

SLIPSTREAMS

EDITED BY
Martin H. Greenberg
and John Helfers

DAW BOOKS, INC.
DONALD A. WOLLHEIM, FOUNDER
375 Hudson Street, New York, NY 10014
ELIZABETH R. WOLLHEIM
SHEILA E. GILBERT
PUBLISHERS
http://www.dawbooks.com

DAW Book Collectors No. 1364.

DAW Books is distributed by Penguin Group (USA) Inc.

First Printing, May 2006
1 2 3 4 5 6 7 8 9

DAW TRADEMARK REGISTERED
U.S. PAT. OFF. AND FOREIGN COUNTRIES
—MARCA REGISTRADA
HECHO EN U.S.A.

PRINTED IN THE U.S.A.

ACKNOWLEDGMENTS

"Coin of the Realm," copyright © 2006 by Fiona Patton

"The Silver Knife," copyright © 2006 by Michael A. Stackpole

"The End of Spring," copyright © 2006 by Russell Davis

CONTENTS

INTRODUCTION

by John Helfers

WHEN THE IDEA for this anthology occurred to me, I will confess that I had at best an infirm grasp on what the definition of "slipstream" literature is. After looking over this collection of stories, I'm not sure I have any better understanding of the term now. I know that there will probably be those who pick this book up and say, "this is about as far from slipstream as you can get," and hurl it across the room, and—hopefully—there will be those who say, "some of these stories are slipstream, some of them aren't," and get at least a meaningful conversation about what the term means (or doesn't mean) out of it.

As near as I can tell, slipstream is a type of fiction that tries to alter a reader's perception of the world around them (in that sense, it is similar to most other forms of literature), or the world that they are reading about in the particular book they have stumbled upon. It seems to blend elements of modern (and postmodern, to give the deconstructionists their due) fiction with some sort of fantasy or magical realism, to create something that is worthy of a new name. Even defining the term takes us back to the parable of the blind men and the elephant, only in this case the elephant is bright pink, and may (or may not) have wings. So even if one of the men would touch every part of it, and assemble that into a picture of the animal in his mind, he still wouldn't have a clear idea of what he was looking at.

I will also confess that I did not give my authors a definition (such as it is) of slipstream literature. I simply asked for stories that combined two (or more) genres of any kind, and give me the result. To me, regardless of whether a novel or short story can be considered slipstream or not, the genre is simply a continuation of the fantastic literary tradition, which has been going on for centuries. The Greek author Lucian of Somostrata wrote his work *True History* in 175 AD, about taking a journey to the moon in a sailing ship carried by a whirlwind. If that didn't make the Greeks reexamine their reality, even with the myths of the gods, I don't know what would. Edgar Allan Poe's masterful tales "The Murders in Rue Morgue" and "The Tell-tale Heart," are to me prime examples of slipstream storytelling, both of which use elements of literature, horror, and psychology to create stunning tales that I would hope shook up the literary establishment in some fashion when they appeared. One could also make the case that the majority of Barry N. Malzberg's work is as slipstream as it gets (although I'm not sure how he will react to this suggestion). My point is that slipstream, in whatever form one chooses to think of it, is all around us, and has been for centuries. It just acquired a name recently.

Therefore, the notion of slipstream isn't really ahead of or outside the mainstream, but rather appears to have evolved into its own subgenre embracing the combination of disparate writing genres, themes, and tropes into a story that becomes something more than the sum of its parts. With that starting point in mind, I then sent out the call for stories.

As I had stated earlier, the twenty stories in this collection vary widely in subject, tone, scope, and just about any other convention one can think of. Some hold very closely to the nebulous slipstream, others stray about as far afield as one can go. What binds them together is, to me, what "slipstream" truly is: the blending of one or more disparate literary genres into a different kind of story, one that falls outside traditional literary conventions, perhaps even those of fantasy and science fiction. Therefore, this collection brings together fantasy westerns right next to science-fiction ghost stories. Romantic time travel disaster tales snuggle up to alternate history science fiction. Hard-boiled detective stories featuring reimagined myths follow up literary fantastic horror stories. And, yes, here and there are at least a few stories that should satisfy slipstream purists, however they define themselves or the genre.

The stories in the following pages represent to me what slipstream was, is, and can be. Whether you agree or disagree, my only real hope is that you enjoy them, since that, after all, is the real purpose of all fiction, no matter what genre it falls into—or between.

VENTING
A Mad Amos Malone story
by Alan Dean Foster

Alan Dean Foster's writing career began when August Derleth bought a long Lovecraftian letter of Foster's in 1968 and much to Foster's surprise, published it as a short story in Derleth's biannual magazine *The Arkham Collector*. His first attempt at a novel, *The Tar-Aiym Krang*, was bought by Betty Ballantine and published by Ballantine Books in 1972. It incorporates a number of suggestions from famed SF editor John W. Campbell. Since then, Foster's sometimes humorous, occasionally poignant, but always entertaining short fiction has appeared in all the major SF magazines as well as in original anthologies and several "Best of the Year" compendiums. Six collections of his short form work have also been published. His work to date includes excursions into hard science fiction, fantasy, horror, detective, western, historical, and contemporary fiction. In addition to publication in English, his work has appeared and won awards throughout the world. His novel *Cyber Way* won the Southwest Book Award for Fiction in 1990, the first work of science fiction ever to do so.

"YOU'RE GOING *WHERE?*" the clerk exclaimed, gaping at his customer. He exclaimed because of what the customer had just told him. He gaped because the individual looming over the service counter was not just a mountain man, but a mountain of a man.

Mad Amos Malone had that effect on people.

It wasn't just his height—a couple of inches short of seven feet. It wasn't just his size—bigger than most men and not a few bears. A lot had to do with his attitude: as if he'd already seen and done most everything, and wasn't ashamed to admit to it. Attitude, and maybe his eyes. They seemed to go in and out of focus, like the lens of a telescope, as if one moment the crazy giant was looking right at you and the next at some far-off distant land ordinary mortals knew nothing of and wouldn't dare visit even if offered the chance of an escorted visit.

"Yellowstone." Methodically, Malone fingered out coins from a leather pouch to pay for his goods. Salt pork and sugar, coffee and beans, tobacco, bacon, salt, pepper, bullets. Really big bullets, each one three and a half inches long. For buffalo, the clerk assumed. For other things, though Malone did not tell him what.

"Colter's Hell." The clerk, who was young, and skinny, and red-haired, and full of the cocky confidence of a youth too handsome and insufficiently wise, shook his head in disbelief. "Hard to believe they just made a park out of it. Who'd want to take a vacation trip to Hell?"

"Folks who git cold easy." The mountain man's massive arms enveloped his supplies and he turned to leave.

"Why you going there?" When Malone turned with a frown, the clerk (who, while not wise, was not entirely stupid) hastened to add, "If you don't mind my asking?"

Malone smacked his lips, two leathery lumps of flesh just visible in the depths of his black beard. The clerk thought he saw something else moving in there, but was chary of staring too long.

"Guvmint agent asked me to check out a certain part o' the new park. Somethin' 'bout some trailbreakers tryin' to chart a new course into the back country. 'Course, the whole park is new country. Fer most folks."

The clerk was unable to keep himself from probing just a little farther. "What about them?"

"Seems they didn't come out again."

The young man had another question or two tingling his tongue. He decided not to ask them, looking on as the giant ducked his head to clear the general store's front doorway and turned sideways to squeeze through. After allowing a discreet few moments to pass, however, he ambled outside. Doc Jensen was there, too, on the plank sidewalk, and Millicent Lawrence, the wife of Samuel Lawrence, the owner of the hardware store. The three of them stared in unison as the huge visitor rode out of town. As the extraordinary figure trotted past them, other townsfolk also stopped to gawp. But not for too long, lest their gawping be repaid in kind.

"Now what do you make of that?" Mrs. Lawrence's voice was a blend of emotions. "I declare, that is the largest human being I have ever set eyes on. And also the strangest. Almost as strange as that odd creature he is riding. I think it must be a horse, but of what breed I cannot for the life of me say."

"Told me he was going into the Yellowstone." Her marital status notwithstanding, the red-haired clerk had on occasion entertained impure thoughts regarding the attractive Mrs. Lawrence, and was pleased at the opportunity, however brief, to show off his knowledge of things passing strange. "Colter's Hell."

Doc Jensen nodded sagely and adjusted his spectacles. "I should say an entirely appropriate destination, from the look of him."

Worthless complained most of the time it took to reach the borders of the proud young nation's first national park. He continued complaining as they entered and proceeded to progress beyond the limits of the first tentative, hesitantly-marked trails, pushing into mountainous back country that was unknown and unsurveyed. It was possible that beneath the camouflaging leather patch on his forehead, the unicorn's trimmed-down horn was irritating him again, Malone knew. The next time they stopped, he would put some of that special ointment on it, the golden goo he had bought in a bazaar in Jaisalmer some considerable time ago, when crossing the Thar Desert.

It certainly was an outlandish place, this new park. In parts down low between the mountains, the ground steamed and hissed and suppurated, so that in the chill of autumn clouds rose upward to air-wrestle with those descending. The result was a climatological confusion that often left him squinting to see through the resultant heavy fog. The surveyors and soldiers who had forced fitful penetration into this isolated pocket of the country feared stepping into concealed pools of water hot enough to fry man and mount alike, or being swallowed by steaming mud that would boil off a man's boots before he could reach proper ground. Such concerns didn't worry Malone. Even with one eye locked in a permanent squint, Worthless could sense and avoid dangerous earth long before he put his hoof in it, so to speak.

Days had passed since Malone had seen another human being. Bears and elk, yes. Fox and beaver in plenty. Even wolves, who came close, perhaps drawn by the prospect of prey, perhaps by the wolf's skull cap that adorned Malone's head. When that cap winked back at them, the paralleling pack hesitated. When it threw back its half head and howled, they took off running so fast they left more than one unintentional longitudinal marker behind them in the shallow snow.

It wasn't yet deep. Too early in the season for that. But if the party Malone had been deputed to find didn't get out quick, they'd be trapped by some of the coldest, snowiest weather on the continent. That was what Malone had been hired to do: find 'em, and bring them out. Difficult work, given the first snow and the absence of much in the way of trail spoor. If anyone could do it, he and Worthless could. The unicorn was not pleased with the undertaking. This time of year, he much preferred the company of a warm stable and compliant mares. Or, not being particularly particular, t'other way around.

The faint tracks of those who had preceded them eventually led man and mount down into a valley furiously alive with the earth's breath. Intermittent geysers spewed hissing whale spouts of water into the crystal-clear air of morning. Noxious gases vented from fumaroles while mud pits bubbled and stewed like the paint pots of the maddest of damned artists. Lush evergreens blanketed the surrounding mountainsides. High overhead, an eagle screamed. Searching diligently for prey, it saw only a lone rider on horseback: too big to carry off, too big to ignore.

Sympathetic to the plight of any creature whose daily foraging amounted to endless searching for moving needles in a geologic haystack, Malone threw back his head and screamed a reply. This so startled the eagle that it banked in midair sharply enough to shed a feather. In the way of eagles and hawks, their consequent conversation was shorter than Hawthorne or Melville would have countenanced.

Eagle: Seen any vermin?

Malone: Nope

Eagle: 'Bye.

He continued on, moving ever deeper into the valley of mist and ground-hugging fog. The trail of the party he was tracking grew fainter and fainter, until even he had trouble telling the difference between particles of soil that had been disturbed by man and horse and those that had simply been roiled by the unsettled Earth. It was when he was turning back, with an eye toward retracing part of the trail already traversed, that a noise most peculiar made him pause and look to his right.

Worthless was plodding gingerly around the fringe of a vast bubbling and popping mud pit. Nothing out of the locally ordinary there. It was only when a portion of the pit studdenly rose up and assumed human shape to confront Malone that he took serious notice.

The mountain man thought he was more than middling familiar with the general panoply of demonic manifestations, but this was the first time he had ever seen a mudunculus. Point of fact, he'd never even *heard* of a mudunculus. But that surely was one looming there before him, its feet sunk deep in the bubbling gunk and its distorted, lopsided, coffee-hued head flashing fangs at him from the midst of a mouth of muck. It had heavy, muscular mud arms that reached all the way to the ground; a tapering, wickedly whiplike tail; a bald, slick skull; long ears that drooped like those of a bloodhound from the sides of its head; penetrating eyes of blazing brown; and a nose that was as pointed as its glare. It grinned down at Malone from a very great height indeed. Strong men would have panicked at the sight, and women fainted.

Not Mad Amos Malone. He'd done seen quite a bit.

The mudunculus was certainly impressive. Steam rose and curled from its huge body which, though quite naked, was covered in thick searing sludge that contributed a thankful modesty.

"Oho!" it burbled delightedly. "Another surveyor. And just in time for breakfast."

"Don't mind if I do." Sliding down out of the saddle, Malone commenced to rummaging in one of the hefty saddlebags that was slung across Worthless' back. As the creature of the depths stared, the mountain man unlimbered skillet, spoon, and fixins.

Instant insanity the demon expected. Insouciance was not a reaction to which it was accustomed.

"You pathetic human, I was not issuing an invitation. *You* are to be breakfast! You, and that toothsome-looking nag you rode in on."

Busy setting up his skillet and accoutrements, Malone glanced idly in his mount's direction, then back at the mudunculus. "I've heard Worthless called a sight many things. I've called him more names than most, myself. But I reckon 'toothsome' is a new one." Using kit from his saddlebags, he carefully began to build a fire under the skillet, making a cooking pit of stones to contain it. "I believe I rightly heard you call me 'another' surveyor. By that I'm supposin' you have some knowledge of them that come here afore me?"

The mountain man's curiosity restored the demon's grin. "Truthfully, I do. They were not welcome." Dripping mud of different colors and extreme temperature, enormous arms spread wide, as if to encompass all that man and demon alike could see. "This is my home. None may come here without my permission. All who trespass are doomed to meet the same fate." One long, thick finger pointed meaningfully toward a nearby geyser mound. "Behold the fate that is to be yours, master of some small courage."

Leaning slightly forward as he crouched by his skillet, Malone was just able to see around the edge of the built-up mound of sulfates and silicates and such. It shaded a pile of bones. Human bones, roughly disarticulated and bleached white as chalk. At least three skulls stared back at him. There might have been more. He nodded slowly to himself.

He had found the missing party of surveyors.

Showing foot-long fangs, the mudunculus leaned forward. "Do you not tremble at the sight? Are you not melting with fear? You have but a moment longer to live before your flesh is boiled from your living bones, as was theirs!"

Having stood, Malone returned to hunting through a saddlebag. "Y'know," he declared absently, "there's a real trick to carryin' eggs on horseback." One hand full of henfruit, he headed back to the skillet. "Takes jest the right kind o' packin', and the right kind o' horse."

"Unworthy one! You have no respect. I think perhaps you are already mad." A great sucking sound ensued as the demon took a giant step forward. Not toward Malone, but past him, to his left. "Watch then, as I consume first your beloved animal, so that you may see what is in store for your own body!"

Eggs sizzling in the cast-iron skillet, Malone glanced up. "Wouldn't try that if I were you."

The progeny of the pit ignored him. Leaning forward, mouth agape, it brought its jaws down hard on Worthless's hindquarters. Turning its head, the horse looked back and, as usual, squinted.

There was a snapping, crunching sound. But it came not from Worthless' legs or pelvis, nor from his spine. Rather the sound was of one fang snapping. Letting out a cry of hurt and surprise, the demon drew back sharply. One massive hand felt of its upper jaw. A great tooth had broken in half, and its orthodontic companions were throbbing painfully.

"What manner of monstrous beast is this?"

Malone eyed Worthless, who had gone back to nibbling at the ground. "A tough one." His gaze shifted to the still stunned demon. "I reckon y'would have figured that out if you'd taken the time t'notice thet he's croppin' calcite, not grass." Eggs well on their way to cooking in the skillet, he added bacon. "Settles his stomach, it does." His gaze narrowed. When Amos Malone's gaze narrowed, anything in the vicinity that had an ounce of sense turned and fled. It did not speak well for the demon that it remained where it was.

Malone continued. "Now you harken to me, Mister Mud-Face. This here piece o' ground has been declared the first national park o' this young country by none other than President Grant himself. It's to be open to all." With one powerful, calloused hand, he gestured at the seething, steaming landscape spread out before him. "Myself, I don't have no problem with you keepin' yer house here. I pride myself on gettin' along with every sort o' critter, no matter how disagreeable their personal habits. But this here consumin' o' visitors, that's gonna have to stop."

Used to being feared, the mudunculus was so furious at the mountain man's words that he forgot the loss of his half a fang.

"Miserable little human! Worthless worm that burrows in dung! You dare to dictate to Nagaroth, Lord of Heat and Fire? I have changed my mind. I will not boil you alive. I will melt the meat from your bones—slowly—leaving your vitals for last, and begin consuming them while you are still alive!" Reaching down into the swirling stew of boiling earth and water at his feet, he dragged up a handful of blazing, glowing dust. "The flesh of your face will be first to burn!" Drawing back its arm, it flung the handful straight at Malone.

Putting up a fair-sized hand of his own, the mountain man caught the flaming dust before it could strike him. Carefully, he deposited a pinch or two in his skillet before dumping the rest aside. Smoke rose briefly from his thick-skinned palm.

"Thankee fer the brimstone. 'Tain't good Mexican spice, but it'll do. I like a little zest in my eggs."

Eyes bulging with barely controlled fury, the demon took a long, deep breath. Then it pursed its ugly lips, and spat. A stream of boiling water shot right for Malone. Though the spray was hot enough to sear the paint off the front of an unlicensed saloon, he only leaned slightly to his left.

The water struck him face on. For a moment, he was completely obscured by the resulting gush of steam.

Nagaroth's grin, which had been absent for a number of minutes, now returned as he waited to see the results of his scalding aqueous assault. When the steam cleared, his face fell in full-featured flabbergastment—fell literally and almost to his chest, in fact, as it oozed downward.

Malone sat, intact and sturdy, behind his skillet. Steam rose from his fringed leather jacket, from his pants, from his boots and from his face. Turning his head to his right, he sniffed at one underarm before looking back at the astonished demon.

"Thanks, there. First time in a month this outfit's been proper clean, and that I've had a decent bath." Leaning forward, he squinted down at the top of one boot. "Even killed the lice, I do believe."

It was at that point that the demon Nagaroth went slightly berserk; thrashing the mud in which its feet were immersed, howling at the sky, beating its broad chest, and causing huge bubbles of mud to rise and burst all around it. Geysers erupted and fumaroles belched, while the very earth underfoot quivered fit to suggest the great Missouri quake of 1811.

The demon threw fire at Malone. It only made his bacon cook faster. He threw hot stones. The mountain man effortlessly dodged them, save one nicely shaped one he grabbed to employ as a seat. Only then did the thwarted, frustrated fiend do something so horrific, so terrible, that it finally drew Amos Malone's undivided attention.

Leaning far forward and reaching out, it roughly slapped the skillet to one side.

Worthless looked up immediately. Normally utterly unflappable, the half-horse, half-unicorn's eyes grew wide. It began backing up, away from the scene of the tragedy. High above, a certain eagle looked down sharply, took notice of something singularly unpleasant, and hightailed it for the biggest tree it could find.

His gaze fixed on his ruined breakfast, Malone slowly rose. Not as high as the demon, but high enough. He eyed the ruins of the nearly crisp bacon and the almost ready eggs for a long moment. Then he turned his attention wholly to the one who had committed the unforgivable sin.

You can shoot a mountain man more than once. You can cut him with a knife, or filch his goods, or impugn his ancestry, or question his manhood. But you do not, not ever, mess with his breakfast.

"That," Malone declared in a low tone of voice that similarly caused the earth underfoot to tremble slightly, "was a dang near impolite thing to do."

"Suffer!" Pleased (and perhaps a mite relieved) to have finally unsettled his unexpectedly unimpressed victim, Nagaroth shook a fist in the mountain man's direction. "Soon you too will be part of the soil, and no more."

"Now you lookee here, my overheated unhygienic friend. Because I were raised polite, I'm givin' you one last chance to agree to the requirement I've laid down. Otherwise, it's banishment forever from this valley, an' to a place where I guarantee you'll get no rest."

Nagaroth shook his head slowly. "You are a fit opponent, I avow. Yet you are but mortal, while I am of one with the eternal elements. You will die here, as will all who come after you: man, woman, or child." The demon raised both arms skyward. "I will build terraces of their bones."

"Have it your way, then." It was Malone's turn to shake *his* head. "I swan, but demons are stubborn folk." As the mountain man lifted one foot high, Nagaroth prepared to parry what it expected to be a blow of feeble and futile strength.

But Malone did not kick out. Instead, he brought his foot down hard; once, twice, several times in succession. Rattled, the earth shook underfoot, and the resulting concussion knocked bewildered squirrels out of their trees for a mile around.

Six times Malone stamped the ground, then six times again. By the third set of six, Nagaroth was sensing the imminency of his coming triumph. If kicking dirt was the best this insolent human could muster by way of a defense, then their confrontation was nearing an end before it had even begun. Lifting first one leg out of the mud, then the other, he started forward, great hands outstretched. No slow boiling for this one, he decided. He would smother it, fill its impudent mouth with hot mud until it choked.

A fountain of flame erupted between Malone and the oncoming demon. So hot was it that the very rocks themselves seemed to draw back in fear. A blast of sulfur corrupted the clean mountain air. Worthless looked on a moment, then dropped his head and went back to cropping calcite.

Out of the fire and the heat and the flame stepped a singular figure. It was impeccably garbed in the oufit of a professional gambler, and a successful one at that. Ruffled white shirt with neatly looped black string tie, gleaming black vest beneath black jacket, black pants and boots, all shone as if just lifted from the haberdasher's shelf. The narrow, vulturine face featured a small, perfectly pointed goatee complimented by a thin mustache the end curls of which defied logic as well as gravity. The teeth were pointed, as was the switching, ever-moving tail that protruded from the seat of the black pants, and the two small horns on its head punched neatly through the custom tailored, wide-brimmed black hat. As it approached the mountain man, smiling a smile of immaculate, eternal evil, it extended a hand.

Malone did not shake it. Instead, he nodded a curt greeting.

"Mornin', Nick."

"Good morning, Mr. Malone. Good to see you again."

"Wish I could say the same. You remember that little scrape I got you out of not long these many years ago?"

"Ah, yes." The figure in the gambler's outfit murmured softly. "I never forget such things. Could have been most personally embarrassing."

"Well, I'm callin' in that card today." Lifting his gaze, he nodded at the still figure of the demon Nagaroth, who had been shocked into immobility. "This here property is now a park. Its plenty big, with room enough for all manner o' critters—but the nature o' the real estate notwithstandin', I reckon there jest ain't no room for bone-scourin' demonics." He smiled thinly. "His is a presence that might have a tendency to dissuade folks who might otherwise be inclined to come a-visitin'."

The gambler turned to confront the demon, who quelled visibly. "Sire, I was only being myself. By all the sacrosanct laws that govern. . . ."

"Shut up." Eyes no ordinary human could meet and survive locked on the now quaking demon. Their owner sighed. "This is what comes of giving the immortal impious a measure of individual independence. They invariably overreach themselves." He raised a hand, the nails of which, while pointed and sharp as knives, were exquisitely manicured.

"*Sire, no,* I beg of you, I . . . !"

Thunder, dark and nasty, rolled across the valley. By the time it had died away, so had the formerly invincible demon Nagaroth. Using both hands to give a little tug-down on the hem of his fine vest, the gambler turned back to the one who had summoned him forth.

"You're a piece of work, you are, Amos Malone." Eyes flashed. "I now consider my old debt to you to be repaid. The next time we meet. . . ." His expression, that had begun to darken, was once more replaced by a smile of suave iniquity. "I look forward to the day when our respective positions of strength are reversed, and I can summon *you*—for a visit to my place of dwelling."

Malone snorted. "Good thing you're immortal, 'cause I reckon that's about how long you'll have to wait. And even when thet time cometh, I plan on plantin' my backside elsewhere." He glanced skyward. "Still, it's a fine morning, if a bit chilly. Would be ill-mannered of me not to offer to share breakfast with a fellow traveler, however mean and rotten be his immortal soul." He indicated the overturned skillet. "Have to start all over agin, though. Your minion made a mess o' things."

Taking a seat on the ground, the gambler indicated his acceptance. "I'm *always* chilly, up thisaway. I like my bacon and eggs well done, if you please, and my toast . . ."

"Burnt. I know." Malone started back for his saddlebags. As he did so, the Devil called after him.

"It is no small matter for one to summon me, much

less to freely cancel so powerful an obligation." He looked back to the place that had formerly been the home of the now banished and disgraced demon Nagaroth. "Something of considerable consequence must have ensued for you to do so."

Returning with eggs and bacon and bread, Malone whispered a few words to the upended skillet, causing it to tumble and bounce its way across the ground until it was once more comfortable situated above the circle of rocks that surrounded the cooking fire. Occasionally, a flicker of flame would burst forth from beneath the heavy cast iron to caress one of old Nick's boots, like a cat licking its master.

"Why, I should think it would be obvious, in a place like this." Tossing the bacon onto the skillet, Malone watched as it started to sizzle. He began cracking eggs. "Your former underling, why, he got me good and steamed."

FROM GEHENNA

by Isaac Szpindel

Isaac Szpindel is an award-winning author and screenwriter who is also a producer, electrical engineer and medical doctor/neurologist. His short fiction includes the Aurora-Award-winning "When the Morning Stars Sang Together" from the DAW's *ReVisions* anthology that Isaac co-edited with Julie E. Czerneda; and "Ineffable," a horror fantasy that recently appeared in DAW's *In the Shadow of Evil*. Isaac's screenwriting has been translated into many languages and has credits including Warner Bros. and Disney. Isaac is also a frequent academic lecturer, and an on-air guest on Canadian television. Visit his website at www.geocities.com/canadian_sf/szpindel/

THE JEWISH SABBATH DESCENDS upon the work week at dusk and in graceful modesty, like a bride. And on the eve of this most holy day it is said that the Holy Name endows the world with a second soul of sanctity that adheres to only the most virtuous and most pious. So it would be for her, knew Fruma-Malka the butcher's widow, as she ripped through the flesh of the freshly slaughtered chicken that lay prostrate on the worn cutting block before her. The centerpiece of a fine feast to welcome the bride's weekly return to Fruma-Malka and to her sweet son Baruch, her world entire. Even in this dying day of a consumptive London August of the gentile year of 1888 and even in this kitchen of this miserable Wentworth Street tenement left to her by her late husband Jacob, may he rest in peace.

With great care and with great skill, Fruma-Malka drained the last drops of blood from the fowl's carcass and commenced removing its organs in the manner in which she had been instructed by her husband the butcher in the years that had followed their marriage. And although it was, after all, a Jewish woman's duty to support her husband in all his business, Fruma-Malka had discovered she had both a talent and a taste for such work. The feel of freshly slaughtered flesh, the oily smell of the fat appealed to her in ways that even her husband did not, so that Fruma-Malka gave herself wholeheartedly to her husband's work if not to her husband himself.

Over the years the tissues of the butcher's trade had attached themselves to Fruma-Malka and she had grown greatly in girth. Yet, in the service or her work, her stout arms and plump fingers moved with uncanny speed, unhampered even now by the smothering bulk of the leather butcher's apron that enveloped her five-foot frame and that had rightly belonged to her Jacob when he had so passionately inhabited this world. These lustful passions, knew Fruma-Malka, had caused everyone to both love and respect the man, but they had also been responsible for hastening him to paradise. Fruma-Malka, however, had little interest in such nonsense and little passion for flesh that was not ritually slaughtered. For this reason, Fruma-Malka had been careful to confine her duties to the butcher shop and to the kitchen. Jacob had understood this, but had been nevertheless unable to govern his passion and Fruma-Malka knew that he had been given dispensation by the Rabbi to relieve his urges among the Low-London *kurvehs* whose diseases became the means of her Jacob's death.

For this Fruma-Malka harbored no guilt. What else was she to do? Fruma-Malka had attempted many cures for her husband's affliction. On one occasion she had even entertained the possibility that a lustful *Dybbuk*, a departed wandering soul guilty of some horrible crime, had attached itself to Jacob. Why else would a man want a woman for such constant nonsense beyond the required act of procreation? Fruma-Malka had gone to great lengths and great expense to procure a rare kabbalistic text that was said to contain a cure and a protection from such possessions, but this, too, failed to exorcise Jacob's distasteful passions. Fortunately, Fruma-Malka had never succumbed to these desires. The Holy One, praised be His Name, tests the flesh in many ways, and where Jacob, mercy upon his soul, had failed, Fruma-Malka had managed to succeed.

Better Jacob should seek his pleasures in the next world, thought Fruma-Malka, than to have shared with her his affliction in this one. And even so, she was not the one to be blamed, for had she not, as required, borne Jacob a son soon after marriage? Had she not been the one to suffer both the pain of Jacob and the pain of childbirth within the same bed, just as the Holy Name had promised would be the fate of all the daughters of Eve on the expulsion from Eden? Still, such a perfect son, such a reward as Baruch, seemed just reparation for even such great indignity and pain.

"Yes," said Fruma-Malka aloud. "For such suffering, I am not to be blamed, for nothing."

And it was a sign from the heavens, thought Fruma-Malka, that at that very moment, she should be removing not just the slaughtered hen's innards, but that she should be removing its reproductive organs. "A most kosher hen for the Sabbath. Blessed be The Name," she incanted, "who created heaven and earth, man and woman."

With dutiful alacrity and pious respect she placed the hen's womb over the carcass's left shoulder in the manner proscribed commemorating the ancient sacrifices made at the Holy Temple in Jerusalem before the Jews had been expelled and spread to the corners of the earth. The womb was the holy of holies within which The Name performed miracles. Baruch had been one such miracle and so was to be treasured and protected, especially in these solemn *days of awe* that preceded the Jewish New Year and the terrible Day of Atonement where all sins were to be accounted for. With no father, it fell to Fruma-Malka to protect this miracle, their Baruch, from the outside world and from the world on high as this ultimate day of judgment, Yom Kippur, approached.

"Mamma?" Baruch's voice nearly startled the bloody knife from Fruma-Malka's hand as it startled her thoughts back from her reverie. Surely, this was another sign, thought Fruma-Malka as she regained control of the knife and composed herself, that Baruch should pick this moment to approach his loving mother. His face glistened with the fervor of study, and the scraggle of beard that refused to take hold upon his milky chin made him appear like a child in Purim makeup. *Too thin,* thought Fruma-Malka. It made his dark eyes look sunken and sullen. She would fatten him up properly, for was he not now eighteen years old and in need of a wife?

"A snack, my sugar and spice?" she offered, and pecked Baruch on the forehead, leaving behind a strand of spittle that attached the two for an additional instant.

"No, Mamma, Nahum and I were meditating on a passage, we didn't hear you come in and then, the hacking . . ." Baruch looked down at the bloody corpse with an expression of disgust. He was much too delicate for such things. He could never be a butcher like his father, nor would he likely succumb to the same distractions his father had. Baruch's passion was for Torah, not for flesh. He was a gifted student, like a hummingbird over his books, who even the Rabbi trusted in the guidance of his own son, Nahum. This was the source of much *naches* to Fruma-Malka and of much respect from within the Jewish community of Spitalfields. As the two had become inseparable, Fruma-Malka *kvelled* with bursting pride—the Rabbi's boy! Such a son as Baruch guaranteed Fruma-Malka, and even her errant Jacob, an honored place in the afterlife. So it was said. Still, Fruma-Malka knew well that jealousy often follows a boy such as hers like a hungry dog follows the butcher's wagon, and for this reason she had on every day placed a slender crimson thread as bright as blood upon her son's person in order to blind the evil eye and to stifle wagging tongues. Perhaps she should have done the same for her poor Jacob?

"And what of my hacking and tearing, it disturbs your

precious studies?" Fruma-Malka teased her Baruch. "You work so hard, both you and Nahum, it is almost Sabbath, time for rest."

"The Holy One, blessed be His Name, rested only on, and not until, the Sabbath," countered Baruch.

Fruma-Malka beamed with a satisfaction that overcame her disappointment in Baruch's lack of appreciation of the Sabbath meal she was preparing for him. "So smart you are, my boy. With the wisdom of Solomon and the beauty of Joseph. *Ptoo, ptoo, ptoo.*" She spat three times onto the floor to ward off any evil spirit that might now be listening and looking for an unsuspecting victim as perfect as her son. "Go back to your studies and to Nahum. I will be quiet so you shouldn't be disturbed."

Baruch turned and left, his dark locks bouncing before his ears and below his skullcap, his dark disheveled jacket topping half-buttoned pants with the prayer fringes spilling over and making it appear as if he'd only now wakened late and had dressed too hastily. *Time only for Torah, that one,* thought Fruma-Malka, *I will reward his dedication, so he will forgive my disturbance.*

Deftly and with the back of the blade Fruma-Malka herded the chicken's organs onto a square of wax butcher's paper, which she then wrapped into a package tied with string and which she marked with a chalk X to identify unkosher remains meant for disposal. From the breadbox on her left she removed a dark and spongy loaf of pumpernickel and with artistic grace she withdrew a wooden-handled bread knife from a nearby block and sliced two even pieces out from the center. Seeds scattered and the bread released a pungently sour aroma that intermingled with the salty odor of sweat and work. From the ice box she removed a jar containing sediments of a waxy pale gelatin separated by layers of yellow fluid: her best chicken fat. The fat's sweet oily scent completed the fragrant symphony that was to be her gift to Baruch and Nahum.

And as she buttered the glossy layers of fat onto the bread, Fruma-Malka knew that with this generous delicacy that she prepared now for such two perfect boys, and without a thought for herself, she had become once again worthy of inhabitance by an additional Sabbath soul.

On her best porcelain serving dish left to her by her grandmother, Fruma-Malka carefully laid out the two slick slices of fattened bread. She then pulled back the gray-brushed auburn nest that was her hair and wove it into a tight bun. Through all her troubles, Fruma-Malka had managed to retain a stout beauty as was befitting a woman of her child-bearing age and girth. Her pale hazel eyes lay even now like pearls within rich beds of cream separated by a thin slice of nose. Fruma-Malka might have attracted another man, a widower perhaps, but she had no desire, and even less time now that she cared alone for Baruch, for such an inconvenience. Fruma-Malka's only concern remained to appear presentable before the Rabbi's son and her own.

Removing the apron from the fullness of her frame, and with the dish held before her like the treasures of Solomon, Fruma-Malka padded quietly down the hallway that connected the kitchen to the other rooms of the apartment, including the study that harbored her son. She would drift in while they studied and would wordlessly place her fatty confection before them as a bee offering honey to its queen. And just as silently she would exit without a word of thanks, not even a pardon for her previous disturbance. Her reward for this generosity, along with many others, would be hers in the next world. And, true to her expectations, as she floated toward the thin study door, Fruma-Malka could now perceive the ecstatic exhortations of the boys' passionate prayer to the extent that it filled her with a spirit of such joy and contentment that left no room for that of the coming Sabbath bride.

With surprisingly elegance, but fitting speed for a butcher's wife, Fruma-Malka unlatched the study door and slipped through the opening she had newly created between the secular and the sanctified.

Fruma-Malka was then rendered completely dumb. She remained paralyzed by the sight before her, for a time that seemed to her to rival the forty years the Israelites had wandered lost in the desert. Another less pious, less virtuous, soul might easily have been struck blind by that which she beheld, but not Fruma-Malka, who remained transfixed like a pillar of salt for what seemed like an eternity. Like Lot's wife gazing upon Sodom.

SMASH.

Fruma-Malka's porcelain serving dish that had once been her grandmother's had not survived witnessing the horror. Like the snapping of a hen's neck, it shattered against the floor with a great and brief explosion that scattered its shards to the study's four corners.

"Mamma!" gasped Baruch. He stumbled off Nahum the Rabbi's son, turning away to hide his nakedness, and likely his shame, from his mother.

"No, no," whispered Fruma-Malka, "not my boy. This is not my boy. Such a thing . . . my perfect boy, like unblemished cream, your skin was. Those nights I endured your father, those nine months I carried you, and then the two days whole I suffered to bring you into this world. And now, this!"

Nahum the Rabbi's son stood erect between the two, saying nothing and grinning haughtily, like a drunken *Moshgiach* expecting his customary bribe for blessing the day's slaughter. Fruma-Malka fixed him in her hazel eyes. "You enchanted my perfect boy?"

"Mamma, he didn't," Baruch interceded, "I wanted—"

"Your father, then, I should spit on his grave. He did this to you? Did he take you to those two-shilling *kurvehs?* They put their disease in you now, too?"

"Mamma, Papa tried, but I couldn't. I didn't want, and he understood, they understood. Won't you now understand?"

"I am to you like those *kurvehs*. You perform these acts because whores, they understand? The words of harlots are higher to you than those of the Torah?" Tears rusted the razors of Fruma-Malka's eyes as she searched the study shelves around her. The many volumes, texts, and manuscripts were all witnesses made unclean by the acts performed within their embrace. What works had they defiled? The holy Torah itself, its various commentaries, the writings of Miamonides, even the kabbalistic text with which she had tried to cure her Jacob. And on this book, all at once, it became clear to Fruma-Malka. She knew immediately what had occurred and what was to be done. The mystic text and its presence in this room was a sign as surely and as clear as the Holy Name's rainbow after the flood.

"I know you now, *DYBBUK!* I have found you out!" she cried out and snatched the kabbalistic text from its perch.

"No, Mamma, I am not possessed, there is no dybbuk."

"I should believe you now, dybbuk? You perform such crimes and I should not expect you also to lie?"

"Mamma, dybbuks are for fairy tales and stories. Superstition like your crimson threads. Please don't do this. Sit down, let me dress, and let us discuss."

Fruma-Malka ignored the creature that had been her son and thumbed the pages of the kabbalistic volume until she reached the passage that she had previously marked and that she knew so well having attempted it so many times in the case of her Jacob. This time, however, she would not fail. Her Baruch, her world entire, was at stake. With divine justice and holy fervor at her left and at her right Fruma-Malka incanted the words proscribed in the book of exorcism in a voice devoid of melody. And when she had completed the passage, she started anew, repeating it over and over, fervently, desperately.

"You see," pleaded Baruch, "nothing. It is only me and Nahum. Now will you please, stop and listen to us?"

Fruma-Malka ignored him. She had no patience for the lies of a dybbuk, no matter its host. No doubt it intended to trick her by appealing to her love for her son.

Turning to the Rabbi's son, Baruch continued. "Go, Nahum, it's no use now. Better my mother shouldn't share this insane *mishigas* also with you."

But Nahum the Rabbi's son did not go. He had, however, changed. The expression had fallen from his face and his countenance had gone wan. A few years Baruch's senior, he had retained much of his baby flesh and now that flesh trembled. The trembling rose to a shaking that threw the skullcap off the curls of his head and that swung his earlocks like violent pendulums from his temples.

"Nahum?" Baruch's lips trembled and distorted his lover's name.

Fruma-Malka, seeing the change overcome Nahum, stopped for one brief moment, shocked by her own success, then intensified her refrain with the renewed hope that she would soon also drive the possession from her Baruch.

A lump the size of a fist suddenly appeared as if it had burrowed in and stretched the skin of Nahum's abdomen. It then commenced to traveling about under his skin, bobbing and weaving a sinister subcutaneous path.

Baruch stumbled back and fell to his knees as the lump rose and settled in Nahum's throat. Nahum's mouth opened, and through lips that did not move a shrill voice that was not Nahum's emanated from his body. "Stop, Jewess. Do not cleave me from this host. I have left your son in peace. He has acted only according to his nature."

"You are a liar, dybbuk!" cried Fruma-Malka, halting the incantation and commencing the next stage of the exorcism. She must now force from the dybbuk its confession. "Speak! What crime denied you the next world and made you this?"

"Three hundred years ago," the voice began, "as a young man full of passion for the Torah, I studied at the feet of the great Rabbi Luria in the holy town of Safed nestled among the mountains of the Galilee. It was said that the *Shehina*, the Holy Spirit itself, resided above Safed after the destruction of the Temple had razed its home. But the *Shehina* and the Torah were not enough to slake my thirst for the flesh. And so, in time, I found another who was full of similar passion and I took a lover from among my fellow students. And until now, I had not found another like him. His skin tasted of coriander and his complexion was like the purest milk, and when he spoke his words were as honey to my ears.

"But at this time there was a merchant with whom my lover boarded, and this merchant, he had a daughter. She was dull of thought and plain to the eye, but she offered my lover one accursed boon where I could not—and this was a child. And so, with the promises of a harlot and a rich dowry befitting a merchant's daughter, my lover left me and was wed to her.

"Good to her whorish promise, the bitch was soon fat with child. And as her belly grew, they took to fulfilling the good deed of accepting guests, myself included, to their Sabbath table. So also did my rage grow at the love that had been stolen from me and at the lover who had forsaken me even though his passions, I was sure, remained only for me.

"At one such Sabbath meal where I was the guest, I could bear no more. I rose from the table, and seizing the ceremonial knife with which my former lover and host intended to perform the ceremonial blessing of the bread, I engraved the enormity of my jagged rage upon their flesh. First I slashed the life from my lover's bosom so that I could watch his heart bleed as he had caused mine to. This proved too much for his false bride to endure, so that I found the whore senseless and waiting for me to rip the unborn abomination and her thieving womb from her body, for were they not the cause of my misfortune?

"I shed no tears for her or for what might have been their daughter, but finally I was overcome with remorse over the loss of my lover. So, in my final act I turned the blade upon myself to reunite with my lover in the paradise of the next world.

"I had erred terribly. And while my lover, his wife, and their daughter frolicked in paradise, I was denied. When not even the accursed depths of Gehenna would open their gates to me, I was forced to return from there to become what you find before you, a dybbuk, condemned to wander from host to host, to inhabit the bodies of the weakest-minded and the nonbelievers among us.

"Far too many souls provided ready purchase for my *attachments,* with their disbeliefs and their doubts and I became downhearted until, after a time, I discovered that in some instances I could pursue my passions for the flesh once more. Yet, as I recommenced my activities, the accursed Luria found me out and cast me from my next victim. But with so many hosts at the ready, and doubt inhabiting minds that even Luria thought safe, I had little difficulty in fleeing elsewhere to exercise my passions for masculine flesh and for revenge upon the feminine. I was especially vicious with the harlots who were to me like my lover's bride whose womb had stolen my love. And just as Luria found me out once again and prepared to destroy my soul utterly, merciful fate delivered me in the form of a terrible disease that swept him as well as many others from this world. With the Rabbi wandering the heavenly plane, I did likewise upon this earthly counterpart and began my violent and lascivious travels. And so, over time, I have come to London and to you."

With this story completed, and as described within the kabbalistic instructions of Fruma-Malka's text, the body of Nahum the Rabbi's son fell to the floor in fierce convulsions. And as the shaking continued, the lump ascended Nahum's neck toward his open mouth. Nothing appeared, but the body stopped its flailing, given over to naked sleep upon the boards of the tenement floor.

Fruma-Malka turned to Baruch. "Now, you are safe. He will not bother you again."

But before Baruch could respond, Fruma-Malka watched in horror as Baruch's body flopped to the floor and began floundering like a fish removed from water. And as he gasped for air, a lump appeared in his throat and descended to his abdomen.

"No!" Fruma-Malka screamed. "He is innocent." Fruma-Malka's voice quivered with fear, and confusion. Her world entire was the dybbuk's host now, and it was because of her.

Suddenly, taking advantage of Fruma-Malka's momentary lapse, Baruch the dybbuk sprang to his feet and with preternatural speed, reached out to rip the mystic manuscript from her quivering hand. The shrill voice emanated through Baruch's motionless lips and naked body now. "He is innocent, whore, and his soul resists me with much strength. I prefer much stronger bodies and much weaker souls."

"Then leave him," she pleaded.

"I intend to, by my own will, and without the words

of this filthy book," stated the shrill lipless voice, then Baruch's arm shot out, sending the text flying past Fruma-Malka and across the room. "Once I have found a better host."

Fruma-Malka thought on this. Surely there was an orphan or a simpleton or a nonbeliever in this very tenement, but it would take time to find him and she could not abide the demon within her naked son's form one moment longer.

"Then take me, instead, and I will find you a new host," offered Fruma-Malka. A dybbuk was as trustworthy as a *Moshgiach* drunk on unkosher wine, but what choice had she?

"I have never worn a womb-bearing garment before. I am not so sure you will suit me, whore, even for a short while."

"I am no *kurveh!* I am a woman of valor, beyond rubies and pearls, and I have never given myself freely to another man. It is a *kurveh* who made you this. *Kurvehs* who took from me my husband and also now my son." Fruma-Malka spat on the floor. "I hate them as you do. Take me and do as you will, but understand, I do this only for my son, I will be blamed for nothing."

Baruch the dybbuk reached out and curled his fingers about Fruma-Malka's wrists. The lump rose up his throat and disappeared through his open mouth. Immobilized by her son and by her terror, Fruma-Malka accepted the dybbuk within her as she had accepted no other man before.

She felt a momentary chill of ice and a sharp pain as she lost control of her shaking form.

With the taste of blood in her mouth, Fruma-Malka awoke beside the unconscious forms of Baruch and Nahum on the floor beside her. Like lambs they slept, their chests rising and falling lightly now without the weight of the dybbuk upon them. As she regarded them, so peaceful in their sleep, she looked up through the study window to see three stars appear in the night sky, heralds of the Sabbath.

And on this twenty-fourth day of Elul in the year 5648, Friday, August 31, 1888, to the gentiles, Fruma-Malka knew that she was not alone. She knew that a second soul had indeed attached itself to her own, and she rose, feeling strong and full of revenge in these *days of awe* before the High Holy Days. Then she retraced her steps to the kitchen and reclaimed her leather apron. Once there and with care, she wrapped her knives in wax paper and tied them lovingly with string. And perhaps out of habit, she marked the package with a chalk X.

This time the shrill voice of the dybbuk spoke within her. *We are strong and skilled, my dear, a fine garment for our work this Sabbath.*

Fruma-Malka nodded silently, slipping the chalk into the pouch of her apron. Together they would rip retribution from the *kurveh's* wombs as they had ripped her husband and her son from her. Perhaps she would start tonight with the one called Mary Ann. The one that had come upon them that night in London as they had returned from synagogue, and that had so immodestly propositioned her Jacob before his own wife. At the time Fruma-Malka had found the familiarity with which the *kurveh* had addressed her husband disturbing, but that was before she had learned of the rabbi's dispensation. Still, she should not have referred to him by the gentile name of Jack.

Yes, cooed the voice inside her. *She will have her Jack, my dear, they will all have their Jack as we author our revenge upon them. Together we will do this, and together, Jewess, we will not be blamed. . . .*

"For nothing," replied Fruma-Malka the butcher's widow through lips that were her own and in a voice that was also her own, as she and the second soul that was upon her loped out onto the sweat-slaked streets of Spitalfields and Whitechapel.

BIDING TIME

by Robert J. Sawyer

Robert J. Sawyer of Toronto is one of only sixteen authors in history to win both a Hugo Award for best novel (for *Hominids*) and a Nebula Award for best novel (for *The Terminal Experiment*). His latest novel is *Mindscan,* and more of his short stories can be found in his collection *Iterations.* For more information about Rob and his work, visit his million-plus word Web site at sfwriter.com.

ERNIE GARGALIAN WAS FAT—"Gargantuan Gargalian," some called him. Fortunately, like me, he lived on Mars; it was a lot easier to carry extra weight here. He must have massed a hundred and fifty kilos, but it felt like a third of what it would have on Earth.

Ironically, Gargalian was one of the few people on Mars wealthy enough to fly back to Earth as often as he wanted to, but he never did; I don't think he planned to ever set foot on the mother planet again, even though it was where all his rich clients were. Gargalian was a dealer in Martian fossils: he brokered the transactions between those lucky prospectors who found good specimens and wealthy collectors back on Earth, taking the same oversize slice of the financial pie as he would have of a real one.

His shop was in the innermost circle—appropriately; he knew *everyone*. The main door was transparent alloquartz with his business name and trading hours laser-etched into it; not quite carved in stone, but still a degree of permanence suitable to a dealer in prehistoric relics. The business name was Ye Olde Fossil Shoppe—as if there were any other kind.

The shoppe's ye olde door slid aside as I approached—somewhat noisily, I thought. Well, Martian dust gets everywhere, even inside our protective dome; some of it was probably gumming up the works.

Gargalian, seated by a long worktable covered with hunks of rock, was in the middle of a transaction. A prospector—grizzled, with a deeply-lined face; he could have been sent over from Central Casting—was standing next to Gargantuan (okay, I was one of those who called him that, too). Both of them were looking at a monitor, showing a close-up of a rhizomorph fossil.

"Aresthera weingartenii," Gargalian said, with satisfaction; he had a clipped Lebanese accent and a deep, booming voice. "A juvenile, too—we don't see many at this particular stage of development. And see that rainbow sheen? Lovely. It's been permineralized with silicates. This will fetch a nice price—a nice price indeed."

The prospector's voice was rough. Those of us who passed most of our time under the dome had enough troubles with dry air; those who spent half their lives in surface suits, breathing bottled atmosphere, sounded particularly raspy. "How nice?" he said, his eyes narrowing.

Gargantuan frowned while he considered. "I can sell this quickly for perhaps eleven million . . . or, if you give me longer, I can probably get thirteen. I have some clients who specialize in *A. weingartenii* who will pay top coin, but they are slow in making up their minds."

"I want the money fast," said the prospector. "This old body of mine might not hold out much longer."

Gargalian turned his gaze from the monitor to appraise the prospector, and he caught sight of me as he did so. He nodded in my direction, and raised a single finger—the finger that indicated "one minute," not the other finger, although I got that often enough when I entered places, too. He nodded at the prospector, apparently agreeing that the guy wasn't long for this or any other world, and said, "A speedy resolution, then. Let me give you a receipt for the fossil . . ."

I waited for Gargalian to finish his business, and then he came over to where I was standing. "Hey, Ernie," I said.

"Mr. Double-X himself!" declared Gargalian, bushy eyebrows rising above his round, flabby face. He liked to call me that because both my first and last names—Alex Lomax—ended in that letter.

I pulled my datapad out of my pocket and showed him a picture of a seventy-year-old woman, with gray hair cut in sensible bangs above a crabapple visage. "Recognize her?"

Gargantuan nodded, and his jowls shook as he did so. "Sure. Megan Delacourt, Delany, something like that, right?"

"Delahunt," I said.

"Right. What's up? She your client?"

"She's *nobody's* client," I said. "The old dear is pushing up daisies."

I saw Gargalian narrow his eyes for a second. Knowing him, he was trying to calculate whether he'd owed her money or she'd owed him money. "Sorry to hear that," he said with the kind of regret that was merely polite, presumably meaning that at least he hadn't lost anything. "She was pretty old."

" 'Was' is the operative word," I said. "She'd transferred."

He nodded, not surprised. "Just like that old guy wants to." He indicated the door the prospector had exited through. It was a common-enough scenario. People come to Mars in their youth, looking to make their fortunes by finding fossils here. The lucky ones stumble across a valuable specimen early on; the unlucky ones keep on searching and searching, getting older in the process. If they ever do find a decent specimen, first thing they do is transfer before it's too late. "So, what is it?" asked Gargalian. "A product-liability case? Next of kin suing NewYou?"

I shook my head. "Nah, the transfer went fine. But somebody killed the uploaded version shortly after the transfer was completed."

Gargalian's bushy eyebrows went up. "Can you do that? I thought transfers were immortal."

I knew from bitter recent experience that a transfer could be killed with equipment specifically designed for that purpose, but the only broadband disrupter here on Mars was safely in the hands of the New Klondike constabulary. Still, I'd seen the most amazing suicide a while ago, committed by a transfer.

But this time the death had been simple. "She was lured down to the shipyards, or so it appears, and ended up standing between the engine cone of a big rocket ship, which was lying on its belly, and a brick wall. Someone fired the engine, and she did a Margaret Hamilton."

Gargalian shared my fondness for old films; he got the reference and winced. "Still, there's your answer, no? It must have been one of the rocket's crew—someone who had access to the engine controls."

I shook my head. "No. The cockpit was broken into."

Ernie frowned. "Well, maybe it was one of the crew, trying to make it look like it *wasn't* one of the crew."

God save me from amateur detectives. "I checked. They all had alibis—and none of them had a motive, of course."

Gargantuan made a harrumphing sound. "What about the original version of Megan?" he asked.

"Already gone. They normally euthanize the biological original immediately after making the copy; can't have two versions of the same person running around, after all."

"Why would anyone kill someone after they transferred?" asked Gargalian. "I mean, if you wanted the person dead, it's got to be easier to off them when they're still biological, no?"

"I imagine so."

"And it's still murder, killing a transfer, right? I mean, I can't recall it ever happening, but that's the way the law reads, isn't it?"

"Yeah, it's still murder," I said. "The penalty is life imprisonment—down on Earth, of course." With any sentence longer than two mears—two Mars years—it was cheaper to ship the criminal down to Earth, where air is free, than to incarcerate him or her here.

Gargantuan shook his head, and his jowls, again. "She seemed like a nice old lady," he said. "Can't imagine why someone would want her dead."

"The 'why' is bugging me, too," I said. "I know she came in here a couple of weeks ago with some fossil specimens to sell; I found a receipt recorded in her datapad."

Gargalian motioned toward his desktop computer, and we walked over to it. He spoke to the machine, and some pictures of fossils appeared on the same monitor he'd been looking at earlier. "She brought me three pentapeds. One was junk, but the other two were very nice specimens."

"You sold them?"

"That's what I do."

"And gave her her share of the proceeds?"

"Yes."

"How much did it come to?"

He spoke to the computer again, and pointed at the displayed figure. "Total, nine million solars."

I frowned. "NewYou charges 7.5 million for their basic service. There can't have been enough cash left over after she transferred to be worth killing her for, unless . . ." I peered at the images of the fossils she'd brought in, but I was hardly a great judge of quality. "You said two of the specimens were really nice." 'Nice' was Gargantuan's favorite adjective; he'd apparently never taken a creative-writing course.

He nodded.

"*How* nice?"

He laughed, getting my point at once. "You think she'd found the alpha?"

I lifted my shoulders a bit. "Why not? If she knew where it was, that'd be worth killing her for."

The alpha deposit was where Simon Weingarten and Denny O'Reilly—the two private explorers who first found fossils on Mars—had collected their original specimens. That discovery had brought all the other fortune seekers from Earth. Weingarten and O'Reilly had died twenty mears ago—their heat shield had torn off while reentering Earth's atmosphere after their third trip here—and the location of the alpha died with them. All anyone knew was that it was somewhere here in the Isidis Planitia basin; whoever found it would be rich beyond even Gargantuan Gargalian's dreams.

"I told you, one of the specimens was junk," said Ernie. "No way it came from the alpha. The rocks of the alpha are extremely fine-grained—the preservation quality is as good as that from Earth's Burgess Shale."

"And the other two?" I said.

He frowned, then replied almost grudgingly, "They were good."

"Alpha good?"

His eyes narrowed. "Maybe."

"She could have thrown in the junk piece just to disguise where the others had come from," I said.

"Well, even junk fossils are hard to come by."

That much was true. In my own desultory collecting days, I'd never found so much as a fragment. Still, there had to be a reason why someone would kill an old woman just after she'd transferred her consciousness into an artificial body.

And if I could find that reason, I'd be able to find her killer.

My client was Megan Delahunt's ex-husband—and he'd been ex for a dozen mears, not just since Megan had died. Jersey Delahunt had come into my little office at about half past ten that morning. He was shrunken with age, but looked as though he'd been broad-shouldered in his day. A few wisps of white hair were all that was left on his liver-spotted head. "Megan struck it rich," he'd told me.

I'd regarded him from my swivel chair, hands interlocked behind my head, feet up on my battered desk. "And you couldn't be happier for her."

"You're being sarcastic, Mr. Lomax," he said, but his tone wasn't bitter. "I don't blame you. Sure, I'd been hunting fossils for thirty-six Earth years, too. Megan and me, we'd come here to Mars together, right at the beginning of the rush, hoping to make our fortunes. It hadn't lasted though—our marriage, I mean; the dream of getting rich lasted, of course."

"Of course," I said. "Are you still named in her will?"

Jersey's old, rheumy eyes regarded me. "Suspicious, too, aren't you?"

"That's what they pay me the medium-sized bucks for."

He had a small mouth, surrounded by wrinkles; it did the best it could to work up a smile. "The answer is no, I'm not in her will. She left everything to our son Ralph. Not that there was much left over after she spent the money to upload, but whatever there was, he got—or will get, once her will is probated."

"And how old is Ralph?"

"Thirty-four." Age was always expressed in Earth years.

"So he was born after you came to Mars? Does he still live here?"

"Yes. Always has."

"Is he a prospector, too?"

"No. He's an engineer. Works for the water-recycling authority."

I nodded. Not rich, then. "And Megan's money is still there, in her bank account?"

"So says the lawyer, yes."

"If all the money is going to Ralph, what's your interest in the matter?"

"My interest, Mr. Lomax, is that I once loved this woman very much. I left Earth to come here to Mars because it's what she wanted to do. We lived together for ten mears, had children together, and—"

"Children," I repeated. "But you said all the money was left to your *child*, singular, this Ralph."

"My daughter is dead," Jersey said, his voice soft.

It was hard to sound contrite in my current posture—I was still leaning back with feet up on the desk. But I tried. "Oh. Um. I'm . . . ah . . ."

"You're sorry, Mr. Lomax. Everybody is. I've heard it a million times. But it wasn't your fault. It wasn't anyone's fault, although . . ."

"Yes?"

"Although Megan blamed herself, of course. What mother wouldn't?"

"I'm not following."

"Our daughter JoBeth died thirty years ago, when she

was two months old." Jersey was staring out my office's single window, at one of the arches supporting the habitat dome. "She smothered in her sleep." He turned to look at me, and his eyes were red as Martian sand. "The doctor said that sort of thing happens sometimes—not often, but from time to time." His face was almost unbearably sad. "Right up till the end, Megan would cry whenever she thought of JoBeth. It was heartbreaking. She couldn't get over it."

I nodded, because that was all I could think of to do. Jersey didn't seem inclined to say anything else, so, after a moment, I went on. "Surely the police have investigated your ex-wife's death."

"Yes, of course," Jersey replied. "But I'm not satisfied that they tried hard enough."

This was a story I'd heard often. I nodded again, and he continued to speak: "I mean, the detective I talked to said the killer was probably off-planet now, headed to Earth."

"That *is* possible, you know," I replied. "Well, at least it is if a ship has left here in the interim."

"Two have," said Jersey, "or so the detective told me."

"Including the one whose firing engine, ah, did the deed?"

"No, that one's still there. *Lennick's Folly*, it's called. It was supposed to head back to Earth, but it's been impounded."

"Because of Megan's death?"

"No. Something to do with unpaid taxes."

I nodded. With NewYou's consciousness-uploading technology, not even death was certain anymore—but taxes were. "Which detective were you dealing with?"

"Some Scottish guy."

"Dougal McCrae," I said. Mac wasn't the laziest man I'd ever met—and he'd saved my life recently when another case had gone bad, so I tried not to think uncharitable thoughts about him. But if there was a poster boy for complacent policing, well, Mac wouldn't be it; he wouldn't bother to get out from behind his desk to show up for the photo shoot. "All right," I said. "I'll take the case."

"Thank you," said Jersey. "I brought along Megan's datapad; the police gave it back to me after copying its contents." He handed me the little tablet. "It's got her appointment schedule and her address book. I thought maybe it would help you find the killer."

I motioned for him to put the device on my desk. "It probably will, at that. Now, about my fee . . ."

Since Mars no longer had seas, it was all one landmass: you could literally walk anywhere on the planet. Still, on this whole rotten globe, there was only one settlement—our domed city of New Klondike, three kilometers in diameter. The city had a circular layout: nine concentric rings of buildings, cut into blocks by twelve radial roadways. The NewYou franchise—the only place you could go for uploading on Mars—was just off Third Avenue in the fifth ring. According to her datapad, Megan Delahunt's last appointment at NewYou had been three days ago, when her transfer had actually been done. I headed there after leaving Ye Olde Fossil Shoppe.

The NewYou franchise was under new management since the last time I'd visited. The rather tacky showroom was at ground level; the brain-scanning equipment was on the second floor. The basement—quite rare on Mars, since the permafrost was so hard to dig through—was mostly used for storage.

"Mr. Lomax!" declared Horatio Fernandez, an employee held over from the previous ownership. Fernandez was a beefy guy—arms as big around as Gargalian's, but his bulk was all muscle.

"Hello," I said. "Sorry to bother you, but—"

"Let me guess," said Fernandez. "The Megan Delahunt murder."

"Bingo."

He shook his head. "She was really pleasant."

"So people keep telling me."

"It's true. She was a real lady, that one. Cultured, you know? Lots of people here, spending their lives splitting rocks, they get a rough edge. But not her; she was all 'please' and 'thank you.' Of course, she was pretty long in the tooth . . ."

"Did she have any special transfer requests?" I asked.

"Nah. Just wanted her new body to look the way she had fifty Earth years ago, when she was twenty—which was easy enough."

"What about mods for outside work?" Lots of transfers had special equipment installed in their new bodies so that they could operate more easily on the surface of Mars.

"Nah, nothing. She said her fossil-hunting days were over. She was looking forward to a nice long future, reading all the great books she never had time for before."

If she'd found the alpha, she'd probably have wanted to work it herself, at least for a while—if you're planning on living forever, and you had a way to become super-rich, you'd take advantage of it. "Hmmph," I said. "Did she mention any titles?"

"Yeah," said Fernandez. "She said she was going to start with *Remembrance of Things Past.*"

I nodded, impressed at her ambition. "Anybody else come by to ask about her since she was killed?"

"Well, Detective McCrae called."

"Mac came here?"

"No, he *called.* On the phone."

I smiled. "That's Mac."

I headed over to Gully's Gym, since it was on the way to my next stop, and did my daily workout—treadmill, bench press, and so on. I worked up quite a sweat, but a sonic shower cleaned me up. Then it was off to the shipyards. Mostly, this dingy area between the eighth and ninth circles was a grave for abandoned ships, left over from the early fossil-rush days when people were coming to Mars in droves. Now only a small amount of maintenance work was done here. My last visit to the shipyards had been quite unpleasant—but I suppose it hadn't been as bad as Megan Delahunt's last visit.

I found *Lennick's Folly* easily enough. It was a tapered spindle, maybe a hundred meters long, lying on its side. The bow had a couple of square windows, and the stern had a giant engine cone attached. There was a gap of only a few meters between the cone and a brick firewall, which was now covered with soot. Whatever had been left of Megan's shiny new body had already been removed.

The lock on the cockpit door hadn't been repaired, so I had no trouble getting in. Once inside the cramped space, I got to work.

There were times when a private detective could accomplish things a public one couldn't. Mac had to worry about privacy laws, which were as tight here on Mars as they were back down on Earth—and a good thing, too, for those, like me, who had come here to escape our pasts. Oh, Mac doubtless had collected DNA samples here—gathering them at a crime scene was legal—but he couldn't take DNA from a suspect to match against specimens from here without a court order, and to get that, he'd have to show good reason up front for why the suspect might be guilty—which, of course, was a catch-22. Fortunately, the only catch-22 I had to deal with was the safety on my trusty old Smith & Wesson .22.

I used a GeneSeq 109, about the size of a hockey puck. It collected even small fragments of DNA in a nanotrap, and could easily compare sequences from any number of sources. I did a particularly thorough collecting job on the control panel that operated the engine. Of course, I looked for fingerprints, too, but there weren't any recent ones, and the older ones had been smudged either by someone operating the controls with gloved hands, which is what I suspected, or, I suppose, by artificial hands—a transfer offing a transfer; that'd be a first.

Of course, Mac knew as well as I did that family members commit most murders. I'd surreptitiously taken a sample from Jersey Delahunt when he'd visited my office; I sample everyone who comes there. But my GeneSeq reported that the DNA collected here didn't match Jersey's. That wasn't too surprising: I'd been hired by guilty parties before, but it was hardly the norm—or, at least, the kind of people who hired me usually weren't guilty of the particular crime they wanted me to investigate.

And so I headed off to find the one surviving child of Megan and Jersey Delahunt.

* * *

Jersey had said his son Ralph had been born shortly after he and Megan had come to Mars thirty-six Earth years ago. Ralph certainly showed all the signs of having been born here: he was 210 centimeters if he was an inch; growing up in Mars's low gravity had that effect. And he was a skinny thing, with rubbery, tubular limbs—Gumby in an olive-green business suit. Most of us here had been born on Earth, and it still showed in our musculature, but Ralph was Martian, through and through.

His office at the water works was much bigger than mine, but then, he didn't personally pay the rent on it. I had a DNA collector in my palm when I shook his hand, and while he was getting us both coffee from a maker on his credenza, I transferred the sample to the GeneSeq, and set it to comparing his genetic code to the samples from the rocket's cockpit.

"I want to thank you, Mr. Lomax," Ralph said, handing me a steaming mug. "My father called to say he'd hired you. I'm delighted. Absolutely delighted." He had a thin, reedy voice, matching his thin, reedy body. "How anyone could do such a thing to my mother . . ."

I smiled, sat down, and took a sip. "I understand she was a sweet old lady."

"That she was," said Ralph, taking his own seat on the other side of a glass-and-steel desk. "That she was."

The GeneSeq bleeped softly three times, each bleep higher pitched than the one before—the signal for a match. "Then why did you kill her?" I said.

He had his coffee cup halfway to his lips, but suddenly he slammed it down, splashing double-double, which fell to the glass desktop in Martian slo-mo. "Mr. Lomax, if that's your idea of a joke, it's in very poor taste. The funeral service for my mother is tomorrow, and—"

"And you'll be there, putting on an act, just like the one you're putting on now."

"Have you no decency, sir? My mother . . ."

"Was killed. By someone she trusted—someone who she would follow to the shipyards, someone who told her to wait in a specific spot while he—what? Nipped off to have a private word with a ship's pilot? Went into the shadows to take a leak? Of course, a professional engineer could get the manual for a spaceship's controls easily enough, and understand it well enough to figure out how to fire the engine."

Ralph's flimsy form was quaking with rage, or a good simulation of it. "Get out. Get out now. I think I speak for my father when I say you're fired."

I didn't get up. "It was damn-near a perfect crime," I said, my voice rock steady. "*Lennick's Folly* should have headed back to Earth, taking any evidence of who'd been in its cockpit with her; indeed, you probably hoped it'd be gone long before the melted lump that once was your mother was found. But you can't fire engines under the dome without consuming a lot of oxygen—and somebody has to pay for that. It doesn't grow on trees, you know—well, down on Earth it does, sort of. But not here. And so the ship is hanging around, like the tell-tale heart, like an albatross, like—" I sought a third allusion, just for style's sake, and one came to me: "like the sword of Damocles."

Ralph looked left and right. There was no way out, of course; I was seated between him and the door, and my Smith & Wesson was now in my hand. He might have done a sloppy job, but I never do. "I . . . I don't know what you're talking about," he said.

I made what I hoped was an ironic smile. "Guess that's another advantage of uploading, no? No more DNA being left behind. It's almost impossible to tell if a specific transfer has been in a specific room, but it's child's play to determine what biologicals have gone in and out of somewhere. Did you know that cells slough off the alveoli of your lungs and are exhaled with each breath? Oh, only two or three—but today's scanners have no trouble finding them, and reading the DNA in them. No, it's open-and-shut that you were the murderer: you were in the cockpit of *Lennick's Folly*, you touched the engine controls. Yeah, you were bright enough to wear gloves—but not bright enough to hold your breath."

He got to his feet, and started to come around from behind his funky desk. I undid the safety on my gun, and he froze.

"I frown on murder," I said, "but I'm all for killing in self-defense—so I'd advise you to stand perfectly still." I waited to make sure he was doing just that, then went on. "I know *that* you did it, but I still don't know why. And I'm an old-fashioned guy—grew up reading Agatha Christie and Peter Robinson. In the good old days, before DNA and all that, detectives wanted three things to make a case: method, motive, and opportunity. The method is obvious, and you clearly had opportunity. But I'm still in the dark on the motive, and, for my own interest, I'd like to know what it was."

"You can't prove any of this," sneered Ralph. "Even if you have a DNA match, it's inadmissible."

"Dougal McCrae is lazy, but he's not stupid. If I tip him off that you definitely did it, he'll find a way to get the warrant. Your only chance now is to tell me *why* you did it. Hell, I'm a reasonable man. If your justification was good enough, well, I've turned a blind eye before. So, tell me: why wait until your mother uploaded to kill her? If you had some beef with her, why didn't you off her earlier?" I narrowed my eyes. "Or had she done something recently? She'd struck it rich, and that sometimes changes people—but . . ." I paused, and after a few moments, I found myself nodding. "Ah, of course. She struck it rich, and she was old. You'd thought, hey, she's going to drop off soon, and you'll inherit her newfound fortune. But when she squandered it on herself, spending most of it on uploading, you were furious." I shook my head in disgust. "Greed. Oldest motivation there is."

"You really are a smug bastard, Lomax," said Ralph. "And you don't know *anything* about me. Do you think I care about money?" He snorted. "I've never wanted money—as long as I've got enough to pay my life-support tax, I'm content."

"People who are indifferent to thousands often change their ways when millions are at stake."

"Oh, now you're a philosopher, too, eh? I was born here on Mars, Lomax. My whole life I've been surrounded by people who spend all their time looking for paleontological pay dirt. My parents both did that. It was bad enough that I had to compete with things that have been dead for hundreds of millions of years, but . . ."

I narrowed my eyes. "But what?"

He shook his head. "Nothing. You wouldn't understand."

"No? Why not?"

He paused, then: "You got brothers? Sisters?"

"A sister," I said. "Back on Earth."

"Older or younger?"

"Older, by two years."

"No," he said. "You couldn't possibly understand."

"Why not? What's that got—" And then it hit me. I'd encountered lots of scum in my life: crooks, swindlers, people who'd killed for a twenty-solar coin. But nothing like this. That Ralph had a scarecrow's form was obvious, but, unlike the one from Oz, he clearly *did* have a brain. And although his mother had been the tin man, so to speak, after she'd uploaded, I now knew it was Ralph who'd been lacking a heart.

"JoBeth," I said softly.

Ralph staggered backward as if I'd hit him. His eyes, defiant till now, could no longer meet my own. "Christ," I said. "How could you? How could anyone . . ."

"It's not like that," he said, spreading his arms like a praying mantis. "I was four years old, for God's sake. I—I didn't mean—"

"You killed your own baby sister."

He looked at the carpeted office floor. "My parents had little enough time for me as it was, what with spending twelve hours a day looking for the god-damned alpha."

I nodded. "And when JoBeth came along, suddenly you were getting no attention at all. And so you smothered her in her sleep."

"You can't prove that. Nobody can."

"Maybe. Maybe not."

"She was cremated, and her ashes were scattered outside the dome thirty years ago. The doctor said she died of natural causes, and you can't prove otherwise."

I shook my head, still trying to fathom it all. "You didn't count on how much it would hurt your mother—or that the hurt would go on and on, mear after mear."

He said nothing, and that was as damning as any words could be.

"She couldn't get over it, of course," I said. "But you thought, you know, eventually . . ."

He nodded, almost imperceptibly—perhaps he wasn't even aware that he'd done so. I went on, "You thought eventually she would die, and then you wouldn't have to face her anymore. At some point, she'd be gone, and her pain would be over, and you could finally be free of the guilt. You were biding your time, waiting for her to pass on."

He was still looking at the carpet, so I couldn't see his face. But his narrow shoulders were quivering. I continued. "You're still young—thirty-four, isn't it? Oh, sure, your mother might have been good for another ten or twenty years, but *eventually* . . ."

Acid was crawling its way up my throat. I swallowed hard, fighting it down. "Eventually," I continued, "you would be free—or so you thought. But then your mother struck it rich, and uploaded her consciousness, and was going to live for centuries if not forever, and you couldn't take that, could you? You couldn't take her always being around, always crying over something that you had done so long ago." I lifted my eyebrows, and made no effort to keep the contempt out of my voice. "Well, they say the first murder is the hardest."

"You can't prove any of this. Even if you have DNA specimens from the cockpit, the police still don't have any probable cause to justify taking a specimen from me."

"They'll find it. Dougal McCrae is lazy—but he's also a father, with a baby girl of his own. He'll dig into this like a bulldog, and won't let go until he's got what he needs to nail you, you—"

I stopped. I wanted to call him a son of a bitch—but he wasn't; he was the son of a gentle, loving woman who had deserved so much better. "One way or another, you're going down," I said. And then it hit me, and I started to feel that maybe there was a little justice in the universe after all. "And that's exactly right: you're going down, to Earth."

Ralph at last did look up, and his thin face was ashen. *"What?"*

"That's what they do with anyone whose jail sentence

is longer than two mears. It's too expensive in terms of life-support costs to house criminals here for years on end."

"I—I can't go to Earth."

"You won't have any choice."

"But—but I was *born* here. I'm Martian, born and raised. On Earth, I'd weigh . . . what? Twice what I'm used to . . ."

"Three times, actually. A stick-insect like you, you'll hardly be able to walk there. You should have been doing what I do. Every morning, I work out at Gully's Gym, over by the shipyards. But you . . ."

"My . . . my heart . . ."

"Yeah, it'll be quite a strain, won't it? Too bad . . ."

His voice was soft and small. "It'll kill me, all that gravity."

"It might at that," I said, smiling mirthlessly. "At the very least, you'll be bedridden until the end of your sorry days—helpless as a baby in a crib."

CRITICAL ANALYSIS

by Tanya Huff

Tanya Huff lives and writes in rural Ontario with her partner, four cats, and an unintentional Chihuahua. In addition to sixteen fantasies, she's written two space operas, *Valor's Choice* and *The Better Part of Valor,* and is currently working on a series of novels spun off from her Henry Fitzroy vampire series. In her spare time she gardens and complains about the weather.

"YOU! YOU'RE A POLICE officer, aren't you?"

Detective Sergeant Michael Celluci stared down at the pale, long-fingered hand clutching his arm and then up at the tall, unshaven, young man who'd stopped him on the steps of police headquarter and asked the question. "I am."

Pink-rimmed, bloodshot eyes locked onto Celluci's face. "I need your help."

"With what?"

"Someone's going to kill me."

"Uh-huh." The man was sincerely frightened. Celluci'd seen frightened often enough to know it. Sincere . . . well, not so much. Not in his line of work. He nodded toward the doors where condensation beaded the glass barrier between warmth and January in downtown Toronto. "You want to talk about this inside?"

* * *

"His name is Raymond Carr and it started with threatening e-mail." Celluci passed Vicki the file folder and headed over to the coffeemaker. "It escalated to someone hacking his system and sticking the threats into his work."

"What's he do?"

"He's a writer. Did you make this when you got up, or is it sludge left over from this morning?" The mug of coffee he'd just poured stalled halfway to his mouth.

"What do you care? You'd drink the sludge anyway. What's he write?"

"Pretty much anything people will pay him for. Of course, people are paying him a lot less when their ad copy comes complete with death threats."

"You'll save, save, save while we beat in your head with a bat?"

"Less wordy. Oh, and he's working on a book."

"Yeah, isn't everyone." She frowned at the top printout. "I assume the word *die* isn't meant to be in here?" A few more pages in. "Or here? Actually, since it's repeated about a dozen times, forget I asked. What did he do and who did he do it to?"

"He doesn't know."

"Well, he clearly pissed off someone with some hacking abilities," she muttered, scanning the rest of the file.

Celluci pulled out a chair and sat down on the other side of the kitchen table. "He says he didn't."

Fingertips against the edge of the table, she leaned back, balancing on two legs of her chair. "So you think it's some kind of a sick joke? Just some bored techno-nerd getting his jollies by screwing with a stranger?"

"That's possible. Point is, Carr's terrified. We wrote him up, but there's not much we can do until we have more to go on than electronic threats."

"Don't you guys have techno-nerds of your own now?" She beat out a drum roll. "Several someones who can trace an e-mail like this back to the sender?"

"Apparently, we can't do squat without Carr's computer and he won't hand it over. Says his whole life is on that machine."

"Really? I hope he remembers to do backups." She flipped the folder closed and let her chair drop flat.

"What does he expect you—where 'you' refers to Toronto's finest, not you personally—to do?"

"Protect him."

"I think I just figured out where this is going."

Cellcui smiled and drained his mug. "Carr's address is on the outside of the folder. I told him you'd be by this evening."

"Mike, I'm not hired muscle."

"Did I say you were? You have special abilities."

"Special abilities?" Her smile was both threat and invitation.

He cleared his throat. "And," he continued emphatically, ignoring the invitation and disregarding the threat, "you may be an undead creature of the night, but you were a cop, and a good one, for years. Use *those* skills for a change. Find out who's threatening him. Do some detecting. While you're there, see that no one beats his head in with a bat."

Raymond Carr lived on Bloor Street in a third-floor flat over the Korona Restaurant. As Vicki made her way up the steep, narrow stairs, she avoided touching the grimy banister and wondered if he could afford her services. Mike sometimes forgot she wasn't on the public payroll anymore. Or he was indulging in some weird passive-aggressive "let me take care of you" macho thing. She wasn't sure which.

The apartment door had been painted a deep blue sometime in the distant past. It wore a grimy patina of hand-shaped smudges fading down into black scuff marks probably caused by shoving it open with a booted foot.

Hand raised to knock, Vicki paused, and frowned. With millions of lives surrounding her—and, more specifically, with the half dozen lives close at hand behind inadequate walls of ancient plaster and lath—it was difficult to separate out the sounds coming from inside Carr's apartment. Sifting sound, disregarding everything that wasn't life, focusing, she picked out a heartbeat. It was slower than it should be. Struggling.

Not even burning onions on the second floor could mask the smell of blood.

The door had a deadbolt on it and a security chain. Both were screwed into a doorframe that had probably been installed at the turn of the century. The wood gave way with a sound like a dry cough. The mulitiple layers of cheap paint hung on a moment longer, then Vicki was in the apartment and racing down the long hall toward the front room, following her nose.

This door was also locked.

And was unlocked just as quickly.

A young man—blond hair, pale skin, late twenties, approximately six feet tall and a hundred and seventy pounds—lay sprawled on the linoleum, blood spreading out from under his head along the artificial watershed of the uneven floor. He was alone in the room.

Between one heartbeat and the next, Vicki knelt beside him, his head cradled in one hand, a folded towel from the bathroom in the other. Had any assailants still been around, they might have wondered when she'd had time to get back down the hall but had they still been around, she'd have dealt with them first, so the question would have been moot. The room was empty except for the injured man. No one was hiding under the desk. No one lurked in the tiny turn-of-the-century closet.

A couple of mouthfuls of spit on the towel—easy enough to work up under the circumstances, the smell of blood was making her mouth water—and then both spit and towel applied to the wound. As the coagulant in her saliva went to work, she pulled her cell phone from her pocket, flipped it open, and dialed one-handed.

"So you broke down the door?"

"That's right."

"Because you could smell the blood?"

"Yes."

"From out in the hall?"

"That's what I said."

"Just trying to get my facts straight, Ms. Nelson."

Vicki forced her lips back down over her teeth as the earnest, young constable went over her statement for the fourth time.

"And then you broke down the inner door as well?"

"Yes."

He gave her what he probably considered an intimidating stare. "You forced the lock right out of the wood. Splintered the wood. So not only do you have a rather unbelievable sense of smell, you're unusually strong."

"I work out." While she appreciated he was just doing his job, enough was enough. Locking her eyes on his, she smiled. "Now go away," she said softly, "and stop bothering me."

"I . . . I think that's all I need to know."

"Good." A more normal tone. A slightly more normal smile.

He backed up two steps, then turned and scuttled down the hall toward the apartment door, nearly bouncing off Mike Celluci.

"Vicki . . ."

"I was cooperating."

"You terrified him."

"So? Back in the day, I used to terrify the uniforms all the time." She sighed as they fell into step heading toward Carr's tiny office. "When did they start hiring children?"

"About the time I started going gray."

They paused to allow the crime scene team to leave, and Vicki reached up to push the curl of hair back off his face. She'd gotten rather sentimental about his scattering of gray hair—after she stopped being furious at it. Raging at the years that took him farther and farther away from her. She would age but slowly. She'd changed at thirty-four. It would be centuries before she saw forty. Sunlight and the occasional idiot Van Helsing clone allowing.

She stepped aside so the head of the crime scene unit could have a talk with Celluci and, well beyond normal eavesdropping distance, eavesdropped shamelessly.

"So," she said when they were finally alone in the apartment. "The door was locked from the inside, the window was painted shut, and they think they've only got one person's prints, although they'll have to get back to you on that. Didn't I once read a Miss Marple book with this plot?"

"You read a book?"

"Funny man."

Celluci shoved his hands in the pockets of his overcoat and scowled at the room. A battered office chair, more duct tape than upholstery, lay on its side against the outside wall. "He could have just tipped over backward and hit his head."

"With the chair over there and this kind of a spatter pattern? Stop playing idiot's advocate, Mike. Looks to me like he pushed away from the desk, spun the chair around . . ." Vicki sketched the arc in the air. ". . . leaped out of it, and was on his feet when he was hit. Whoever it was came in through the door . . ."

"The locked door."

"We don't know for certain that the door was locked when the assailant *arrived.* Came in through the door," she repeated when Mike nodded reluctantly. "Walked very, very quietly around to about here . . ." She indicated a spot by the desk.

"It didn't have to be that quiet. If Carr was writing, he could have been distracted. Lost in his own world."

"Fair enough. But the assailant didn't just sneak in and attack him from behind, or he'd have fallen forward, over the keyboard. He got Carr's attention first. There must have been a fight. Maybe the neighbors heard something."

"Gosh, Vicki." Celluci's voice dripped heavy, obvious sarcasm. "I would never have thought to ask the neighbors if they heard anything. It's a good thing you're here. And frankly, I'm more concerned with how the guy got out, not in." A long stride took him to the other side of the red-brown puddle. He frowned at the window and the layers of paint that had clearly not been cracked. "Last time this was opened, Trudeau was Prime Minister."

"No one here but Raymond Carr when I broke in. No one passed me on the stairs, and no one came out of the building with a bloody weapon while I was close enough to see the door."

"Would you have seen the weapon under a winter coat?"

She smiled at him. "If it was bloody, I'd have known it was there."

"If. He could have left before you got close."

"Not at the rate Carr was bleeding out. It had to have happened just before I got here or the coroner'd be slabbing him right about now."

He shrugged, accepting her explanation. "Don't these apartments have a back exit into a courtyard?"

"The uniforms checked it. Locked. Three bolts thrown. Impossible to do from outside. And the window in the kitchen has as much paint on it as this one. Plus a layer of grease."

"I hate this kind of shit." Celluci dragged both hands back through his hair, dropping the curl over his forehead again. "I don't suppose our perp turned to mist or smoke, or there's a bat hiding out in a dark corner that we missed?"

"Don't be ridiculous."

"You telling me vampires don't exist?"

"I'm telling you that even if Hollywood didn't have its collective head up its ass, we wouldn't have wasted the blood." Carefully avoiding the splatter trail, she moved to the desk and looked down at the monitor. It was a new model, one of the liquid crystal screens made by a company she didn't recognize. From across the room, it had looked blank. Up close, there was one word, dead center on the screen.

"Mike."

He leaned in for a closer look. "Die."

"It's not an e-mail. They had to have typed it when they were in the room."

"I'll make sure they dust the keyboard when they bring the machine in. What are you doing?"

She frowned at an oval of drying blood nearly invisible on the black plastic of the monitor housing. It was shaped like a thumbprint, but she couldn't see a pattern.

"So you're eyeballing hills and valleys now?" he snorted when she pointed it out to him. "Good work, Vicki, we've got the son of a bitch. Our bad guy had to have left it there when he was typing. Left hand holding the monitor, typing with his right. If you can find another one of these, we might be able to piece together how the fuck he got out of the room."

"If I can find another one?"

"You know, sniff it out."

"Sniff it out?"

He turned to scowl at her. "Would you quit repeating everything I say?"

"I'm not repeating everything," she told him, "just the stupid parts. This room is saturated in blood scent, Mike. And before you ask," she cautioned, "I can't track the bad guy. I'm not a bloodhound."

One dark brow rose.

"Not funny."

"You're right. I'm sorry." Hands shoved deep in his pockets, he looked around the room. "So, what do we have?"

"You have an unsolved assault. And I have to find another client."

"He's not dead."

"You want me to guard him in the hospital?"

"That's up to you."

"I hate hospitals."

Vicki'd disliked hospitals before she changed and she'd started disliking them even more, after. Light-sensitive eyes found them far too bright and no amount of disinfectant could keep them from reeking of death. That they also reeked of disinfectant was not a selling point.

Raymond Carr was in a private room at the far end of a quiet corridor, the room the hospital unofficially kept for ongoing criminal cases. Sometimes it held the criminals. Sometimes the cases. With budgets cut and then cut again, the police department hadn't the man-power to guard an unsuccessful writer from an unknown enemy. They'd do their best to turn the unknown to a known, but as long as Carr seemed safe in the hospital, he'd remain unguarded.

Vicki stood in the room's darkest corner and watched the pale man on the bed draw in one short, shallow breath after another. He was sleeping—not entirely peacefully. Long fingers twitched against the covers and his eyeballs bounced behind his lids. Vicki wondered what he was dreaming about.

He'd told the police he couldn't remember what had

happened. That one moment he'd been writing and the next he was in the back of an ambulance staring up at a pair of EMTs. It was all still in there, though. Trapped in the dark places.

Vicki did some of her best work in dark places. Unfortunately, Carr was wired—she wouldn't be able to question him without setting off the bells and whistles.

"Who's there?"

Might as well try it the old-fashioned way. The Hunter carefully masked, she stepped out of the shadows. "My name's Vicki Nelson. Detective Sergeant Celluci told you I was coming over tonight."

"What happened to me?"

"You got hit on the head."

His eyes widened and he stared up at her with dawning comprehension. "You're the one he was sending to protect me!"

"Sorry; I got there a little late." And anyone else would have knocked and gone away. "For what it's worth, I kept you from bleeding to death."

"My computer!"

Apparently, it wasn't worth much. "The police have it."

"My book! My God, they have my book!"

"Calm down." A quick glance at the monitors showed a rise in heart rate. "You'll get it back when they finish the investigation."

"It'll never be finished."

She wasn't entirely certain if he meant the investigation or the book. "You must have backup copies."

"It's on disk." The bandage whispered against the pillowcase as he rocked his head from side to side. "I meant to burn it, but . . ." The rocking stopped. His pupils were so dilated his irises had nearly disappeared. "Why do you want my copy?"

"I don't. I was just reassuring . . ."

"You're trying to steal it!"

"No, I'm not." She let her eyes silver just enough to force him calm.

He panicked instead. The heart-rate monitor screamed as he tried to scramble back through the head of the bed.

Vicki was in the stairwell before the nurses left their station. She waited, the door open a crack, listening as they tranquilized him and strapped him down. He kept yelling that his book was in danger.

"Quite the imagination on him," one nurse muttered to the other as they left the room, her tone suggesting that "quite the imagination" could be translated as "total paranoid nutcase."

As Vicki slipped away, she thought it might be time to find out what else "quite the imagination" might mean.

The yellow crime scene tape remained across the door, but in the still, dark hours of the morning when Vicki returned to Raymond Carr's apartment, the police were long gone. Because of the manner of Vicki's original entrance, the apartment couldn't be secured, so they'd taken the trouble to put a padlock in place—a lot cheaper than keeping a uniform around until the landlord could arrive and make repairs. It was a good lock. It took Vicki about two minutes to pop it.

As well as the computer, the police had cleared Carr's desktop and taken all the drawers, hoping for a clue amid the debris. While she appreciated their thoroughness, she was a little annoyed by the need to pry a copy of the book out of official channels. Official channels were notoriously narrow.

And speaking of narrow . . . since she was there, she leaned her laptop case against the wall and stepped into the closet to check the ceiling for trapdoors leading to a closed-off and forgotten attic. Nothing. The cheap linoleum was solidly attached in all four corners, so there was no chance of a trapdoor to the apartment below.

On her hands and knees, peering under the desk at a floor unmarked by secret passageways, she snickered, "Who's the paranoid nutcase now?"

Paranoid nutcase . . .

Carr had thought she was going to steal his book. Had believed it so strongly, the hysterics had protected him from her ability to get into his head.

Vicki twisted and looked up at the bottom of the keyboard slide.

The masking tape that attached the square mailing envelope was almost the same color as the pale wood of the desk. The label on the single disk inside simply said, *Book.*

"The blood on the monitor wasn't a print."

Vicki glanced up from her laptop as Celluci came into the living room and dropped down beside her on the couch. "I'm sorry, Mike."

He grunted a noncommittal response to her sympathy. "What are you reading?"

"Raymond Carr's book. It's weirdly good. He starts off by massacring almost an entire village just so the hero—Harticalder—can go off and kick ass, so the plot's mostly a series of violent encounters strung together on a less-than-believable travelogue, but even doing the most asinine things, the characters are strangely believable. These guys read like real people."

His hand closed around her shoulder, warm even through the fleece of her sweatshirt. "Where did you get that?"

"Calm down, I left the original where it was." She popped the disk out of the side of her computer. "*This* is a copy." Pushing it back into the drive, she set the machine aside and pivoted in place until she faced him. "There's something else."

"What do you mean?"

"I know that look. It's your *I've come to a conclusion* expression."

He sighed and ran his hand back up through his hair. "The lab says there's no weapon, that the floor was the point of impact. One bang."

Vicki snorted. "No one hits their head that hard on a floor. It's a flat surface. Essentially flat," she amended, remembering how the blood had spread.

"And there's no indication of anyone else ever being in that room."

"Except for the blood on the monitor," she pointed out, poking him in the thigh with her bare foot.

"A random splatter. Raymond Carr got tangled up in his chair, fought to get free, and fell. That's why the chair was over by the window. No one pushed him, no one slammed his head down—there isn't another mark on his body."

Carr's skin was so pale that bruises would show almost instantly, blood from crushed capillaries pooling under the surface. "What about the threats?"

"We did a little background check, and it turns out that Raymond Carr is a paranoid schizophrenic. If he was off his medication, the odds are good he was writing the threats to himself."

"And?" Vicki asked pointedly.

"And what?" His hand closed around her ankle before she could poke him again. They both knew he couldn't hold her, but that wasn't the point.

"And you've had all day; is he off his medication?"

"Doesn't seem to have been. But . . ." He sketched uncertainties in the air with his free hand.

"But even paranoids have enemies."

He smiled then and pulled her close enough to kiss. "I knew you were going to say that."

"What about the blood on the monitor?" she asked when they pulled apart.

Celluci's turn to snort. "You know as well as I do that sometimes not all the pieces fit. You know better than I do that weird happens."

That was an impossible point to argue with, so she didn't bother and later, after he fell asleep, she checked that the bite on his wrist had closed over and slid out of bed to finish the book. Or at least to finish all of the book there was.

The fight scenes continued to be contrived, but the dialogue rang true and as she closed the last file, Vicki had to admit she believed in ol' Harticalder and his people. Almost buried under the preposterous plot, Carr had real talent.

On a whim, she went online and ran a search on the brand of monitor on Carr's desk. Her laptop was almost five years old and, even with the monitor dimmed down as far as it would go, it was still hard on light-sensitive eyes. Odds were good that new ones like Carr's had new features.

According to the official Web site, they did everything but make toast.

It seemed that Quinct, the company, had developed an amazing new technology for manufacturing the liquid crystal screens. They'd produced them for almost a year, claiming the new screens provided a viewing surface a minimum sixty percent sharper than the competition. And then, they'd gone bankrupt.

A bankruptcy sale explained how Raymond Carr had managed to afford one.

The site gave no reasons for the company's fall, and the best Vicki managed to find elsewhere on the Web was a Live Journal thread discussing the monitors. Apparently they weren't just sixty percent sharper—according to the half-dozen people in the thread who'd owned them, they made images so clear new details came into focus in the background and even the written word seemed somehow real.

Real. There was that word again.

As she shut down her machine, she decided not to repeat the word to Mike. Although forced to become more open-minded than he'd been, speculation outside the boundaries covered by the crime lab and some good old-fashioned legwork still annoyed him, and an annoyed Mike Celluci was no fun to live with.

Besides, no one knew better than she did that reality came with qualifiers.

But she popped the copy of the book out of her laptop just to be on the safe side.

No one attacked Raymond Carr in the hospital, and the day he was released, the police handed back his computer.

"There was no crime committed," Celluci explained that evening when Vicki commented on the speedy return. "Just a man who slipped off his meds and had an accident."

"You told me it looked like he was taking his meds."

"Let it go, Vicki." Elbows braced on the kitchen table, he rubbed his temples. "I've got two teenagers dead because some asshole in a car thought it would be fun to shoot at strangers. I don't have time to protect Raymond Carr from himself. You think he needs supervision, you do it."

She thought it wouldn't hurt to drop by.

This time the door was unlocked and the blood scent was stronger.

Carr hadn't had time to put a new lock on his office door and his landlord's rudimentary repairs hadn't included replacing the latch mechanism. When Vicki laid her palm against it, it swung open, unresisting.

The only light in the room came from the monitor, but even before the change that allowed her to miss his heartbeat and the song of his blood, she would have known Raymond Carr was dead. The living were never so completely still.

His chair had been tipped back—flung back considering the distance from the desk. He was still in it, his arms outstretched, fingers curled. His feet in old-fashioned, scuffed, leather slippers were in the air, his head rested in a puddle beginning to dry to a brackish brown around the edges. It was difficult to tell for certain without moving the body, but the back of his head looked flat and there were three distinct points of impact.

The police would assume they'd been wrong. That there'd been an assailant the first time. That this mysterious assailant had somehow gotten into and then out of a locked room in a locked apartment and that today—late afternoon by the smell—he or she returned and finished the job. If they'd found no evidence of a second person in the room, they had to have missed something and, blaming themselves for Raymond Carr's death, they'd work like hell to make up for their mistake.

Except . . .

Vicki pulled a latex glove out of her pocket—even the bloodsucking undead left fingerprints—and walked to the desk. There was a single word in the center of the monitor.

Dead.

She moved the cursor down to the next line and typed *Harticalder?*

Then she felt a little foolish when nothing happened.

"Right," she muttered, deleting the name and snapping off the glove. "Vampires exist, werewolves exist, wizards exist, so therefore it's logical that characters can be made so real that they climb out of new and improved monitors and bash in the brains of the bastard who put them through so much shit. Which is not to say," she added to Raymond Carr, "that you didn't deserve it. You slaughtered the entire village, for Christ's sake!"

Then she frowned as his eyes flared silver for an instant, reflecting the light of the monitor.

When she turned, there was still only one word on the screen.

Dead.

There'd be no marks on Carr's body because no matter how real they seemed, imaginary characters didn't leave marks. Or fingerprints. Or worry about locked doors. Or climb out of monitors and take vengeance on the creator who killed their wives and children to make a plot point.

Vicki pulled the glove back on and reformatted the hard drive. Pulled the plug on the machine, then took a cheap pen from the desk and drove a hole into the corner of the monitor. The part of her that had been a good cop for all those years hated the thought of compromising a crime scene. The rest of her slid the book's backup disk out of its hidden sleeve, snapped it in half, and put the pieces into her pocket.

Half a block away, from the payphone inside the front door of the Brunswick Hotel, she made an anonymous phone call.

"Obviously, it had to do with the book. This time the hard drive was reformatted—not just erased but refucking formatted—and the copy taken. Carr must have written something that really pissed someone off. I guess it's a good thing you made that illegal . . ." Celluci paused in his pacing to stress the word, ". . . copy, or we'd have nothing."

"Sorry, Mike." Vicki moved a red queen onto a black king and looked up from the laptop. "I copied my notes from the voodoo case onto the disk."

"You what?"

"Well, how would I know you'd need it? You said the lab determined he fell. That it was an accident."

She could hear his teeth grinding. "The evidence at the time . . ."

"Except for the missing book," she interrupted.

"And the destroyed monitor!" he interrupted in turn.

They stared at each other for a long moment.

"You never mentioned a destroyed monitor," Vicki sighed at last. "Fine, except the missing book *and* the destroyed monitor, what evidence do you have this time? Prints? Witnesses? Fibers? Anything?"

"Vicki, no one accidentally slams their own head into the floor three times with force enough to flatten the back of their own skull!"

The volume as much as the content of his protest answered her question; he had nothing. The police had nothing. She set the laptop to one side, stood, and crossed the room to lay a sympathetic hand on Mike's arm. "I'm not saying it was an accident. Maybe he destroyed his own book and then killed himself."

He caught up her hand in his and pulled her around to face him. "No one kills themselves by slamming their own head into the floor three times! Where the hell did you get that idea?"

"I don't know." Raymond Carr had created a village filled with amazingly real characters and then slaughtered almost all of them to make a plot point. Harticalder had ridden away to wreak vengeance on those who'd done the slaughtering. Maybe he'd traveled a little farther than planned. And if not him, well, there'd still been half a dozen other characters left behind to mourn.

"Vicki?"

She shrugged. "I guess I read it in a book."

MENU FOR LIFE . . . AND DEATH

by Jane Lindskold

Jane Lindskold cooked her first roast at age seven. She has been interested in cooking ever since, and hopes to someday be as good a cook as her mother. In addition to cooking, her interests include writing. She is the author of over fifty short stories, and fifteen or so novels, including the recently released *Child of a Rainless Year*, the five volume Firekeeper saga (*Through Wolf's Eyes, Wolf's Head, Wolf's Heart, The Dragon of Despair, Wolf Captured*, and *Wolf Hunting*), and the archaeological adventure fantasy, *The Buried Pyramid*. She resides in New Mexico, where she has learned to make a great meatloaf that includes green chile and piñon nuts. She is writing another novel.

TEA FOR TWO

Take two, male and female, mingle with sweet cakes, strong tea, soft music, and suitable glances. Warm thoroughly with strolls through flowers in midsummer gardens. Garnish with unexpected confidences.

Nectar and Ambrosia Deluxe

Remove all outer peel, arrange in layers. Ingredients may include oranges, bananas, and coconut, but feel free to be inventive, even exotic. Top with thick cream, whipped until stiff. Sprinkle with sugar and the smallest pinch of salt.

Wedding Feast

Cake of wheat or rice flour (or whatever grain is held sacred in the given land), usually baked by the bride, although sometimes by the groom. Wine or other respected beverage, often blessed in some fashion.

Once the wedding feast was highly symbolic, evolving from a simple exchange of bread between the bride and groom, symbolizing their promise to support each other and the offspring of the union.

Later, this simple exchange evolved into elaborate banquets, often invoking in their varying courses hopes of fertility and prosperity for the newlywed couple. Today, the symbolic elements have been reduced to the rice thrown upon the bride and groom as they emerge from the church. With the recent trend toward replacing symbolic grains with birdseed or confetti, even this lingering element of sympathetic magic has sadly diminished to nothing.

Since the bride and groom will find time to eat very little of this meal, they should be open to suggestions from their caterer as to what to serve, rather than seeking to please themselves. Regional dishes are always nice, but the traditional rubber chicken serves just as well. No one comes to a wedding expecting a good meal.

More essential to the celebratory mood are liberal applications of champagne and other alcoholic beverages. These will create the appropriate levels of hilarity and high spirits, which, in turn, will convince the exhausted bride and nervous groom that they are having a wonderful time.

As mentioned above, the wedding feast was once highly symbolic, and some small remnant of this symbolism lingers in the wedding cake. Until recently, this multitiered extravaganza was made from dry white cake coated with heavy, nearly inedible frosting. However, within the past two decades, there has been a tendency toward making this cake edible, even enjoyable. Consider chocolate cake with fruit filling between the layers or perhaps a sophisticated spice cake. The whiteness of the frosting (symbolic of purity) can be preserved by the use of whipped cream or buttercream frostings.

Much has been discussed about the significance of the

ritual feeding of a bite of cake by the groom to the bride and vice versa. Most agree that this practice is rooted in ancient fertility rituals. Indeed, even today, there remain ethnic groups where the couple is considered wed upon the exchange of some item of food.

In the modern United States, however, the mutual feeding of cake has become a power play, with both parties holding the belief that whoever smears more cake on the other will somehow be dominant in the relationship to come. We cannot help but feel this is a sad and even dangerous development, for in the light of the nearly complete loss of sympathetic magical rituals in any other part of the marriage feast this twisted parody of the once sacred exchange of bread has become symbolic of future strife rather than of any more positive element, and the question of dominance rather than union within the new marriage takes on primary importance.

Surf and Turf

Traditionally, this meal consists of seafood (usually lobster) and a high-grade steak, served side by side with a variety of side dishes. The meal can be quite expensive, and best enjoyed in an exotic setting. Consider the Caribbean, with steel bands playing in the background or perhaps the French Riviera.

Tuna Casserole, Hamburger Stroganoff, Hot Dogs and Beans

All too soon, the young couple must face the sad reality that the honeymoon is over, and living within a budget is a necessity. Still, with love and cooperation, even mundane ingredients can be given that special flare. Couples wherein both members of the family work should consider preparing meals ahead, and exploiting the versatility of the freezer and microwave.

Perennial budget stretchers can be enhanced. Try spicing the tuna casserole with green chile or salsa (now more widely available in the Mexican foods section of your grocery). That old favorite, Hamburger Stroganoff, can be made exotic with the addition of a few portobello or shiitake mushrooms. At the very least, use fresh ingredients, never, ever canned!

Giant Popovers

Take eggs, milk, butter, flour, and salt. Mix at low speeds, gradually adding the melted butter. Bake for one hour. Is there anything more wonderful than seeing such ordinary ingredients rise and swell?

Pickles, White Chocolate, Mango Ice Cream, and Other Cravings

The pregnant woman's cravings for peculiar foods during her pregnancy have become legendary. Interestingly, despite the increased nutritional guidelines given by obstetricians and pediatric specialists, these cravings have increased. Denied coffee, chocolate, alcohol, and numerous other little pleasures, the pregnant woman finds her body suddenly craving other foods. Often these are foods in which she showed no interest before, and so are not usually found in the well-stocked household pantry.

No husband should ever make the mistake of believing his wife is merely being difficult with her little requests for, say, mango passion fruit sherbet or vinegar chile potato chips. She is undergoing intimate chemical changes that affect her biological needs. No matter how put out her husband may feel about being sent out on a rainy evening after a long day's work, when he is longing to put his feet up, rest, and watch a ball game on television, his wife is not exercising a power play.

Really.

Goldfish Crackers, Creamed Vegetables, and American Cheese

The coming of a little one (or two or three) to a household can lead to changes in the family diet, especially once the darling child has been weaned from baby foods and joins the family at the table. It is a fact of life that children's palates often are not suited to the foods adult members of the family enjoy.

Highly spiced foods and strong flavors are often rejected by children, but adaptations can be made that will enable the family to share one meal. Substitute bland American cheese for cheddar or pepper jack, and watch the kids gobble down their macaroni and steamed veggies. Eliminate vinegar, lemon juice, and most spices in favor of neutrality. Fast food is always a hit with the little darlings. An added bonus is that the restaurant's varied menu allows Mom and Dad to add some otherwise forbidden flavors to their meals.

Beware of abusing the fast food option. Regular indulgence in fast food will not supply sufficient nutrition for a growing child. Fast food also has an alarming tendency to pad out the hips and waistline. Many a mother has been astonished to find that regular dining with her children has transformed her once svelte figure into something that can only be called "matronly." Her husband, less intimately concerned with these duties, somehow manages to maintain his earlier weight.

Of course, the wife and mother—who has doubtless given up work outside the home to tend to her little darlings—can cook one meal for herself and her husband, and another for the children. There is considerable labor involved in this effort, but the effort may be worthwhile, especially if the husband starts finding more and more excuses to take his meals away from home.

Cheesecake

This rich dessert is certain to please the most discerning husband, especially when attractively topped, perhaps with grated chocolate or fruit compote. Some connoisseurs hold that the minimalist variation holds its own sensual attractions. A wise wife is advised not to permit overindulgence in cheesecake lest her husband's heart become adversely affected.

Lobster, Oysters, Love Apples, and Bittersweet Chocolate Fondue

The aphrodisiac elements of certain foods are much lauded, and should not be underestimated. Remember the joys of savoring surf and turf on your honeymoon? Remember when a meal was enjoyed without small, piping voices screeching for attention in the background? Try the following menu to stimulate your love life. We suggest you make reservations in advance, and request a private booth.

Start with oysters, served raw if possible, and accompanied by a tangy, spicy dipping sauce. Seafood in general has the reputation for tremendous aphrodisiac qualities. Of all seafood, oysters top this list. There is an indefinably sensual quality to eating raw oysters. Some connoisseurs go so far as to say that this process invokes other, more intimate, erotic practices. Even cooked, however, oysters still retain their aphrodisiac qualities.

Follow the oysters with lobster served with plenty of melted butter. Have the chef crack open the shell, but otherwise extract the sweet, tender meat yourself. Try feeding succulent chunks to your partner, or licking butter from each other's fingers. Accompany the lobster with some light side dishes: a chewy French bread and fresh love apples—as tomatoes were once known.

Should you include wine with your dinner? By all means, but restrict yourself to a crisp and delicate white wine that will not overwhelm the other flavors. Perhaps the sommelier might recommend a vintage not typically found at your local grocery store. Remember to restrict yourself to a glass or two. Alcohol increases desire, but reduces performance.

Conclude your meal with a selection of fruits and pastries dipped in hot, melted chocolate. Banana sections are particularly provocative when fed by the gentleman to the lady. The lady might enjoy serving her date thin slices of apple, playing Eve to his Adam. A good coffee is a fine accompanying stimulant. Avoid accompanying liqueurs for reasons mentioned above.

Simmered Heart, Braised Heart, Boiled Tongue

Prepare heart by trimming away coarse fibers at the top and inside. Simmer covered in water infused with various herbs. Thyme and onion are recommended. Rosemary and rue and even wormwood are interesting alternates.

For braised heart, prepare as described above, then stuff the cavities with herb dressing. Stitch shut, then roll in seasoned flour. Sear in hot fat in a Dutch oven. Add enough liquid to partially cover, probe with fork until it proves done.

Tongue requires skinning, boning, and trimming away of gristle. Scrub fresh tongue with brush. Add to kettle along with whole cloves, peppercorns, bay leaves, and onion. Cook until tender. If necessary, remove skin. Serve with horseradish, tartar sauce, or hot mustard.

Tomato aspic makes a suitable side dish with any of these meats. Try banana or peach flambé for dessert.

When He Carves

Prepare the roast according to directions. Remember the roast should "rest" for anywhere up to a half hour before carving. Precautions should be taken that the meat not grow cold.

Despite the increasingly egalitarian nature of the modern kitchen, carving remains largely within the masculine purview. Never mind that the "little woman" may have already trimmed and scored the roast. Nothing brings out the atavistic male more readily than a succulent haunch of freshly roasted meat impaled upon the "crown" in the center of the carving board.

The carving knife should be razor sharp before the task is begun. However, as sharp items have an immemorial fascination for the gentleman, keeping his tools prepared should be a pleasure rather than a chore.

There are different methods suggested for carving different cuts of meat. The general rule is that if there is a narrower portion (as in a leg of lamb or tip of tongue) this should be placed to the carver's right.

Remember to give the carver a clear field for work. Carving knives are very sharp, and meats have different degrees of density through which the blade may move with greater or lesser ease. Another hazard that may occur in the course of carving is for the blade to encounter bone and slip. In such an instance, the blade may emerge from the roast at an unpredictable angle. An observer, watching from too close at hand, might be injured, perhaps severely.

Once again, remember, carving can be dangerous! Take care to avoid accidents and keep yours a happy kitchen.

Cold Meats for the Funeral Table

Sliced roast beef or turkey. Cheese. Various condiments. Pickles. Various breads, including at least white and whole wheat. Deli salads. Sheet cake. A selection of soft drinks, possibly wine and beer.

It is a sad fact that nearly every family will need to host at least one post-funeral reception. Sometimes these are held for only close family members. Other times all the mourners are invited to come by the house, and share their memories of the deceased with the family. These receptions have their roots in ancient rituals and rites by which the dead was appeased, in order that the soul would not linger to haunt the survivors.

Although a simple menu, easily supplied from the local grocery, is suggested at the opening of this section, the nicer side of this uncomfortable social reality is that even in the modern United States, people respond to grief with gifts of food. Women who have not cooked for years find themselves pulling out casserole dishes or baking pans. Those who cannot manage to cook still visit the grocery to purchase some offering.

Especially if the chief mourner is a widower, he may find himself overwhelmed with kettles of soup, casseroles, and trays of sweets.

Some of his guests may even supply cheesecake.

WINGMEN

by Jean Rabe

Jean Rabe is the author of more than a dozen fantasy novels, and three dozen fantasy, science fiction, and military short stories. Her latest novels include *The Finest Choice* and *Return to Quag Keep*. She is an avid, but lousy, gardener; a goldfish fancier who loves to sit by her pond in the summer; and a movie goer . . . if the movie in question "blows up real good!" Visit her Web site at www.sff.net/people/jeanr.

STAPENHORST SWORE HE could taste the oil spitting off the engines, could feel the wind whistling shrilly past his ears, cold as ice so high this late morning in November. If only he could be up there!

He craned his neck farther out the truck's window and tipped his chin back to catch a glimpse of a Fokker barrel-rolling to come behind a Spad. The tiniest sparks of light, the Fokker's machine guns, and the wounded Spad banked away, Stapenhorst's eyes following it.

"Catch him," he breathed. The Fokker pursued, as if following Stapenhorst's orders. "Finish him. Bring him down and . . . *hurensohn!*" The curse came as the truck Stapenhorst was riding in hit a deep rut, making him momentarily lose track of the two planes.

"My apologies, Leutnant Stapenhorst. The road here is very bad."

"Though not so bad as your driving I think, Feldwebel Gerhtz."

"Leutnant, I . . ."

Stapenhorst gave the driver a dismissive finger wag and again focused on the aerial battle to the west. Eight pilots from Jasta 11 that he could count. Nine a few moments ago, but one plane spiraled down trailing thick gray smoke and then a puff of white—a parachute.

The Jastas, distinguishable at this distance only by the blush of color and the three wings of their Fokkers, were sparring with a mixed French bag—better than two-dozen Spads and Nieuports. The Frogs had wing guns that could flip up and shred the bellies of any Fokkers above them. Probably what had happened to the unfortunate German plane that should be nosing into the ground about now, Stapenhorst thought.

The truck turned left down a narrow and less bumpy road, the new direction giving Stapenhorst a little better view of the dogfight.

"They're outnumbered," the driver offered. "Frightful odds. There'll be more than a few widows tonight, damn the French. The Jasta will certainly need you, sir. Need more than you to replace all the pilots who will not be coming home."

Stapenhorst watched a pair of Spads sandwich one of the Fokkers, taking top and bottom angles in an effort to shoot out the German plane's engine. A Nieuport was banking in to add to the misery.

Suddenly a lone Fokker came down from the clouds. It sideslipped toward the offending Nieuport and spit slugs in the French's fuselage, sawing the tail off. As that Nieuport spun out of control, the Fokker continued to the high Spad, then, after finishing it, dove on the bottom one to save his wingman. The odds were impossibly altered in but a few heartbeats.

Stapenhorst's breath caught as the rescuing Fokker leafed down on another French plane.

"Richtofen," Stapenhorst said. That able pilot could be none other than the vaunted leader of Jasta 11, Stapenhorst's new commanding officer. Stapenhorst's hand tapped the orders in his pocket, and he allowed himself a satisfied smile.

The truck turned again, now following a tree-lined road that effectively blocked Stapenhorst's view of the deadly aerial ballet. He cursed again and pulled his head inside.

It was more than two hours later that the truck rolled onto a cleared field.

The Fokkers he'd watched in the dogfight had arrived well before him and were spaced evenly in front of a row of large tents. The setting sun was striking the blood-red paint and canvas, making the planes practically glow. The color was said to frighten the allies, particularly the inexperienced ones.

Each triplane had slightly different markings, so the pilots could recognize each other in the air and so that spotters stationed along the German lines could more easily confirm the kills of specific pilots. Mechanics were working on only two of the planes, meaning little damage had been suffered in the dogfight—save the plane Stapenhorst saw going down.

"Leutnant Stapenhorst, this is the Jasta 11 aerodrome. Will you be needing. . . ?"

"*Nein*. Nothing else, Feldwebel Gerhtz." Stapenhorst slid out of the truck and shouldered his duffel, slammed the door, then motioned the driver away.

It wasn't what he had expected, this aerodrome. Stapenhorst pictured the famed Jasta 11 having permanent buildings, hangars for the planes and warm quarters with well-stocked bars for the officers. An aerodrome that would be the envy of every German pilot. But there was nothing here save tents—for the planes, and smaller, shabbier looking ones for the men—all of which could be quickly taken down and moved on a moment's notice.

"Of course." Stapenhorst mentally chastised himself. Many Jastas moved often so that the French and English could not easily target the aerodromes. And Jasta 11—fighter squadron *jagdstaffeln* 11—moved in particular. The Flying Circus, the unit had been dubbed, because it traveled across the countryside like a German circus—by rail. The planes were carefully dismantled so they could fit on railway wagons. Any observers would think it nothing more than a circus traveling on to the next engagement. The Jasta stayed no more than a few days in any one place, then the planes and the men were loaded onto railway wagons again, always late at night, and taken to another field. Stapenhorst noted there were train tracks nearby.

Since Bloody April this Jasta had become the most decorated and most successful. Baron Manfred von Richtofen and a few of the other Jasta 11 pilots held the coveted *Pour le Merit*, the Blue Max, for obtaining twenty "kills."

Stapenhorst had only two kills to his name, both Brits, though he had many commendations for assisting in bringing down enemy planes.

"But I will get many, many more kills on my own serving here," he said. Squaring his shoulders, he headed toward a large tent at the end of the row of planes, his breath feathering away from his face in the chill air. He spotted two pilots ducking through the entrance. Tapping the papers in his pocket, he hurried after them.

The men inside were haloed in cigarette smoke, and the smell of beer and of spiced sausage cooking on a small stove hung heavy. Stapenhorst blinked to take some of the sting out of his eyes. Like a dream, the greatest pilots of the Jasta were all gathered here—Hintsch, thin-lipped Festner, Emil Schaefer, Otto Brauneck, Kurt Wolff, Georg Simon—who Stapenhorst had met a few years back and who had recommended him for this Jasta—Esser, Krefft, Lothar von Richtofen. And in the center, like a king holding court, was Jasta 11's leader—Manfred von Richtofen, the famed Red Baron.

They'd all been talking, and though Stapenhorst was paying only slight attention to the loudest buzz, he could tell they were discussing the late afternoon battle. Someone near the Baron was making a toast. *"Der Tog!"* To the day.

Stapenhorst stepped farther inside, and the conversations ceased. All eyes turned to him. Peering through the fog of smoke to get a better look, Stapenhorst was struck with their appearances—all of their faces planes and angles, their pale skin tight across their cheeks and jaws, their eyes dark and unblinking. Every aspect gave them the miens of predators.

One of them finally spoke to him, but he wasn't sure who or what was said, and he cocked his head, hoping it would be repeated.

After several beats of silence, he removed the orders from his pocket and walked toward the Baron. "Leutnant von Stapenhorst reporting per orders."

The Baron, smaller than Stapenhorst thought he looked in photographs, took the papers and idly glanced at them. "You were expected yesterday." The words were smooth and melodic. "We could have used you this afternoon."

"There was no available transportation."

"Always the problem." The Baron handed the papers back. "Welcome to the Circus, Leutnant."

Stapenhorst gave a curt nod. Outward, he presented a stoic mask. But inside his stomach churned. Face-to-face with his idol—all of Germany's idol. Inches away. "Where do I . . ." Stapenhorst glanced at his gear.

"Do not bother to get comfortable." This came from Simon. "We move tonight."

The railway wagon had benches bolted to the bed. After trying several seats, Stapenhorst decided the benches were all equally uncomfortable. The track was uneven and added to his suffering. The other pilots in the cabin were engaged in hushed conversations and did not think to include him. Two were trading cigarettes and taking turns with a flask of whiskey.

They had all been reasonably polite to him, though they did not go out of their way to make him feel truly welcomed. Perhaps that would have to wait until he became an ace.

Simon told him that would happen soon. All of Jasta 11's pilots—save Stapenhorst—were aces. The Jasta's record was impeccable and incredible. The pilots defied all the desperate odds thrown at them, particularly when they were against French planes.

"Ah, it is heaven to be a part of this," Stapenhorst had told Simon an hour or so earlier.

"Heaven?" Simon shook his head. "*Nein.* Not even close. But you will see that soon. When you're an ace. You will truly be a part of the Jasta then."

Stapenhorst asked Simon to explain further. But the elder pilot shook his head and instead questioned Stapenhorst.

"Would you do anything for Germany? Anything?"

Stapenhorst nodded.

"I told the Baron as much. That is why you were invited to join us. Anything for victory, eh?" Simon smiled grimly and excused himself to another train car.

Stapenhorst watched some of the other pilots leave through the cabin's rear door. The door at the front led to wagons where the planes were kept. After a while he decided to see where the other pilots went.

"Odd." Stapenhorst stood at the head of the next cabin. It was lit only by a pair of oil lanterns. There were benches along the side to his right, the left had bins for storing duffels and supplies. He pressed to the next cabin, also empty, balancing himself as the train rocked back and forth, bracing himself as he stepped on the platform between the cabins and again felt the wintry air.

He paused at the next door, though he couldn't say what held his hand. Nor could he explain why he pressed his ear to it, as he hadn't at the previous cabins. Nothing. Wait. There was something other than the keening of the wind and the ratcheting sound of the railway wheels. Concentrating, he picked out voices, some high-pitched and excited, some deep, one melodic—the Baron's. But he could make out none of the words.

Stapenhorst smoothed at his uniform and squared his shoulders. He opened the cabin door and quietly stepped inside. It was darker than the other cabins, and longer. Stapenhorst could barely see the silhouettes of the pilots. Everything was indistinct in the light of a lone lantern that had been turned as low as possible. He swallowed to moisten his throat, intending to step forward and offer a greeting—but he stopped himself. For an instant he thought he saw other shapes—small, deformed ones. The lantern flared a little brighter and they were gone.

Simon looked up and spotted Stapenhorst. *When you are an ace*, he mouthed.

Stapenhorst had flown more than fifty missions, but he'd never flown a tripe before. His was designated Dr.

I 144/17. His last plane had been an Albatross DIII, which he found comfortable and responding, if sometimes ponderous. This new Fokker Dreidecker was . . . snug, and it made him both giddy and nervous at the same time. It looked small inside and out, with three wings of descending length, the largest with a span of about ten meters. He had considered requesting a familiar plane, even an outdated DII. But he didn't want to ask any favors of the Baron. Besides, he told himself, the other Jasta 11 pilots were flying these contraptions.

For a brief moment he recalled the shadows of the previous night, then he focused on the hum of his plane's engine, not so loud as what he was used to. He nudged the throttle forward. In an instant the plane leaped off the field. Stapenhorst expected the Fokker to drag with its three wings. Instead, they provided an astonishing lift. He was angling upward faster than he had in any other plane. Its engine was a 110 Le Rhone rotary, built and supplied to Germany under license by Thulin, a Swedish firm. The cowling was enclosed to just below the airscrew boss and had two cooling holes. The ribs and leading edges were plywood, everything else fabric-covered, and the trailing-edges were wire. Balanced ailerons were fitted to the top wing only, and the center wing had two cutouts. Lightweight, highly manageable, and with exceptional upward visibility—as it lacked the bracing wires that could be shot away on biplanes.

Stapenhorst knew the plane had its champions—Werner Voss last year demonstrated that it was outstanding in a dogfight and that nothing matched its climb rate. It had its detractors, too, as many pilots, including the famous Heinrich Gontermann, had died from wing failures. He'd heard there'd been structural improvements since those days. He certainly hoped so.

The twin Spandau machine guns were perched in front of him. "Easy to aim," he noted.

Opening the throttle, the plane sped forward, catching up with the rest of the squadron—all on the way to the front for a strafing run. "To slaughter the *frontschwein*," he said with a smile. The enemy frontline pigs.

The Dr. I was faster than he expected, and the rudder moved effortlessly. He tried a roll, discovering that the ailerons had a stiff feel, and he worried if that could prove a liability.

"Let's try something else," he said, staying at the back of the formation, as the Baron had suggested. Richtofen wanted Stapenhorst to experiment with the Dr. I a bit—while still keeping the other Jasta 11 pilots in sight.

He attempted a slight turn, the wings producing still more lift and giving him a quick heading change. He circled the plane back and worked the rudder to keep it from rolling too much. No aircraft could possibly turn better than this! Amazing, he thought, as he adjusted his goggles tighter.

So the ailerons were a bit stiff, so it lost some maneuverability when the tail dropped. Ax-handlelike skids had been added to the lowest wings so that if the tail dipped too close to the ground, the plane would not easily crash.

"Heaven!" Stapenhorst was caught up in the speed, the excitement, the glory of flying. Nothing matched the sensation, and the cold could do nothing to trounce his spirits. God bless the war that allowed him to experience this, and to be in the Baron's squadron. He opened the throttle wider, and he followed the others to the front.

The landscape changed dramatically the farther they flew. Farm fields, barren this time of year, gave way to scabrous, ugly land pockmarked with craters from bombs and artillery fire.

The forward planes angled down, and Stapenhorst matched them, still marveling at how the Dr. I moved.

"Heaven," he repeated.

They paralleled a river, then flew over a ruined bridge. Above the drone of the engines, he could hear the boom of flak cannons and the whistle of bombs. An instant more and he could see manmade clouds of weapon smoke rising into the early morning sky. The Allies were hunkered down in the trench, and the lead Fokkers dove on them, machine guns spewing lead.

The strafing run lasted only minutes, though it felt much longer than that. Time twists during combat, Stapenhorst knew. The Jasta was astonishingly successful in taking out several banks of antiaircraft guns and well-entrenched machine-gun emplacements, and only one plane was damaged in response.

It was unnervingly easy. But Stapenhorst was an expert pilot, and he was flying among Germany's very best. And so he told himself that skill won the day. He ignored the shiver that danced down his spine, and he somehow managed to set aside any qualms about the victory.

And that night, when Simon and several other pilots retreated to the rear train car, Stapenhorst tried to follow them.

"Nein," Simon scolded. "When you are an ace."

A few days later, Stapenhorst scored his fourth kill. One more would give him the coveted title and entry into the private gathering at the back of the train. They were getting more dogfight missions close to the front, and tomorrow morning they were going after a French balloon. Just before sunset they would go out again, this time to strike at a French squadron. The squadron seemed to fare the best against the French.

Stapenhorst thought of that fifth, magical kill as he lay in his bunk, cold despite the wool blankets. The Jasta was camped in a clearing near the tracks this night. Winter was deepening, and its winds were chasing away some of the joy he felt at being in the midst of these great pilots. Winter and the curiosity of what he would find in the rear cabin when he was invited into their little circle. He shuddered as he nestled farther under the covers and tried to fall asleep.

He listened to the snores of his fellows, and he heard the rustle of clothes and the grunt of a pilot pulling on his boots. Moments later, he heard the tent flap open and close. There was the sound of boots crunching over gravel and the frozen ground.

Perhaps the pilots were excited about the prospect of flying two missions tomorrow. Couldn't sleep and so they decided to take a walk and perhaps share some whiskey and smokes. Stapenhorst threw off the blankets and struggled into his boots. He would join them. He drew his coat tight around him and stepped outside and glanced across the field, the full moon making it easy for him to see the planes and the other tents—and still more pilots that were striding toward a copse of trees.

Some sensible part of him insisted he go back to bed. But Stapenhorst ignored the warning and started off at a trot.

The trees ahead were a mix of evergreens, looking like black cutouts under the bright moon. He wondered why the pilots would come all the way out here.

The sensible part of him complained louder, but he only picked up his pace, brushing past the first evergreen and knocking frost off its branches, pieces of lace flittering to the ground. Two pilots were just ahead of him, and one of them turned—Festner. Caught in the moonlight, Stapenhorst froze.

Festner motioned for him to come closer.

There was no threat in the gesture. Indeed, Festner was smiling. But the smile didn't reach his eyes.

"Nein," Stapenhorst said. "I think it is too cold out here tonight."

"You are persistent," came a voice from behind him. "But in a little while you won't be minding the cold." Simon prodded Stapenhorst forward. "We were waiting for you to become an ace before we introduced you. That's been our custom. But I suspect you'll get your fifth kill tomorrow, with all the action we'll be seeing. So we might as well introduce you now and settle your curiosity."

There was a campfire burning merrily just past a column of tall pines. Esser, Wolff, Krefft, and Richtofen were the highest-ranking of the eight seated around the fire. Simon prodded again, and Stapenhorst complied, finding a spot next to Esser. Simon sat to his left.

"See? It's not cold around the fire," Simon laughed.

Stapenhorst nodded, feeling his throat constricting and his chest tight. Nerves. He glanced quickly about. There were no cigarettes or flasks of whiskey, none of the trappings of fellowship. The only conversation was between Richtofen and Wolff, and it was soft and in a language Stapenhorst couldn't understand.

Simon slapped him on the back and went to say something else. But he stopped as Krefft stuck his hand in the fire and pulled out a blackened stick. He started tracing a pattern across the hardened ground and mumbled in the language Richtofen and Wolff spoke. Some words had a familiar sound, and Stapenhorst futilely tried to pick through the jumble.

"It is old Norman," Simon finally whispered. "It is a chant that calls them."

Calls who? Stapenhorst mouthed, though instantly he knew the answer. The small shadows he saw in the railway wagon.

"The lutin."

Lutin. Lutin. Lutin. Stapenhorst knew the word, and his mind stretched back to tales of his childhood. Goblins! Mischievous folklore beings who at one instant could be a fully equipped mount, a *Cheval Bayard*, and at the next a housecat. Some were said to be good spirits meant to protect German houses, and at the worst would twist a child's hair into locks so tangled they had to be cut. But others were of a dark nature, so the tales said.

Lutin here? How could they be real? Not possible!

Simon was saying something else, but Stapenhorst was too lost in thought. It wasn't until the fire flared that his thoughts came back to his surroundings.

The wisps of smoke rising from the flames formed shapes and spun away, coming to ground and circling the pilots and giggling maniacally. There were a dozen, each different. The largest was nearly two meters tall and looked like the misshapen skeleton of a man, red skin pulled close across the bones. Another looked like a small gorilla, fur as scarlet as the flames and eyes solid black. A few were rats, with glowing red fur that melted away to become gray and mangy. They cavorted behind the pilots, making clacking and hooting noises, slapping each other and occasionally wailing like prowling wolves. There was music to their sounds. It had a primal rhythm that was interspersed with complex dissonant rifts. Some of the pilots were swaying to it. Krefft was trying to sing along in the old language.

Despite himself, Stapenhorst found he enjoyed the dance and the melody, closed his eyes and let the sounds overtake him. He felt pleasantly warm and welcomed, and suddenly the hard ground was comfortable.

Then the music stopped and the creatures stood still,

forming a circle inside the pilots now. One of the beasts, a large rat, settled itself in front of Stapenhorst and rose on its tiny hindquarters, waving its claws in the air.

With the music gone, Stapenhorst's will was returning. "I–I–I don't think I want to take part in this," he whispered to Simon. "This isn't real."

"Oh, it's very real. And you've no choice, brother." Simon made a tsk-tsking sound. "You said you'd do anything for Germany."

"Anything," Stapenhorst admitted.

"This is a small sacrifice, my friend."

Stapenhorst made a move to get up, but Simon slammed a hand on his leg.

"Anything for Germany, you said."

Stapenhorst swallowed hard, but nodded. *Anything,* he mouthed.

"Good. When you joined this very special Jasta, you signed on for this. We're careful who we let into our ranks. I recommended you, remember. Don't disappoint me. Besides, it won't hurt much."

The rat crawled up Stapenhorst's leg, nose quivering and eyes shining. It opened its mouth to reveal snow-white teeth. As he stared at the creature, it appeared slightly fuzzy and out-of-focus.

Around the circle the other creatures were selecting pilots, Richtofen and Wolff each getting two.

"What will happen?" Stapenhorst risked.

"Take off your coat, brother. And unbutton your shirt. As I said, it won't hurt much. And it is the least you can do for the war."

Stapenhorst shook his head, one last, vain attempt at defiance.

"They want our blood. It is a special treat for them." Simon dropped his voice so Stapenhorst had to strain to hear. "In return, they serve as our most valuable wingmen. With them, no odds are too great." Then Simon was doffing his coat and rolling up a sleeve, offering his arm to the creature that had chosen a miniature gorilla form.

Stapenhorst couldn't remember loosening his clothes, but he could tell his chest was bare to the winter air.

The rat clung to a fold of his shirt and stared up into his eyes. It chittered something in the old language, then it sank its tiny teeth into Stapenhorst's breast, and it feasted.

Stapenhorst wanted to know how often this ritual was performed, and how often he would be expected to take part. But he decided those questions would be for another time. So nothing was said during the walk back to the tent, nor at breakfast. Stapenhorst had no scar from the odd encounter, and the only souvenir from the night was the dissonant tune he kept hearing in his head.

They would be running on the French balloon within the hour. It was reported near the front and spotting German gun emplacements. It needed to be brought down quickly to protect the infantry, and Jasta 11 was the closest squadron. They should expect the balloon to be heavily protected—with antiaircraft guns and machine guns, and of course with planes. Richtofen selected himself and only ten other pilots for the mission . . . the men who were in the clearing last night.

Stapenhorst opened the throttle and stayed even with Simon. The plane handled effortlessly this morning, better than ever perhaps due to the damaged aileron being replaced. They climbed high, nearly to the Fokker's ceiling of more than six thousand meters. It should have been unbearably cold this high up in January, but Stapenhorst felt only the slightest chill.

"Is it the wingmen?" he mused aloud, meaning the lutin goblins. "Could they possibly. . . ?"

"Yesss." The word was a hiss coming from over his shoulder. "We help you." A rat, Stapenhorst assumed it was the one who fed on him last night, came down his chest and settled in his lap. "We give you warmth. And what you call luck."

It wasn't speaking the old language now. It was crisp German, though the words sounded tinny because of the creature's high-pitched voice.

"And you do all of this—for us and for Germany—for a bit of my blood?" Stapenhorst cursed himself for talking to the thing. He looked away from it and focused on the other planes in the formation. In the distance below, the oblong form of a dirigible was faintly discernible through a thin layer of clouds.

"For that," it replied. "And for a bit more."

Stapenhorst's plane sped up, though he hadn't moved the throttle. The others were moving faster, too, and had started their dives. He double-checked his machine guns and warned himself: *don't get too close to the top of the balloon, as it could burst into flames and catch me.*

A side shot, he decided, watching Simon barrel-roll down with the same intention. Richtofen was diving straight down for the risky shot on the top. Perhaps he had nothing to fear. Perhaps there was a lutin in his plane protecting him.

"Closer," the creature urged him. "There. Faster."

Again the plane sped up of its own volition, and Stapenhorst opened fire, the bullets ripping into the silk. He heard machine-gun fire all around him—from the other Fokker pilots and from emplacements on the ground. There were rifle shots, too, these coming from the observers in the basket beneath the balloon. It all sounded like he'd swept into the middle of a giant hornet's nest.

And in the background, he heard the dissonant music from the clearing.

"Now onto the other planes," the lutin told him. "They're coming up from the ground. There are two British planes with them, but you will not shoot at them. Sometimes the British station pilots at French aerodromes. We did not know they would do so today."

"We?"

"My fellows," the creature sneered. It looked slightly out-of-focus to Stapenhorst.

Indeed there were two British Bristols amid French Breguet fighters. Slower and larger than the Fokker Dr. Is, the Breguets were nevertheless more formidable. They were two-seaters, meaning there could be double the firepower and double the chance of dying to them. There were a couple of Morane-Saulniers in the mix, monoplane two-seaters that were not as maneuverable and that had Hotchkiss machine guns that spit copper bullets.

"I'm not to shoot the British. Why?"

"Because I said so. Because I say you only shoot Frenchmen today."

Stapenhorst shook his head. "I don't understand."

"You are not meant to," the lutin purred. It had become a fuzzy cat, snuggling on Stapenhorst's lap. He studied it, seeing some of its features indistinct. "They have many, many planes up today, the French. But you are not to worry. You will shoot them."

Stapenhorst nosed down to meet the climbing Breguets. Four other Fokkers had broken off from the tattered balloon and were joining him. He was warm in the high, cold, January air. He was unduly confident. And he was thinking it more than a fair trade for a bit of his blood.

"And a bit of something more." The cat intruded on his thoughts. "Get closer, I say."

Stapenhorst did, though not as fast or as close as Simon had managed.

"Are the others not to shoot the British, too?" As Stapenhorst prepared to take aim on one of the two-seaters, he saw Simon's plane out of the corner of his eye. A small, red gorilla was climbing out of the cockpit and walking along the wing. Then it was spreading its arms and taking flight toward the nearest Breguet, latching onto its wing and scrambling toward the fuselage. It was clear the French pilots didn't see the lutin, which was climbing in with the observer now and dismantling his twin machine guns. A moment more, and it was headed for the pilot's guns.

"My God," Stapenhorst whistled. No wonder the Jastas had few fatalities and little damage to their planes. The creatures disarmed their opponents. "The French can't see you, can they?"

"Nein," the cat said in thick German. "Not unless we want them to."

"And you do this all the time? Ruin their guns?"

"Break their spars and poke at their engines. Shred their canvas and steal their breath."

"For the glory of Germany."

"For the glory of Germany," it parroted snidely. "For the glory of Jasta 11."

"And all for a bit of my blood? And a bit of something else?"

"A bit of your soul. The small piece you keep for yourself. That piece that hasn't been given to the Fatherland."

The warmth fled Stapenhorst's body and he pulled back hard on the stick, taking his Fokker higher, narrowly missing Wolff's wing.

"A piece of my soul."

"You won't miss it."

A lump formed in his stomach, and he took his plane higher still, past what was left of the balloon that was being winched down.

"A small price to pay for the glory of Jasta 11." The cat started kneading his leg. "Now return to the battle. I'll make you an ace today. Isn't that what you wanted?" The cat gestured with a paw. "The pilot in the Morane-Saulnier there, and his observer. Their guns are useless now. An easy kill, Ace Stapenhorst."

"But what about the Bristols?" The dissonant music of the clearing became loud in Stapenhorst's ears, competing with the sound of machinegun fire.

"You ask too many questions," the lutin grumbled. "Pilots who ask too many questions do not fly long. We have not taken enough of your blood, Stapenhorst. We have left you with too much will."

"What do you. . . ?"

"The day you joined the Jasta. Do you remember it?" The lutin didn't wait for a reply. "The Jasta lost a pilot that very morning. He asked too many questions. He was too willful. Like you." The lutin became a rat again and wriggled its nose at Stapenhorst. "That Morane. Dive on it and become an ace."

"Anything for Germany," he whispered.

But he would have to talk to someone tonight, Simon or Richtofen. Winning this way wasn't settling right with him. And why wasn't he to fire on the Bristols? Why couldn't. . . ?

"Nein. Nein. Nein." Tittered the rat. "You will talk to no one. And you will stop asking questions."

"Get out!" Stapenhorst shouted. "I will talk to anyone I please. Get out of my plane!"

"Perhaps Simon was wrong to request you in this squadron. None of the others have complained of our tactics. All they think about are the kills and the medals." The rat yawned and scratched its nose. "I think you are too much of a risk."

Stapenhorst stared at it, seeing nothing else and all at once seeing something truly fuzzy about the creature. It opened its eyes wide in surprise.

"What are you?"

"Pity you look so close," the creature taunted. "So few of you Germans have the presence to truly see us. We should have taken much more of your blood last night."

"Get out!"

"If you insist, Leutnant Stapenhorst."

"Get out now, you little demon."

The creature complied, scurrying up his chest and onto his shoulder, then around to the back of his collar, where it began digging into the parachute. Stapenhorst tried to grab it, but the feat proved impossible while still flying.

The parachute destroyed, the rat scurried out onto the fuselage. It seemed the creature had no fear of speed or height or gravity. It crawled down the nose and started scratching at the engine casing. It turned back, once, to glare at Stapenhorst. Then it proceeded to dismantle a piece of his plane's engine. When it was finished, it turned into a childlike creature with pastel wings.

"Not a lutin," Stapenhorst breathed.

It shook its head and grinned, somehow looking innocent and mischievous at the same time. "Unfortunate that you looked so close. And now you'll join the few others who saw us for what we really are."

"Fey."

The child-creature nodded. "From the Unseelie Court. We take a bit of your soul, and we let you think you are winning for Germany. But we are stealing your secrets and we are using you, paying you back for the Saxon invasion."

"And using us to kill the French."

"We never liked the French," the fey smiled. Then it leaped into the air and disappeared.

Stapenhorst threw all of his being into leafing the plane down with a dead engine. Had the plane not been so lightweight, and had he not been such a gifted pilot, he would have flown into the earth.

He had just enough lift to get him well behind the front—and into British territory, where he suspected there would be fey waiting.

Leutnant von Stapenhorst of Jasta 11 was captured January 13, 1918, when he was forced down in allied territory. His Fokker Dr. I 144/17 was the first intact plane of its kind captured by the British.

YANKEE BOY

by Alexander B. Potter

Alexander B. Potter resides in the wilds of Vermont, editing anthologies and writing both fiction and nonfiction. His short stories have appeared in a wide variety of anthologies including the award-winning *Bending the Landscape: Horror* volume. He edited *Assassin Fantastic*, the award-winning *Sirius: The Dog Star*, and *Women of War* for DAW Books.

1775

THE BRANCHES WHIPPED around him as he scrambled up the mountainside. His feet slid on the pine needles and leaf litter covering the ground and his arm flailed to maintain his balance, almost losing his grip on his musket. Ben caught hold of a low branch with his other hand and used it to lever himself up another few steps, then leaned against the tree trunk to catch his breath and listen for pursuit.

He hadn't heard anyone behind him for some time now, but he needed to be sure. Chasing the Boys down wasn't really the Yorkers' style, much as they threatened to, but they were still damn persistent, no matter their cowardly, thieving ways. Every man who called himself a Green Mountain Boy had learned so with each renewed order coming out of Albany to take back the New Hampshire land grants, each sheriff and surveyor sent in, and each new settlement of Yorkers moving in on Yankee land. Worse even were those already living on the grants, who would just as soon give over to New York ownership for nothing more than a questionable promise to be left in peace. Just the thought of those who would meekly accept New York rule made Ben's guts twist.

Or maybe it was just that he hadn't eaten in a while.

Ben sucked in a breath and calmed himself, then peered around the tree, back the way he'd come. Nothing. Just more trees and the long sloping fall of the land toward the base of Mount Moosalamoo, slowly giving in to the encroaching dusk. He pushed his hat back off his forehead and scrubbed at the sweat running down his face with his sleeve. Another minute or two, just to be sure.

His heart quieted in his chest, and still the woods stood silent. Twilight settled all around him, and under the tree cover it darkened quickly. He knew he'd best get moving again if he wanted shelter. He thought he was close, but he'd never had to find the cave on his own in the dark before.

Splitting up to melt back into the land had seemed like the best idea at the time, in the face of surprisingly well-armed Yorker resistance in Cornwall. In retrospect, Ben wondered if splitting up in twos would have been smarter. Not that there'd been that many of them this time out. Probably shouldn't have even tried the raid without more men, without Ethan along. But Ethan wanted them on guard, keeping the Yorkers in line even when he was elsewhere. Ben thought he'd have approved the attempt, even if it did fail.

Settling his hat more firmly, he straightened from the tree, shouldered his musket, and started off again. Wasn't like he was scared or anything. Green Mountain Boys didn't know fear, damn it. Not outside on their own lands. Not even at night. So it was getting a little dark and he was alone. He snorted and kept walking, scouting for the landmarks in the growing dusk.

Exhaustion sang in his muscles, and his knees hurt after all the running, then climbing uphill for the last hour or so. The dark thickened, the moon rose, and still he walked.

Ben tried to keep from complaining to himself, even counting his footsteps for distraction. Complaining didn't do a bit of good and was unloyal besides. Wasn't like he didn't believe in the cause, and Ethan. He definitely believed in Ethan. He wanted to keep hold of his family's land too, just as much as any of the Boys.

But sometimes, Ben just wanted to go home and stay there. Somewhere inside him, he was getting tired of the fighting.

Raiding the Yorker settlements had started out fun. Exciting, even. He'd picked up a few extra cattle for his father, so . . . couldn't complain. Running off the New York officials made decent sport, and fed the anger smoldering under his breastbone. But that last fire'd taken it out of him. Watching the flames—that he'd help set—eat the log home that someone actually lived in . . . it made him stop and think. Think of his own home crumbling to glowing coals, his mother and father watching it with the same stricken faces as the evicted tenants had done.

Wasn't like it couldn't happen. Hell, it could happen any day. He shuddered and walked faster, pretending to himself that he was just cold.

Bible said one thing. Well, actually, Bible said a whole lot of things, not a lot that made sense to Ben. And one too many things that seemed to be saying the exact opposite of what the page before said. But *preachers* said the Bible said one thing . . . Ethan said something else altogether. Ethan made plain sense, and Ben liked the big man something fierce. He'd admired him even before his father had become one of Ethan's biggest supporters. Ben particularly liked it when Ethan grumbled about making the Green Mountain territory its own province, a real republic all on its own. Not part of New York, or New Hampshire, or Canada.

Deep down, he just didn't know if he was cut from the same cloth as Ethan, was all. Ethan never tired of campaigning against the claims of New York, rallying the Boys, chasing out any settler who had Yorker sympathies and support. Ben wanted that kind of passion, the kind Ethan had in abundance.

Ofttimes he felt it, boiling up inside him like sap going to sugar, when he stood in Ethan's presence, listening to him speak. Watching him raise that big fist and shout. It was just times like these, alone, none of the other Boys around to keep him focused on the fight, the loyalty, the pride.

Alone.

He paused and listened, staring up through the branches at the moon. Owls. Small rustles of night rodents. He breathed in deeply and felt the chill spring air flow through him. *Just need to calm down. You know it's not far. You can do this.*

He supposed he should just be glad it wasn't raining. And he walked on.

His perseverance paid off when he saw the familiar rocky outcropping. Breathing a sigh of relief—which did *not* indicate he'd been scared, just *tired*—Ben approached the rocks and ducked down to squeeze through the almost unnoticeable opening. Slipping into the small cavern, he plunked himself down on the ground with a rush of weakened knees, pulling in deep shaky breaths. He leaned the musket against the cave wall close at hand. As confident as he'd tried to be, he'd lost count of the number of times the little voice in his head muttered that he might not be able to find the cave.

The dark of his shelter wrapped around him and whispered safety, even as the cold of earth and rock seeped through his breeches and kept him from lying down. He pulled his coat tighter. Late April might be warm enough in the sun, but not after nightfall. Especially up here on Moosalamoo. Slowed the rattlesnakes down, which came in handy, but he'd be lucky if he could get to sleep at all. Still, wouldn't be the first time with less than ideal bedding since he'd taken up with the Boys.

He sighed and leaned his head back against the cave wall. His cocked hat pushed forward over his eyes and he left it, the familiar feel of the brim resting against his nose when trying to sleep increasing his sense of comfort. Made him think of catching some rest in the corner of some warm, lamp-lit tavern with the smells of baking bread, roasting meat, and drinking men in his nose. Leaned up against a wall while the other Boys talked and drank and laughed and planned . . . the rise and fall of familiar voices lulling him even as they got rowdy and a little too loud. Safe in their company. Safe in their passion, their purpose.

The soft scraping noise off to his left in the cave chased every bit of comfort and safety clean out of his head.

Snatching his hat off, he whirled, coming up into a crouch with musket in hand, eyes scouring the depths of the darkness. It was useless. Whatever moonlight made it through the trees to illuminate the narrow opening and spill through the crack in the far end of the cave didn't cut through the deeper shadows at all. He only hoped that whatever was in here with him couldn't see better than he could. He aimed his musket in the direction of the noise, best as he could guess.

Another scrape; something moving closer. Person? Animal? The Boys jested often enough about a bear taking up residence in the cave. Wouldn't a person have spoke up soon as he came through the cave mouth? Would a bear even fit through the opening? *A scrawny, underfed,* hungry *bear would*, his mind muttered. He cursed the thought as his knees trembled.

Whatever it was stopped moving again, and he finally cleared his throat nervously and managed "Who's there?" in the sharp kind of voice he thought Ethan might use under these circumstances. The cracking of his voice didn't quite have the ring of authority of Ethan's. He could feel his palms sweating against the musket. Between one breath and the next, the low pulse of a headache throbbed between his eyes.

After a pause, a raspy voice answered, "Who's . . . there?"

Person. Ben almost dropped to the floor in relief again, lowering his gun, only just remembering that "person" didn't necessarily mean "friend." The cave wasn't obvious, but also not impossible to find. He doubted a Yorker would be stumbling around this far in territory, but never could be sure. "Are you one of the Boys?" he whispered harshly, the long barrel rising again.

Another oddly extended pause, and Ben wondered if the man might be injured. *Or just coming up with a plausible story to spin on me.* Or maybe just as scared as he was, although he somehow doubted that. He blinked, wondering why the pressure of the headache suddenly hurt so bad when it hadn't bothered him at all during his escape up here.

"Yes," came the answer in that same rough voice. "One of your . . . boys."

Ben sagged against the wall. The man might still be lying, but how would he know until he saw him? "Hold on there, step into the moonlight," he ordered.

Silence held for long moments. Then more movement, and more scraping, this time in the other direction. Finally a short, slim figure stepped into the weak light falling through the crack in the rocks. The moon gilded the light hair almost blue.

Ben tilted his head, trying to make out the shadowed features in the gaunt face. They looked almost familiar. Something about the eyes was . . . off. His head hurt. Something just seemed wrong. In the strange light the figure almost looked like a woman, a young one anyway, smaller build with finer facial features than he was used to on any of the Boys. But the figure wore breeches not skirts, and that voice . . . too deep by far for a woman or girl.

Besides, his eyes must be playing tricks, Ben thought, because now the face looked fuller, and the eyes as normal as his own. Probably this thrice-damned headache pushing directly between his eyebrows, lodging behind his eyes, making his vision funny.

Squinting, he moved closer almost without meaning to, trying to place the familiarity. The musket drooped in his hands. With every step closer the face looked more and more—

He stopped dead in spite of an overwhelming urge to keep moving forward. His breath caught in his throat. The other's bones seemed to shift under skin even as he watched, even as he swore it had to be a trick of the moonlight. With each second the face looked more . . . like his own. The squaring jaw, the light hair that darkened even as he stared at it. Even the body looked different, taller, the form stockier, shoulders broadening.

"Ben," said the voice, low and careful, and now instead of rasping, it exactly mimicked his own.

"Who *are* you?" he breathed, unable to stop the steps that he now definitely did *not* want to be taking, bringing him closer to the man who could be his brother. His *twin*. The pressure in his head pulled him forward, as if a fishing hook lodged deep in his brain and reeled him in like a trout.

The man—*man?*—extended a hand, and Ben stared, uncomprehending, at his own fingers reaching toward him, only belatedly realizing his arm was rising to meet the grasp though he'd given it no such permission.

"I'm Ben," said his voice, so calm, so perfectly reasonable, from that other mouth.

But I'm Ben, his mind insisted as his fingers grasped his fingers and he sank to the ground. The pressure in his head increased like an ax driven between his eyes. The dark cave went darker around him.

It-Ben waited until full light to leave the cave. Though night vision offered no impediment to it, this land was too new to its kind to be roaming in full dark. Stepping out into the early morning, it leaned the weapon against the cave and looked out over the view from the mountain. Staring at the lake far below in fascination, it wondered idly where the other First Advancers landed and how they fared.

It knew many arrived before it, as it had been one of the last to enter a pod and escape the disabled ship. It almost waited too long.

Standing before the cave, It-Ben released the disturbing memory. Nothing to be done about the ship, so no benefit in wasting thought. It stretched its new form, staring down at the hands and arms with something like satisfaction. Not only a sentient creature, useful, too. Definite improvement over the first creature it took. Flexing fingers carefully, it looked back at the cave.

Was-Ben still lay on the dirt floor, and It-Ben knew

it should do something about the body. The memories and experiences absorbed from the taken form told it that burial was expected. But it had nothing to dig with, and had no intention of digging with its new hands.

It had not expected a . . . human?—*human*, the new memories confirmed—to come to it in the temporary hideaway. It expected to have to seek longer, watch and wait. It had seen humans already, had touched one mind earlier while still in the form of the first creature taken. The small human—smaller than the current specimen, and lighter, too—had run screaming from it when it shuffled out of the woods. It touched the mind long enough to know the fear its then-form inspired in this new species, and to touch the possibilities held in that small skull.

It knew in that moment of contact that this would be the species it needed. No doubt, the others of its kind had already reached a similar conclusion. It left the small one, returning to the woods to continue to acclimate to the world and practice taking on the form it had seen so briefly.

The results were conclusive. More contact definitely required. More mind exploration, and touch contact.

It wasn't at all prepared for Was-Ben to stumble in on it. Still, it knew opportunity when it presented, and Was-Ben carried a . . . it searched the new memories for the word, matching image with language . . . a musket. Technology, of a sort. Confirmation of its earlier suspicions. An excellent place to begin.

But no technology to assist with digging. It-Ben pondered leaving the body where it lay. That didn't sit well, though. That was not the way of its kind. Proper respect to those who gave of their essence for perpetuation was due. The first creature expected nothing. Leaving it to the elements fit. This time, the absorbed experiences of Was-Ben resisted that very idea with a strength It-Ben found surprising.

Finally, it reentered the cave and dragged the body out into the sunlight. It had already removed the clothes during the dark time and wore them now. It could project a vision of expected coverings for a short time but simply maintaining basic form, and using the form's own coverings, proved much more efficient and conserved energy. Staring down at the current body, it realized the first creature, despite the mental limitations, could serve well for these needs. Carefully removing each garment it wore, it set them on the ground, then reached back for the molecular structure of the first creature it encountered on this planet.

Bear, supplied the Was-Ben's memories, with a similar sense of fear as the small one. It started to form the word, but it had already reassumed the bear form. Only a low growl emerged. Again looking down at the front appendages, wide paws with thick claws appeared much sturdier and more suitable. Digging this creature understood. It ambled a short distance from the still form of Was-Ben and began to dig. When the shallow hole looked large enough, it shuffled back to the body and, gripping an arm in the strong jaw, dragged the body to the hole.

Filling in the hole took much less time.

Allowing the bear form to recede and the Ben form to coalesce, It-Ben redressed the new form. It had paused long enough. It needed to find others of Was-Ben's clan and begin to look for the others of its own clan, and they must begin to establish. Cataloging each entry in Was-Ben's memory, it examined the familial and societal ties carefully. With the honed instinct for power structures common to all of its kind, it knew immediately which clan member it should seek.

Ethan.

It even knew where to find the Ethan. Or at least a likely place to start.

It-Ben picked up the musket and began to walk.

Time registered differently in Was-Ben's recollections, and It-Ben understood the concept of measuring the passage by the coming of the dark and the light, which it simply associated with the planet's rotation toward and away from the large star at the center of this solar system. Two of the rotations passed before it reached Sudbury, with a few stops to revert to bear form for easier feeding and nourishment.

During the walk it practiced the movements held in

muscle memory, the speech patterns of this form's adaptation, and spent most of the time studying Was-Ben's perceptions of the power structure and system of deference among the clan members it would soon find. By the time It-Ben crossed into Sudbury, it knew exactly how to respond to each known Green Mountain Boy, and had a fair idea of what the others of Was-Ben's clan expected from him. More would come from interaction directly with the clan members.

With its current form known in town, acquiring a horse became a simple matter. It-Ben visited the town stables, watched the stable master, and temporarily assumed a close enough semblance of his appearance for long enough to walk out with one of his charges.

Riding the horse proved nowhere near as simple. The animal sensed something, and shied again and again. It-Ben finally forced calm on the beast with a direct mental invasion that left the horse somewhat devoid of personality, but quieter and docile enough to ride.

It supposed, as it worked to relax into the animal's gait, that it could have just assumed a faster, less easily tired form, such as the horse itself. It found, though, that the human form held the lure of increased interest, with the complicated thought processes and self-awareness. Once established, it was reluctant to give it up for other than short times to forage for sustenance.

No question, it had found the species it needed.

The ride south toward Bennington progressed quickly, until halted unceremoniously by the arrival on the road of representatives of the very man it sought. It-Ben reined in as the riders heading north hailed it with familiarity. Greeting the newcomers with casual aplomb, it thrilled to see not one second glance from any of them.

"Ben, excellent luck! Have you heard already, then, and come to meet us? No? Muster's been called! Ethan wants us in Castleton by Sunday. It's to be Fort Ticonderoga! There's been blood in Lexington, we're taking the British fort!"

Listening to the babble of voices from all sides, It-Ben recognized the identifying information from Was-Ben's experiences. Still, it took some time to assimilate the fact that the Ethan was in fact heading directly to it. Had it been human, it would have been amused by the turn of events. Not being human, it simply appreciated the concept of humor.

Listening more than speaking, observing the small knot of men, It-Ben readily agreed to return with the riders to the northern direction, and meet with Ethan there. It knew the camaraderie so highly prized in Was-Ben's experiences colored its perceptions of the fellow riders—"the Boys" it corrected itself—but observation on the ride would provide excellent opportunity with little risk of exposure. It could absorb the human milieu without needing to do more than nod and stretch its new mouth in the teeth-baring social ritual.

It hardly needed to exercise its mind touch to continue learning. So much information these humans had to impart, and all without asking anything in return.

The ritualistic teeth-baring came easier each time it did so.

Meeting up with the Ethan on the road before Castleton brought It-Ben into the presence of the one it sought. Given the crowd and the circumstances—they all immediately rode into Castleton proper—it realized that no migration to the Ethan form could occur immediately. Was-Ben had strolled among the Green Mountain Boys with ease and acceptance in his time, but he had not struck up regular conversation with the Ethan and it might attract undue notice if it did so now.

It recognized in the varying shades of deference that Was-Ben felt a distinct difference in station, and held the Ethan in highest regard. Higher perhaps, than was fully deserved, given its own observations.

He was impressive, though, this Ethan Allen. A passionate orator, and demanding of loyalty in such a straightforward manner, his men gave it without reserve. It-Ben watched the spectacle in Castleton in silent fascination, where the Committee of War presented the Ethan with field command of the Ticonderoga scheme. As just another Green Mountain Boy, It-Ben saddled up and rode out to Shoreham with the rest.

It consistently maneuvered as close to the rebel hero

as possible, this being perfectly acceptable Was-Ben behavior that the other Boys looked upon with tolerant amusement. Still no opportunity arose. It supposed this was not the best time, all things considered, and resigned itself to a longer stay in the current form, low on the power structure though it was. The overwhelming sense of strength of will and purpose reached out to it, tantalizing, every time a mental brush or focused mental push could be directed at the Ethan. The sense of self—and self-importance—intrigued it greatly. Even more so, the fealty pressing in on it from all sides, pouring out of the Boys toward the Ethan.

Upon settling in Shoreham for the night to make preparations for the onslaught, it continued to observe all, and watch for opportunity. It stayed alert long after the other Boys slept, its kind not needing the same sort of dormancy the human form required. But no matter its efforts, the Ethan remained in close proximity to at least three other humans at all times.

The first hint it received that anything might be going other than to plan came the following morning, with the sudden rushing about of the other Boys. Confusion presented opportunities, and it immediately made its excuses and left the company of the Boys it sat with, studying the new concept of "poker."

It again recognized the application of the human concept of humor at the startled reactions of the other Boys to "Ben's" apparently sudden ability to keep "his" face completely expressionless. Others of its kind might disagree, but It-Ben thought poker playing constituted a safe enough arena in which to extend somewhat out of character traits for its chosen form. Especially when those traits were required by the rules of the game. It was certainly within the realm of possibility that Was-Ben *could* have matured some since the Boys' last interaction with him.

Possible, no matter how improbable. It allowed the small ritualistic teeth-baring even though no human stood close enough to appreciate it.

Once outside, it realized in an instant that confusion was not all that stalked the small town of Shoreham.

Something that in a human would be termed excitement coursed through it.

Another of its kind was close.

Before it could even ascertain the correct direction to move in, shouts to assemble rang out. It counted no surprise when the direction the Boys moved to assemble matched the direction it soon sensed it needed. Assembling with the Boys, It-Ben jockeyed with the eager crowd to move itself closer to the Ethan, and realized suddenly that perhaps another of its kind had usurped its own chosen target, and taken the Ethan for itself.

That would not do. Despite its own second thoughts about the Ethan as a choice, now that it had more experience of the man, it would not simply give him up to another.

But when It-Ben made it to the front of the assemblage, the Ethan was safe. Or relatively so, for next to the Ethan stood what appeared to be a human man, resplendent in a blue uniform far too clean for the quaint form of travel this species used. The subservient one just behind and to the right of the newcomer explained the immaculate nature of the uniform.

It-Ben recognized at once its other, and saw the head of the other rise and seek it out as well. Meeting eyes, the mental touch came immediately, and welcome contact flooded through both. It-Ben felt the greater length of time its fellow had spent in the human form it stood in, and marveled at the experiences it must have already had.

But now the Ethan spoke, calling loudly above the muttering, shifting mob, and It-Ben turned its attention to its target, tearing itself reluctantly away from the fleeting contact with its other. It knew its other understood, and indeed, it was coming to attention itself, taking on a decidedly arrogant posture.

"Boys, for those of you who don't recognize, this man standing before you is Colonel Benedict Arnold, of the Connecticut Footguards. He's got an official commission from the Massachusetts Committee of Safety to seize Fort Ticonderoga. He'll be leading our forces into battle."

The instantaneous hue and cry surprised It-Ben not at all. It noted its fellow, It-Benedict, had no such foreknowledge and lost all expression for long enough that It-Ben knew it was perplexed. It wondered if It-Benedict did not know much about the Ethan, and the Boys, or if it had allowed the experience of its host existence to color its expectations of other humans.

Something to think about. And be prepared against.

Despite the Ethan's calls to quiet, the crowd took some time to settle, and random men continued to holler out, "Be damned if I serve under anyone but Ethan!" It-Ben remained quiet and listened with interest as the Ethan explained they would all still be paid the expected amount of two dollars each, and the plan itself would go just as they had decided.

It-Ben watched the Ethan's reactions carefully as the Green Mountain Boys protested, vocally and at length, and threatened to simply go back to their homes if Ethan didn't lead the attack. It reached out as subtly as possible to the mind of the Ethan, and felt the satisfaction and smugness borne of sure knowledge his Boys would do just this. One of the Boys pushed to the front of the crowd, put down his musket, and refused to pick it back up unless Ethan commanded the mission. One by one, all the Boys followed suit, until a large stack of weapons formed.

With a calming thought to its other, It-Ben joined the line and laid his musket with the rest. *Wait. Agree. Share thoughts.* Sensing disgruntled agreement, It-Ben decided to definitely have a conversation with It-Benedict at a later point about being careful of taking on a host's perspective. For now, it sent reassurance and reformed with the other Boys. In a matter of minutes it was clear nothing would happen without Ethan and Benedict Arnold coming to agreement, which they finally arrived at some hours later. The Ethan would command the mission, and Colonel Arnold ride alongside him.

As afternoon stretched to dusk, It-Ben joined the other troops on the march from Shoreham to Hand's Cove, from where the attack would be launched. With It-Benedict at the front alongside the Ethan, It-Ben chose not to try to communicate until arrival. Sure enough, as expected, as soon as the troops assembled at the cove, It-Benedict found reason to "inspect the troops" and wander among them. As his other moved without disturbance through the men, It-Ben spoke mind to mind, no longer fearing to break its other's concentration. *You have obviously found one of power. Well done.*

Yes. Until now, have been doing quite well. It-Benedict's reply was short and still irritated. It was a young one, It-Ben realized.

The Ethan has power as well. Of a different sort, I believe, but a potential I may have interest in pursuing.

I do not care for the Ethan. There are others much more interesting. Was-Benedict had much knowledge and experience of them. Look . . . see. As It-Benedict drew closer, it opened its mind, allowing the warm flow of information to inundate It-Ben.

It-Ben's eyes widened. The young one was right. Others, indeed. *I see.* It-Ben met the gaze directly as It-Benedict stopped before it, and the contact deepened. *You have done very well.*

It-Benedict made a good show of glancing over the troops closest to It-Ben, then looked back and nodded. *It is the one they call George Washington. He is the one.*

Indeed. It-Ben nodded in return. *Ticonderoga, then. Ticonderoga first, then we bring the George Washington the cannon he desires. The George Washington will be pleased.*

It-Benedict risked once more meeting It-Ben's eyes.

They shared a ritualistic teeth-baring moment between them.

MARROW WOOD

by Nina Kiriki Hoffman

Nina Kiriki Hoffman has sold more than two hundred stories and a number of novels. Her works have been finalists for the Nebula, World Fantasy, Mythopoeic, Sturgeon, and Endeavour awards. Her first novel won a Horror Writers Association Bram Stoker Award. In addition to writing, Nina works at a bookstore, does production work for a national magazine, and teaches short story writing through a local community college. She lives in Oregon and has cats.

HEW AVERY DA SILVA HAD had his ears docked and his eyebrows reshaped three planets and four lifetimes ago, when the last known member of his race killed herself. Better to blend with the larger mass of somewhat human population, he felt, not knowing that a fashion for pointed ears and winged eyebrows would sweep the cultureweb, and even youngsters on the backwater colony planet where he lived at the time would shift their looks toward his. How strange was that, his looking the way they were born, and they looking like members of his race? But it was a passing fad, and just as well he'd revised his looks before it came and went.

His craft, woodwork, kept him jumping worlds, following the colonist wave as it spread outward through the galaxy. Hew never followed on the colonists' heels; he let each colony get established and hungry for trade before he arrived. While he waited, he collected information about what sorts of woods the new planets supported. Wood data flowed outward on trade ships, in plant catalogs, at curiosities sites on the cultureweb. When he saw something that excited him, he moved. A new kind of wood brought him out of the dull gray doldrums. A new kind of wood, or a circus ship.

Hew had a woodshop on Despirada, a planet with six thriving settlements—a population of perhaps thirty thousand, with the largest concentration of them in Landing, where the spaceport was—and at least four good new sorts of wood. One of them, marrow wood, had properties for which he had been searching for more than four hundred T-standard years. Little by little, he used his accumulated wealth to buy sections of marrow-wood forest. There wasn't much competition for the forest lands, as marrow-wood trees were hard to clear, and once cleared, would return; their roots were uncanny and persistent. The farmers among the colonists were satisfied to clear easier lands for their crops.

Hew loved the trees' stubbornness as much as he loved their wood. Finally he had found a world to host his dream.

People, that broad-spectrum word for everyone in the Alliance, had been living on Despirada for almost two hundred T-standard years. Hew had lived there seven years when T. Moody's Compendium of Unnatural Wonders and Mysterious Phenomena landed.

The scanner in Hew's shop was set for port traffic control, so Hew heard the request to land. The captain, Moody, had a voice so full and fruity Hew wanted to eat it like dessert. "We're delighted to be in your skies again, Interface Cory," Moody said to the port overseer. "Our performance visas are in order. We've had all our shots. We've honed new marvels for your people's delectation. Would you be so kind as to assign us a landing spot? We'll have the port fee ready for you."

"Hey, Theo," said Cory Duomopolis, usually the most laconic individual Hew knew. She sounded almost happy. "Welcome back. Do you still have the bears?"

"Most assuredly, my lovely. In fact, we've added two cubs and an adolescent since our last visit."

"Hallay! I'm assigning you Space Seventeen. See you soon." She switched him over to the automated air traffic controller.

Hew turned off his scanner.

His apprentices, Mina and Lore, paused in their wood sanding and watched him.

"Holiday," Hew said.

"I'll close up, boss," said Mina.

"Get us tickets," Lore said.

Hew put on his dark-green spring cloak and his broad-brimmed hat, then gripped his latest staff. This one was made of marrow wood, fine grained and full of dark-red-in-cream swirls. Its head was that of a Salia dragon, with inset eyes of emerald flame jewels from Cask.

Hew nodded to the youngsters and headed out. Before the door quite closed behind him, he heard Lore ask Mina, "Why does he rush off every time a circus lands? Do you think he wants to join one?"

Mina had been with Hew longer than Lore. "No," she said.

The door hitched itself closed then, and the rest of her answer was muffled, even to his superior hearing. Never mind; no one could work for him long without making things up. He had told his apprentices very little about himself, so of course they had to fill the fact vacuum with speculations.

The spring rain was more of a mist this afternoon, but Reuben, at the teashop next to Hew's Woodworks, had his door open despite the damp. "Hey, Hew." He came toward the open door, drying a glass with a towel. "Another circus landing?"

"A Captain Theo Moody," Hew said. "Sounded like he's been here before. Do you remember?"

"Moody." Reuben stared at the ground, his hands motionless around the tea-glass. His brows rose. "Moody? Oh, yeah! Ten years back, must have been. Before you got here. Best circus I've ever seen. He's got flyers who scoot through the air so fast it looks like they're trailing flame. And animals—best animals, Hew. Some I've never seen anywhere else, and you know I watch all the animal channels. People who leap from one horse to another, midair somersaults. Bears and tigers and even a Salia dragon." He hurried back to his counter, put down the glass, picked up a handful of scales, and returned to hand them to Hew. "Buy me five tickets, will you?"

"Sure."

"The women," Reuben said. "Shaped like women in dreams, and their eyes are silvery gray, like yours. I dreamed about them for months after they left."

Hew felt his eyebrow crook. It wouldn't look the way it used to, when he had used it to denote a wry, amused dismay or curiosity. The muscle worked, and the revised brow shifted, but he didn't know any longer what it communicated. What did he want it to say?

That he entertained foolish hope again? How he wished he would find other members of his race, who could speak the language of fine facial signals, though he was crippled since the surgery; he would be able to interpret, but they wouldn't be able to understand him.

He put his hand on the top of his staff's dragon head, felt the wood wake under his palm. There was a heat in it, a flow of energies, formerly foreign; he and the wood had been working toward understanding each other since he first cut into a chunk of downed tree. Despirada had given him back languages lost since the gates to the other world had closed on Terra and all his people dispersed.

"We are doomed to lead half lives," his lover, Kala, had told him before she left him, years and worlds ago. "The quickening is gone."

"Maybe it's alive somewhere else," he'd said. They had only been to five new planets then.

"It is dead, Hew. Earth was its only home." She stroked the branch of a small tree. Their apartment on Hearthstone had been full of local plant life, none of it green; the spectrum of Hearthstone's sun was different, and the plants had red and purple leaves. They grew well indoors as long as they got enough light. Kala cut skylights into their roof, and brought one of every plant she could find nearby, raised it, waiting, hoping, seeking for a plant to respond the way the plants of Terra used to before the gates closed. Hearthstone plants, like Earth plants since the gates closed, were just plants, dumb, slow-growing, light-eating barbarians.

"I can't live like this," Kala had said.

Hew had made love to her and fed her cherries and silver, hoped he had driven her depression away; but two days later he found her in the bathing pool, her blood mixed with water, and her eyes closed in true death.

He wished she had seen Despirada.

Hew slipped Reuben's scales into his pocket. "I'll find out when the performances start."

"Good chance to you," Reuben said.

"What?" asked Hew.

"I know you're looking for something. I hope you find it."

Startled, Hew said, "Thank you." He headed for the port, mulling over the fact that Reuben knew more about him than he had suspected.

"Hey, Hew," called vendors in the open-sided market stalls of the communal square, where the growers and gatherers brought produce every day.

"I need a good chair," said a red-fruit farmer.

"I need a new tide fork," said a fisherwoman.

Hew pulled a notebook from his pocket and made notes of commissions. Maybe he should walk around more; obviously work was all around him. Winter was ending, and more people were coming into his shop to ask for things, preparing for the activities of the spring. Mina and Lore could use new projects. Mina had mastered two of Despirada's lesser woods. Lore was still clumsy; he had no natural feel for wood, but Hew believed he could learn.

When he had moved to this planet, Hew had thought his business would involve crafting curios to sell to offworld collectors. But the colonists had settled here for a reason. They were backsliders who wanted to live with the tech of earlier times; they wanted woodcraft in their furniture and tools. The locals didn't pay what offworlders would, but they gave him other currency, welcome and respect, things he hadn't had in a couple of lifetimes. He had trained four apprentices and sent them out to start their own shops in other towns, and there was a waiting list of youngsters who wanted to learn wood when Mina and Lore moved on.

He was not sure how all this would play out against his own dream for Despirada. If he could find other members of his race, he wanted to make this their home-world. He had always thought that would mean buying the whole planet and kicking the humans off. But he had friends now everywhere; people had talked him into joining the government and taking part in land-use and development decisions. The planetary assessor, who took his money and wrote deeds to his new lands, knew more about Hew's financial situation than Hew wanted anyone to know. How could Hew hide his circumstances and still do everything legally? The only way he knew was to proceed slowly. Wait for a new assessor to be elected before he bought another section of forest; use his powers to fuzz facts in the minds of the assessors and the memories of the colony computers; and take government jobs so he could direct policy to protect the forests and keep the planet clean of the ravages of heavy industry. Fortunately, most of the colonists were interested in environmental protection, too.

He had never joined a planetary government before. Let the humans do what they would; he was looking for a place beyond them, something they wouldn't be able to recognize when he found it.

Despirada was different from everything in his past.

He waved off more requests for woodwork at the market and passed through the security tunnel that guarded the way to the spaceport. Mats and Leandre were on guard at the portside end of the tunnel. "This is the new staff?" Mats asked. Everything Hew wore or carried had been scanned as he walked through the tunnel, so the guards knew the staff was wood alone, but Hew handed the staff to Mats to examine. "Fine work," Mats said. "How much do you want for it?"

"It's not for sale yet," said Hew. "It's too new, and I like it too much."

"When you decide to sell, tell me first, will you? I love your work. The wife still adores the leaf-man face I bought for our anniversary."

"I'll tell you," Hew said. "Thanks."

Leandre dug some scales out of his pocket. "Will you buy me tickets to the circus? I've still got hours of shift left, and I'm worried they'll all be gone by the time I'm off."

"Sure," said Hew. Mats dug money from his pockets, too. Hew made more notes.

"I wondered how soon you'd get here," Cory said, when he stopped by the port office to get permission to visit the new arrivals. She smiled at him; it was the first time he'd seen her smile wide enough to reveal teeth.

"You like the circus?" he asked. She hadn't been interested in the previous ones.

"This one I do. They treat their animals well. Sit with me a while, Hew. They won't be through quarantine for another hour." She handed him a pocketknife. He smiled and took a small chunk of marrow wood out of his wallet, dragged the waste container from her desk to his chair with his foot, and sat back to whittle, letting the feel of wood and the tool in his hands soothe his anxious anticipation. He had waited hundreds of years to find other survivors. The longer he waited, the more hope faded. Sometimes he didn't know how he himself survived. A spark in wood here, a glimpse of a phantom there, a thread of melody in a marketplace or theater that reminded him of the world beyond the gates. Small moments stitched together into a quilt of hope he could almost wrap around himself.

Despirada had changed everything.

"They've passed the checks," Cory said, palming her interface to view different displays. "Let's go meet them."

Hew handed her the knife and a bear made of marrow wood, the red-and-white grain in the wood ordered along the bear's back and limbs and head like fur.

"Oh," she breathed, turning it over in her hands. The grain had been straight when he started, but marrow wood responded to his intent. "Thank you." She set the bear on her console.

A small wind gathered in his chest, brushed along his nerves, whispered of fear and delight. He had the wood.

He had the land. All he needed, all he searched for, were remnants of his own people. Maybe this time . . .

He gripped the marrow-wood staff and followed Cory from her office to the travelers' center, another gateway between Despirada and the commerce of space. The spaceport was a world apart from colony life; it housed all the machinery of interface between Alliance Traffic and Despirada. There was a thin ring of businesses between the gates to the world and the gates to the spaceport that catered to offworlders exclusively: hotels, gambling houses, brothels, restaurants, and specialty shops, all under a weatherproof dome. This part of Despirada was like almost every other world Hew had ever visited or lived on. Many of the people who worked in the ring were transients, experts in their own disciplines who lived in the ring and didn't mingle with the colony settlements outside.

The landing field itself was open to the sky; ship shuttles could land there, but nothing could leave the forcefield-shielded port except by coming through the travelers' center, where people and machines checked offworlders for dangerous invaders of all sorts. The travelers' center was one of the few structures on Despirada built from universal building blocks, safe, self-sealing, impervious segments that could be shaped with purple light when they came out of their wrappings, but set harder than anything once sprayed with setting compound. Most of the colonists had opted to build from native materials, despite the cheap utility of the building blocks. The center was a big white structure, visible for miles. Just now the front doors, big enough to accommodate vehicles and all sorts of other traffic, were open wide.

A group of more than thirty people, some tugging looming freegrav carts, spilled out of the portal.

A large, bear-shaped man in a red cloak over a brown suit swept his tall hat off and bowed low as they approached. His head was covered in a waving wealth of red-and-orange-streaked hair. "Interface Cory! Again I behold your celestial countenance!" he said as he straightened, his smile broad in his weathered, dark face. The corners of his rain-gray eyes crinkled.

Hew gripped his staff so tight the marrow woke in his hand.

"Captain Moody! Welcome to Despirada. I hope you'll stay longer this time," Cory said.

Moody nodded. "Entirely possible, divine one. We've always found your planet hospitable." His gaze shifted. "Will you introduce me to your friend?"

Cory laughed. "This is Woodworker Hew, new since the last time you came. He's obsessed with circuses and couldn't wait to meet you. Hew, Captain Theo Moody."

"Captain," Hew said, though his voice caught in his throat. He took his hat off.

Moody's winged eyebrows spoke: You are one of us? But you don't look like us. Ah, you are hidden! Hidden but waiting for us?

"Captain," Hew said again. "All of that."

Men and woman let go of their burdens and charges and gathered around him. Everywhere he looked, he saw family, though they had many colors of hair and skin. Most had gray eyes and peaked brows; most had enough hair to hide their ears from sight. They reached to touch him, a brush of fingertip on his cheek, a pat on his hair, a tug on his shirtsleeve.

"Captain?" Cory said, her voice alarmed.

Someone touched the staff and cried out, and all the others murmured, a language Hew had not heard in ages, a music of news and wonder.

For the first time in centuries, Hew spoke his native tongue. "You're here. You're alive!"

A rush of voices answered him with the same words.

They moved back a step, and Moody approached him. Hew handed him the marrow-wood staff. The dragon head turned to stare into the captain's face, and the captain laughed, a startled chuckle. The others gasped and whispered to each other. Those nearest touched the staff, fingertips lingering on the wood. The captain handed the staff to someone else, and they passed it on.

"I thought this might be the planet," the captain said in standard. "Gods and shadows, Hew! Well met! Where have you been hiding?"

"Everywhere I thought obvious," Hew said.

"Hew?" Cory said. "Hew? Captain?"

The people who surrounded him moved back, one of them carrying the staff. Hew smiled at Cory, who stood there looking suspicious, her stunner in her hand. "It's okay, Cory. Captain Moody is my cousin. I've been searching for him."

"Your cousin?" Cory said. She glanced between Hugh and Moody. "I suppose. Well, welcome to Despirada again, Captain Moody and company. Let's go to the main gate. Will you set up in the fairgrounds again?"

"All arranged," said Moody. "I contacted the city commissioners; I've got performance permits. Here's my paperwork and the port fee, my lovely. And, Interface Cory, if you will direct your attention here?" He led her back to one of the freegrav carts, and its attendant stroked a hand across one pearly side. The material cleared, showing a group of bears, startled by the sudden light.

"Oh!" she cried.

The bear handler, a stocky woman in a green suit, pressed something into Cory's hand.

"Thank you," Cory said. She lifted two rainbow-colored tickets, read the information. "The first performance is tonight? I'd better let you go, then. You remember the way to the fairgrounds?" She set her thumb to the pad beside the main gate. The field shut down.

"We have a map," said Moody.

"And a local guide," Hew said.

"We'll look for you tonight," Moody called to Cory, who waved as they walked the tunnel to the city.

All these years I've waited and hoped, Hew wanted to say to them with gestures. He had to speak it aloud, in the lost language.

We, too, have hoped, said the others.

Children waited in the light rain outside the gate and cheered as the circus arrived. More of those pulling freegrav carts shifted the cart sides so that the animals inside were visible. Vendors left their stalls in the market to come and stare. Patrons in teashops and restaurants came out to see and wave. Moody greeted everyone.

The fairgrounds administrator settled them with a minimum of fuss. A scarlet-and-white-striped tent erected itself, and Moody led Hew inside. Two or three of the others followed, the rest busy setting up exhibits and performance tents.

"I've spoken to the forests," Hew said. "The marrow wood is quick. It doesn't speak the same language as our old forests, but it's a language we can learn. I'm building us a haven."

Moody glanced at a red-haired woman in a yellow dress. She placed long-fingered hands over her stomach and smiled an inward smile.

"The news is amazing," Moody said. "We are overjoyed to find you, Hew."

"Not as happy as I am to find you. I've been alone a long time."

"Some of us will settle. Some of us will keep searching. We find scattered others every so often, and usually they join the circus; so far this is the only home we've found. A haven. A stationary home at last. With waking wood?"

Hew laughed. He dug in his pocket for an unshaped chunk of wood to show them, but his fingers stumbled on all the scales people had given him as he walked to the port. He pulled them out, along with his book. "I have commissions for tickets," he said. He checked his notes. "Twenty-three. May I buy that many? I don't know what you charge."

Moody's eyebrows danced. We've made a homecoming at long last, after centuries of searching, and you're concerned with tickets? We must get to know each other better!

Hew shifted his cheek, his brow. No, he couldn't speak clearly this way. He said: "I thought we could make this a place just for us, but they're here, too. They were here first. Is there room for all of us?"

Moody's gaze went around the room, meeting the gaze of all the others. "Don't you know?" he said at last. "We're all entwined. There's no other way." He pulled a sheaf of tickets from his pocket and handed them to Hew. "I honor your entanglements, Hew Alone. Well met. We've got a show to prepare for, and a future to rethink. Can you show my wife the wood?"

"Oh, yes," said Hew.

"I am Frida," said the red-headed woman. She took his arm and they left the tent together.

The warmth of her fingers, her cinnamon-and-jasmine scent made him homesick and happy. He took her to his shop, waving to neighbors on the way but not stopping to converse. He got out the electric cart he drove to the forest to collect wood. She sat beside him on the seat. An ancient, familiar, long-absent energy surrounded her, waking its sibling in him as surely as he woke marrow wood with a touch. He drove her out of town, past the fields, into his forest.

She leaned against a marrow-wood tree and looked up through the fretwork of scythe-shaped green leaves toward a damp gray sky.

Hew placed his palms on Iri Grovemother, felt her energies wake and gather, then shoot down to seethe through all the other trees in this grove. Hello. Hello, small moving part. Hello!

"Oh!" Frida cried. She turned and pressed her cheek to a tree trunk, hugged the tree. "This *is* home!"

Home now that you all are here, thought Hew. He leaned against Iri Grovemother, waded in her welcome until his shadow twined with hers. Almost he sensed the edge of a gate to somewhere. He didn't know where it would open, but now that others had come, people to be his anchors, maybe he could explore.

CLAUS OF DEATH

by Michael M. Jones

Michael M. Jones graduated from college with a degree in the technical aspects of theater. As soon as he found out that theater in the real world was a job, rather than fun, he went back to school, and concentrated on his other love, writing. Operating under the philosophy that he can't die with things left unread, he's busy collecting comics, books, magazines, action figures, and music at such a rate that he's effectively immortal. The rumor is that he bought a house just for the bookcase space. Contrary to popular belief, he is not part of any government conspiracies, or shadowy groups seeking to control the world. He currently lives in Roanoke, Virginia, with many cats, none of whom have any respect for books whatsoever, and his overly patient wife, who does appreciate books.

IT BEGAN, AS THESE things always do, with a woman. She strolled into the dingy, cramped room I laughingly call an office these days, pausing at the door to cast a contemptuously dubious look around at the mix-and-match Salvation Army decor. I could just imagine how it all looked through her eyes: the scarred mahogany desk overflowing with papers and empty coffee mugs, the dented green file cabinet on which sat a single fern barely clinging to life, the bare wooden floor, the couch with its assortment of stains and old cigarette burns, the mismatched wooden chairs, and the faded paint on the door that read, "Nicholas St. Claus, Private Investigator." Yeah, I knew just how this lady would look upon her surroundings and despair. I knew her tastes, and this was as far away from them as you got. I couldn't even imagine what she made of me, so I slammed the door on that line of thought immediately.

In fact, before I even looked directly at my visitor, I opened the minifridge I kept behind the desk, and pulled out some liquid courage, a half-empty bottle of spiked eggnog that had kept me company through the long Christmas nights. Splashing a liberal amount into the nearest coffee mug, I drained it quickly. I needed it. Courage was all I had left. Like some bizarre reverse Wizard of Oz, the lady'd stolen my heart, messed with my head, and caused me to leave home once and for all. My hand shook, and I took that as a sign to pour another shot. The lady started to speak, but I held up my free hand, stopping her words in their tracks. I tossed back the drink, and slammed the mug down on the table, pinning down an overdue electricity bill.

"Hello, Ginny," I said. Where my ex-wife is concerned, I wanted the first word, and whenever possible, the last.

"Hello, Nick," she replied, not waiting for an invitation before settling down gingerly on the seat closest to my desk. She crossed her legs, her little black skirt riding up to grant me a highly enjoyable view of smooth, pale skin. My hand tightened around the empty mug. No, two shots was already pushing it on an empty stomach. She went on before I could find the right words to ask her what the hell brought her down from her ivory tower to my hole in the wall, the hole I'd crawled into five years ago and hoped never to emerge from again. Ginny was by far the last person I'd ever expected to see in here. "I need your help," she said. Words I'd never thought to hear, followed by words I'd often heard only in my most bitter fantasies: "Jack's dead, Nick. He was murdered. And I need you to find out who did it."

Jack Frost. The guy who'd been nipping at more than Ginny's nose since I left, and some time before that. My former protégé turned rival. My replacement, in more ways than one. Funny. I'd always thought I'd feel a lot better with him dead, but Ginny's cold, matter-of-fact words left me feeling just a little emptier inside, like someone'd taken an ice pick to my heart. I looked up to meet her eyes, truly seeing her for the first time in half a decade, and my power instinctively rose to the occasion, telling me everything I needed to know about her. Within a heartbeat, I knew exactly how she'd been nice, and how she'd been naughty. I knew if she'd been bad or good, and what she'd have gotten in her stocking if I still filled stockings on that one magical night of the year. I thought of peaches to go with the cream of her skin, a gold necklace to match her hair, and sapphire earrings to match her eyes. I thought of—aw, hell, I had to stop thinking along those lines. But it had been a long time, and I was still a man. I looked closer, and within another heartbeat, I could read between the lines, and see the true anguish in those eyes. She was keeping it together for appearances' sake. Calm, cool, and collected, like an ice sculpture, but brittle. She was going to tell me everything she knew, take advantage of our shared history and the embers of my love for her, and then she was going to go home and shatter with grief. Her presence here meant that she had no one else she could turn to. I sighed mentally, took all of those old feelings and desires and bitter memories, shoved them all into a tiny box in the back of my mind, and locked it. Leaning forward, I tried to sound professional as I said, "Tell me everything, Ginny."

And she did. Her recitation of the facts was mechanical, her voice tightly controlled, and I watched her knuckles grow white as she clutched the arms of her chair. There wasn't much to tell, really. He'd been melted with a heating spell, a very focused, very personalized bit of magic that hit the guy where it counted, counteracting the magic that had brought him to life and granted him human form in the first place. Ginny, no expert when it came to spellwork, could only tell me that it had been long-range, possibly even delayed release, something that struck out of the blue while they were in bed. I read between the lines, and gathered that they hadn't exactly been asleep at the time. God, what a mental image. One I didn't need. But anyway, no muss, no fuss, exit Jack Frost as a puddle of water, stage left. With a little better timing, it might have taken days for someone to notice his absence. I wondered if the killer had wanted Jack's demise to be noticed immediately.

Once Ginny'd finished telling me what little she knew, we haggled briefly over terms of payment and compensation. We both knew I was doing this as a favor, in memory of what we'd once shared, but neither of us were foolish enough to say so. Things between us were . . . complicated on both sides. She'd broken my heart, but in the end, I wasn't entirely blameless. There was plenty of pain and anger to go around, but real feelings still existed also. It was a mess. My payment for this case, though, would keep me in rent and 'nog for a while. It was a relief when she left and I could lock the door behind her and shut out the world for a while.

It took an hour or so, but finally I felt ready to get to work. I grabbed my overcoat (still bemoaning the recent loss of the old red-and-white parka, but that fur trim had proven way too flammable for my own good, and that's another long story) and left the office. Going down two flights of stairs and out the front door put me out on the streets of Holiday, and onto the case of Jack Frost's murder.

Holiday, Alaska. Sitting right on the border between where the mundane world ended and the magical one began, it was a frontier town where the Northern Lights cast dark shadows, and beings both mundane and supernatural ended up when they had nowhere else to go. It was the ends of the earth for people like me, a refuge for the weary of heart and heavy of soul. It was also the closest island of civilization to the realm I'd once ruled, and saw a lot of traffic from the North Pole's inhabitants. Somehow, I just couldn't see myself living in warmer, sunnier, more pleasant climates. Everyone in Holiday had their reasons for being here. Everyone had their secrets, most of them dirty and sordid and downright unpleasant. Lucky me, I knew most of them already.

My first stop was The Confessional, which, while not the only bar in town, was the only bar worth visiting for people in the know. I'd been drinking there for a very long time, which made me as much of a regular as anyone ever got in a place like this. The Confessional was a dark little place, an afterthought shoved up against the back of St. Peter's, an old church of indefinite denomination that catered to just about anyone willing to believe in a Christian god. In one of those strange twists that so characterized Holiday, the priest at St. Peter's and the bartender at The Confessional were one and the same, with Father Aaron saving souls one day a week, and serving spirits the other six, and you had to be careful what you let him know and under what circumstances, for while he respected the sanctity of the church's confessional, anything else he heard was fair game.

This early in the day, the place was fairly empty; in Holiday, most people don't get down to serious drinking until after sunset. I bellied up to the bar, parking my butt on my usual stool down at the end. Father Aaron finished polishing a glass and came over to check on me. We exchanged our usual snappy repartee, acknowledging that yeah, we were both still alive and kicking, and yeah, that a life of celibacy was still working out for him, which I found amusing since rumor has it that before he put on the collar, he was quite the ladies' man. We weren't what you'd call friends; I had a rather dubious relationship with the whole Christian faith, and my roots were all too pagan. But we had an understanding, and got along fine for all that. He was one of my best sources of information in town. Over a stiff eggnog, I outlined the problem.

"Yeah," allowed the good Father, nodding thoughtfully and scratching at his chin. "I seem to remember hearing something of a hitter here in town. Supposedly one of the Mysteries," he added somewhat disparagingly. He wasn't too big on the mystic, for all that many of his patrons came from one supernatural tradition or another. "Didn't pay it much mind, on account of not my business." That, we both knew, was patented bullshit. Father Aaron remembered everything, assigning it a value in his mental bank, and all it took to get him to share was knowing his prices.

"A hundred bucks to the poorbox," I said thoughtfully, "would go a long way, right?"

"Two hundred would buy a lot of hot soup and blankets," agreed Father Aaron amiably.

We settled on one fifty, which I wrote off as expenses, and Father Aaron agreed to arrange a meeting for me with the hit man, an out-of-towner called Mr. Tuesday. On my way out, I stuffed my "donation" into the box Aaron'd helpfully set out by The Confessional's door. "Thank you. Thank you very much," Father Aaron recited as I left.

Next stop was the factory itself, a place I returned to with an extreme reluctance. I'd built it from the ground up, and nurtured it for a long time, and just thinking about it tore the scabs from my heart. The good memories had all been overlaid with bad ones, such as me catching Ginny in bed with Jack and too much tinsel. Yeah. Not a very merry Christmas, or a happy New Year.

It didn't take me long at all to get there; one of the little magic tricks I still possessed was an ability to get where I wanted to go without actually crossing any distance. I hated it; these days, it made me queasy and reminded me of happier days. Walking was better for me anyway. But short of a magic sleigh, there weren't many other ways to get where I was going. The factory doesn't exist in the real world.

Suffice it to say, nosing around the place was a mistake. There was nothing new to be learned there. Everyone loved Jack. He'd brought modernization to the factory, and it hummed like a well-oiled machine. Things had changed drastically since the old days, had been changing well before I left. It had become impossible to manufacture all the toys kids would get on Christmas. Hell, you couldn't even fill up the stockings with fruit and baubles anymore. The population explosion in the past century combined with the rise of an industrialized, consumer-oriented society meant that our role in the holiday had become almost entirely ornamental. Ironically, the more I'd become a cultural icon, the less I was actually needed. The world wanted the image, not the man. Ultimately, we'd abandoned the old system. Now the factory worked to gather magic from all over the world year-round, distilling it into "the Christmas spirit," which was then infused into little objects and ornaments and redistributed to spread the cheer. Warm fuzzies, Christmas miracles, happy family reunions, that sort of thing. Random acts of kindness and senseless acts of beauty.

Yeah. Pretty abstract, I know. I never could wrap my mind around it. That's about the time I brought Jack on board and let him handle business matters along with Ginny. I was a hands-on kind of guy, clinging to the old ways, such as actual gift giving and the annual Christmas Eve Ride. Is it any surprise I let my attention slide on the other matters? It's certainly no surprise that I missed what Jack and Ginny were up to behind my back. I think, on some level, I didn't want to know.

I nosed around the factory long enough to be made profoundly uncomfortable. I conducted a few half-hearted interviews with some of the senior staff, the elves that had been with me since the early days, the ones who'd moved up in the ranks and successfully weathered the transition of methods and management. The longest of those interviews was with Gunter, one of the Germanic tribe that had first come to work for me back when I needed skilled craftsmen and dedicated laborers. These days, he had an office all his own, and an official position as head of Magic Distillation, making him one of the busiest, most important people there. All courtesy of Jack's restructuring of the company's internal workings. I spent fifteen, maybe twenty minutes with him, all of it forced and awkward. As I finished the interviews, I allowed myself to admit that in some ways, I was hurt that so many had stayed on despite the change in regime; I'd half hoped more would have left with me. But why risk a good job in a dwindling market? Just for old times' sake, I poked my head in the reindeer quarters, which were pretty much ceremonial these days, and then I called it a day. I'd had enough.

Everyone had liked Jack. Great guy, very charismatic, very hip. Knew all the latest slang and fads. The more I heard, the more I felt like an old fossil, one who'd overstayed his welcome by a century or two. The more I was confronted by the radical changes brought about in recent years, the more it twisted in my gut. People were doing just fine without me. Any hope I'd had that they'd all been pining for my return was dashed. Sure, they were polite and welcoming, but . . . it wasn't the same anymore. Honestly, though, I didn't know what I'd hoped to learn here anyway. I hadn't stumbled across any books entitled *Melting People for Fun and Profit,* at any rate. It looked like my best bet was to meet with Mr. Tuesday, and see what he had to tell me, willing or no. With any luck, he'd be the link I needed to get to the heart of things.

I departed the factory weighed down by my thoughts, the suspicion that I'd missed something nagging at the back of my mind. I wanted to dismiss it, call it the disconcerting feeling of being back in old surroundings and finding everything changed, the familiar turned unfamiliar. Such was my mood that when I exercised my little spatial twist to transition back to Holiday, I accepted my stomach's lurching as just another attempt of the world to make me miserable.

Of course, there was no rest for the weary; a message waited for me on my answering machine.

Father Aaron had come through for me. Mr. Tuesday was willing to meet me tonight, at eight. According to my clock, that gave me just enough time to clean up and trudge on over.

That's how I ended up back at The Confessional, this time tucked away in one of its tiny booths, nursing yet another spiked eggnog and nibbling unenthusiastically on a plate of freshly-baked chocolate chip cookies, one of Aaron's house specialties. I'd arrived just a few minutes early, wanting to get settled in before my "guest" arrived. I'd dug up a little about the man who called himself Mr. Tuesday, rummaging through my files. Like me, he was one of the old gang, a Mystery fallen upon hard times and forced to find another line of work to keep from vanishing altogether. Probably Norse, if his pseudonym was any clue to his original identity.

Lost in my thoughts, still puzzling over who had the motives to want Jack out of the picture, I wasn't paying attention when Tuesday silently slipped into the seat across from mine. He was a sharp man, both in features and in clothing, well-dressed and almost painful to look at. Hard angles and cold eyes made his face one I'd never forget. As he rested his arms on the table, I couldn't help but notice the way his right sleeve draped loosely, calling attention to his missing hand. Yeah. I offered my left hand to shake, trying to downplay how his arrival had startled me.

He shook it, and then leaned back in his seat. "Nick St. Claus. I have to admit, your request surprised me. I can't even imagine how naughty someone must have been to require my services."

I was glad he didn't waste any time. After the way today had beat me down emotionally, and kicked me where I'd be sure to feel it, I wasn't in a mood to beat around the bush anymore. Leaning forward over the table, I replied, "I didn't call you because I want someone killed. I called you because someone's already dead, and you were in town when it happened."

Tuesday arched an eyebrow, and watched me, evenly. "Is that so." He took a cookie, and bit into it fiercely. Once he'd swallowed, he continued. "And this concerns me why?"

Screw it. I knew how he wanted to play this, but I was in no mood to play cat and mouse with an old god turned professional killer. I steepled my fingers, and met his icy eyes with my own, once again unlocking that coil of magic deep within my mind. With a familiar mind, it's easy and gentle, my power slipping right on it. Mortals are even easier, their minds defenseless, and children practically scream their secrets to any who'll listen. No, with Tuesday, it was hard and focused and violent, like a drill going through concrete, and later I'd feel ashamed of myself for it. I broke through his barriers before he caught on, and read his soul mercilessly, finding every stain and secret. Who he'd killed, how, why, all the sordid details. I discovered that while he was in town to eliminate a problem, it wasn't Jack Frost. I dug just deep enough to discover he was contracted to knock off a local Mystery-turned-drug lord, and then I retreated. I didn't care what happened to Frosty; that icy bastard and I had history as well, none of it good. The important thing was that Tuesday knew nothing at all about Jack's murder, and I was back to square one.

The abuse of my power left me exhausted and dirty

inside, too tired to react with anything other than grudging acceptance when Tuesday responded by sticking a gun in my face. Hell, I'd earned it.

"What the hell?" he exclaimed, features turned ugly with rage. Yeah. Serves me right for pissing off an old war god. "You've got three seconds to explain before I ventilate your skull, you ass. You've got some nerve, rummaging through my head. I should empty yours for it."

Eyes closed, trying to banish the new headache and erase the image of the cold metal oblivion positioned inches from my face, I explained as succinctly as possible. "My ex-wife's lover got killed, and she hired me to investigate. I was an idiot to take the case, and it's been eating me up inside ever since. I'm done, Tyr. I'm all torn up, and tired of the whole thing. Go ahead and shoot. Hell, let's do this outside, so Aaron doesn't have to clean up the mess."

There was a long pause, and the metallic clunk of a gun being placed on the table. "Relax," he ordered. I opened my eyes, and caught him watching me with pity in his eyes. "You're a mess, Nick. But believe it or not, I understand you. I'm not happy about what you did, but . . ." He shrugged. "We all do stupid things from time to time. Look, obviously I didn't kill your guy. You're barking up the wrong tree here. If this is your idea of detective work, you need a new job." No kidding. I never claimed to be a great detective. I fell into the job when I first came to Holiday. But Tuesday wasn't done. "My advice to you is simple: Ask yourself 'who benefits?' Who gains from having your guy out of the way?"

"I've already done that," I protested, knowing what I said was a lie. I hadn't thought that deep, because honestly, I didn't want to be here, doing this, and it showed. I'd gone about this like a drunken man in the dark, sloppily stumbling through the motions, picking my angles of investigation almost at random, and had gotten nowhere. If I wanted to see this thing through, I'd have to go back, try harder, look deeper, and most likely, learn something I didn't want to know about someone I liked.

Tuesday looked disappointed. "Don't lie, Nick. You're

a decent guy who's made a few really bad choices. But you could make a good detective, if you actually tried, rather than wallowing in self-pity and stupidity. I remember you from the old days. You were one of the greats until you let it all slide. Don't be a loser." He stood up, grabbing his gun. "I have work to do. So do you." A pause. "Oh, by the way. If you ever try that shit with me again," and here he tapped his forehead, "I'll make sure your death is slow and painful."

"Hold on," I said quickly, my mind racing. "One last piece of business."

"Shoot," he said curiously.

I told him what I needed and, though surprised, he was willing to oblige, fairly cheaply. Then he was gone, the bar seeming empty in his wake. Father Aaron watched the door shut behind Tuesday, before glaring at me in disapproval. I mumbled my apologies, not wanting to hear his thoughts on the matter, and left as well. I had to return to the factory, one last time, and put an end to things.

As I closed the distance between myself and the factory, letting the cold crunch of frozen snow underfoot punctuate my thoughts, I ran through the list of suspects, thinking about what I'd seen, heard, and learned during my first visit. I threw in all the niggling suspicions and gut instincts, some of them going back years, and let it all simmer. By the time I twisted through space and arrived at the factory, I knew where I had to go, and who to find.

Gunter was in his office, like a good little workaholic, a quality that had led to his current success.

"Evening, Gunter," I greeted him, entering and closing the door behind me.

"Mister Claus!" he replied, clearly startled. He jerked a hand across his desk, sweeping a pile of papers into an open drawer, slamming it quickly. "What are you doing back? Do you need something? Have you found out who killed Mister Frost yet?"

I nodded, sadly. "Yeah. I know who did it. What I don't know is why, Gunter. Why'd you go and kill Jack Frost?"

Just like that, the cards were on the table. He'd known

he was busted the second I entered, and looked almost relieved to have it out in the open. "For you, boss," he said promptly. "I did it so we'd get you back. I knew that if Mister Frost was killed, Miss Virginia would go to you, and you'd take the case, and then you'd have to come back here, and maybe we could go back to how things were before. You don't understand, it's just not the same without you."

"Oh, I understand completely," I agreed. "I know things have changed. But you really couldn't have expected it to work, could you? It seems a bit . . . well, simplistic. Kill Jack so I'll return?"

"I knew once you and Miss Virginia saw each other again, you'd patch things up. Especially with her in need of comfort," he explained earnestly, eyes wide and hopeful. "Please, boss. We all want you back."

There it was. It was too easy, too pat. Too much like what I wanted to hear. He was trying too hard. "It's not that simple, Gunter. You can't heal the past so easily."

He continued to cajole me, half-desperate, half-pathetic, and I watched him lie to my face, his eyes flickering back and forth rapidly. I knew he was hiding something, and while he talked, I reached deep with my power, uncoiling it like a snake in the sun, slow and subtle. It was easy; I'd known Gunter for centuries, and the only reason I hadn't done this earlier was because, well, it was Gunter. I didn't want to suspect him. I hadn't wanted to see into his heart. We'd worked together for so long. But I probed, and unraveled the threads of his soul, letting his sins spill out for my perusal. He'd been very, very naughty. "Oh, Gunter," I said, suddenly bone-weary and ready to cry. "I wish you hadn't been so obvious."

He blinked. "I—what?"

"I know everything, now. How you've been embezzling magic from the factory for years. Abusing your position. It was easy when I was here, I gave you free rein and things were simpler. Jack, though, he liked paperwork and checked up on things. He found something, didn't he? Noticed some discrepancies and dug until he found your secret stash. So you killed him, but you were too hasty, and things didn't go as planned. Sloppy. Impatient." I recited the facts dully, taking no joy in how his expression went from indignant to resigned. "You didn't expect Ginny to turn to me and drag me back into this mess. You thought you'd have more time to clean up your tracks with someone who didn't know you. Another day, and you'd have been in the clear, I bet. And here I am, stumbling through your half-assed coverup, and whoops, it's all over."

"Like you even cared about Jack Frost?" snapped Gunter. "Come on, boss, you wanted him dead as much as anyone. You should be dancing on his grave, not pointing fingers at me! Merry early Christmas! Jack's dead, and you didn't have to do a damned thing!" His tone turned agreeable, wheedling. "And you know, you could walk away. I know you want to. For old times' sake. We split the magic, you turn your back, and you never see me again. You're happy, I'm happy, end of story."

"You're right," I agreed reluctantly. "I wanted Jack dead. I really thought it would make me happy. He stole Ginny, took the company, replaced me, and did better than me in every regard. I hated him with a passion, especially at first." I jammed my hands deep into my pockets, shaking my head. "But I don't feel satisfied. Just hollow inside."

"So what now? Arrest me? Come on, Nick, we could all come out on top if you take the deal!" insisted Gunter. I could tell he was getting antsy, especially with me blocking the only exit. I saw his fingers twitch, and felt magic stirring in the air. Yeah, he was desperate, and lord, I was tempted to take the offer. Walk away from this train wreck and never look back.

"What it boils down to," I said slowly, "is that I hated Jack, but dammit, he made Ginny happy, and when you killed him, you hurt her, and that's the one thing I can't stand. It's why I left in the first place. You made Ginny cry, Gunter. You killed Jack, stole from the company, and made me walk waist-deep in the shit of my life. You've been extremely naughty." And before he could finish whatever spell he had on tap, I pulled Tuesday's gun from my pocket. I was all out of coal, so I filled Gunter with lead, instead, in the twinkling of an eye. He dropped before the last shot finished echoing in the small room, and I tossed the gun onto his corpse, done with it.

Just like that, it was over. I left the room, and went to go find Ginny and tell her how it had all gone down. I was going to get my money, and then I was taking a long vacation to somewhere warm and far away.

I was tired of being cold.

MARKED MEN

by John Mierau

John Mierau lives and writes in southern Ontario with his very patient partner Nikki, and a dog that hogs all his footspace when he writes. "Marked Men" is his second sale: his fantasy "Mountain Challenge" was published in *Fantastic Companions*, edited by Julie E. Czerneda, volume 2 of *Realms of Wonder*.

Laramie Mountains, Wyoming
1869

"GET UP!"

Rough hands yanked Daniel from his hiding place behind a crate of buffalo pelts bound for the East. Half asleep, he was thrown from the train car into prairie and scrub brush. He tried to break his fall, and his hands were slashed on the rock bed of the tracks. He screamed and came all the way awake. He wanted to run but could only cradle his hands to his chest, gasping at the pain. A tall man jumped down after him, kicking him in the ribs before tying his wrists together. "Y'all picked the wrong train," the man drawled.

The sun already hung at the top of the sky, shrouding his captor in shadow. Daniel looked up the tracks and saw the square timber of a mine entrance cropping out of a low foothill; his guts turned cold. *The mountains? I'm not even out of Wyoming!*

It would come that night. He was running out of time.

His captor herded Daniel to the gleaming black-and-red caboose at the rear of the train he'd just been thrown off. His legs were kicked out from under him. Head spinning, he stayed where he was put, blowing on his bloody hands. Behind him, an army of Chinese in straw hats were hauling all manner of goods from the mine onto the train, watched over by hard-looking white men with rifles.

On the porch of the caboose stood a man with his back turned. The collar of his tailored white shirt was undone and he was lathering his face to shave. A thin Chinese boy stood a step away holding a mirror. From behind, someone approached Daniel's captor. The new voice was Irish, the same brogue Daniel had worked so hard to banish from his own mouth. Moments later a stocky Irishman stepped into view. He tipped his dented felt hat to the man on the caboose.

"Travis caught him riding your rail for free, Mr. Bock," the new man reported, then spat brown tobacco juice onto the tracks.

The skin of his Marked left hand tingled, and Daniel clamped his right over it. He quaked, having learned to fear whatever the Mark delighted in. Daniel looked around for the source.

The one named Travis had walked past the train to the rusted steel stop at the end of the tracks. His cruel eyes were now on the crowd of Chinese breaking their backs loading Bock's train. He was stroking the leather of his holster as he watched them. *A gunman.* But he was not the source: the Mark was celebrating a greater evil.

A whip cracked, and Daniel turned in time to watch two white men kick a fallen Chinese. The man huddled on the ground and did not resist the blows. The remaining workers kept their heads down, likely hoping not to attract similar attention.

Forget his bad luck, Danny-boy, find a way to improve your own!

Daniel cleared his throat, already dry from the hot sun. "I sure do apologize for how this looks, sir, me being on your train and all. My name is Downey, Daniel

Downey. My father's big in—" Daniel licked his lips, the blarney close to stillborn on his lips. "In the fur trade! I was robbed collecting goods for him."

Now the juices were flowing, Daniel thought. "I see you're hard at it, sir." He levered himself to his feet. "I'd be glad to lend a hand in exchange for a seat back to the next station. I would make full restitutio—"

Something hit him hard behind the knees and Daniel collapsed. The Irishman spat tobacco next to his head.

"I—I assure you all I'm no hobo." He plucked at his tattered vest. "Oh, this," he laughed. "I can easily replace—"

"I doubt that. Damnation, stand still, boy!" Bock raised the back of his razor-wielding hand to the child holding the mirror. "You know I don't approve of trespassers, Mister Jessup," he said, before wiping the razor blade carelessly on a towel draped over the boy's shoulders. The boy's eyes never left the blade.

Jessup, cleared his throat. "I was thinking the mine, Mister Bock?"

Bock shaved another strip, then turned and bent his hooked nose down toward Jessup and the prisoner. As Daniel met his eyes, the Mark *burned.*

The Mark exposed the darkest secrets of men, reveled in them, and forced them on Daniel. It showed him nothing bright or beautiful. Nothing Daniel would want to remember with crystal clarity long after, perhaps forever. As he stood staring up at Bock, such a knowing was forced on him.

The opium-tinged sweat of the workers faded, replaced by the phantom scents of cigars and scotch. The aromas filled Daniel's nostrils as the Mark's workings took hold: the inner thoughts of Leland J. Bock played out before his eyes.

The smoke and liquor were the pettiest of Bock's vices, but he demanded the best of both. He hungered after the best and the finest in all things. It was that hunger which had driven him to his fortune, using every means at his disposal. It was that hunger that returned him now to the Laramie mine, the first of his businesses. He was here to recover its buried treasures. Prizes a lifetime of theft, violence, and death had accrued.

The train shuddered through the night, carrying Bock

closer to his mine. "They will be here in two days, Jessup," Bock had said. Smoke curled from his lips and along the windowpane of the caboose. Jessup stood behind Bock's high-backed chair, hat in hand. "Don't find out what happens when I am disappointed." Bock savored the effect of his words. Fear had always been his favorite motivator.

He'd paid a prince's sum to the newly minted rail line inspector of the newly minted Trans-Continental Railway, but it had bought him only two days. Two days to haul every work of art, every nugget of gold, every stolen moneybag out of the long-dead coal mine he was steaming toward. Two days to get it aboard this train and away, before less corruptible men uncovered the booty that had financed his empire. Two days to save all he could before he buried that secret life forever.

The Mark shuddered, its vision at an end, thrusting Daniel back into his own skin. His stomach turned. All thoughts of self-preservation were lost in the face of the horror set to come. "You can't do it!" But he would, Daniel knew it. Bock's darkness was etched in him now, an invisible tattoo never to be forgotten.

Daniel sprang toward the rail car. "You can't—" Travis was suddenly there. His hand blurred and an iron blow sent Daniel back to his knees. He followed it with another, and another. The gunman hummed while he worked.

Jessup chuckled. "Day's work in the mine won't kill you," he lied.

Aboard the train Bock turned away, disinterested. He pocketed his razor, took the mirror from the boy, then yanked the towel off the boy's shoulder. The waif stumbled against Bock. "Use this one too, he's getting sloppy," he snarled, pushing the boy down the stairs. "Get it *done!*" He slammed the door against Jessup's simpering.

Jessup yanked Daniel by his bonds toward the cave mouth, but Daniel wrenched the rope free of the fat Irishman. Reaching up, Daniel caught the boy stumbling off the train, clawing his fists into the pajama-like top the kid wore. "Run! Clear out of here! Get into the mountains and stay there!"

The boy stood frozen as Jessup yanked Daniel away by his roped, bleeding wrists. He stumbled, and Jessup pulled harder. Struggling to stay on his feet, Daniel looked back as Travis waved on a powerfully built man to take hold of the boy. *No!* He hadn't known the words to reach the boy, had received no glint of understanding from his young eyes.

The faces Daniel passed all seemed indifferent, uncomprehending. "Run!" Daniel shouted, but nobody listened or cared. Some sniggered at the sight of a white man being pressed to labor. Close behind now, the boy tried to wriggle free, staring curiously at Daniel.

"Stop working and run, they're going to seal—"

The back of Daniel's head exploded and he fell. Jessup walked around him, spat more tobacco from the wad in his mouth and pointed at him with his metal-filled leather sap. "Shut it or I'll bury you right here, son!"

Daniel crawled in the dust. He couldn't work his mouth to shout, but his eyes pleaded with each of the Chinese he passed.

"Jaysus," the big man slapped the boy and he fell to the ground in a crowd of dust in front of Daniel. "The little shit *bit* me!" he yelled.

"Get him moving, Hawkins," Jessup barked.

Daniel looked up. "How can you do this?"

"Do what, boyo? We're just cleanin' out Bock's piggy bank before the new owners come along." Jessup said coyly. "Haven't you heard? The *Trans-Continental Railway's* done. Last spike's goin' in up at Promontory, a pretty gold one, so I hear 'em say."

The boy, Jun, cried out. Daniel turned too late to fend off Hawkins, whose massive arms wrapped around his chest. Jessup moved in close with a knife drawn. "I've got no more track to lay. Why feed all these Chinee?" the foreman whispered harshly. "An' I can't have you scare 'em before they're finished this last job!"

Daniel squirmed but couldn't get free. "They're gonna bury you," he wailed, nothing left to lose. "Don't let 'em do it, please, you gotta—!"

The knife came in. Just in time, a second metal gleam sliced down Jessup's arm. Bock's straight razor, in the hands of the boy!

Jessup squealed and dropped his own blade, dancing away from the boy. Hawkins tossed Daniel to the side and he struggled to stay on his feet. The boy stood frozen, staring in horror at the blood and bits of flesh on the razor. Perhaps used to cries of pains, Jessup's screams hadn't drawn any attention from the workers.

Hawkins drew his pistol and pointed it at the boy. Daniel charged and smashed the hand down. The sound of the gunshot did reach the workers, who scrambled away from the two men as blood geysered from Hawkins' leg. Workers rushed for the mine entrance, away from the white man shooting in their midst. Daniel pushed himself against the cave wall and silently urged them on. An old Chinaman pressed against the wall close by, his wizened, intelligent eyes puzzling out what was happening.

Daniel saw Jessup draw and shoot, and the stampede slowed, confused. Hawkins, on his knees, somehow clung to consciousness and pointed his gun at the boy again. Daniel ran forward and kicked the big man in the face, knocking him onto his back. He scooped up the gun and pulled the Chinese boy close to the wall.

Jessup fired into the air twice more, and the rush toward the cave mouth froze. "Jaysus Chri—" he squealed. The hand holding the pistol was shaking and coated with blood. "Travis, get in here!" He waved the gun at anyone that got close. Low words passed from mouth to mouth among the workers held at bay by that single gun, building courage. Feet began inching forward, until the cocking sounds of rifles echoed from the mine entrance.

Travis ran into the cave slow and careful, cocking a rifle. Daniel stepped protectively in front of the boy, even as he thought of running. *No, stick it out and pay a debt, for a change!* He'd get the boy out, then get clear himself.

Travis shot a thunderous round, and some of the workers turned and ran.

Daniel felt the Mark writhe, as it only did when feasting on the commission of horrific acts. He feared the guns would hold the Chinese at bay long enough to seal their fate.

Daniel shouted again. "They're going to seal you in!" *Don't any of them speak English?*

Jessup fired wildly into the air, assaulting every ear. "Back to work!" Sure enough, people began to turn away.

Back into the mine.

Jessup hurried over to a stack of barrels and pulled a small box from the top of one. "We wanted 'em ignorant, kid. No English, a-tall." His good arm held the box close to his chest. The cut arm trembled but kept the pistol up.

Daniel saw that string was tied to the box. Not string, he decided, some kind of black cord. It snaked to the mouth of the cave before climbing up the wall and sticking into a bundle of red sticks.

Dynamite.

"Ain't you the hero, Downey. Too bad none of these bastards know it." Jessup spat out a lump of tobacco. "Travis, don't let any of 'em by on your side. Hawkins, get off your ass and bring that Chink kid here, I owe him sumthin' special." Jessup ratcheted a T-shaped handle out of the top of the box.

More railroad men collected near the cave mouth. With each burst of the rifle, the Chinese fell back. Daniel felt his odds become grimmer and grimmer. As the spurs of Travis' boots chimed closer, the boy patted a small hand against Daniel's back. "Mister?" he whispered. "Foreman Jessup will hurt us? Bury us in the cave?" Jun spoke in a refined British accent, not struggling with Daniel's words, but in naïve disbelief.

Daniel hugged the boy. "Yes, yes, he will. He's a very bad man, please tell them!"

The boy spoke the words Daniel could not, and the Chinese roared.

The mob surged toward Jessup and Travis. Daniel saw the old Chinaman's eyes widen, his hand pointed toward the front of the cave. His shout was lost in the roar of the mob, and then he was carried away by it, too. Daniel followed to where the finger pointed. Past Travis, firing into a wave of broken fingernails and calloused hands, Jessup was almost out of the cave.

Daniel raised the gun without thinking. He aimed for

the chest. The big man spun a bolt open on the box to feed the second cord into it. Daniel's hand shook, and he pretended it was just from months of liquor. He pretended he was sighting squirrels with his father's shotgun, held a deep breath, and fired.

Jessup dropped the second cord as if he were surprised by something, and made to stand up. Daniel sighted again, but right then the fat squirrel fell backwards, on top of the half-set detonator.

The world shrieked and came apart.

He relived the nightmare with every slumber.

They let go of Daniel and he fell. Blood dripped from his mouth as he rolled over, holding up his hands, pleading for them to stop hitting him.

Nelson Grainer laughed.

Stephen's boot lifted Daniel, hurling him against a crate of rotting lettuce. Nelson fanned the cards his bodyguards had pulled from Daniel's sleeve. "I can't stand a cheat, Mr. Downey. Especially a poor one." He threw the cards in Daniel's face.

Nelson knelt before Daniel, pulling the white glove of his left hand free. "I'm going to tell you something very important," he giggled. The giggle stretched, and Nelson pressed his left hand to his forehead to collect himself.

Red, glowing marks swirled on the back of Nelson's hand.

Daniel jerked himself awake. He immediately regretted it: his ears rang, and everywhere something ached.

By dim lantern light he could see dozens of Chinese men sitting or lying injured along the walls of a round cavern, damp and chill. Somewhere close gunshots roared, the screams coming after them muffled by their echo.

The boy!

"There—there was a boy," he croaked to them.

An old man turned to face him. "No question asking!" The words were thickly accented, but the meaning clear. He stamped closer and Daniel could make out wizened features and clear eyes. It was the man who had spied the charge of dynamite before the explosion. "Lots dead, maybe because of you! And more still dying, didn't you hear!" One of the injured limped closer, blood twisted in the long black hair of his mustache and the matted ponytail draped over one shoulder. He slid a knife from a fold of pajama top and slashed it toward Daniel. His words were lost on Daniel, but not the grief they held.

The old man silenced the knife wielder with a raised hand. An angry murmur spread through the crowd, but when the eldest turned to them quiet descended again.

Daniel tried to stand and just barely managed. He remembered the rain of stone smashing down on the Chinese workers. A rain he'd loosed by killing Jessup. He gasped as he remembered the sounds the rocks made as they collided with flesh.

Daniel squeezed his eyes shut and sipped despair. He tried to let just a little out, like he'd once rationed whiskey. Just like whiskey, he found himself wallowing in the despair more and more. He thought of his parents, good Irish farmers who saved a lifetime to send him to school in Boston. Only Daniel had squandered their money, been expelled that first year and evicted from his rooms.

That was when he took up cheating, and put himself on the road to the Mark.

The old man held his hand up to keep the mob at bay. Daniel saw blood staining them. He looked down and saw matching red stains on his vest. "You carried me out? You saved my life."

The old man shook his head. "Yes, old fool Shen saved you from the rocks. Better maybe I let you die!" Shen pitched his voice low. "I know what you run from, I saw the Mark. You carry great debt of sin. You are damned."

Daniel stuck his hands into the pockets of his trousers to hide the Mark. *What did Shen know?* The mob was bent on his death, Daniel could feel it. It was not the time to ask. "Please, I did not bring the mountain down on us."

Shen stalked closer. "We saw you fight with foreman Jessup, and the explosion. So many missing, we dare wait for them no longer. Lots of us think you done it.

Lots want to die." He walked closer and whispered. "Maybe better for you, die here, before *it* takes you!"

"I'll take my chances," Daniel said, swallowing his need to ask more. He had to save his life first. "Bock wanted you all buried, Shen!"

The enraged man came closer, poking the air with his knife. Shen spoke sharply to ward the man off a second time. "Young's brother died today. Maybe Jun, the boy, dead, too. You shot Jessup, started all this. So say to me why I don't let Young have a revenge!"

Shen returned to the survivors. He shook his head at a whisper, but the questioner spoke louder, more forcefully. Shen raised his eyes to meet Daniel's across the cavern, then finally nodded. At once the man with the bloody mustache started across the floor.

Shen grabbed the man's knife arm spoke softly. The man began sobbing, barely checking his advance. The old man crossed back to Daniel's side. He tapped his ears. "I planted lots of dynamite for railroad. Hear little, unless it is quiet. Easy to pretend no English, and sometimes lets me hear secrets." Shen leaned in, placed a hand on Daniel's shoulder. "I wish I can say you didn't make the explosion like I can say you protected the boy."

Daniel swallowed.

"Very sorry, Daniel." Shen's eyes fell away. "Very sorry," he said again, and turned and walked away.

The Mark seethed, sensing the danger. Daniel felt its fear, took courage from it.

If this is the last hand . . .

"Shen," Daniel called out, and the man stopped in place. "The Mark. Tell him to bleed me clean. Don't let him touch me."

The old man's head bowed ever so slightly. He uttered a sharp command, slid his hand across his throat. Young nodded, his eyes not straying from Daniel's. He raised the knife blade high over a shoulder in a backhand grip, ready to carry out the sentence his grief demanded.

Daniel listened for the inner voice that always looked for the out, counted the cards. He was surprised to find his greatest sorrow was not for himself, but for Jun, and

Shen, and the others whose mountain grave he would share. Jessup had been right about one thing. *Helluva time to become a good Samaritan.*

As the knife came slicing down he felt fury rise in the Mark. It realized he planned to rob it of a new host, to take a small victory in burying the debt of evil in the bowels of this mountain along with his flesh.

Daniel took cold comfort: the evil would die with him. He jutted his chin out to make for a clean cut.

The knife whistled close. A shot rang out. The tip of the blade barely pricked Daniel's throat as he watched a drop of red appear on Young's chest. He staggered backward and turned to face Travis and Hawkins, the flat of their palms cocking their pistols to fire.

Young screamed between Daniel and the guns. He jerked with each impact but kept on going, raising his blade and burying it in Hawkins' neck. The dying man emptied his pistol into Young.

"Damn y'all!" Travis cursed in his Southern drawl. "You especially, Downey! Bock won't dig us out till we kill all your Chinese friends." Daniel heard the metallic scraping of bullets being jammed into a six-shooter.

Someone doused the lantern. People scattered, terrified, in the dark.

"Boulder nicked my right hand, too," Travis said, indignant. The chamber snicked closed, then Daniel heard him cock the hammer. "Gonna cost that rich bastard more fo' healin'-up time." Travis fired into the dark again.

Daniel heard a man fall and cry out. Daniel searched for him in the dark and hauled him to his feet. He followed the sounds of the fleeing Chinese, reaching a wall and skinning his hand along it until he felt a cool breeze and his hand sank through empty space. Another gunshot lit the room and he saw Shen scoop the bleeding man out of his arms and pull him through the opening.

"You sure pissed off Bock, Danny boy! Don't worry 'bout him, though, I'm gonna sort you out myself." Daniel scrambled through the hole just before Travis' next shots chipped the far side of the wall. A lantern glowed ahead of him, and he saw Shen beckoning him to follow.

"Gonna hunt you down if I have to go through every slant-eye first. I got the bullets, boy!"

Daniel stopped. The lantern, hid by the backs of the fleeing, faded.

Travis was a killer. Daniel heard the scuffle of boots as Travis stalked carefully closer, searching for the opening. Travis would follow the light ahead and spend every bullet he had in the pursuit.

Daniel thought back to the first moonless night after he'd been Marked. The Thomason gang had laughed at him when he'd come to them for sanctuary, and Daniel had hidden with the rats beneath the saloon they called home. They were the toughest and cruelest of Boston's gangs, but when the collector had arrived, they cried for their mothers and fell before it. Daniel had listened to it all, biting on his fist and voiding himself . . . and walking numbly away when daylight came.

The next moonless night, Daniel had hidden behind the jail cell of a man waiting to be hanged. Earlier that night the saloon had been full of the man's victims. Their sobbing accounts of his cruelty and slaughter reminded him of the Thomasons, and gave him an idea. Daniel waited beneath the window of that prison cell, ice in his bowels but with nowhere left to run and no more cards up his sleeve. Then it had come, and he'd listened to the murderer whimper and hammer at the bars in vain as the collector descended upon him, silencing him forever. He saw the shadow of the thing, thrown by fluttering candlelight on the ground before him, and it was more than he ever wanted to know of it. Then the light had been snuffed out, and once again Daniel waited in terror for the light of day. At dawn he fled, grief-stricken by what he'd done.

"It only takes sinners," he kept telling himself, but the words rang hollow. He had spent every sleepless night since watching the moon fatten and wane, wondering if he could sacrifice another.

Daniel might have been spared this moonless night, too, with the likes of Travis close by. But the Mark was quiet yet; the collector was not close enough for Daniel to ambush the gunman without risking a bullet, and he would not buy time with the lives of innocents. That was something, at least. *Something* still good in him.

"No more good folk die before I do," Daniel whispered. He turned around, built up speed, and barreled past the opening just ahead of a bullet's crack.

"Would'a thought you a crack shot," he taunted over his shoulder. *Get him angry, that was Daniel's hope. Draw him away from Shen and the others.* "Getting old, Travis?"

Travis screamed. More bullets caromed through the passage as Daniel ran for his life. *Maybe I can live through this,* Daniel thought. Maybe Shen knew a way out. *And maybe I can pull an inside straight out of my—* His foot sank in a deep groove filled with water and he tumbled hard to the ground.

His lungs heaved, and his legs felt weighted with lead. He struggled to his knees and listened hard. He knew Travis would be close, now. He had to keep running, but the water in the puddle was cool. It took him back to that night three months past; the thing he could not banish from his dreams and spent every waking hour running to escape.

Nelson leaned over Daniel in that alley, close enough for the glowing Mark, hungry and alive, to light both their faces.

"Do you like my Mark?" Nelson reached into Daniel's sodden lap and lifted his left hand, clasping it with his own. Writing scrawled along the flesh of the side of Nelson's palm and stretched tentatively toward Daniel's. Letter by arcane letter leaped across. Each new touch was agony, like barbed wire tearing, like flame licking and burning.

"It likes you!" Nelon hissed breathlessly.

Daniel's eyes jerked, uncomprehending, from the words crawling onto his flesh and back to Nelson's tortured eyes.

"I am dying, and I begin to understand that something comes after this life. I have done terrible things, but *you* will pay for them."

Something cold, something malevolent entered him, and Daniel gasped as the last of the red glow fell from Nelson's hand.

"Yes, take it all!" Nelson wept, and Stephen stepped close to help him to his feet.

Darkness seethed through him, spirits of hatred and cruelty and all mortal sins. "Why?" Daniel begged.

Nelson stood taller now freed of his burden. "You earned it, my boy! You are a liar and a cheat, I could not have passed it on otherwise."

A carriage turned the corner and hooves clattered to a hasty stop. Nelson climbed in. "I doubt there is enough magic left in the world to unmake that Mark, that makes it yours for life," Nelson called.

The horses started moving.

"You will feel the collector when it comes!" As the carriage turned the corner, Nelson cried out the window. "It will seek the Mark on the darkest night each month. Hide among sinners when it comes, it may win you time." Nelson's voice became tearful once he was out of sight. "Thank you, my boy! Thank you!"

Daniel lay gasping in his nest of fetid trash, scratching in terror at his hand.

"Daniel!"

He wrenched away from the memory, hearing his name. It was Jun's voice, crying out in pain.

"I got your little Chink friend, Danny, want to watch me gut him? No more running, now! Get on back, and you can die instead."

Daniel had already turned back when the Mark flashed brilliantly. Words began to form, layered circles within circles, and the glow flared bright enough to light the way.

Time.

"Let him go, Travis. I'll take his place.'

Travis laughed from inside the cavern littered with the bodies of the Chinese and Hawkins. "There's my huckleberry!" His laughter choked off when Daniel stepped through the low opening. The gunfighter stared in amazement at the glyphs projected about the cavern.

"Let him go," Daniel said. "If you're worth your word."

Travis, hypnotized by the light, let his hand fall away

from Jun. The boy ran to Daniel's side, wonder instead of fear lighting the boy's face.

"What is it?" Travis laughed away his awe, became once more the wary killer. "That a Chink trick? Won't help you escape. I know the yella's got a way out. Bock didn't believe me, but I know there's one. Won't help you none, though."

"No, not me," Daniel agreed, watching a familiar shadow grow behind Travis, the light of the Mark unable to pierce its veil.

"Not the kid either," Travis promised, his voice ugly.

"Care to make a bet?" Daniel asked, jutting his chin at a patch of shadow growing just past Travis' right shoulder.

"You're too far away to make that chestnut work," Travis laughed, and cast a relaxed look over his shoulder. He saw the blackness growing there and jumped away from it.

Jun began to cry and tugged at Daniel's hand. "Let's away, please," the boy begged.

The blackness took shape. "Danniell," it whispered. Something stepped out of shadow to be kissed by the light of the Mark. It was almost a man, tall and pallid gray. Seven feet or more, naked but for a light cloak cast to the side. Daniel held his hand toward it, illuminating the cloak that trailed behind in a messy tangle reaching to the dirt. *Not a cloak.* It was a set of rotting, feathered wings.

It stopped between the men and knelt to smile at the boy. Daniel yanked Jun away. "And what plans have you made for me this moonless night?" it rumbled.

"He is not for you!"

It nodded. "I doubted you would hide behind a child." It rose and turned to Travis. "But this is a morsel I will take."

Travis shook his head, fear twisting his face. "Wh–what are you?"

"I am neither risen or fallen, mortal."

Travis sunk to his knees, frantically trying to pray around the butt of the gun he'd worshiped so long. "No. I don't want to die!"

"How unfortunate for you," it said. Travis screamed and started shooting.

Bullets passed through it. Daniel grabbed Jun, shielding his body and pulling him toward the opening. Lead chipped the walls around them. "Run, find Shen!" The boy was scared, and couldn't free his eyes from the wailing gunfighter and the creature advancing on him. Daniel shook him hard, and Jun snapped out of the spell. *"And don't come back, hear?"* Travis was firing faster now, screaming wordlessly. Daniel pushed the boy out into the passage and shoved, watching to make sure he was running before leaping back into the cave.

"Wait!" Daniel shouted, too late. The creature placed his hand on Travis' chest. The gunman begged one last time as his skin began to wrinkle and blacken.

Daniel closed his eyes and pressed his forehead to the cool rock, sickened. The hammer fell impotently a few more times as Travis' moans dimmed to a childlike mewling, then to silence.

It was kneeling in the center of the cavern when Daniel could make himself look again. He watched it lower what had been Travis *into* a perfect circle of shadow on the floor. When it was all the way through, the circle shrank around the point of the creature's finger and disappeared. It stood and smiled.

"You have come back? A shame. I rarely have such clever prey, and there are more in this mountain I would have taken."

Daniel shook his head. "You can't have them."

It sighed, a completely human sound, and the desiccated wings quivered behind it. "I sense your own stain has grown little. You bear the Mark well; without it, you may have suffered only purgation."

A question came to Daniel. "Who do you serve?"

It bristled, growled. "No one. That is *my* sin." And it reached a gray hand out, finger pointing.

"Please!" Jun stumbled in between them and threw his arms around Daniel. Daniel struggled to move him away, too late. The creature's hand touched the back of the boy's head. White light flared where they touched.

The creature gasped, and staggered back, its face

transformed by rapture. The look faded quickly, as if remembering something painful. It heaved a single sob, then looked at the boy and smiled. "I had forgotten. Thank you, child."

Then it carried the smile to Daniel. "I cannot pass such innocence. You are safe this moon. Live well until we meet again."

The wings rustled, seeming fuller in a way Daniel could not fathom. It stepped back into the shadows falling from the Mark's dying light, and was gone.

The train was close by, and slow enough as it steamed uphill. Time to go. Daniel stooped to pick up Jun and place him in the back of the wagon next to Shen and the others.

"Please come, Daniel. I will protect you again," Jun promised.

Daniel shook his head. "Can't, kiddo. It wouldn't be right."

Shen tousled the boy's hair and winced. The Chinese escape route had been a natural chimney to the top of the mountain, and it had been a hard climb for the old man. "I will take Jun to California. My family will keep him safe." He gestured to the Mark, faded to coal-red now in the light of day. "This land, everything is steam and steel and telegraph! No way to fight Darkness. When I was small like Jun, in China, there were men who fought it. Maybe you go there?"

Daniel smiled gingerly. "Takes more than a moon to get to China, Shen. No, I think it's time to head back East."

Shen's eyes narrowed. "The old man, Nelson? You will find him?"

Daniel hefted the sack of food and clothes Shen had collected for him and shook his head. "Nelson Grainer died peacefully in his sleep three days after I met him. I hear of a big shindig planned for railroad folk, though, next month in New York. Care to wager our friend Bock likes to hobnob?"

Shen cackled, and raised a fist with his good arm. "I hope you good hunting. And if you need a place to rest?"

"I know where to find you. Take care, Shen."

He reached into the wagon and hugged Jun tight. "Thank you, little man. I owe you one, and I don't welsh on my debts. Not anymore."

"I will pray for you, Daniel," Jun sobbed into the shoulder of the silk shirt Shen had given Daniel, but quickly wiped the tears away when Daniel turned away and started down the side of the foothill with a wave.

"Ai, a Christian!" Shen muttered as the horses snorted and jerked the wagon into motion. "I tell you *all* about gods, Jun, just wait!"

Daniel hurried down the foothill. A fellow freerider waved to him from an open car and he broke into a jog down to the tracks. He enjoyed the wind on his face and the whistle of the train.

If all went well, he could be in New York in two weeks. That would give him plenty of time to find Bock and plan the next moonless night.

All the time in the world, if he played it right.

PSYCHO PHYSICS

by Donald J. Bingle

Donald J. Bingle doesn't worry about genre when he writes. His first novel, *Forced Conversion* (call your library now!) mixes speculative fiction with a healthy dose of military fiction and a touch of theology. He is currently novelizing his latest screenplay, a dark comedy about the environmental movement, and writing a mystery novel. Don has fantasy, science fiction, horror, romance, and comedic stories in a variety of thematic anthologies and has written gaming materials for Timemaster, Chill, Bond, Paranoia, Dream Park, Battle Cattle, and, of course, Dungeons & Dragons. His full writing and gaming resumes can be found at www.orphyte.com/donaldjbingle.

"IN THE BEGINNING was the Word . . ."

Detective Neil Barrett watched from the opposite side of the interrogation room's two-way mirror as his well-educated suspect muttered the phrase again and again. Sometimes the guy stared at the table and sometimes he gazed blankly at his own reflection, but the murmuring never stopped.

"In the beginning was the Word . . ."

The suspect, Dr. Pavel Kaminsky, was alone in the room with a paper cup of lukewarm vending-machine coffee, two straight-backed chairs, and a wooden table. Previous miscreants had managed to carve a variety of graffiti and anti-police declamations in the table despite having been searched for sharp objects before being ushered into the police station, but the doctor paid no attention to the offensive scrawls. Pavel merely sat passively in one of the two chairs and repeated his mantra.

"In the beginning was the Word . . ."

Barrett had left the interrogation room a few minutes earlier, after having dropped off the lukewarm coffee. He retreated to the adjoining room to gaze through the transparent side of the two-way mirror and attempted to collect his thoughts before proceeding. He didn't want to mess things up and he wasn't sure if he needed to call in a shrink before he asked any more questions.

It had all begun simply enough just this morning, with a call from the head of the national laboratory outside of town. He didn't know what was said; the captain had taken the call. All he knew was that he had been sent out to the laboratory to deal with a 6-0-2, theft of property, shortly after the captain had hung up.

It had seemed so trivial as he drove out to the lab. Now he was clearly in over his head.

The bored security guard defending the flimsy, teeter-totter guardrail blocking the entrance to the lab couldn't find "Neil Barrett" on the green sheet of paper on his clipboard, but a quick flash of his detective's badge was all Barrett needed to get by that minor obstacle. The kid gave a tug on the counterweight and the gate guardrail swung up.

"Security here sucks," Barrett muttered to himself as he moved on up the driveway, past the well-tended, but water-wasting landscaping toward the main building. The kid at the guard shack hadn't even studied his badge. He could have gained access to this place with one of the toy badges from the cowboy costumes Marge had bought for the kids two Halloweens ago, if, of course, Marge hadn't taken them, everything she could cram into a large U-Haul truck, and the kids when she left that Christmas eve. He didn't miss the stuff . . . or Marge . . . but the kids were occasionally cute and actually seemed to like him.

He came to the end of the landscaped drive and parked his secondhand Oldsmobile in one of the overly abundant, unused "handicapped" parking spaces near the front door to the administration building. What? He was going to give himself a ticket? Besides, ever since Marge left, he had felt a bit handicapped. No family, no support structure; just a crappy apartment and a thankless, tedious job with lots of hours but no overtime budget to pay for them.

He went through the main doors, the sterile chill of institutional air-conditioning replacing the already fierce heat of the Arizona sun. The receptionist was apparently away from her post, so he grabbed the building diagram from underneath the clear plastic top of her desk blotter and navigated his own way to the office of Patricia Broadhurst, the Laboratory Director. He waved off the secretary typing outside Ms. Broadhurst's spacious office and barged in through the office door without being announced.

"If I was a terrorist with an AK-47, you'd be dead."

Broadhurst looked up from her papers, startled, as her secretary skidded to a stop behind Barrett. He shrugged his large head back toward the secretary, whose name was Melanie according to the security identification pinned to her blouse and who was surprisingly stacked for having a lady boss. "So would she."

"Captain Fresno said you were uncouth, but effective," said Broadhurst, quickly regaining her composure in a way only professional flak-catchers and bureaucrats can. "So far he's half right. Sit down." She motioned to Melanie, who had one eyebrow raised in confusion and residual fright. "It's okay, Melanie. I was expecting Detective Barrett. Close the door as you leave, will you, dear?"

Barrett snorted lightly. If he ever called one of the gals in the steno-pool "dear," a reprimand would be dropped in his permanent file and he would be shipped off to a gender sensitivity training session run by some dyke with a bad attitude and more testosterone than his last partner. He smiled insincerely and slid into one of the teak-and-leather chairs across the desk from Broadhurst as Melanie retreated to her typing.

"You know, you shouldn't be surprised you had a theft here," Barrett gruffed. "Security is a joke. Anyone can just walk in and go where they please. So what is it? A purse? PDA?" He looked around the office at the classy furniture. "Some chairs or a picture?"

Broadhurst frowned. "This is of a slightly more serious nature, Detective."

Barrett leaned forward in his chair. "Jesus, don't tell me you lost a laptop with 'sensitive' data on it. I don't want to spend two weeks going through trash at the landfill 'cause some bozo left his laptop in an unlocked car and it got boosted by some kids who wouldn't know what to do with a scientific formula if their lives depended on it."

"No . . . er . . . uh . . . even somewhat worse, I'm afraid. We're missing some specimen."

Barrett crinkled his brow in confusion. "Some specimen? You mean, like for drug testing? You made me drop everything and drive out here 'cause somebody peed in a cup and you can't find it?" He was pissed, but not so pissed he didn't appreciate the irony of that emotion being applied in this circumstance.

Broadhurst stood up and moved around the desk, speaking softly, but with authority. "Please shut up and just listen for a moment, Detective. 'Specimen' is what we call 'fissionable material' in our research here." She looked at his blank, stupid face. "Radioactive material, Detective. This is a nuclear research facility, after all."

"You lost a bomb?" said Barrett, thunderstruck.

Broadhurst closed her eyes and spread her hands for a moment before answering, her tone strained. "Not a bomb. We don't have bombs. We don't make bombs. We're a research facility, not a munitions factory. But, yes, we did lose track of some fissionable material—plutonium, to be precise."

The first thought that flashed through Barrett's mind was that Melanie, the secretary with the frightened doe-like eyes and big hooters, must not know, 'cause if Barrett barging into her boss's office had frightened her, knowing that there was missing plutonium would have sent her fleeing back to her parents' house. He dismissed Melanie to the back of his mind, though, at least till later, and asked the next obvious question.

"Enough for a bomb?"

Broadhurst sighed and leaned on the corner of her desk. "I . . . I'm a laboratory administrator with a background in chemistry, not a nuclear scientist, but no, I don't think so. But it could be enough to make a 'dirty bomb.' "

Barrett got up from the chair and turned away from Broadhurst in an effort to quell his anger, but he couldn't bottle it up. He spun back toward her, his voice rising to match his emotions. "You lost enough plutonium for a fucking dirty bomb and you called the local cops to report a 6-0-2? What are you, lady, some kind of psycho? What has to happen before you call the feds, Armageddon?"

"Look, Detective, Captain Fresno said you were effective. It probably was just moved to another experiment without being properly recorded. I can call the Feds and they can swoop in here and shut down the facility and fire everyone, and threaten to incarcerate everyone, and all that will happen is that everyone will get scared and start lying and the specimen will be hidden somewhere and never found and everybody loses."

Barrett looked at her. Sure, she was covering her own ass, but she was probably right.

"Or," she continued, "you can ask a few discreet questions without giving away why you're asking them, so word doesn't leak and start a panic, either among the employees or the public at large, and maybe we can resolve this without any fuss."

Barrett didn't immediately respond. She was right and he was cocky enough to think that he might be able to pull it off, not that this was a tale he could ever tell anyone.

She gave him a once-over. "You're probably close to your twenty, right? Eligible for a pension soon, but no prospects besides the force."

Broadhurst must have guessed at his thoughts. You could do that sometimes, if you were a good interrogator. Maybe that skill helps in the civil service, too. "You've got the lingo right, anyhow. Next thing, you'll be telling me to watch my six."

She ignored his banter and continued on, smoothly, too smoothly for his taste. "You know, a senior security gig at a national laboratory can be a nice job. Good benefits, regular hours. A person with a police background and familiarity with the lab would have a leg up getting such a position."

Barrett knew enough not to take the bait overtly, but a job roaming the secretary-filled hallways at some government facility beat the hell out of busting skanky hookers at the truck stop and chasing dope-heads down alleyways.

"Let's focus on the crime. Who had access?"

Broadhurst managed to return to her chair without winking or gloating over her success. She picked up a sheet of paper with several names on it and handed it across the desk before sitting. "Not that many. Dr. Pechelnik was conducting some tests on the impact of environmental factors—humidity, temperature, freeze-thaw, and the like—on canisters which transport the fissionable material. Some zealous bureaucrat in Washington decided the tests would be invalid unless the containers actually had specimen inside. Pechelnik, his assistant, and just a few others have access to the secure testing lab."

Barrett looked over the short list. "So, Pechelnik, he reported the stuff missing?"

"Oh, no. No one from his lab knows, at least as far as I am aware. The problem was discovered in a routine security audit conducted after hours last night."

Barrett raised his eyebrows. "Who did that?"

"Lawrence Michelson," replied the Laboratory Director. "Senior security officer. He verifies the weight of the sealed container during each security audit. It was light by precisely the weight of the specimen."

Barrett noted the name at the bottom of the list. "And you don't think he filched it."

Broadhurst shrugged. "Why report it, if he did? He has a good gig here, though he will be retiring soon, I understand."

Jesus, she is really waving the flag, thought Barrett. Better get to work. "Okay, I'll have a chat with the people on the list . . ."

Broadhurst started to interrupt, but he waved her off. ". . . without giving anything away."

* * *

Barrett made his way to the Chemical Engineering Building, Number 415, and walked in through the double glass doors. He glanced briefly at a bulky device in the vestibule that could be used to scan hands and feet for radiation before one exited the building, then moved past it and through a second set of doors. Inside, above a box of yellow booties that a placard announced "must be worn at all times" in the building, was a glassed-in, black placard with movable white letters listing the resident scientists and their room numbers. He consulted the list and moved left down an empty hallway with shiny linoleum flooring, past metal, institutional doors with tiny windows crisscrossed with reinforcing wire, his uncovered shoes thudding against the tile.

Most of the doors were marked with the name of the occupant or the description of the lab. One had a large decal on it that read: "Do NOT open door if closed." Barrett looked at it quizzically for a moment, but resisted the temptation to open it. He moved on past another door, this one painted red, with a sign hanging down on short chains from the hallway ceiling depicting a large arrow. In even larger type, it read: "Emergency Decontamination Showers." He tried to imagine Melanie in the shower, but the door still gave him the creeps.

Finally, at the end of the hallway, on the right, he came to Pechelnik's office, straight across from the Environmental Testing Lab. He rapped lightly and immediately let himself in. Behind the government-issue metal desk sat a pale, mildly plump, slightly balding man. He wore practical glasses and a white lab coat. He was chatting with a leggy young woman in a similar lab coat. The woman had striking green eyes unencumbered by eyewear.

Yeah, this could be a real nice gig.

Pechelnik, at least he assumed it was Pechelnik, looked up, peering over the top of his glasses expectantly. Barrett didn't care what color his eyes were; he was still thinking about the green-eyed lady.

Barrett forced his attention back to his task and spoke up. "Ms. Broadhurst asked me to speak with you regarding some . . . uh . . . administrative matters."

Pechelnik looked genuinely startled for a second, but then quickly covered it up. "I really don't know why it should be so difficult to change my 401(k) contribution rate," he said, managing to sound both mundane and defensive at the same time. Barrett said nothing, going along, while Pechelnik turned back to the leggy lab assistant. "Grace, we'll have to discuss the decay rates after lunch. If I don't take care of this, I may never be able to afford to retire and leave all this to your capable hands."

Grace smiled artificially at both of the men. "No problem, though how you can afford to put anything away on a government salary is beyond me, Casimir." She moved toward the door, passing Barrett with what he dreamed was a once-over. As she left, she looked back over her shoulder, "I'll be in the lab."

Barrett looked at Pechelnik, letting him stew for a moment. Then, without offering his hand, he simply announced, "The name's Barrett. I'm not from the accounting department. I'm from the police department." He flipped his badge open and shut with a lazy, familiar motion. "But you knew that, didn't you, Dr. Pechelnik?"

Pechelnik looked down at his desk and pretended to sort his papers. Finally, he looked up, fear in his eyes. "Um . . . yes . . . I guess I did." His eyes flicked nervously between the detective and the open door to the hallway. "Uh . . . could you close the door?"

Barrett reached back with his left foot and, without looking, nudged the door shut. He kept his eyes boring into Pechelnik.

The door *whoomphed* lazily shut and the latch clacked into place.

"And you know I'm not here about your 401(k) plan, don't you, doctor?" This was going to be easy, too easy.

Pechelnik shifted in his chair.

Barrett pressed on. "But you do know why I am here, don't you?" Barrett was already picturing himself walking the rounds down the clean hallways of the complex, chatting up the secretaries and lab assistants, then driving home to a nice, new apartment in his shiny, new sports car.

Pechelnik's imaginings were apparently of a more unpleasant nature. Beads of sweat were beginning to form on his shiny, pale brow, despite the uniform, air-conditioned coolness of the building. But as the physicist thought, his composure began to steady. Finally, he spoke.

"I've really got nothing to do with it."

"With what?"

"With Dr. Kaminsky's disappearance, of course."

Now it was Barrett's turn to think in silence. Who the hell was Kaminsky? He wasn't even on the list Broadhurst had given him. Had Kaminsky pilfered the plu . . . the specimen? He decided to go with the flow.

"So you know why I'm here. That just makes me believe you did have something to do with it, but I'm a reasonable man. Just tell me what you do know and we'll see how it turns out." Barrett casually reached down and picked up a stack of computer printouts from the spare chair in the office. He dropped them to the floor, then slowly sat down and leaned back. "Take your time. I like a good story."

Pechelnik feigned irritation. "I'm sure I wouldn't know where to begin."

"The beginning is always good," said Barrett. "What's your relationship with Kaminsky?"

"Pavel . . . he's my counterpart here at the lab. We've worked together for years, even before we came here. He's more of a theorist and I'm . . . well . . . I'm more of a technical fellow. You know, crafting the experiments to test out his hypotheses, setting up the equipment. That kind of thing."

"What kind of theorist?"

"He's a physicist, like me. You know, quantum mechanics . . ."

Barrett gave him a stern look. "Do I look like I know anything about quantum mechanics?"

Pechelnik's voice took on a more relaxed, professorial tone. "It's really quite exciting, you know. Mainly, on the physical side, it's all about really small particles, the particles that make up atoms. Scientists smash atoms together at really, really high speeds, close to the speed of light, in cyclotrons and accelerators, then study the trails that the component parts make in order to determine their characteristics."

"And Kaminsky, he 'theorized' about what these trails would be?" Barrett was lost, but it was best to keep the interviewee talking.

Pechelnik's hands fluttered with enthusiasm as he warmed to his tale. "Oh, no. Much broader, much more cosmic than that. What do you know about wave theory, Detective?"

Barrett shrugged. "You tell me what I need to know to understand Kaminsky's work."

Pechelnik picked up an empty file folder and pushed a pencil through the center of it, then held it up sideways. "If I were to shine a bright light through this hole and the room were dim, what would I see on the opposite wall?"

"A small circle of light, I guess."

"Right, Detective. Now, if I were to punch a second hole in the folder and shine the light again, what would I see, assuming the holes were close enough and the source was bright enough?"

"You're the scientist. You tell me," said Barrett. This was not how he imagined this interrogation going.

"You would see light and dark stripes. It's called an interference pattern. The light waves from the two different holes interfere with one another to form the pattern."

"And that was Kaminsky's big discovery?"

Pechelnik laughed a nervous little professional chuckle, the kind Barrett reserved for the captain's jokes. "Don't be absurd. Everyone's known that for centuries. The more interesting thing is that they can do this same experiment on a quantum scale, where only one photon—one light particle—is emitted by the light source at a time and then, after it goes through one or the other of the holes, it hits a sensor. And do you know what happens, when they do that a bunch of times?"

Barrett simply shrugged.

"Nothing changes!" exclaimed the doctor in triumph.

Barrett thought about the cutbacks at the department and where his tax money was being spent, but he simply said "Uh-huh."

"Don't you see? The photon has to go through one hole or the other and only one is sent at a time, so there's no other photon or wave to cause the interference pattern."

"Uh-huh."

"But, when they actually set up a device to track which hole the photon goes through and they do that a bunch of times, instead of an interference pattern, they get two circles of light on the other side."

"Wait, I got this one. So the tracking equipment is affecting the results, right?"

"Even more mysterious. If they keep the tracking equipment on, but erase the results before they can be read, the light-and-dark-band interference pattern returns."

It was all getting too bizarre for Barrett. "And what does this have to do with Kaminsky?"

"Well, he was among those who theorized that every quantum event that can occur does occur, at least in some universe. The photon can go through the left hole or the right hole, so it does both, one in one universe and the other in another universe. When we don't know the hole the photon went through, that probability wave collapses back onto itself, the two universes merge, and it is as if the photon went through both holes. It interferes with *itself*."

"You mean . . ."

"Exactly. If we know which hole it went through, then the universes don't merge. We are in a universe where the photon went through one hole and there is another universe exactly the same as this one, but where the photon went through the other hole."

Barrett was perplexed. The physics was confusing enough, but what exactly did this have to do with Kaminsky and his investigation? He tried to get back on track. "I'm confused. You and Kaminsky are doing that stuff here? I thought you worked on environmental testing of nuclear canisters."

Pechelnik's excitement over his scientific explanation faded quickly. "We do. We did the other work . . . before, when we worked at one of the accelerators."

"You left together to come here?"

"Yes."

"But now Kaminsky is missing?"

"Yes."

"Since when? How long has he been gone?" Now they were getting back on track.

Pechelnik scrunched up his face momentarily. "Since yesterday afternoon."

"How do you know? Maybe he's just out sick this morning."

"No, he's missing, I tell you. I would know. Pavel and I . . . well . . . we're very close. I . . . er . . . checked his apartment and he's not there."

"And you think this theoretical stuff has something to do with him being missing?"

"I'm sure it does. You see, he's been working on the implications of a multiple universe theory in his spare time. If you accept that a universe splits off whenever something happens here that is physically different and that difference is perceived, then you can create new universes at whim."

Crap. Why hadn't he taken more science courses? "You lost me there, doc."

"Well, medical science tells us that thought has a chemical component. Neurotransmitters fire, releasing chemicals that cause other neurotransmitters to fire or not fire. That is how thought occurs."

"So, every time I think something, I create a new universe?" Barrett paused a moment to think of Melanie and Grace soaping up in the shower in his apartment. Yeah, it was a great dreamworld, but he couldn't believe it was really a *world*. "I don't know, doc."

"It's actually quite consistent with religion, if that makes you feel any better about it, Detective."

"How so?"

"Well, Christianity teaches us that improper thoughts are a sin and that that sin is as bad as actually acting out the improper thoughts. Maybe that is because by having such thoughts, you create a universe where they occur."

"So, in some parallel universe, Jimmy Carter isn't just lusting in his heart, huh?" Barrett couldn't help but chuckle.

Pechelnik put a stop to Barrett's laughter. "And all the homicidal thoughts of raving lunatics come true—

the tortures, the murders, the genocide, the sadistic side of man, fully realized."

The thought was sobering, but his mind couldn't really grasp the concept. Barrett snorted lightly. "You don't believe this . . . theory, do you doc?"

"Dr. Kaminsky's a very bright fellow—a genius in my mind. I've never known him to be wrong. Tell me this, Detective. Do you believe in the power of a positive mental attitude?"

Jeez, now the guy was sounding like the counselor Marge dragged him to the year before she split with the kids. Barrett shook his head. "I don't know. Seems to work for some, I guess."

"Did you ever think as to why it works?"

"I don't know. Positive thinking causes endorphins that make you work harder or something?"

"If a positive-minded person is constantly thinking positive thoughts about themself in happier, richer, more successful circumstances, wouldn't they be creating universes where they actually were happier, richer, and more successful? And in all those universes, they're thinking even more positive thoughts about their future, creating more and more universes in which they are more and more successful, until there are so many universes in which they are happy and successful, that odds are that in any universe they look at, any one they exist in, they are happy and successful. It's self-reinforcing. All the permutations of themselves create a practically infinite number of universes in which they are successful."

"If wishing makes it so, how come the positive attitude people need all those self-help books?"

"Kaminsky believed that putting things down in print helps strengthen the reinforcement mechanism. The written word inculcates others to have the same or similar thoughts and ensures that the universe of your thoughts outlives you because your thoughts are perceived and thought by others."

"Are you saying Kaminsky wished himself away to a happier universe?" Try to put that in a report and he'd need to find a new job, that's for sure.

"Not at all. You can't move to a new universe, except one second at a time, by the choices you make or the words you write. Again, religion is consistent. 'In the beginning, was the Word,' Detective. Why couldn't our universe have started from someone's words?"

Barrett was determined to keep the odd scientist on track. "Sure, whatever. But what has this got to do with Kaminsky being missing?"

Pechelnik was becoming visibly agitated. He wrung his hands and stood and began pacing behind the desk. "He became very interested in the reinforcing power of writing. By causing great numbers of people to think something, you could, he believed, create a probability of a permanent universe where it was so."

Barrett thought of all the crappy writers in the world, banging away at their keyboards, and all of the god-awful stories they had produced. Then he thought of all the insipid sitcoms, stupid comics, and bad movies he had experienced and winced hard at the prospect of universes where they were real.

Pechelnik continued, both his tone and his pacing increasing in tempo. "I write a bit, you know. Upbeat, optimistic stuff. Poetry. That kind of thing. Bit of a romantic, I guess. I want the worlds to be a better place, you know." An emotional tremor crept into the physicist's voice. "Of course, I don't have any impact compared to the science fiction writers. They not only create universes where our world has a brighter future, they create whole new worlds—utopian places without crime or hunger or war . . ."

Pechelnik's eyes quickly misted over as he talked. "It's really quite a sacred calling, you know, to imagine a better world and call it into being with your words and share it with others." By this time, the self-proclaimed poet was crying liberally as he spoke. He suddenly seemed to notice the tears with embarrassment. "I'm sorry, Detective, it has just been such a strain today, with Pavel missing and all." He tilted his head toward a small restroom adjoining the office. "Do you mind?"

Barrett nodded and Pechelnik retreated to the restroom. The door closed and Barrett could hear the water running. No doubt that was why Pechelnik didn't hear the rap on the office door from the hallway. Barrett stood and turned toward the door as Grace let herself in.

She seemed startled that Barrett was still there. "Oh, I'm sorry. I thought Casimir would be free by now."

"No problem. He's just in the john." There was an awkward moment of silence before Barrett decided to make small talk. "Have you worked with Dr. Pechelnik long?"

"Several years," answered the lab assistant.

Barrett didn't really want to interrogate her now, not with Pechelnik's interview still in progress. But it never hurt, professionally or socially, to be nice to a good-looking interviewee of the female persuasion. He grasped for additional chit-chat.

"I understand the doc's a writer. Ever read any of his stuff?"

Grace stiffened suddenly. A look of fear flitted in her eyes. "What do you mean?" She glanced nervously at the restroom door, but it was still shut tight and the water was still running.

Barrett misinterpreted her fear. "Hey, I won't tell him you saw anything. Can't have the boss knowing you read his poetry about chirping birds and croaking frogs, can we?"

"Is that what he told you," she spat out with surprising vehemence, "that he writes poetry?" She lowered her voice to a conspiratorial whisper, her eyes never leaving the restroom door. "He writes *pornography*. Disgusting, nasty, violent stuff. I came across it once when I was using his terminal. Tons of it. I couldn't even keep reading . . . didn't want to keep reading. I just ran out of the room. It's no wonder he got fired at the accelerator—I heard that there was an incident there, but never guessed what it might be until I saw that awful filth."

"So it was him that got fired and not Kaminsky?"

She was so startled by the reference to Kaminsky that her eyes flicked to Barrett's for just a moment, her pupils wide, before returning to guard the door. "What do you mean, Kaminsky? Where did you hear that name?"

Barrett was confused, more confused than during the

explanation of quantum wave theory. "Kaminsky. His counterpart here at the lab."

She looked Barrett straight in the eye. "There's no Kaminsky here. Never has been. That's his goddamn pen name." With that, she glanced back at the bathroom door and fled the room, disappearing down the hallway.

Barrett looked after her in astonishment for just a moment, the water still running in the restroom the only sound breaking the silence of the small office. Then he spun quickly and kicked in the door to the restroom.

The hot running water had steamed up the small room. At first, all he could see were the phrases "Too late . . ." and "the Word . . ." written in the condensation on the mirror. Then he looked down and saw Pechelnik. The psycho had wrapped a towel around his neck and twisted it until he had passed out. It was the kind of half-assed suicide attempt that first-timers were known for; Barrett had seen this kind of thing before. The physicist had hit his head slightly when he fell, but he was breathing.

Barrett's mind kicked into overdrive to try to get a grasp on the situation, but any universes he might be creating with his thoughts now would surely be chaotic, a dance of revelations and quantum theories overlaid on a stark, nuclear reality filled with uncertainty and unanswered questions. All Barrett knew was that he had to get this guy to a controlled environment and sort things out before the asshole tried something even more stupid and more lethal.

Barrett shook the dazed doctor awake and walked him quickly out to the dented Oldsmobile, still parked in the handicapped spot, and drove quickly to the station house.

Attempted suicide was a crime.

It would do for a start.

Now Barrett stood on the other side of the glass in the interrogation room and tried to parse it through. He had called Broadhurst from the car and had her access the physicist's computer. It was full of sick, violent stories, just as Grace had indicated. Clearly, Pechelnik/Kaminsky was a whack-job and, for his money, that meant that odds were he was a whack-job with a bunch of plutonium and the knowledge to use it. But the psycho physicist had clammed up after the suicide attempt. He just kept muttering to himself and that wasn't getting Barrett anywhere.

Suddenly, it came to him. He had seen a puff piece on the television just this morning about the big, worldwide, science fiction convention in Phoenix. Barrett strode back into the interrogation room and looked the muttering scientist square in the eye. He spoke with firm authority. "Kaminsky doesn't like science fiction, does he?"

The physicist quivered as he whispered, "In the beginning was the Word . . ." But Barrett noticed an almost imperceptible shake of the head.

He grabbed the cradle off the wall phone. "Call the Phoenix convention center and have them evacuate. We have a possible bomb or airborne radioactive particles being released at the science fiction convention."

Barrett hung up the phone and relaxed just a bit. He had made his call—either he would get a commendation for saving the geeks at the sci-fi fest or he would need that job at the national laboratory after the department got sued over an unnecessary evacuation. Sure, he knew that Kaminsky, as he had thought of him since he kicked in the restroom door, probably hadn't built a nuke, but he could easily have cooked up some conventional explosives and laced them with the plutonium so as to kill all those utopian universes that the science fiction and fantasy authors would create in the future.

The local police would either stop it in time or they wouldn't . . . or both.

Now, Barrett just had to see which universe he would be living in.

Funny thing, it was neither one.

Barrett was caught by surprise—everyone was caught by surprise—when a massive explosion shook the main convention center on the Vegas strip later that evening, shattering the windows in thousands of hotel rooms and the neon lights in dozens of casinos, slivers of deadly glass slicing down on the revelers below. There was chaos and cursing and blood. And all that was before the authorities realized that a fine plutonium dust had been propelled with the shockwave of the explosion. The heavy radioactive particles settled out relatively quickly in the blocks surrounding the convention center, but not before condemning all of the conventioneers to grisly, painful death.

Barrett cursed himself with a vehemence usually reserved for his ex-wife. Vegas was almost as close as Phoenix. He should have checked into it; he might have guessed it if he had known the main two conventions in town that evening: a sado-masochism bacchanalia for porn writers and a group of military strategic planners and war-gamers.

The bomber wasn't Kaminsky. It was Pechelnik—the timid poet, the counterpart that wrote verse about fluffy dogs and who hated the other part of himself, the part that had descended into perversion and gotten him fired from his dream job on the cutting edge of quantum physics, ruining his life, ruining his world, ruining other worlds.

Light and dark? Or just two damn assholes from one source? Barrett didn't know the physics. He just knew that Pechelnik believed the theory and so believed that Kaminsky's sick writing was creating universes of unimaginable horror and depravity.

So he interfered with *himself*.

The next day, the attendees at the science fiction convention in Phoenix returned to their seminars—rescheduled after the unnecessary and inconvenient evacuation of the day before. Some of them discussed the horrible terrorist attack in Vegas. As with most grisly tragedies, the nervous, survivor-syndrome jokes had already begun: The sadists had never dreamed anything so cruel. The masochists had never had it so good. And, the military planners, naturally, never saw it coming.

But most of the sci-fi conventioneers put aside the headlines of the moment. Instead, they discussed better worlds and, in doing so, helped create them.

Broadhurst was, of course, fired. The military took over responsibility for security and research at the national laboratory.

Pechelnik was put in a padded room, doped up heavily, and denied any writing instruments.

As for Barrett, he became a devotee of positive mental attitude.

And it worked.

His new, better-paying job wasn't necessarily proof of that, but his honeymoon with Melanie was definitely in a world of its own.

EVEN IN DEATH

by Marc Bilgrey

Marc Bilgrey has written short stories that have appeared in numerous anthologies, including *Merlin, Crafty Cat Crimes, The Ultimate Halloween,* and *Far Frontiers.* He has also written for magazines, television, and comedians. His humorous fantasy novel *And Don't Forget to Rescue the Princess,* was recently published.

I FOUND OUT ABOUT Fred Neilson's death the same way everyone else did, by seeing it on CNN. I'd just gotten home from a client meeting downtown that had run long. I hadn't even had time to check my phone messages, when I flipped on the TV and there it was.

I sank into a chair and stared at the screen as the news anchor read the words: "Fred Neilson, computer software billionaire and founder of NornTech Systems, is missing and presumed dead. His twenty-five-foot fishing boat was found today, off Cape Cod, Massachusetts, by the Coast Guard. A massive search has been called off due to a severe storm. A spokesman for Neilson was quoted as saying that his staff had not heard from Neilson for twenty-four hours before contacting authorities. Neilson had told executives at NornTech Systems that he was going to spend a week on his boat fishing and would check in daily. Neilson was not married. Neilson founded NornTech Systems twenty-five years ago when still . . ."

I shut off the set and thought about my friend Fred. Was it really possible that he was gone? He was an excellent sailor, knew those waters better than anyone. I was just in denial, I told myself. Accidents really do happen, especially in November when the winds start whipping those waves like a child shaking a snow globe.

I stared out my apartment window at the lights of the buildings across the street. Though I'd been on Fred's boat, *The Babbage*, in calm waters during the summer months, I knew that in winter things were different. If he'd accidentally fallen overboard, even with a life preserver on, he'd only be able to last for an hour at most before he'd die of hypothermia. And now with a storm . . .

Not sure what to do, I unpacked the Chinese food I'd bought on my way home and ate dinner. Afterward, I turned the TV back on to see if there were any new developments. It seemed surreal, somehow, to be looking for news of a friend's death on TV. After a story on a bus accident in the south, they went to a field reporter who was in a raincoat on a windy beach. Behind him were massive waves.

"No progress in locating software giant Fred Neilson, whose boat was found floating aimlessly twenty miles off Cape Cod. I have Colin Delaney of the Coast Guard here. Any word on the search for Fred Neilson?"

The microphone was directed at a dark-haired, stocky man wearing a parka. "No. I'm afraid nothing can get through one of these nor'easters. We can't risk losing any of our people."

"Is there any hope of finding Fred Neilson alive?"

"At this point?" he said, as if surprised by the question. "We'll be lucky if the body turns up at all."

I snapped off the set.

That night I had dark dreams of ancient frigates, sails unfurled, wooden decks creaking, as powerful gusts sent them into murky waters.

When I woke up, it was raining outside—not hard, just a dull drizzle. I only had one meeting that day, a routine advertising job to turn in an illustration for a company newsletter. Thankfully, the client seemed pleased with it and the whole thing lasted less than half an hour.

Just as I walked into my apartment, the phone rang. It was Amanda Harris, Fred's personal assistant. "Hi, Robert," she said, "I guess by now you've heard the news."

"Yes," I said.

"There's going to be a memorial service on Friday at St. Paul's Church on Sherbourne Island."

"I'll be there."

"Eleven AM. Henry will meet you at the ferry. You're welcome to stay the weekend at Fred's cottage."

"Are you all right?" I asked.

"Fine," she replied. "Stiff upper lip and all that."

Two days went by and no body was found. The sky was overcast when I boarded the ferry on Friday morning. I had no trouble finding a seat, unlike the summer months when I often had to stand during the two-hour trip. As the lumbering ship pulled out of port, I stared at the now calm water and watched a couple of gulls swoop down and then fly off into the distance.

I thought back to the first time I'd met Fred. I was unpacking my suitcase in my dorm room when in burst this blond-haired bundle of energy. "Hi," he said, extending his right hand, "I'm Fred Neilson, your roommate." His outgoing jubilant personality was completely sincere, I was to learn. Though he came from old money, he never once treated me like anything but an equal. There was never any talk of lineage except to tell some funny story of an eccentric aunt or dotty cousin. And the word *nouveau* was never so much as uttered. This was certainly a change from my boarding school days where I was never allowed to forget my father's meager beginnings and self-made success as if it rated a scarlet letter.

Why Fred liked me was something I never quite understood. Oh, not that I don't think I'm likeable, it's just that Fred didn't need me. Even in college, everyone knew he was a genius. He never studied. He didn't have to. Meanwhile, I was cramming like crazy. Fred was always busy working on his own ideas, writing pages of mathematical equations. They were as incomprehensible to me as ancient Sumerian. Fred, on the other hand, had no trouble understanding my paintings and indeed was one of my most ardent supporters. Even among the other art majors, I was shunned for nothing more than the sin of wanting to do "commercial work."

Every fraternity wanted Fred, but he didn't join any. I didn't either, but then, I hadn't been asked. Fred may have been a loner but that didn't mean he was alone. Women were drawn to him like metal filings to a magnet. Me, I was not so fortunate there either.

Sometimes, Fred and I would cut school, go into Boston and see a movie or just walk around the Commons, while he'd tell me about the plans for the future. He'd had it all worked out, even then. I remember I used to feel like Igor to his Victor von Frankenstein. People would see us together on campus and look at Fred, then at me and shake their heads. I knew they were wondering what he saw in me. I can't say I blamed them. I used to ask myself the same thing.

When school ended, Fred went on (to no one's surprise) to achieve exactly what he'd set out to do. I, on the other hand, slipped into the Bohemian subculture of New York's art scene (to my father's profound disappointment) and then to a quasi-compromise in advertising and illustration. None of this affected my friendship with Fred in the least. We communicated by e-mail on a monthly basis, and once or twice a year, we would meet, usually at his cottage on Sherbourne Island.

There, we'd spend the days on his boat or bicycling around the island or walking along the beach. Every so often, he'd mention some new thing he'd been working on, software or artificial intelligence. It was all as foreign to me as it had been when we were in school, but mostly we'd talk about other things.

I was met at the dock by Henry Beale, one of Fred's executives from NornTech Systems. He was dressed in a dark blue suit and necktie. His brown hair had thinned since the last time I'd seen him. He was now starting to look his age, which was forty-five. On the ride through town, Henry was silent. When we were past the old captains' houses and on the road out of town, he said, "Before Fred went out on the boat, he told a few people that when he got back he was going to make a major announcement."

"About what?" I asked.

"No one knows. Whenever Fred was working on something new, he always kept it under wraps. Last time he spent a few days on the boat he came back with the prototype for the next generation of product. He goes away for a weekend and suddenly we're fourteen months ahead of everyone in the business. Why he even bothered having an R&D division, I'll never know. He *was* the R&D at NornTech Systems."

We came to a stop in front of the church. Henry and I got out of the station wagon and walked into the white wooden building. There were maybe fifty people inside. Top level employees of NornTech Systems and members of Fred's family. No press, no cameras.

I looked around the chapel and located Amanda Harris. Her chin-length blond hair framed her thin face and she seemed very composed in her black dress and short pearl necklace. I figured she was now about thirty. She nodded at me and indicated where Henry and I should be seated.

The minister gave a eulogy which was followed by a few family members' and employees' memories of Fred. When it was over, we all got into cars and headed over to the other side of the island.

Fred's cottage was unchanged since I'd last seen it six months earlier. He liked to call it rustic. I'm not sure thirty rooms with an ocean view qualifies as rustic in anyone's lexicon.

I wandered around, shook a few hands, and made polite conversation with Amanda and with some of Fred's management people whom I knew only slightly. On the lawn outside, I caught up with Fred's mother and offered my condolences. She seemed to be holding up well.

A little later, we all went to the water's edge while the minister said a few words, and then, Fred's mother tossed a wreath into the Atlantic, where the waves carried it off to parts unknown.

* * *

By nightfall, the crowd was dispersing and people were saying their good-byes.

"Where do you go from here?" said Amanda, as I stood looking out a picture window. "Back to New York?"

"I thought I'd take you up on the offer to stay for the weekend," I said. "How about you?"

"I suppose the Framingham office can do without me for a day or two, so I'm staying as well."

Later, when all the others had left, Amanda and I had dinner in the main dining room. Ellie, one of Fred's household staff who lived on the grounds, had prepared and served a superb bluefish almondine.

After dinner, Amanda and I walked down to the water near Fred's dock.

"Where's Fred's boat?" I said.

"*The Babbage* is at South Wharf in town having some repairs done."

"Of course."

Amanda looked at the ocean and said, "Fred had the most brilliant mind I've ever encountered."

She continued for a while on this tract. It was obvious to me that, like so many who knew or had come into contact with Fred, she worshipped him. And, as I had done so many times before, I became akin to a confessor while she heaped her praise upon him. When she finally emerged from her testimonial, she seemed for the first time to become vaguely aware of my presence.

"It's getting late," she said. "I'll say good night now." With that, she turned and headed back into the house. A few minutes later I went in and found my room.

When I woke up at six in the morning, it was still dark. No one had thought to turn on the heat and I shivered. I considered trying to go back to sleep, but I felt oddly energized. It occurred to me to take a walk. I got dressed and at first thought to go down to the water, then decided instead to drive into town.

I took one of the station wagons and drove onto the deserted road. As I headed toward town, I saw the first glimmers of dawn in the sky. When I got to Main Street, it was empty. No people, no cars, not even parked ones. The street lights were still on. I got out and started walking. A block later, out of the corner of my eye, I thought I saw something move. At first I figured it was Wally, the town cat, then I turned and saw Fred Nielson standing on a side street.

For a few seconds I stood transfixed, too stunned to do anything. Then he waved, smiled, called my name, and said, "I found it."

I began moving toward him. As I did, I saw him start to fade away like a wisp of smoke. By the time I reached him, he was gone.

I stared at the sidewalk where he'd stood as if expecting something else to happen. When, after a few minutes, nothing did, I went back to the car, got in, and drove out of town.

A couple of hours later at breakfast, over Ellie's best homemade pancakes, Amanda said, "Are you okay? You don't look rested."

"I didn't sleep well," I admitted. I had no intention of discussing what I'd seen or thought I'd seen with anyone. It did cross my mind that the stress was taking its toll. The only problem with that theory was that I didn't feel particularly stressed. And yet, what *had* happened? Had I hallucinated a ghost or, bizarre as the notion was, had I actually seen a real one? I was not taken to flights of fancy despite my artistic temperament. There had to be a logical explanation.

"I slept surprisingly well." said Amanda, breaking my train of thought. "You'd think I'd be forlorn with grief, but such was not the case. Maybe the fact that it's all over gave me some sense of relief."

"I wanted to ask you, Amanda, did you know what Fred was working on when he died?"

"No, not exactly, but I do know that he'd been amassing a lot of material on mythology."

"Mythology? What area?"

"Norse."

"Getting back to his roots, eh?"

"Apparently, but I don't know what any of it had to

do with NornTech Systems, though. That's not to say he couldn't have been researching something for other reasons, maybe personal ones."

"Personal reasons?"

"Sure, Fred loved to invent mathematical problems and then go about solving them. You were his friend. I thought you knew that."

The words stung. "We didn't talk much about math." Mostly because of my barely rudimentary grasp of the subject, I thought.

"I can't imagine that," said Amanda, almost starry-eyed, "that's *all* Fred and I ever talked about."

Then I wondered if her relationship with her employer had been more than professional. But I discarded it immediately. Fred was true to his own code of morality. One of his ironclad rules was he did not prey upon his employees. I now knew what Amanda's story was. I'd forgotten the signs, not having seen them since school. She was infatuated with Fred. Smitten by his intelligence like an idealistic freshman with a learned professor.

"Did you know that Fred could do advanced calculus and trigonometry problems in his head?" said Amanda.

"Much call for that?" I said, then thought better of it and said, "Sorry." It was as if I weren't even there.

"There are people that can play chess without a board, but how many can play three-dimensional chess or even multiple games?"

I mumbled what I hoped was a polite "excuse me," and got up from the table. A minute later, I wandered into Fred's office, a room he'd set aside for work. As expected, everything was immaculate. Neatly stacked books, papers, software. His computer consoles, six in all, were completely devoid of dust. He was no absent-minded scientist, I thought, as I looked at the few volumes on his desk. They were heavy tomes, in weight and content. I opened a couple and flipped through some pages. I found, as advertised, long passages on Loki, Odin, Thor, Balder, and all the other deities which made up the Norse pantheon. One book had woodcuts of Asgard, Valhalla, and a depiction of Ragnarok, the end of all things.

"If you're trying to figure out what Fred was up to,

you've been beaten to the punch," said Amanda, walking into the room.

"You—?"

"Among others, half the top brass of NornTech Systems was in here yesterday turning the place upside down. They looked through every bit of software, even rifled through notes. Why are you staring at me that way? It's not as if we were looting. You do know that Fred gave his top people stock, don't you?"

"I'm not a complete idiot," I said.

"Sorry, you've just seemed a bit, uh, uninformed, that's all, no offense."

"None taken."

"I think you are the only one of his old friends who isn't or wasn't working for him."

"It's not for want of an invitation," I blurted out, realizing immediately the full extent of my faux pas.

"You mean," her lip visibly trembling, "you turned down an offer from . . . do you realize what you . . ."

"Yes, yes," I said, "I wasn't corporate material. Besides, I didn't know anything about computers. And I didn't want to have to answer to anyone but myself."

"Answer to anyone?" she said, raising an eyebrow. "A lot of people would've killed—"

"You'll excuse me," I said, and left the room.

I spent the afternoon driving aimlessly around the island, looking at deserted beaches, the lighthouse, the cranberry bogs, even the old graveyard where a few Revolutionary heroes were buried.

When night came, I found myself in The Harbor Bar, sitting near a few locals, listening to stories about how to build the ideal lobster trap, and what *exactly* was wrong with the summer people. As I sipped my second scotch, a football game I had no interest in came on the TV, which seemed to excite the natives. After that, a new group of people wandered into the bar, talking of outboard motors, Sheetrock walls, and deer hunting.

Against my better judgment, I ordered something to eat. The blackboard menu indicated that it was codfish, but the deep-fried object on my plate resembled neither cod nor fish. After consuming it, I still had no idea what I'd eaten. Time passed. I endured jukebox music, rowdy laughter and even a few attempts at conversation which I was able to politely deflect.

Eventually, I paid my bill and left. Outside, I was hit by a cold burst of winter air. Invigorating yes, but also cutting. Having nothing to do and feeling a bit in my cups I began strolling down the dark, empty street. At the foot of Main, I happened to glance toward the docks where, standing in the shadows, I saw Fred. He was translucent, like a wrinkled piece of cellophane.

"I found it," he said.

My inhibitions now sufficiently dulled, I approached him without hesitation. "What have you found?" I asked.

"The multiverse."

"What's that?"

Fred started walking in the direction of the docks. I kept pace with him. "It's what I've been looking for," he said. "It's a problem that physicists have been trying to solve for years."

"Okay, hold on for a second. I know I've been imbibing tonight, but correct me if I'm wrong, aren't you dead?"

"You're wrong, sorry to disappoint you. I'm no ghost. I'm as real as you are. That's what I've been trying to tell you. I've been investigating the strange traits of certain elementary particles that seem to contradict Newton's laws by being in two places simultaneously."

We approached the dock and then I heard the wood planks beneath my feet. Fred's steps made no sound.

"I'm not sure I follow you, Fred," I said. "I'm no mathematician, let alone a scientist. Maybe you should be telling this to Amanda or Henry or one of your executives."

"Everybody has a vested interest in NornTech Systems except you. I want to make sure what I say is heard by someone I trust implicitly. The multiverse is not that complicated, really. These elementary particles I was telling you about, somehow they can start before they arrive, be in two places at the same time. Physicists call them superstrings, and have speculated on other dimensions, overlapping dimensions, that occupy the same time and space that would allow this phenomenon to happen."

"Other dimensions?" I said, as we passed empty slips and the occasional fishing boat.

"That's right, all of which sounded to me a lot like the worlds or dimensions that the skalds mentioned."

"Skalds?" I said, thinking I was probably asking very foolish questions.

"Yes, the bards and poets of the ancient Norse mythological texts. They spoke of nine dimensions coexisting, each with its own sentient beings and advanced civilizations. All I've done is combined the science with the mythology by way of mathematics."

"You mean you're there right now?"

"Exactly, but the door to the worlds is about to close, so I won't be able to communicate with you anymore. What I need you to do is retrieve my laptop from *The Babbage.* It's in a false bottom of a desk drawer in my cabin. It has all the formulas that will allow travel here and back. In my haste, I left before I could take it with me. Make a backup of it, and give a copy to Henry. He'll know what to do with it. If I haven't returned in six months, take a copy to our old math professor, Dr. Clemmons."

Then Fred faded and vanished like a dissolve in a movie. I turned and saw that I was standing in front of *The Babbage.* It was bobbing gently up and down in the dark water. In the summer months it would have been surrounded by a plethora of pleasure craft with a variety of silly names. Now it stood alone.

I climbed aboard. I remembered that Fred always kept a duplicate key to his boat in a little box hidden in a compartment under the railing. Despite my night of drinking I now felt curiously sober. I found the key, passed the wheelhouse, and went below decks. As I rummaged around, searching for the laptop, I speculated on what Fred had said.

Though it stretched the bounds of credulity, it *did* seem to have an odd sort of internal integrity to it. I certainly did not feel myself capable of conjuring up a mirage with that kind of articulation.

One's conscious or subconscious must contain the facts that the imagination can build on. My knowledge of Norse myths was limited to reading Thor comic books as a preadolescent. As for Newtonian principles, there was, I could safely conclude, no frame of reference for Newton in my memory at all, beyond an apple hitting him on the head. And whatever advanced mathematical equations that had even been alluded to were so far beyond—

And then I found it. It was just as Fred said it would be, in the false bottom of a desk drawer. I switched on the laptop and quickly found the file labeled: "Skalds—Walking the Rainbow Bridge." A perfunctory look uncovered pages of complicated figures and numbers. Then more pages of mathematical theory and Norse references to other dimensions. Still further, I found instructions on how to open, as Fred put it, the interdimensional door, with directions to specific longitudes and latitudes. I guessed it was where his boat had been found.

I shut off the machine and snapped it shut. No need for further speculation, I thought, as I slipped the computer into its carrying case, turned off the cabin's light switch, and started up the stairs. Reality had made all conjecture obsolete. I hopped onto the dock and began walking back to the car.

The next day I arose early and fixed my own breakfast. I was hoping to avoid Amanda, not being in the mood to hear any more dewy-eyed monologues about her dearly departed idol. My stealth paid off, and, as I got into the cab I'd called, I let out an audible breath.

It was my plan to take the ferry back to the mainland, rent a car, and drive to Framingham with my valuable cargo. There, as per my instructions, I would hand deliver the package to the right party. I figured I could make the backup disks when I got there.

I bought a one-way ticket at the steamship office, then boarded the ferry. Twenty minutes after leaving the dock, I was standing on deck braving the chill when I heard a female voice address me.

"There you are," said Amanda, placing her arms on the railing not far from mine. "What happened to you this morning?"

"I was seized by a sudden bout of homesickness," I replied, staring out at the choppy water.

"I remember riding this ferry so often with Fred."

"Oh?" I said, trying to brace myself for the onslaught that was sure to follow.

"Fred was among the wealthiest men in the world, but he still enjoyed taking the ferry. Said it reminded him of when he was a child and his parents used to summer on the island."

I mumbled an unintelligible grunt as I thought about myself finally becoming a hero of sorts. Resurrecting the "dead" software CEO and bringing his most important discovery to light. I pondered the success that had eluded me all my life.

I considered the book deals, the change in status, and even the women I'd meet. It was a chance to emerge from the shadows, to shed Igor's hump, and finally walk tall and straight.

"Did you know that I started a campaign to get Fred nominated for the Nobel Prize?" said Amanda. "Now I'll organize a suitable memorial to him. It'll keep him alive."

And then I realized that I would be left with nothing. Just as the bearer of bad news in antiquity was killed, so would the contemporary messenger with good tidings be soon forgotten as well. Paradigm shifting news, Fred Neilson opens up a gateway to other worlds. But I would be destined to be a footnote, a fifteen-minute pop celebrity, the fodder of newspaper stories for a few days and then, once again, relegated to obscurity, filed away as a Trivial Pursuit question. Name the man whom Nobel Prize winner Fred Neilson, the discoverer of interdimensional travel, credits with saving his life. Oh, darn, it's on the tip of my tongue. Who? Never heard of him.

"Amanda," I said, "I talked with Fred last night."

"What?" she replied.

And then I told her everything. The first sighting, the second, the mythology, physics, mathematics and the subsequent search and discovery of the laptop.

"This is beyond fantastic," she said, somberly.

"This *is* the laptop, isn't it?" I said, removing the machine from its case.

She examined the computer and nodded. "It certainly is, and I ought to know, it was a birthday present from me."

I pulled it out of her hands and threw it over the railing and watched it sink into the dirty, green water without so much as a discernible noise.

"Why?" said Amanda. "Why'd you do it?"

"So you'll think about me sometimes."

"You son of a bitch."

"Ah, I see I've already made an impression," I said, and walked inside to buy a cup of tea.

HOMESPUN AND HANDMADE

by Dave Smeds

Dave Smeds, a Nebula Award finalist, has authored novels such as *The Sorcery Within, Piper in the Night, X-Men: Law of the Jungle,* and the collection *Embracing the Starlight*. His short fiction has appeared in *Asimov's SF, F&SF,* and *Realms of Fantasy,* and in such anthologies as *In the Field of Fire, Full Spectrum 4, The Best New Horror 7, Sirens and Other Daemon Lovers,* and *Return to Avalon*. His work, called "stylistically innovative, symbolically daring examples of craftsmanship at the highest level" by *The New York Times Book Review,* has seen print in over a dozen countries.

IN ITS OWN WAY, winter is a season of bounty. Insulated by technology, people of our time usually fail to appreciate that. While I lived with Daniel and his children on their long-ago farm, I would stroke the icicles hanging from the fence rails. At night I would stand outside gazing at the crisp clarity of the stars until my teeth chattered. The harshness of the season was my ally; it brought my dear ones into an even tighter circle around me, the better to savor their company.

Daniel harvested ice the morning of Groundhog Day. He brought the load on the sled to the outside hatch of the cellar. The girls and I came down by way of the pantry stairs. I hung the kerosene lamp from its hook and we gathered in the pool of light to watch him work.

The blocks came sliding down the ramp, each successive one crashing into those below, flinging tiny shards of ice into our faces. Perched in my arms, Murancy giggled at the bracing pinpricks of sensation. To a three-year-old, it was pure entertainment.

"Our mama used to worry we'd get poked in the eyes," Sarah commented. "She always made us stay upstairs."

"Now, now. Your mama was only looking out for you." I tried to sound firm. I was determined that the fondness my stepdaughters had for me did not come by diminishing their esteem for their birth mother. But inwardly, I glowed.

When the last of the blocks had made its journey, Daniel slid down the ramp himself. He lifted away the slats that covered the ice bunker and fetched a shovel from the rack. I handed Murancy into the care of her older sister and reached for a second shovel.

"You'll get your apron dirty. Mind the girls," Daniel said.

I blinked at the curtness. "Of—of course," I stammered, and returned to the stairs. Murancy climbed into my lap as Sarah and I sat on the treads.

Daniel worked quickly, mucking out the bottom of the bunker with robust scoops and dumping the sludge into two large buckets.

While I sat there, I fought to keep my expression smooth, even managing to smile indulgently whenever I felt the girls' attention on me. But I was stung. Daniel might be a nineteenth-century man, but he had never before used gender roles to shut me out. The Pecatonica River Valley had been newly settled when Daniel's parents arrived; he'd seen his own mother guide a plow across a muddy field with the rear end of the pull-horse in front of her nose the whole while. Just a week past, he and I had worked elbow to elbow to clear the snowdrifts from the barn door after the big storm.

I silently condemned the meddler who had spoiled that harmony.

When the bunker was clean, Daniel exchanged the shovel for a pair of ice hooks and maneuvered the blocks across the floor. One by one they dropped into place. He covered them with an insulating layer of fresh straw, then replaced the slats, hiding the storage cavity away for another year. Done, he smiled at Sarah and Murancy.

"Those'll keep a good long time," Daniel announced, slapping the ice-melt from his gloves. He said it as someone who relished a cool serving of canned peaches after a day's toil under a hot summer sun. We all shared his approving glance at the jars of fruit, jam, and preserves on the shelves, the reward of the hours I had spent over the stove at harvest time.

My spirits were rising until I saw what he was really staring at: the corner containing the remnant left from the previous year, a legacy not of my work but that of his late wife.

I glanced down, pretending to be absorbed in checking the slats to be sure they were seated evenly over the bunker. When I looked up again, Daniel had climbed the ramp to empty the buckets into the snow beyond the woodpile.

In the afternoon, I baked bread. The girls kept me company, churning butter and cracking walnuts, their young faces aglow with the anticipation of sampling the first loaf hot from the oven. Their father avoided me, remaining outside to top off feed bins and patch the hen coop.

He came in at suppertime, of course, but he was not his usual ebullient self, brimming with observations about the day. He ate quickly and left early, offering the excuse that he needed to fetch more wood for the stove. He said it as if I'd wasted what was there before, as if my breadmaking were some sort of whim and not a necessary and regular contribution to our lives.

The rift yawned even wider at the end of the evening. I came into the bedroom after settling the girls in the loft and found him already beneath the blankets and the room dark. I had to relight a candle in order to put away my slippers and let down my hair.

I left the candle burning as I slid, shivering, beneath the many layers of flannel and wool. I wanted to see Daniel while we talked.

I knew he was awake. His muscles hadn't relaxed nor

had his breathing become rhythmic. I waited. Finally, he opened his eyes. He stared at the rafters, not at me.

"You didn't have to store ice in your cellars, where you come from. You had other ways to keep food cold."

"Yes."

"You had all kinds of incredible things. More'n I can begin to guess at."

"Things don't make a person happy. What I have here is what I find incredible."

"But it ain't a true life. Ain't the one you were born to live."

"When a parent adopts a child, is the child any less precious because it didn't arrive the usual way? Just like I adopted Sarah and Murancy, I've adopted you and this place."

"Ain't no 'just like' about it. It's not the same at all." His voice went hoarse. "Is Annabeth even your name?"

"I—" I couldn't answer. The question upset me too much. I knew I was going to break down. I fled for fear my hysterics would awaken the girls.

No place in the house was soundproof enough. I bolted outside and high-stepped, bare feet on packed snow, to the outhouse. I shut myself in and gave up all attempts at self-control. I sobbed so hard I strained an abdominal muscle. The tears poured down until I nearly choked.

"You poor dear." The voice came from the darkness beside me. I yelped in surprise.

I flung open the dampers of the pot-bellied stove. The glow of the embers through the grill revealed the household's gray tabby sitting on the bench beside the toilet lid. Or that is to say, it appeared to be the household's gray tabby, but I had just left the real cat in the bedroom, curled up in its basket on the cedar chest.

I made a guess. "Vivica?"

"Yes."

My tear ducts snapped shut. I continued to shudder a little, but that was because all I was wearing was a nightgown. I thrust more fuel into the stove. I was tempted to throw the cat in as well. "Were you the asshole that blabbed to Daniel?"

"No, that was Kenneth. I was opposed to the idea,

actually. I figured it would just make you dig in your heels."

"You were right about that much."

"Terri, Terri, Terri," the faux-cat said. "So we can't force you to withdraw, but that doesn't mean it's right for you to stay. Come to your senses."

"You know how judgmental that sounds?"

"It's called intervention. It's an act of concern."

"Yeah, everybody's willing to butt in now that I'm happy. When I could really have used some cheering up, you all were nowhere to be found."

"Maybe that's true," Vivica suggested, though it didn't sound like a concession to my ears. "Or maybe you didn't give us a chance. Tell you what. I'm going to the gymnastics championships on Luna in a couple of weeks. I have a spare ticket. You could tag along. I've booked a great suite at the Hilton. Dori and Sam are gonna show up for the finals. Be like old times."

"Spare me the pity gestures, Viv. I like it just fine where I am."

"Oh, for fuck's sake, Terri. Look around. This is so primitive. So . . . *filthy*." The cat lowered its nose to the gap between the bench and the closed toilet lid and snorted at the fumes wafting up from the cesspit. "You can't tell me you like having to put up with this stench every time you go to the bathroom. I have to believe you'd see how much you don't belong here if you were in a rational frame of mind."

The fact is, outdoor plumbing was one adjustment to life in the 1880s that I didn't cope with as gracefully as I accepted others. But I wasn't about to give Vivica the satisfaction of hearing me say that.

"This isn't intervention," I said. "It's just intrusion. You've had your say. I want you to leave."

"Your money's almost gone, you know," Vivica said. "What will you do then?"

"My credit is excellent. Now I believe I asked you to leave?"

The cat rolled its eyes, not at all a feline mannerism. "All right, all right. The timer's running down anyway. But this isn't over, Terri."

"Bye-bye," I said.

I shut the dampers, restoring the darkness. When I opened the outhouse door and the moonlight shone in, the cat was nowhere to be seen.

In the morning, Daniel came in from milking the cows, ate his breakfast, and headed for the barn again almost before he had finished swallowing the last bite. As he crossed the yard, Sarah's gaze followed him through the frosted kitchen window. She glanced at me, then down at the floor.

Only after Murancy went down for her nap did Sarah summon the courage to speak. I was at the sink peeling potatoes. She was at the kitchen table, grating cheese.

"It's been so good since you came," Sarah said. "Pa was so sad when Mama died." Once she might have added, "and even before Mama died," but I had weaned her from such talk. "Did you two have a fight?"

"A fight? Not exactly."

I put down the peeler and moved to the chair across from her. I reached out and cupped her hands.

"He's . . . upset with something he learned about me. He's disappointed in me," I said.

Sarah's brows drew together until a pair of vertical wrinkles scored her normally doll-like forehead. "Pa thinks you're his Helen of Troy. He told me so."

"He said that before he knew certain sides of me."

"What's so awful about you? What didn't he know?"

To my surprise, the words came easily. "Do you know what an addiction is?"

"No, ma'am."

"It's when someone has a craving for something that makes them feel good. They want it all the time, and they do anything to have it. They get so they can't help themselves."

"Like Uncle Caleb, and his drinking?"

"Like that." I had not met Daniel's brother-in-law. Daniel didn't allow him to come 'round anymore. Caleb might even be dead; he hadn't been seen in Stephenson or Green County in quite some time.

"But you don't drink more than a sip of cordial, now and then," Sarah protested.

"My problem is not alcohol."

"Then what do you hanker for?"

"All this." I waved my hand at the hand-carved dining table, the knothole in the rafters, the rag carpet in the hallway, woven by Daniel's grandmother when she lived back East. Things unique to this house, and to this particular juncture in time. "I can't stop wanting to be with your father, wanting to be with you. Wanting to be here."

"That doesn't sound so wicked."

"No. No, it doesn't," I answered. "I don't believe it is."

"Pa shouldn't worry about it, then."

"I agree," I said. I offered her my lap. She climbed into it and I held her tight. "I promise you everything will be fine soon. One way or another."

She cuddled, and for a moment I thought things between us would be fine. But she was so quiet, and the frown hadn't gone away.

Once again, I found an intruder in the outhouse when I arrived. This time the avatar was a weasel. Weasels were a common enough sight on the farm. After all, we had hen's eggs to steal. This one, though, didn't run away upon being discovered.

"A varmint. How appropriate," I said.

"I don't think Sarah quite believed your explanation of the difficulties between you and her father," the weasel said. Small and rodentish as the voice was, I recognized it as belonging to Andrew, from my old therapy group. "She's a bright child. I imagine she's going to keep digging until she gets a thorough explanation, don't you think?"

"And I suppose you plan to help her along with that?" I snapped.

"Oh, no. That would be out of line. I'm not Kenneth, you know."

"Thank goodness for small favors," I replied.

"I've taken a look at your session logs. You handle your responsibilities so well as Annabeth. You should try that as Terri. You do have responsibilities, you know. People you should be there for."

"So you say. Right now my responsibility is to empty

my bladder. Are you planning on helping me with that, too, or can I have some privacy?"

The weasel hesitated. Andrew had clearly come to say more, but perhaps he had been expecting that I would be more willing to listen. He wasn't great at being a point man. "As you wish," he finally said. He hopped off the bench and down the wooden step.

He turned around when he reached the footprint-littered snow. "You know, you were a real help to me when I was in over my head. I wish you could take some of the advice you gave me then."

I shut the door.

At lunchtime, I sent the girls out to the barn to fetch their father. He hadn't come in all morning.

I watched through the window. Daniel met the children at the barn door. But he didn't accompany them as they set out for the house.

The girls stopped midway back, confused. They waved for him to follow. Still he stood there.

What I saw confirmed my fears. I had lost him. He wasn't able to be my Daniel anymore. His matrix couldn't adjust enough to deal with the information Kenneth had given him. He was too aware of the nature of his existence. He couldn't forgive me.

Sarah was picking up on the dissonance. At any moment, she might begin to ask him questions I couldn't have her knowing the answers to.

"Goddamn it," I murmured.

I had no choice. I went to the kitchen wall and placed my palm against it. "Access," I said.

The interface appeared. I quickly reset the Character Parameters to baseline. I'd lose the enrichment incorporated since then, but it couldn't be helped.

I also authorized Highest Level Security. The modification would ding my account more than I had planned, but my credit was adequate, if not as robust as I'd implied to Vivica.

My "friends" would not be able to hack in again, not even to view the logs as Andrew had. Their measures had inconvenienced me, but I wasn't done here yet.

I restored the wall to its 1880s look and returned to

the window. Out in the yard, Daniel and the girls were now behaving as they should. Daniel was grinning as he swung Murancy in a circle. Sarah was giggling. Soon all three headed for the house, full of good cheer and looking forward to their midday meal.

I opened the oven. As the aroma of potato and cheese and onion poured out, smiles beamed all around. I put the casserole on the table, served everyone's portions, and we began to eat.

The cheese contained an authentic pungency that few of my era would know, but that wasn't what made the meal special. Its value came from the lack of pretension, from the company, from the setting, from the sheer comfort of familiar ingredients prepared in a familiar way. No declaration of approval from some culinary maven was needed to know I had done well. This recipe and way of enjoying it fulfilled the soul.

In this place and time, I knew where I stood.

Not a hint of the recent troubles tainted the scene. Sarah had no questions. Daniel exuded his traditional good humor. When he stood up from the table, he gave me a little kiss that set the girls to grinning behind their hands.

"I'd better get the team hitched up if we're going to make it to over to Buster Hasting's place on time," he said.

Sarah brightened. "We're going visiting?"

"That's right," I said. "Didn't you notice the extra casserole?"

The children cheered and scampered out to the barn at their father's heels.

I followed more sedately, filling a wicker basket not only with the second casserole but a loaf of the bread I'd baked the day before. Charity for an old widower who lived nearby.

By the time I came out, Daniel was in the midst of positioning the horses in front of the sleigh. The animals tossed their heads and whinnied, eager to be heading out after days of confinement. I helped the children tie bells to Meadow's tail. The mare tolerated it with only a twitch or two. Dusty, the gelding, snorted his disdain at the prospect. "One of these days," Sarah promised him, but she wasn't ready to force the issue this time, nor would I have let her.

The song praises the delights of an open sleigh, but an open sleigh is hardly meant for comfort. Ours was closed, its chassis rounded inward to form a cockpit. Daniel filled the footwarmer with hot charcoal and set it down in the front with a metallic clunk. He draped it with the fitted flannel cover and we climbed in. The heavy sleigh blanket went round us, supplementing the smaller ones around our bodies. I fastened the cover by its hooks and we were cozy in our cocoon, only our muffed heads and Daniel's gloved hands poking through into the chill air. Daniel flicked the reins and we were off.

Buster lived close by. In a later day and age, the distance between our dwelling places would be inconsequential, but for us it was a shift from the everyday world to the special. The girls shouted hurrahs as we rounded the hillock and saw the old farmhouse, smoke rising from its chimney, golden retriever barking in the yard to announce our arrival.

Buster limped onto his porch. "Jake!" he bellowed at his pet. "Get over here." Fortunately he was obeyed, or the hairy beast might have licked us to death as we fetched the casserole and bread from the luggage compartment.

As we paraded inside, warmth enveloped our weather-reddened noses and made them glow. Buster had a glow of his own, a bright-eyed energy as his loneliness was broken, at least for the next hour. "You two have growed an inch since Christmas," he declared with enthusiasm, patting Sarah on the head. He didn't bend to do the same to Murancy; his stiff spine didn't allow it.

We continued in to the kitchen to put the food down, and found a ham lying on the table. "That's for you," Buster said.

"You didn't have to do that," Daniel protested.

"It's little enough in return," the old fellow insisted. "I have a little too much of some things, now that Myrna's gone. No use it going to waste here." He patted the ham. "I may not be much good in a kitchen, but I do know how to hang a pig in a smokehouse."

The old farmer sounded pleased with himself, and he had a right to be. "We're grateful to you," I said.

"Any word from that son of yours in California?" Daniel asked.

Buster opened a drawer and lifted out an envelope. I made out a San Francisco postmark.

"Still making a good life for himself," Buster informed us. "Wants me to come and live with him now that his eldest is gettin' married. I told you about young Will, right?"

"Yes." Daniel chuckled. Buster had mentioned his grandson's engagement the last five visits in a row. "So are you going?"

"Shucks, no. I'll stay right where I am, thank you. Couldn't imagine it any other way."

Buster had homesteaded this farm. It had never been owned or operated by anyone else. I knew he would stay until the day the dog trundled in and found him laid out stiff and cold in his bed, a tintype cameo of his wife on the nightstand beside him.

"Neither could we, Buster. Neither could we," I said, squeezing his hand.

He blushed to have a woman touch him. "You're right good neighbors to me. Keeps a body goin'."

We stayed as long as Buster remained talkative. He made sure we understood we were welcome to stay longer, but we didn't want to wear him out.

The old man escorted us out to the sleigh. As we approached, Jake padded up and looked at us with a regard that I found disturbingly human. I studied him to be sure his behavior didn't resemble that of the cat and the weasel in the outhouse.

The retriever's tail wagged and the exuberant tongue made its traditional assault on little Murancy's face, much to her delight. The dog was a dog. The integrity of the milieu was secure. Everyone was behaving according to pattern.

On the way home, we let Meadow and Dusty set their own pace, the horses' natural laziness balanced by their desire to get back home to their stalls. Buster's farm slipped over the horizon, and we cruised along beside sparkling white fields.

Murancy climbed into my lap and leaned back against me. Sarah leaned in from the side, and together we settled against Daniel. My big handsome man wrapped his free arm around my shoulders and braced so that we were all steady and could, if we chose, remain nestled all the way home.

Daniel's gaze swept over the landscape. He looked at me and smiled. "Ain't it a wonder, Annabeth? Could it be any better?"

A family outing. A good deed accomplished. Beauty all around. And a simplicity and peace I'd never found in the twenty-second century. No, it couldn't be any better.

"It's like a dream," I replied.

The words carved out a chunk of me below my sternum. It added to the awful, hole-in-the-middle sensation already there. I wanted to blame Kenneth and Vivica and Andrew for creating it, but the truth was, the hollowness had taken root well before the first intervention episode.

A dream. Yes. And only a dream. For months my life as Annabeth had seemed to be the greatest sort of wakefulness. No more. An illusion only has power when one can't see the man behind the curtain. I could hold firm against my friends' doubts about the choices I had made, but not against my own.

It was time to do what I'd decided to do when I'd accessed the interface. I'd needed this last sliver of an afternoon to savor, but the clock had run down.

"I love you, Daniel. I love you, Sarah. I love you, Murancy."

Deep within the compartment of the sleigh, beside the dwindling warmth of the foot warmer, I clicked my heels three times.

The sleigh ceased to move. The moment was as frozen as the ground had been: Clouds of breath—human and equine—hung in the air as if painted. Murancy's eyelids were poised half down, captured in mid-blink. Sarah was preserved in the midst of lifting the blanket, curious to learn what I was doing with my feet. Now she would never find out.

Daniel's right hand was forever steady on the reins, keeping our course true.

I closed my eyes. As soon as I opened them, the details of the room around me grew more distinct, became impossible to ignore: The equipment, the blinking indicators, the glow of the clock.

Outside, beyond the smartglass and walls programmed to keep the climate at bay, snow was falling. It was winter, for those who troubled themselves to notice. I could still hear the tinkle of bells on a horse's tail.

HOT

by Sarah A. Hoyt

Sarah A. Hoyt has sold over three dozen stories to places that include *Asimov's, Amazing,* and *Analog.* She has written a Shakespearean fantasy trilogy. She has a time-travel/ adventure novel (a collaboration with Eric Flint) and a Three Musketeers mystery trilogy forthcoming.

SHE SMELLED HOT when she came into my office. She looked hot, too: curvaceous body encased in a tight, bright red dress; high-heeled Italian leather pumps; bluish-black hair falling down her back in waves.

If the world hadn't been coming apart at the seams for some years now, if it were still the sort of world in which my parents had grown up—with white picket fences and a nice little house in the suburbs—this would have been the type of woman I'd want to settle down with and have a dozen or so brats.

"How may I help you?" I asked, as I sternly told myself I just couldn't—couldn't—sit up and bay at the moon. It wasn't done.

"My friend, Electra Jones, said you dealt with a certain type of problem."

The mention of Ms. Jones, for whom I'd taken care of an embarrassing enough problem, made the hair at the back of my neck rise. But I had to be sure. Even Electra must have friends who'd been untouched by all the changes, of course.

"I take care of investigations for divorce and find runaway teens and missing persons, just like the sign says."

I gestured broadly toward the neon sign affixed beside my narrow, fly-specked third-floor window, where the name, Jack Peters, PI, and my specialties scrolled nonstop in vivid violet and glaring green.

She barely gave it a glance. "I don't mean that," she said, with the sort of throaty laughter that, no doubt, turned the minds of more stable men than myself. "I mean, other problems. The kind that . . ."

I looked at her with helpful incomprehension.

Look, humanity has never been any good at dealing with those who are different among them. Racism, the whole problem of racism, stems from superficial differences amid human populations.

How much more racism would arise if humans discovered that, starting about thirty years ago, the world had been bombarded by alien viruses which, when they attacked pregnant women, caused mutations usually associated with the deepest, darkest legends of mankind? And mankind's deepest, darkest fears. How would Mr. Joe Mundane like the idea of werewolves, dragons, weretigers, vampires, harpies, and salamanders living all around him, in his safe suburb?

As one of those mutations, who grew embarrassingly hairy when the moon waxed full, I couldn't afford to have my cover blown.

Oh, sure, this woman was saying all the right words. And there was an "otherness" about her, a "difference" that meant she probably was one of us—in one form or another.

But it was also possible the "difference" was a learned put on.

After all, though the early twenty-first century might be a little late in history for serfs armed with pitchforks storming the castle gates, there were other things true, unmutated humans could do to us. Mental hospitals, hormone treatments . . . and the ever present, dreaded shadow of vivisection had loomed large in my nightmares since puberty, when I'd found out my true nature.

My prospective client opened her purse and fished inside for something. I reached for the desk drawer, where I kept my trusty friend, the Colt.

Truth was the legends had been, to some extent, wrong. Sure, I could be killed by silver bullets. Well, I could be killed by any bullets. And the few humans who'd found out about our kind in their midst had come up with very creative means of killing us.

But what she withdrew from her purse was a paper rectangle, fiery red and headlined Fire House Bank, with an address on Water Street.

I sat back, and she grinned, as though guessing my discomfiture. Dancing toward my desk, she set the paper on it.

Looking at the little square for the amount, I felt my uneasiness grow. A million. The checking account name was Tracci Smith.

"There," she said. "Perhaps now we can stop playing games."

"Perhaps," I said. "Provided that's a real check. Provided that's your real name. Provided the check clears."

She threw her head back and laughed, a perfect, rounded laughter, full of mirth. "You're not a trusting person."

"You learn some things from being a PI," I said.

She reached in her purse, again, and I kept my fingers near the drawer where the Colt was hidden.

I trusted my superior speed against any normal human.

But she pulled out a golden cigarette case, from which she withdrew a long cigarette, which she lit from a golden lighter encrusted in large, reddish stones.

She blew a perfect, round ring into the still, stale air of my office.

In the distance a siren wailed.

I'd always wanted . . . Not so much to blow perfect smoke rings, as to be the sort of person who could, if he wished, blow perfect smoke rings.

Such people, of course, rarely held shabby, one-room offices in downtown Goldport, amid the cheap Chinese restaurants, the abandoned warehouses, and the junkies.

But someone like me needed to. Junkies were more likely to catch infections. And Chinese restaurants were no strangers to dragons and their ilk.

"Well, do you believe in Panspermia, Mr. Peters?"

I barely blinked. Hell, a good thing about reading science fiction is that you know the name of all these theories, all these hypotheses. "If you mean Fred Hoyle's theory that space spores started and influenced life on Earth, I believe the scientific community is still out on it."

She pulled the red-stained cigarette from between her teeth, blew another smoke ring, and expressed a crude opinion of the scientific community. She fixed me with an unwavering gaze, her eyes like two guns pointed at my soul, and she said, "What about diaspora, Mr. Peters? Do you know about the diaspora that started about thirty years ago? The alien viruses that turned humans into . . . something else?"

I blinked. "I've read stories," I said. "Even I must go to the supermarket and when the lines are long, I often read the tabloids."

She laughed again, the deep, rich laughter like yellow yolk oozing out of a soft-boiled egg. It made me hungry. But not for eggs.

"All right," she said. "Believe it, the thing of tabloids, if you will. Or pretend to. Electra said you can perform miracles. And I need one. We all do. And I'm willing to pay for it."

She gestured to the check on the desk, where I'd let it lay, untouched.

"Rumor has it that a Queen dragon is ripe and about to hatch. Do you know what that means?"

I raised my eyebrows at her. I knew a few dragons, in the normal way of things. Like me they were were-mutations. Meaning they alternated between a human form and a form that was anything but.

Like me, most dragons suffered the craving to hunt and kill and tear during their time as dragons. Most of them learned to control it, or to vent it on pigeons and rats and other vermin, as I did. Your self-control diminished when in animal form, but not your intelligence. You still could control yourself, if you made a point of it. And you were still yourself.

Most dragons I knew were decent enough fellows. Of course, I realized with a sudden, sickening feeling, I knew no dragon females.

"It means," my client said, "that for the whole two months of incubation she'll kill prey every day and take it to her lair, and lay it around the eggs, so that the cubs can feed when they wake. She won't be able to control herself." Tracci blew another perfect smoke ring. "I hear that she's just laid her clutch. I want you to find it for me."

I raised my eyebrows again. "What makes you think I can? Dragons, admitting that such a thing exists, are tight-lipped creatures, to judge from all the fairy tales. What makes you think they would talk to me, and, what's more, abet the destruction of their own kind?"

She sighed. "I've heard you can perform miracles, Mr. Peters. And, as I said, I'm willing to pay for it."

She looked pointedly at the check on my desk. "I think you have a couple of days," she said, as she drew herself up, stubbed her cigarette on my window ledge. "It's so hot out, isn't it?" she asked, looking downward, at the city street.

And she turned around and left, her high heels clicking on the aged floorboards.

She slammed my office door shut. Seconds after, I heard the noise—a peculiar high-pitched whine—of the elevator going down.

I got up and looked out the window, to see her retreating along the sidewalk, before I pulled my cell phone from inside the worn leather jacket draped over the back of my chair. I dialed Jonathan's number. Jonathan is a werefox. He's also the president of Fire House Bank. And, customer privacy or not, weres stick together. We have to. Sometimes we're all we have.

Which was what made me so profoundly uncomfortable about betraying another were, about looking for a dragon clutch.

But first things first, I thought. I lived in a tiny, ratty apartment, with no one but my fox terrier, who was great company once every full moon—somewhere between a pet and a best friend. My bills needed paying and Mike, my dog, would like it well enough if I improved our quarters.

So I called Jonathan and waited till his gruff, brisk voice answered, "Hello?"

"Jonathan? Jack here. Question for you."

He ran up Tracci's data and whistled. "More than enough. In fact I'd say that's peanuts to her," he said. "Rich family. We have all their accounts."

"Damn," I said.

Jonathan didn't say anything, but he didn't hang up. His very silence, his refusal to ask me why I reacted this way to the revelation that a prospective customer was wealthy, acted like a question, a pointed query.

"It's what she wants me to do," I said.

Again, Jonathan said nothing. He is a master at keeping his mouth shut. He has a wife and three lovely daughters, none of whom knows dad turns into a small, spry fox at will—and once every full moon for three days, whether he wants to or not.

He's waiting for his daughters' puberty to find out whether they need to know. Until then, "daddy's fishing trips" to relieve the tension of his high-stress job cover up for the inevitable.

"I don't really want to talk about it over the phone," I said. "And I don't think it's anything you can help with."

His silence was so pointed that I could almost see him—on the other side of the phone connection—raise his russet eyebrows and narrow his dark green eyes.

"Give me time to call Marcy," he said. "And tell her I won't be home for dinner. I'll be along. Don't do anything before I get there."

"You don't have to—"

"Look, Jack, I know I don't. That's what friends are for."

And I shut up, because Jonathan and I had been friends since kindergarten. Our mothers were friends and had been pregnant at about the same time. Which explained the twin infections they'd caught and our similar mutations.

An hour later, I was still sitting in my office, but Jack was sitting in the client chair. A small, compact, redheaded man wearing a banker's blue suit, he'd had the forethought and intelligence to bring a cold six pack.

We sat, each with a beer bottle in hand, while I told him my problem.

He whistled.

"I don't want to betray our kind, Jonathan," I said. "Even dragons."

He sighed. "We don't know what dragons are like, Jack, when they reproduce. There is so little in the old legends."

"I know," I said. I had looked up dragons and reproduction on the Internet, taking advantage of my little laptop, before Jonathan arrived. There was nothing. "And the legends are so often wrong. Like the silver bullet thing."

Jonathan laughed, showing the small, pointy teeth that were almost always the mark of a were. "Yeah. But you have to admit silver bullets will kill us."

I made a face. The joke wasn't funny anymore. "I wonder if these legends are fragments, memories from another diaspora."

"That would presuppose," Jonathan said, "that the mutations don't breed true." He looked ruefully wishful.

He would. I refused to give him comfort. "No, it means the mutations didn't breed true that one time. It says nothing about now. Viruses change," I said. "As well as everything else."

He took a swig of his beer. "So we don't know if your client is right, if the clutch and the dragon are truly dangerous."

"Or if my client is up to a game of her own," I said. "Which she might very well be. She could be a religious nut, or a human who has discovered the secrets of our kind and is trying to eliminate us."

He raised his pale eyebrows. "Have you called Electra?"

I nodded. "No answer. And she hasn't shown up at work in a week."

He grimaced. "Which might mean that she is in trouble or simply that the urge has come over her."

I nodded. Electra was what could only be described in legendary terms as a succubus. During that time of the month, she became infinitely alluring and rather compulsively free with her favors.

I'd extricated her from a mess relating to that.

"So, what do we do?"

"We look," I said. "We listen. Or rather, I do. You might want to go home to your family."

He grinned. "Not on your life."

"This might be dangerous."

He grinned. "Isn't everything?"

The restaurant was smoky and dark. Families, most of them actually Oriental, huddled against the small tables, eating chow mein this and lo mein that. I found the proprietor, Li.

Li was an old friend, a good neighbor. He was also the only dragon I knew for sure was one. I'd found that out in the course of his divorce investigation three years ago. His ex-wife remained convinced he'd been having an affair those days a month. I couldn't tell her the truth. Li didn't hold it against me.

"A clutch?" He raised his dark eyebrows. A California Chinese whose ancestors had come over before mine, he spoke perfect English with a west coast accent. "I don't know who's been pulling your tail, Jack. My wife gave birth in quite the normal way."

"But your wife isn't a dragon," Jonathan said. "Quite the difference."

"And pulling my tail wouldn't be worth a million dollars to anyone."

"A million!" Li whistled.

"Are there any female dragons . . . I mean . . ."

"Whose addresses I can give you?" Li asked. "You know how it is, friend, in this thing it's each one for himself. If they want to trust you, they can. I can't do it in their name. Not even for a fellow were."

He signaled one of his waiters to refill the teapot at one of the tables and turned his serious, golden-skinned face toward me. "But I'll tell you if I hear of any clutch. And that's that."

And that was that anywhere else we went. Everyone we suspected of being a dragon turned out as tight-lipped as a well-sewn purse.

Until Jonathan said that he'd always suspected his secretary of being a dragon, and maybe . . .

Just this will show you how desperate we were: I took the bait.

We drove to the small house in the suburbs where his secretary lived.

It was a small, blue house, what is commonly called a starter house—apparently in the hopes that it will grow from a small lump to a large one.

We knocked at the red door flanked by neat flowerbeds.

"She's not married," Jonathan said. "And she might be out."

But, on the very first knock, we heard a fluttering noise inside and something—I'd say something with claws—scratching at the door.

However, the door remained shut.

We knocked again.

On the third knock, as we were about to give up, the door opened.

Jonathan's secretary was a petite brunette. She was wearing a bathrobe and said, "Sorry. I was about to take a shower. Do you need anything?" She looked at Jonathan.

"I thought about the Simons files," he said. "I wondered if you brought them home to work. I couldn't find them at the office."

She looked surprised and denied having brought work home. Jonathan apologized for bothering her.

None of which mattered. None of which meant anything. Because I had smelled her—as probably had Jonathan.

Only to him it wouldn't mean the same thing it meant to me.

She smelled hot.

Really hot.

Like the client who had come into my office.

I exhaled the heated air around her and wondered if this was what happened to dragons when they changed shape. If the heat of the dragon shape came with them.

I barely registered Jonathan's apology.

As his secretary closed the door, I noticed a bunch of white beanbag chairs in her living room, but I gave them no thought.

Jack must have realized I was excited about something. As we got back in his car, he said, "Spill it."

"She smelled like my client."

It took me a while to explain and then Jack sighed. "So your client is a dragon, too. What does that mean?"

"Nothing," I said. "I mean, it might imply that she heard of the clutch through the grapevine. Or . . ."

"Or?"

"Or it might be that dragons, like other sorts of creatures, kill their rivals' egg clutch."

"Oh," Jack said, his eyebrows more arched than ever.

"In either case, I think we need to see my client," I said.

We drove to the address on the check—a high-rise downtown.

It had a doorman and everything, so we had to change shapes to get in.

Not that it's usually any easier to sneak in somewhere in town as a wolf than as a man.

But this particular building had basement windows, with bars. And the windows were open.

The space between the bars was enough for our canid forms, not our human ones, and please don't ask me about the conservation of matter in transformation.

A physicist friend of mine—a weretiger—tells me that the matter doesn't change, only the spacing between the cells.

This might be true, but if so, our canid forms, compact, are powerhouses ready for a potential explosion.

Jonathan changed first, as I watched, fascinated.

There were some weres who got as turned on by watching others change as by watching others undress. I was not one of them, and certainly not with other males. But there was an unavoidable fascination to it. As though one watched an intimate aspect of the other person.

It was strange to watch, too, without feeling the pull and tug of transformation.

It looked painless, almost too easy. There was a blurring of outlines, and then there it was—a small orange-red fox, grinning at me with Jonathan's own grin.

I changed afterward, willing my body into wolf and, as any time this happens without the assistance of the full moon, feeling the tug and pull, the grind of bone, the stirring of rearranged cell, the vague nausea as my insides were pulled and changed into a different shape.

And there it was, Jonathan in front of me, Jonathan who, suddenly was more smell than visual presence. The fox smelled like Jonathan, a smell of dependability and honest friendship.

I always forgot between one time as a wolf and the next how much my nose told me, the things I could know through the senses that I could never know otherwise.

I wagged my tail at Jonathan, and he took the lead, being smaller. He squeezed himself between the bars and jumped into the darkened basement, and gave the small yelp that meant the coast was clear.

I followed.

The basement was dark, musty, with a vague odor of rats, the bare hint of natural gas that said that the heating system was here.

We streaked out of the basement—the door was easy enough to open by coordinating our efforts. Jonathan pushed, while I stood on my hind legs and pulled the knob down.

We took the fire stairs up. Fire stairs are convenient for sneaking around. Very few people ever use them.

Getting into the apartment was another matter.

As though by mutual agreement, we turned back to our human forms and I knocked at the door.

"Yes?" the cool voice I'd heard before echoed from within. It seemed, somehow, to hiss.

"Jack Peters," I said. "I think I have a solution."

There was another hiss, like indrawn breath, then the door opened, on the latch.

She fixed a great gun-metal eye on Jonathan.

"A friend," I said.

She looked skeptical but slipped the latch.

We entered a foyer carpeted in pale silk. "You found it," she asked. And her eyes looked hungry. "The clutch?"

She still smelled hot, but, sensitized by my recent change into wolf, I realized it was a different kind of hot.

I looked past her into her living room—a posh, modern affair with a huge glass door that let out to a nice balcony, overlooking the city of Goldport. In the middle of the living room was a large, square hearth with a gigantic polished-steel smoke hood above it.

Despite it being summer and the air-conditioning going full blast, the hearth was lit and not gas lit, but fed with huge, burning logs.

I looked once, then again.

In the fire, I swear, a creature leaped and turned.

A salamander, I thought. Those mythical creatures said to feed on fire and live only in it.

But then my client must be . . .

But what could she want with the dragon clutch?

Unwonted, there flashed into my mind the image of small, darting lizards feeding on dinosaur eggs.

"Miss Smith," I said, opening my wallet and handing her the check. "I've found that I can't do what you wish. You see, I suspect you of wanting to feed on the dragon eggs, so that you and your friend there can have a clutch of your own."

Okay—as Jonathan has pointed out several times since then—this might not have been the most intelligent thing to say.

Tracci screamed, a scream with an edge of hiss.

I can't describe her transformation, except to say that somehow it prompted Jonathan's and mine, also, and that suddenly I was a small, very scared wolf facing a fiery lizard that had been joined by another, definitely male one.

If it hadn't been for Jonathan, who leaped to the attack, I might well have been frozen by the sheer novelty of it. Not many of us ignite when we change.

But Jonathan, in his fox form, had thrown himself at the fiery creatures and was biting for all he was worth.

Which—as I've told him several times since—might not have been the smartest thing to do.

As I watched, they surrounded him. The tuft on his tail caught fire.

I stared. My best friend was going to be burned to death.

Thoughts of extinguishers flashed through my mind.

I remembered the fire hose in the glass-enclosure outside the apartment door.

Even salamanders can't escape fire regs.

If the legends were right—and, okay, that was a big if—they couldn't live without the proximity of fire.

I threw myself against the door, trying to get it open, before I thought to jump and turn the latch, while I threw myself at it.

It seemed to take hours to run across the small, marble paved hall, years to change to my human shape, centuries to unroll the hose, and pull it tight, and turn the water on, and millennia to get back in the condo.

I was amazed the door hadn't been closed yet and that Jonathan remained alive, if screaming in canine pain while fighting the two creatures.

The salamanders saw the hose and jumped for me.

But the water had started flowing, a strong jet. And I aimed past the salamanders at the fire.

They surrounded me, while Jonathan collapsed on the floor looking dead.

I felt their burning teeth latch onto my neck and my shoulder.

I couldn't defend myself. All I could do was hold the hose aimed at the fire.

It sizzled. It screamed. It died leaving a pile of soggy logs.

Panting, I became aware that the pain on my neck and shoulder had stopped.

Tracci and her friend—a tall, dark-haired, stark-naked gentleman—lay on the floor. Their pallor and stillness were unmistakable.

I dove for Tracci's purse by the door and found a fireproof container with some ashes in it. Probably what she used for a small hearth to allow her to leave the house, to go to my office.

Too bad she hadn't thought to keep some coals in there. Or too good.

I picked up the miraculously unburned check.

Jonathan looked dead, also. A pile of charred russet fur.

But, you see, something the legends had got right.

Weres, when they die, become human again. And Jonathan remained a fox.

I knelt by Jonathan and felt his heart beat strong underneath his furry chest.

Bringing him around and making him change and explaining to the people in the emergency room why he had inhaled so much smoke and how he'd got burned was something else again.

But they let him walk away, eventually, because Jonathan had assumed his most offensively haughty personality and they had to do it.

He was lucky. He had only one third-degree burn. Though that one would make him conduct business meetings on his feet for the next few months. I couldn't even guess what he planned to tell his wife

I joked about it, about the tuft of burned tail, while he winced and sat sideways on the passenger seat of his BMW that he had to let me drive.

Outside my office building, Li was waiting, Jonathan's secretary by his side.

They assumed threatening postures as we arrived, then stared, amazed, as I helped Jonathan's bedraggled self out of the car.

"What happened?" Jonathan's secretary asked.

"You're not going to tell them, are you?" Li asked. "About the clutch. We know you're a decent man and I told Maria we could tell you the truth. That whole thing about feeding the clutch is poppycock, you know. They'll probably be born in human form, anyway. They might be completely human."

It all came out in a rush. I remembered the beanbag chairs in Maria's living room. So white, so almost round. I sighed. I was an idiot.

"I'm not going to tell anyone," I said, and explained the whole thing to them.

They looked from me to Jonathan with what I hoped was admiration, but, perhaps, was amazement at our idiocy.

"So the clutch is yours, is it?" I asked Li.

He actually blushed. "Three boys and two girls." He

said. And added, defensively, "We're getting married next week."

Even with the world falling apart, some things do not change. And even when all goes crazy around them, some people remain pillars of the community.

NITE 2 REMEMBER

by Pati Nagle

Pati Nagle writes science fiction, fantasy, historical fiction, romance, mystery, and whatever else strikes her fancy. Her short stories have appeared in the *Magazine of Fantasy & Science Fiction* and in several anthologies, including those honoring fellow New Mexico authors Jack Williamson and the late Roger Zelazny. She lives in the mountains east of the Rio Grande, surrounded by trees, birds, and coyotes, none of which appear in this story.

BRITTANY IVANS GOT TO PORT three minutes and twenty-seven seconds late, which was a personal best. Usually she was at least ten minutes late, but she had recently resolved to be more punctual. And today she was leading the Nite 2 Remember tour, the top offering in Time Travel Tours' catalog. And there were two single males in her group, so there might actually possibly be a chance that she would hit it off with one of them.

She breezed through the swank titanium doors, tossed a cheery wave to Honey, the receptionist and the boss's current lay (impossibly stacked, totally incompetent with the com panel), and hurried down the hall to Orientation Lounge 7. Her heels thudded softly on the plush carpet of "Liberty Blue," the signature color of Time Travel Tours (Triple T, as the staff called it). Everything from the furniture to the mints on Honey's desk was Liberty Blue.

Brittany paused to twitch her Liberty Blue uniform skirt into place and give her Liberty Blue jacket a tug. Best to make a good impression when first meeting a tour group. You never knew when Mr. Right might decide on a jaunt to the Alamo or Washington's Inauguration or any of the dozens of destinations in Triple T's exclusive catalog. She squared her shoulders, put on a professional smile, and stepped up to the doors.

They spiraled open to reveal her group for the day: three gray-haired old ladies, one of them accompanied by a balding myopic probable-husband; two plump middle-aged gals with their hair (one brunette, one an improbable red) bobbed too short; an Italian-looking fatherly type who seemed embarrassed to be there; and a geek sitting cross-legged on the floor with a workstation open on his lap and wearing full interface mask and gloves. His straw-colored hair stood up in tufts between the mask straps.

Brittany's smile slid south a bit. Mr. Right had obviously failed her yet again. A certain amount of consolation could be bought with chocolates and vidstream chips, but paying for said commodities (not to mention rent and utilities) depended on her commission and tips, which in turn depended on the group's level of satisfaction with their tour. Hence, cheeriness.

"Good morning, everyone! I'm Brittany Ivans, your guide for the Nite 2 Remember Tour. How many of us have been on a Time Travel Tour before?"

The two bob-haired gals shot their hands up, grinning. The others stood still, looking like stuffed dolls, except for the geek who was still in photoelectron land.

Brittany smiled. "Super!"

Still smiling, she stepped in front of the geek and tapped twice on the top of his head with a fingertip. The head jerked up in surprise, then he pulled off the gloves and mask.

"Hi, I'm Brittany, your guide."

"H–hi, I'm Steve."

"Hi, Steve. You did read the travel restrictions, right? About transporting noncontemporary electronics?"

"Oh, s–sure. I just brought this to kill time, I was going to leave it in my locker here. We get a locker, right?"

Brittany addressed the whole group. "Yes, you each get a locker for your clothes and belongings while you're on the tour. They're in the changing rooms. We'll go there in a minute, but first we just need to check you in and go over the schedule and the rules, all right? Super."

Brittany took out her Liberty Blue datapad and tapped it with a fingernail to bring up the tour roster. She waited politely while Steve gathered his gear into a hoversack and picked himself up off the floor. The sack picked itself up, too, and bobbed in the air at about the level of Steve's knees.

"I'm going to give you your passcards now," Brittany said, holding up a glossy Liberty Blue card. "This goes into the special pocket on the inside of your period clothing, over your breastbone. Your passcard links you to the transport beam, so don't ever take it out of the pocket, Okay? Super."

She consulted the roster, then looked up. "Lyla Crumbie?"

"Yo!" cried the gal with the red-bobbed hair. Brittany gave her the card programmed with her data.

"Amber Ferdinand?" One of the blue-hairs. Brittany handed over her card, and proceeded down the list.

"Stephanie Gill." Blue-hair. "Melody Lipton." Brunette-bob gal. "Salvatore Montenegro." Italian guy, Brittany gave him a big smile along with the card. "Melba and Vernon Powell."

"Yes," said the wife half, dragging her hubby with her. Her eyes were sparkling. "It's our fiftieth anniversary!"

"Oh, congrats!" Brittany handed the Powells' passcards to Mrs. P, leaving one. She glanced at the roster. "Steve Shoup."

The geek stepped up, grinning. Brittany gave him the card.

"There you go. Now, before we go to the changing rooms, I need to give you a quick review of the rules." She pocketed her datapad and picked up one of the Liberty Blue folios from a shelf, opened it, and read.

" 'Travelers will refrain from interacting directly with natives of the era except for common courtesies. Please review the courtesy guide provided in your orientation kit. Travelers should avoid giving their names to natives, and may not engage in lengthy conversation or prolonged physical contact with natives.' That means no telling them what's going to happen, and no sex."

Brittany glanced up. They were looking stuffed again, all of them.

" 'Travelers may not bring any objects back from the tour, with the exception of one item acquired legally for era fair-market value, to be kept as a souvenir of the tour. No items may be brought back for resale in departure era. Any traveler who violates these terms is subject to immediate transportation back to departure date. Penalties for violations are as outlined in your travel agreement.' Okay? Great."

"Brittany?" One of the blue-hairs raised a gnarled hand. "Does that mean we can't talk to the natives at all?"

"No, just that you shouldn't get into long discussions. It's too easy to expose your lack of knowledge of the era and attract too much attention. Keep it to things like 'Good afternoon' and 'Pardon me.' "

" 'Pardon me,'" said red-bob to brunette-bob, and tittered. "I just love those quaint old turns of phrase!"

"You'll find a list of useful phrases in your Nite 2 Remember guidelines," Brittany said to all of them, holding up her demo copy, a small booklet of heavy, cream-colored paper with "PRAYERS FOR TRAVELERS" printed on the cover in Liberty Blue ink. "You can take this with you on the tour, but don't let any of the natives read it. It's best not to let them even see it."

"Cool reproduction," said Steve, thumbing through his copy. "I like the variations in the font, suggesting typesetting flaws. Really pro."

"Thank you, Mr. Shoup," said Brittany. "That reminds me, it would be a good idea to start using period courtesy as we're talking. That means we're all Mrs. or Mr. Whatever."

"Or Miss," said brunette-bob. "Wouldn't I be Miss Lipton?"

"Yes, but the era we're visiting has strict social rules for unmarried women, so we're all married ladies today. That way we'll all be free to go around the ship unescorted. Now, please turn to page three."

Brittany cleared her throat. " 'Schedule and Specific Terms for the Nite 2 Remember Tour. 12:03 PM shipboard time, April 14, 1912, tour arrives in starboard Palm Court of RMS *Titanic*.' Oh, each of you will have a replica period timepiece set to shipboard time." Brittany held up her own watch, a dainty gold-filigreed piece on a gold chain. "It's yours to keep as a souvenir of your tour, along with your period clothing."

She went back to reading. "'12:15 PM, lunch in the Café Parisien. 1:30 PM to 5:30 PM, travelers are free to visit any of the following areas: First Class Lounge, First Class Reading and Writing Room, First and Second Class Smoking Rooms, Grand Staircase, Veranda Café/Palm Courts, and the First and Second Class Promenade Decks. Please do not enter the First Class Reception Room, First Class Dining Saloon, or the Turkish Bath. 5:45 PM, meet in starboard Palm Court. 6:00 PM, dinner at the Restaurant À La Carte. 7:30 to 11:30 PM, travelers are free to move about the above-mentioned areas. 11:30 PM, meet in starboard Palm Court. Proceed from there to starboard Boat Deck for viewing of collision with iceberg. 12:15 PM return to starboard Palm Court for transportation back to departure date.' Any questions?"

One of the gray-hairs raised her hand. "Mrs. Ivans, which of those places do you recommend?"

"They're all of historic interest, Mrs. Ferdinand. You should have time to visit them all."

"But do you have a personal favorite?"

"Well, no, since I haven't actually seen them."

The Italian-father guy frowned. "You mean you haven't been there before? They gave us an inexperienced guide?"

Brittany took a deep breath and counted to three. "None of Time Travel Tours' guides ever visits a destination twice, Mr. Montenegro. It could be awkward, bumping into yourself."

Not to mention that *Titanic* was a controlled destination. Licenses for tours there were strictly limited and obscenely expensive. It was the number one destination since the Crucifixion had been closed to tourists, and Triple T was only allowed a small, finite quota of tours. Which was why the Nite 2 Remember tour was fabulously expensive, beyond the ordinary everyday fabulous expense of time traveling at all. Which was why Brittany needed to be nice to the people in her group. Some of them might be a bit weird, but they were all incredibly wealthy.

"Don't worry, Mr. Montenegro," she said, flashing him a beguiling smile. "I've reviewed the reports of every other guide who's led the Nite 2 Remember Tour. I know all the deckplans, and everything else we need to know on board. Any more questions? Great, let's move on."

Brittany hustled her group out the back door of the lounge into a small foyer. To the right and left were doors marked "Women" and "Men," respectively.

"Gentlemen, you're right through there. Ladies, come with me. We'll meet back here when we're dressed."

Brittany led the women into their changing room and helped them find their lockers. As usual, there was much excitement when they saw their period dresses, dripping with lace and accented by rich jewelry. Triple T didn't scrimp on the clothes. Part of the outrageous tour fees went for top-notch fabrication.

The bobs immediately started playing with their hats and gloves, posing in front of the mirror. Brittany hurried into her Liberty Blue day dress with art nouveau sapphire brooch in the shape of Triple T's logo, then went to help one of the gray-hairs who had her corset on backward. When everyone was dressed, Brittany put on a blue hat with enough feathers to populate a flock of quail, grabbed her gloves and shoved her datapad into her reticule, then shepherded the women back to the foyer.

The men were already there. Mr. Powell had on a gray suit and a jaunty straw skimmer hat. Mr. Montenegro was elegant in pinstripes and silk waistcoat with the gold chain of his watch strung across it. Steve seemed less comfortable than the others, but the brown suit and brown bowler hat looked all right.

Brittany smiled brightly. "Well, don't you all look handsome! Everybody ready?"

She led them down a short corridor to the transport room. Taking out her datapad, she brought up group tracking to verify that everyone's passcard was working. Eight little blue blips appeared on the screen, each keyed to a traveler's name, with the ninth white one (hers) close behind. She slid the datapad back into her reticule with the stocking purse of period cash she would use to pay for their meals, and pulled the strings tight.

"All right now, stand together on the pad, please. Inside the blue line. You'll feel a slight buzzing."

Brittany gave the nod to the bored-looking, bleached blonde at the ops panel, who initiated the transport sequence. Brittany braced herself for the sensation of time-transport which, rather than "slight buzzing" (Triple T's official description) actually felt a lot like being flushed down a waterless toilet. When the dizzy whirling in her brain stopped, she opened her eyes and blinked against bright daylight in the *Titanic*'s Palm Court.

"Well, here we are!" she said cheerily.

The tour group looked groggily around. The Palm Court was filled with trellises covered in real vines that must have hated the North Atlantic cold. Mrs. Powell, eyes shining, clutched her husband's arm with one hand and her reticule with the other. The bobs were wide-eyed, whispering and tittering together. Steve the geek was already fingering the wicker furniture, the vines and the trellises. The two single gray-hairs still seemed disoriented. Brittany hurried over to them.

"You all right, Mrs. Ferdinand? Mrs. Gill?"

"Allow me," said Mr. Montenegro, offering his arm to Mrs. Gill. She instantly blossomed from lost sheep into doting matron, smiling as she slid her hand into the crook of his elbow.

"Thank you, young man! How *very* kind!"

How very kind was one of the recommended phrases in the guidebook. Brittany grinned, then shot a grateful look at Mr. Montenegro, who smiled back and twitched his mustache at her.

"Uh, me too," said a geeky voice behind her.

Steve waved his hands vaguely in front of him as if

trying to offer help but not knowing how. Brittany stepped back to let Mrs. Ferdinand take his arm. Since Mrs. Ferdinand outweighed him by a good fifty pounds the idea of his supporting her was slightly absurd, but she seemed to appreciate the gesture.

"Okay, let's hurry now. This way to the Café Parisien."

Brittany led them through the First Class Smoking Room and down the Grand Staircase to B Deck. She'd have to come back here and look around during free time. She had known *Titanic* was lush, but knowing and being there were two different things. The carpets were so thick underfoot it was like walking on clouds, and everything smelled expensive. She could get used to this.

Café Parisien was on the starboard side of the ship, a long, narrow room with wicker tables set for four. Trellises here, too, but no vines, and the dark wood ceiling was elaborately carved.

Definitely could get used to this. This was the *casual* restaurant.

The café's manager was "only too delighted, madame," to seat them at three pushed-together tables from which a similar party had just risen. Brittany was sure the other party had been a tour group, one of Triple T's, probably. The last tour, five years ago, had landed shipboard an hour before hers. Scheduling was planned by the Time Touristry Board so the natives wouldn't notice a sudden increase in the ship's population.

"Ooh!" said brunette-bob, looking around. "It's just like the one at Retro Plaza!"

Brittany gave her an indulgent smile. Retro Plaza was a new mall back home, entirely historic in theme. It was part of the whole time-travel fad. It was even attracting its own tourists.

Lunch proceeded with only one minor hitch, when Steve the geek asked for a Coke. Brittany looked at the waiter.

"Cocoa, he means."

"Oh, that sounds lovely!" chirped red-bob. "I'll have cocoa, too! It's so chilly out on deck!"

"I am desolated to disappoint you, madame," said the

waiter, sounding very French, "we offer only coffee or tea."

"Oh—tea, then."

"Coke exists," muttered Steve after the waiter left.

"Yes, but it's called Coca-Cola, and it's full of cocaine," Brittany said quietly.

"Works for me."

She frowned, but he was fiddling with the menu. He folded it and stuck it in his pocket, then shot her a defiant look.

"That better not turn up on AuctionNet," she whispered.

Steve looked offended. "I know the rules, Mrs. Ivans."

This infuriated Brittany. She picked up her own menu and said, "I wonder what peaches in Chartreuse jelly taste like," while silently repeating her mantra, *happy travelers give big tips, happy travelers give big tips.*

After lunch, she released the group to wander the tour areas while she made a dinner reservation at the Restaurant À La Carte. She then went to the ladies' lavatory to sneek a peek at her datapad. The Powells had gone up to the First Class Lounge, all the single ladies were out on the Promenade, and Steve and Mr. Montenegro had both gone to the First Class Smoking Room, where the sort of trouble they could get into was pretty much limited to alcohol. Relieved, Brittany went out, free to relax a bit.

The Grand Staircase was close, so she walked over and slowly climbed the carpeted steps, admiring the glowing oak paneling and the ornate, curving wrought-iron balustrades. The famous clock featuring the carved figures of Honor and Glory stood at the top of the landing, illuminated by the glow from the glass dome overhead.

Another tour group passed Brittany on the stairs, six people led by a man she didn't recognize in a Liberty Blue suit with a tiny Triple T logo pin in his ascot. Must be a future guy. She returned his nod, and went on up to A Deck.

The First Class Reading and Writing Room was bright and spacious, very girly with pink carpets and drapes.

Only a few ladies were there, writing letters that would never be delivered. Brittany sank into a pink wing-backed chair facing the bow window and watched the people out on the promenade shivering in the cold breeze made by *Titanic*'s speed. They were steaming toward the ice field, heading for collision with the most famous iceberg in history. It was sad, really, she thought, glancing at the other women in the room. Most of them, female first-class passengers, had a good chance of surviving the coming disaster, but more than two-thirds of the people on the ship would die.

Why was it that the most tragic events in history were the most popular time-travel destinations? You'd think people would want to see things like Elizabeth I's coronation or the signing of the Declaration of Independence, but *Titanic* was the number-one dream destination, followed closely by the beheading of Marie Antoinette and the Sack of Rome.

"People are morbid," Brittany muttered.

A woman at a nearby table glanced up. Brittany gave her an embarrassed smile, then looked at her filigree watch. It was 2:26. She decided to go up for a stroll on the Boat Deck.

The stroll lasted three minutes. Sun was out, but wind chill had to be thirty below. Brittany bolted indoors at the first chance, and headed for the First Class Lounge to warm up.

Mrs. Powell waved to her from a Louis XV sofa by the window. Her husband sat beside her, playing solitaire on the ornate coffee table with a deck of White Star Line souvenir cards.

"I hope you're enjoying your cruise, Mr. and Mrs. Powell."

"Oh, it's delightful, dear!" said Mrs. Powell.

"Didn't think the staircase was all that grand," grumbled Mr. Powell.

"Did you come up the one near the Café?" Brittany asked. "It's the forward one that's really beautiful. That's where the clock is."

"Oh—no, we came up the aft stairs," said Mrs. Powell.

"I'd be happy to go see it with you," Brittany told

her, mentally summoning the Grand Staircase trivia she'd memorized.

"After I finish this game," said Mr. Powell.

They waited patiently, Brittany wondering if all marriages that lasted fifty years ended up with the man playing solitaire on an astronomically expensive anniversary trip. She passed the time by chatting with Mrs. Powell about the ship, a harmless topic as long as they were careful to avoid mentioning the little matter of it being destined to sink that evening. The next morning, technically, Brittany reminded herself. Twenty minutes after two. She shivered.

"Do you have a chill, dear?" asked Mrs. Powell.

"No, no. I was just out on deck. It's rather cold."

"We decided not to go out until this evening."

"Might as well stay in." Brittany said, and shot her a warning glance.

Mrs. Powell blinked at her, then seemed to get it. "Oh, oh yes! Nothing to see out there at night. Nothing at all."

"Except the stars," said a British-sounding male voice at Brittany's elbow.

She looked up into the eyes of the most gorgeous man she'd ever seen. He wore a cream-colored linen suit, and had dark hair and blue, blue eyes. Her heart did a flip-flop and her brain immediately started churning, relentlessly calculating the chances of a first-class male passenger surviving the disaster. One in three at best.

Why? Why, when she finally met Mr. Right, did he have to be on a doomed ship, headed for a date with Davy Jones?

Didn't matter. Rule No. 1 for Triple T guides was no getting involved with the natives.

"Forgive me for intruding," Mr. Right said. "I just couldn't resist mentioning the night sky, which is so lovely. Have any of you stepped out in the evenings?"

Brittany shook her head, mute with despair.

"Well, it's charming. All you need do is bundle up in one of the deck blankets, and you'll be snug as a bug. The stars are absolutely amazing. Worth the effort."

"Why, thank you," said Mrs. Powell, obviously delighted at being addressed at length by a native. She gave Brittany a conspiratorial smile, eyes twinkling.

"Y–yes, thank you, Mr. Right," Brittany said numbly.

"How did you know my name was Wright?" He looked startled.

"Er, lucky guess."

Brittany saw that Mr. Powell had finished his card game. She stood up. "Well, we'd better be running along. Good afternoon, sir," she said to Mr. Wright, hoping it was an appropriate thing to say if you hadn't been introduced.

He frowned slightly, but recovered and made a brief little bow. Brittany tore her eyes away from him and tucked a hand in Mr. Powell's arm, turning him toward the exit.

"What a charming man!" Mrs. Powell said with the good humor of someone whose day is going beautifully. "How sad to think—"

"Let's go and see that clock," Brittany said, dragging them both out of the lounge and down toward the Grand Staircase. "You know what they say, time waits for no one, ha ha."

She hustled them to the Grand Staircase, where she told them every boring detail about its design and construction while trying not to think about Mr. Right. She had looked forward to leading this tour so much, but at the moment it was Not Fun. The bob-haired gals joined them on the B Deck landing, cheeks bright red from being outdoors. Brittany thoughtfully repeated all her Grand Staircase trivia for them, then asked if Mrs. Gill and Mrs. Ferdinand were still out on deck.

"No," said brunette-bob. "They went into the Writing—Reading—Writing—that pink room."

"Ah, yes," said Brittany. "That's a room we should all see!" She dragged them relentlessly up the stairs. They passed another tour group; Brittany recognized the yellow-green "H A" logo on the guide's hatband: Historic Adventures, Triple T's biggest competitor. The guide gave her a cheeky grin.

They found Mrs. Gill and Mrs. Ferdinand in the Reading and Writing Room, still recovering from their excursion on the Promenade. Brittany sat them all down for tea, then made a dash to the lavatory to check on Steve and Mr. Montenegro. Her datapad showed Steve's blip still in the Smoking Room, and Mr. Montenegro out on deck. She decided to leave them alone and went back to the others.

Brunette-bob and red-bob (she really should remember their names) were flirting with Mr. Powell, which had vastly improved his mood. Mrs. Powell looked on, a little sharp-eyed but showing no immediate signs of exploding. Brittany sat with a cup of tea going cold in front of her and her brain offering various fantasies of Mr. Wright, none of which made her feel better.

Mr. Wright gallantly giving his place in a lifeboat to a younger man who was newly married. Mr. Wright encouraging a frightened cluster of doomed passengers. Mr. Wright swimming for Nova Scotia, whispering Brittany's name with his last breath.

Snap out of it, Ivans. He doesn't even know *your name.*

"—gobble gobble gobble, Mrs. Ivans?"

Brittany looked up at brunette-bob, who was watching her expectantly. "Uh," she said, panic speeding her pulse.

"Because we overheard someone talking about it on the Promenade Deck, and it sounded like fun," brunette-bob said.

Lipton, that was her name. *Jesus, Ivans, get a grip!*

"I'm sorry, Mrs. Lipton. What did you overhear?"

The bob looked annoyed. "There's a *hymn sing* this evening."

"We wondered if we could go," added red-bob. "It's in the Second Class Dining Saloon, which isn't on the list, but—"

"Sure, sure," Brittany said hastily. "Of course."

A hymn sing should be fairly harmless. Not like any major event could happen there. She searched her tired brain for any reference to a hymn sing being significant, and came up blank.

"Just don't ask for 'Nearer My God to Thee,' " she said.

Mr. Montenegro joined them at that moment, his plump cheeks red from the Promenade. There was a flutter of movement from the ladies, shifting to make room for him. He settled into a low-backed armchair with a contented sigh.

"Did you enjoy the Promenade?" Brittany asked automatically.

"Yes, yes. I spent a good deal of time looking around at the ship, and exchanged a few words with Captain Smith."

The ladies all exclaimed in wonder. Brittany shot him a sharp glance. He winked, and began describing his encounter with *Titanic*'s famous captain in minute detail.

Brittany checked her watch. Almost time to meet for dinner. She had everyone but Steve here. She excused herself and went back to the ladies' lavatory, took out her datapad. Steve was still in the Smoking Room. God, had he fallen asleep in there or something? She decided to check.

The Smoking Room was aft, just forward of the Palm Courts. To get to it Brittany cut through the First Class Lounge, then hurried down a long corridor. The room was splendid, paneled in mahogany with mother-of-pearl inlays, and featured paintings on glass which glowed with daylight, and the famous Plymouth Harbor painting over the fireplace. A hint of cigar smoke hung in the air. She saw men playing cards, reading newspapers, drinking and smoking, but none of them was Steve. The room was U-shaped, so she strolled around the far corner. Other than one young lady rather defiantly smoking a cigarette, there was no one there.

Maybe he'd gone into the Palm Court, where they were supposed to meet for dinner. It was next door, so she might as well look. Passing through the doors, she stopped dead as her gaze fell on Mr. Wright.

He was sitting at a table with a cup of coffee in front of him, looking even more handsome than she remembered. He looked up at her and smiled. Her heart went into overdrive.

"Hello, again," he said. "You're welcome to sit here if you like." He gestured at the open chairs at his table.

"Um, thanks, but I'm looking for someone."

"Oh."

Mr. Wright smiled politely, then picked up his spoon and stirred his coffee. Feeling miserable, Brittany walked past. No sign of Steve the geek. She went outside, onto the deck.

It was colder, getting dark already. She stood gazing out over *Titanic*'s stern, wondering what the hell she was doing here. She wanted to break all the rules, run back inside and tell Mr. Wright that if something happened he should get in a lifeboat at once. She closed her eyes, inhaling cold air through her nose.

Can't do that, Ivans. Look very bad. Lose your job.

"Screw the job," she muttered, but she didn't go back into the Palm Court. Instead she stared at the ship's huge wake, thinking about that old movie where the old woman drops the fabulously expensive diamond into the North Atlantic. She could drop her passcard, and stay here with Mr. Wright.

Except that was nuts. For all she knew he was married, and anyway, he might not survive. *She* might not survive. No Brittanys on the survivor lists, she was sure of that.

She needed a drink. There was a bar between the two Palm Courts. She went back in, pretending it wasn't because she wanted another look at Mr. Wright. He was still there, at the table near the bar door. She could just stroll past, and if she happened to catch his eye she might make a casual remark about how few lifeboats there were on board.

Just as she reached his table, the forward doors burst open and Steve the geek came in. "Brittany! I'm not late," he said defensively.

Mr. Wright glanced up. "Brittany? That's an unusual name for a woman."

A portly man who had just come out of the bar, whisky in hand, peered blearily at her. "Region in France, isn't it? Not a girl's name."

"My parents went there on their honeymoon," Brittany said through gritted teeth. The man with the whiskey looked shocked, and hurried away.

Brittany turned to Steve. "Come along, Mr. Shoup. We don't want to be late for dinner."

He didn't offer his arm, which was just as well because the mood she was in, she'd be likely to pitch him overboard. She hustled him out, not daring to look back at Mr. Wright.

Joining the others, she managed to summon a smile. "Well, here we all are! Shall we go on down to dinner?"

"Oh, yes! I'm starving," said red-bob, who had polished off a plate of profiteroles with her tea.

Crumbie, Brittany remembered. *Mrs. Crumbie. Should be my name, I'm feeling pretty crumbie. Ha ha.*

"Let's go, then," she said brightly.

The Restaurant À La Carte was not crowded at the unfashionable hour of six. More rich wood paneling, with gilt accents, which Brittany rather listlessly pointed out to her party. They were seated at the largest table, with a centerpiece of cheerful daffodils. Four women looked up from a smaller table nearby. One wore a Historic Adventures logo pin.

Jesus, no wonder this sucker sank! There must be a million tour groups aboard!

Brittany stared blankly at her menu while her group chattered about the offerings and glanced surreptitiously at the other patrons, hoping to spot someone famous. She let them order anything they wanted: foie gras, roast duckling, champagne. They'd paid for it, and she had enough in her reticule to cover their wildest possible excesses.

"And for you, madame?" asked the waiter at her elbow.

Brittany glanced up. "Oh. I'll have the same."

She handed him her menu. Not hungry. Feeling miserable. She picked at her duckling and let conversation wash over her.

"A toast," said Mr. Montenegro, raising his champagne. "To our lovely hostess!"

Clinking glasses. Brittany tried to smile, though really she felt like crying.

After dinner, she set them loose again. The ladies all went down to the hymn sing. Mr. Montenegro invited Mr. Powell and Mr. Shoup to play cards in the Smoking Room. Brittany wandered out onto the Second Class Promenade, wishing the night was over. She felt like she was walking among ghosts, which in a sense she was. In a few hours her group would return to their departure date, where all the people here, Mr. Wright included, were long dead.

She roamed B deck, then A deck, peering in windows and through screens, trying to catch a glimpse of Mr. Wright. She argued with herself about whether it was immoral to warn him or immoral not to—and whether it would do any good. For her, none at all, but maybe for him it would make a difference.

You can't change the past, she reminded herself. Whatever influence a time traveler could have was already part of history, already woven in, so whether she warned him or not was really a matter of her own conscience. Whatever decision she made, the result had already played out.

She frowned at her reflection in the windows. Would it make her feel better to warn him, or to abide by Triple T's rules?

"Tell him," she whispered to the ghost-self staring back at her. "Tell him to get in a damn boat."

Feeling better, she took a deep breath and went to look for Mr. Wright. Of course she couldn't find him. She crawled all over the first and second class public areas. On her way back up to A deck, she met her ladies, fresh from the hymn sing.

"We're just going up to the Pink Room for a nightcap," said Mrs. Ferdinand. "Care to join us?"

"Uh—in a bit. You go on ahead and I'll catch up."

She kept searching for Mr. Wright, alternately worrying and being pissed off that she couldn't find him. As the evening wore on, pissed off won out. Finally, she gave up and went to the starboard Palm Court to collect her group for the collision.

Mr. Montenegro was there, having a brandy and chatting with Mr. Powell, who was nursing a tumbler of scotch. The ladies soon tripped in together. Brittany counted heads, then sighed.

"Anyone seen Mr. Shoup? Let me guess," she said, turning to Mr. Montenegro. "Smoking Room."

"Actually he left there rather early in the evening," Mr. Montenegro said.

"Did he say where he was going?"

"Afraid not."

Brittany frowned. "All right, everyone please stay here while I go find him."

She went down to the lavatory and hauled out her datapad. Seven blips in the Palm Court and one in the Smoking Room. Exasperated, she hurried back down the corridor.

The Smoking Room was now thick with cigar smoke. Stifling a cough, Brittany hurried through looking for Steve. Several tables of men were playing cards, but he wasn't at any of them. She didn't want to traipse all the way back to the lavatory, so she found a book someone had left lying on a chair and snuck her datapad in between the pages, then peered at the screen.

It showed Steve's blip in the smoking room, not far from hers. Over by one of the windows, it looked like.

She strolled toward the window in question. Could he be just outside it? No, the passcards were pinpoint precise—they had to be. She walked up to the empty couch by the window and stood frowning at Steve's blip with hers right in front of it.

"Son of a bitch," she muttered.

"Are you looking for your friend?"

Brittany jumped and nearly dropped her datapad. She scrabbled for it, crumpling a page in the book.

"Oh, I beg your pardon," said Mr. Wright, stepping up beside her. He had changed into a svelte tuxedo and white tie. "I didn't mean to startle you."

Brittany stood clutching the book and datapad to her heaving chest. She glared at Mr. Wright.

"You see, I thought, perhaps—" He broke off, glanced at the card players, then gestured at the couch. "Won't you sit down?"

"No, thank you," Brittany said icily, furious at him for being missing all evening and then turning up looking more gorgeous than ever.

"All right."

He knelt down before her and Brittany thought she was going to pass out. Then he thrust his hand between the sofa cushions.

"What, are you looking for spare change?" she hissed.

"No. This."

He pulled out his hand. He was holding a blue card. Steve Shoup's passcard.

"I saw your friend leave this here earlier this evening."

Brittany was tempted to snatch it from him, but she didn't want to tip off how important it was. She stood blinking, trying to think of something to say.

Maybe if she could get Mr. Wright to hold onto it for, say, half an hour . . .

No. Bad idea. Bad, bad idea. Lawsuits. Jail time.

Time! Brittany disentangled one hand and fished out her watch. It was 11:25! In fifteen minutes, *Titanic* would hit its iceberg.

"I have to go," she said. "Thank you for finding that. It's—sort of a memento. I'll return it to Mr. Shoup."

She held out her hand. Mr. Wright gazed at her for a long moment, a smile teasing the corner of his mouth. At last he laid the passcard in her hand.

Brittany turned to go, then stopped and looked back. "Mr. Wright? Are you—um, superstitious at all?"

He smiled. "No."

"Well, I am. Would you do me a favor?"

The smile grew. "Possibly."

"If something happens, will you promise me you'll get into a lifeboat?" she said softly.

His eyebrows rose and he looked as if he was about to laugh. "All right," he said. "I'll promise to do that, if you'll promise to meet me for coffee tomorrow morning."

Brittany swallowed. "Oh. Um—"

"Quarter to eight, Café Parisien."

"Ah—sure. Sure. Yes." She looked up at him, feeling she would sink into his eyes. "I'd love to."

"You'd better go, Miss Brittany," he said softly.

"Oh!" She dashed for the door, turning when she reached it, still clutching book, datapad, and Steve's passcard to her chest. "Thank you, Mr. Wright! Take care!"

He smiled and waved. It actually hurt to turn away and go through the doors to the starboard Palm Court. She felt like fricking Cinderella leaving the goddamn ball.

Steve was with the rest of the group, brimming with false cheer. "Hello, Mrs. Ivans! Heard you were looking for me!"

"Yeah." Brittany pocketed her datapad and let the book fall to the floor. "You lost this."

She slapped his passcard against his chest. He turned red.

"I was just—"

"Save it. We're late. Come on, everyone. We're going to go look at the stars."

She marched them up to the Boat Deck, pausing to raid a storage closet for blankets. Two other tour groups were already there, leaning on the starboard rail.

Disgusting. Morbid. Ought to be illegal.

"Come along, everyone," she said cheerily through gritted teeth. "Who can find Orion?"

They clustered together, arguing over constellations. Other tour groups started showing up, surreptitiously strolling up to the railing. For a second Brittany thought she'd glimpsed Mr. Wright, but it was probably just another tourist. Lots of tuxedos on board, and only the tourists were nuts enough to be out here in the fricking cold, she thought glumly.

She looked toward the bow, trying to spot the berg. The cold draft was making her eyes water. Yeah, the draft. Sure.

When it came, the collision was disappointing. The iceberg loomed suddenly, and a minute later gently bumped the ship. Brittany hardly felt the impact. A long, rattling groan came from below, and a few chunks of ice fell onto the open front of C Deck. That was it.

Brittany took out her datapad and sent the recall signal. As she felt the familiar toilet-flushing sensation, she couldn't help but feel a bitter hysteria. It was an appropriate metaphor for her love life.

The group landed in the transport room, blinking with stunned surprise. Mrs. Powell threw her arms around Brittany.

"Thank you, dear! It was lovely!"

"You're welcome, Mrs. Powell," Brittany said, wiping her eyes. "Let's go, everyone. Gotta make way for the next group."

She herded them back to their locker rooms, collecting their passcards as they went in. Steve the geek gave her a sheepish look as he handed his over.

"I just wanted to see the wireless room, and I knew you wouldn't let me go there. I didn't disrupt anything, honest."

"Yeah, okay," Brittany said, too tired and depressed to get worked up about it. "Never mind."

She'd make a note of it in her report. Have to file a report. Tomorrow, though. Too beat tonight.

She turned in her passcards and datapad, then went to change. The other ladies had gone home, but the two bobs were lingering in the locker room. Strange to see them in street clothes. She'd grown rather fond of them in big hats and lace.

"Ms. Ivans? Brittany?" said red-bob Crumbie. "We just wanted to say thank you. You did a terrific job."

Brittany summoned a feeble smile. "Thanks."

"And we—well, we'd like to ask for you the next tour we take," said Lipton. "Would that be all right with you?"

"Of course. Thank you, ladies."

They smiled in their bobbley way, and traded a glance. "Well, anyway," said Crumbie, "We're going to go over to the Café Parisien now for a sort of farewell drink. Care to join us?"

Brittany frowned, blinking. "Café Parisien?"

"Yeah, in Retro Plaza," said Crumbie. "They've done it up as an old-time espresso place. Haven't you been?"

"Uh, no, I haven't got over there yet."

"We figured we *have* to go tonight, you know, because of the name," said Lipton.

"Café Parisien."

Brittany's heart began to thump. Mr. Wright hadn't seemed very curious about Steve's passcard, had he?

Maybe because he knew what it was.

Lots of people used them, not just tourists. Researchers, watchguards. Anyone who needed to time travel.

"So, you coming?" asked Crumbie.

Brittany looked at her, a slow smile growing on her face. "Not tonight, thanks. But don't worry. I'll try it out soon."

Very soon. Quarter to eight tomorrow morning.

THE CURSE OF THE PENDRAGON

by Irene Radford

A member of an endangered species, a native Oregonian who lives in Oregon, Irene Radford makes her home in Welches, Oregon, where deer, bear, coyote, hawks, owls, and woodpeckers feed regularly on their back deck. As a service brat, she lived in a number of cities throughout the country until returning to Oregon in time to graduate from Tigard High School. She earned a BA in history from Lewis and Clark College, where she met her husband. In her spare time, Irene enjoys lacemaking and is a longtime member of an international guild. Combining her love of history along with a fascination with the paranormal, Irene once again visits medieval England in the world she created for her Merlin's Descendants series.

"HAS TRYBLITH, the Demon of Chaos, taken all of your minds?" Wilfred of Kirkenwood, Don of Merton College, Oxford, shouted at his students. He pounded his walking stick with each word.

Power ran through the staff, begging him to cast a spell over these ignorant savages that would force them to listen and absorb his wisdom.

He swallowed the urge. Forced learning would not last.

The gathered throng of a dozen young men garbed in black gowns with hoods in Merton's colors, cringed with each reverberation of the staff against the stone floor.

That should be enough of a demonstration of power to make them sit up and listen.

They all kept their eyes on their scrolls.

"Not one of you has the sense you were born with!" Doctor Wilfred continued his tirade. His leg ached abominably. Otherwise he might have treated his students' stupidity with a bit more gentleness.

"S . . . sir, may I point out that Dr. Merton said in his Treatise of 1266 that King Arthur did not exist but served as a metaphor . . ."

"What is your name?" Wilfred asked, his voice suddenly as icy as his temper was hot. If he did not get a poultice on his leg ulcer soon, he just might send the boy to the cave where his ancestress had imprisoned the previously invoked demon. He knew the spell. He'd just never had the courage to try it.

His nephew Griffin, Baron of Kirkenwood and Pendragon of Britain, wouldn't hesitate. But then he had more magic in the tip of his fingers than Wilfred would ever be able to conjure in a lifetime.

"I am . . ." the student stammered.

"I don't really care who you are. Nor do I have the patience today to deal with your half reading. Show me the logic in your statement."

"Sir?"

"You are here to learn logic, the finest discipline in the quadrivium. The last discipline you must learn before you can call yourselves masters. And not one of you has the sense to think this through. All you do is quote previous masters." Wilfred pounded his stick once more. This time the act sent vibrations through his feet, connecting him to the earth. The sense of power ready to be tapped calmed him. A bit.

"Sir, is there no logic in quoting masters who have already thought the problem through?"

"Cheeky youngster, aren't you?" Wilfred and the young man began a staring contest.

Wilfred won. The young man looked back to his scroll.

"I could claim descent from King Arthur for myself. Would you believe me?" He could prove it if any of them showed enough interest, and discretion, to appreciate it. His nephew had decided the populace, in general, could not appreciate and might misinterpret such information. So the family kept their ancestry secret from all but the king. King Edward, the first of that name, had a right to know which one of them currently acted the Pendragon and advised his royal personage.

"Such a claim would be suspect," the cheeky student offered.

"At last you are thinking." Wilfred crowed in triumph. "The purpose of this class is to make you think on your own. If we accept everything previous masters believed, we'd still be living in caves with monkeys, eating bugs and not knowing the truth of our God-given talents; never puzzling out the meaning behind the movements of the sun, moon, and stars, never creating or understanding beautiful music, learning to read . . ."

Wilfred paused for breath as he raised his eyes to encompass the entire class. "All of you take yourselves off and finish reading the assigned scrolls before we convene again on Monday. And I mean study them, form your own opinions, don't just parrot the words back to me. You have brains. Use them!" He flung open the door from where he stood with just the power of his mind.

Finally, a release of the energy building within him.

If only he could heal the ulcer on his leg as easily as he opened doors or lit candles. Even if he had the healing talent, he couldn't use it upon himself.

The students scuttled out of his chambers. The young men hastened away. The clatter of their patens on the flagstones made Wilfred's head ache as sorely as his leg.

Wilfred frowned at the lengthening shadows in the quadrangle of the college. Sunset approached on this Friday eve. Simon ben Isaac would not stir from his home in the Jewish quarter this late, even for his old friend Wilfred.

Therefore, Wilfred must go to the good physician and apothecary if he hoped for any relief from the pain in his leg.

He grabbed his walking staff and cloak and stumped out the door of his chambers. The bleak cold of early November in this Year of Our Lord 1289 penetrated his woolen undertrews and set the oozing ulcer on fire. He cursed again, this time in Greek, knowing that any student who overheard him would have to work at understanding the words.

A student, wearing the gown and colors of Merton wove a drunken path across the quadrangle.

Wilfred tried to avoid bumping into the fellow. His painful leg locked in place, then threatened to give way beneath him. This left him a target for the young man's bleary vision. The youth carried a pewter tankard that sloshed dark and fragrant ale.

"You one of mine?" Wilfred shouted peering beneath the boy's hood. "You'll be out on your ear if you are. Drunk this early on a Friday eve. Couldn't you have waited until after sunset?"

"Sorry, sir," the boy slurred. "Been over to the Turf. New ale. Best brewed in whole city." He waved his arms expansively. More of the ale sloshed upon Wilfred's gown.

"Drunken fool." Wilfred brought a ball of cold witch light to his palm, the better to study the boy's face. Too many hours of studying ancient manuscripts had weakened his eyes.

"Strange torch," the boy mused. "Almost magic." He wavered, coming close to toppling over.

Wilfred grabbed his sleeve to keep him upright and center his own vision. "Ulrich of Salisbury. I should have known. You haven't been sober of a Friday since you got here." But he was a damned fine student during the rest of the week. "You'll make a fine scholar if you ever stay sober enough to complete the curriculum."

The world seemed to shift to the left. Wilfred's vision doubled and then doubled again. For a brief moment he caught a glimpse of an older and wiser Ulrich wearing a master's robes, teaching a bevy of younger men in Wilfred's own quarters.

The vision left Wilfred gasping in confusion. "Just a portent. Not a certainty," he reminded himself.

"You say something, sir?" Ulrich slurred.

"Go to confession before you dare darken the door of my chambers on Monday morn."

Ulrich of Salisbury saluted with his mug to his brow. Wilfred doubted he'd remember the order to confess.

But that sacrament was required of all students before Mass on Sunday. Wilfred himself would have to confess his foray into the Jewish quarter. Consort with the tainted Jews was considered a sin.

But no other physician in the city had Simon ben Isaac's skill and knowledge.

"On your way, boy. And stay out of trouble." Wilfred pushed Ulrich toward the student chambers.

"Could you trouble me with one of those hand torches, sir? Stairs are damned dark and twisty."

"Master's secret," Wilfred said rather than admit openly to having magical talent. Bad enough his students spread rumors hither and yon of his alchemical experiments. He didn't need it bruited about that the youngest Don—barely three and thirty—had congress with the Devil, or Jews, or whatever evil currently topped the church's list.

With growing urgency as the sunset fell toward the horizon, he stumped his way across town to the Jewish Quarter.

Suddenly, as if traversing a portal into a new world, the streets became clean, the houses newly whitewashed and thatched and in good repair despite their modest size and appearance. Not one bit of garbage or animal waste marred his passage.

He breathed deeply. This part of town always smelled fresher than the Christian sections. One thing his fellow believers had not learned or improved upon from the Jews was cleanliness. And they weren't likely to in the current political climate.

King Edward Longshanks made noises on a monthly basis about how the Jews corrupted the very air Christians breathed. His Royal Highness also had a fondness for referring to Jews as thieves. One of the few professions open to the Jews was money lending. They had to charge interest to make a living. And every time the king or a great lord defaulted on a loan (without penalty), the Jews had to increase their interest rate to make up the difference.

The Jews were blamed for everything from the decreasing value of a coin to the latest disease to the worsening relations with France to the early and long winters.

Mimicking their cleanliness might become the next great sin.

Wilfred touched his soiled robe with the Celtic cross atop his staff and willed the stains away. The scent of spilled ale and the roast mutton he'd eaten for his dinner evaporated under an orange glow. The embedded mint sauce from yesterday took a little more concentration. At last he felt clean enough to approach his friend, the physician.

"Simon ben Isaac, open your door." Wilfred pounded upon the stout wooden planking with his staff.

" 'Tis Friday eve, the Sabbath. I may not open my door," came a robust reply just on the other side.

"The sun hasn't set yet, you old hen-plucker," Wilfred replied with a bit of mirth.

"How can you tell with those heavy clouds about to dump snow upon us?" Simon opened the door and leaned out, looking at the horizon rather than his friend. A single gray curl dangled before each of his ears. The rest of his hair was clipped short and an elaborately embroidered black prayer cap adorned his head.

"I can tell." Wilfred closed his eyes and concentrated. His body automatically turned to face north. The wind caressed his face and told him everything he needed to know about the heavens. "You've time to poultice my leg before you go to your prayers." Wilfred shouldered the man aside and limped heavily into the stark room.

"Come right in, Wilfred of Kirkenwood," Simon said sarcastically, hands on hips, a glare of disapproval in his eyes.

"Thank you, old friend." Wilfred dropped onto the kist, a small chest with a rounded top, beside the window and stuck his offending left leg out before him. Simon did not waste money on chairs that served no other purpose than a place to sit.

"You've got to do something, Simon. This really pains me. I'll not make it to Monday."

"How do you know the sun has not set?" Simon waved his hand to indicate the bowls of tallow burning feebly around the room. They did little to lighten the gloom of this dark November day.

"My soul senses the movement of sun and stars and

moon. I've studied them too long not to know precisely where they are at this moment. You have half a candle length before the sun touches the horizon. Now please, stop stalling and treat this leg."

Simon remained by the door, his arms crossed across his chest. His mud-brown robes fell to his feet undisturbed by movement.

"I've money to pay, if that keeps you rooted to the spot like some great oak." Wilfred held up the small purse his nephew had sent him so that he might journey home to Kirkenwood to celebrate Yuletide Mass.

"I am not allowed to treat Christians," Simon said simply.

"But you are the best doctor in all of Oxford. Possibly in all of England."

"That matters not. The Archbishop of Canterbury has decreed and the king agrees with him: for a Jew to treat the illness of a Christian only further taints their bodies and disrupts the humors. I may only serve my own people."

"Nonsense. I don't give a misteltoe berry what the king and archbishop think . . ."

" 'Tis the law, Wilfred."

"I am not a physician, merely a simple midwife," a woman said, walking into the main room of the house from some hidden cubby in the rear.

Wilfred stared at her agape. She glided into the room more than walked, graceful, serene, and . . . and beautiful. The most beautiful woman he had ever seen. Her dark hair contrasted delightfully with her pale, flawless skin. And those clear green eyes sparkled with mischief and intelligence.

From one breath to the next, Wilfred, who had never had time or interest in the mousy, stupid, giddy women his family paraded in front of him, fell in love.

"Close your mouth, Wilfred. You will only catch flies with it hanging open like an oubliette," Simon said.

Wilfred managed to lever his jaw upward enough to comply while he studied the woman. She carried a bowl filled with some aromatic substance he could not name. Keeping her eyes modestly lowered, she began bathing the offensive ulcer with a clean cloth which she dipped into the mixture.

No skinny, giggling, maiden this. She had passed the first flush of youth and matured into incredible beauty. The sight of her rounded body filled Wilfred with sweet longing.

"How be it you have managed to keep this glorious angel a secret from me, Simon?" Wilfred finally asked. He knew better than to speak to the woman directly. Jewish ideas of modesty differed from his own.

The first fire of the bathing passed from his ulcer, replaced by a blessed cooling that spread outward from the center of the wound.

"My sister, Miriam, newly come from Flanders." Simon did not follow the information with a formal introduction. Wilfred could not yet speak directly to her.

A secret smile played about Miriam's generous mouth as she applied an ointment to the ulcer. "Simon, tell your patient that this balm will help heal the wound, but he must keep the bandages clean, and he must not drink so much wine or eat too many blood puddings."

Her rich voice washed over Wilfred like a sweet melody.

Simon repeated her words, the same mischievous smile tugged at his mouth as his sister's.

"Simon, tell your lovely sister that I must return here every three days so that she may replace the bandages and apply a new dose of this wonderful balm." Wilfred did not, could not, remove his eyes from her.

Simon repeated those words.

At last Miriam looked up at Wilfred and laughed. "Very well, Wilfred of Kirkenwood. You may return here every three days for more treatment from a simple midwife who has lived too long among Christians to fear them."

"Miriam, no," Simon protested. All trace of amusement left him. "They'll burn you for a witch if he heals too quickly and too well."

"Or they'll brand and exile us all, Jews consorting with a Christian. And a Christian who is rumored to deal with dark powers and alchemy." She rose from her crouch to her knees and glared at them both with hands on hips and her mouth pursed in disapproval.

"Will you marry me, Miriam?" Wilfred blurted out. "I love you."

"Nonsense. You are grateful for the release of your pain. Now return to your studies and your philosophical arguments with your fellow Dons before the sun truly sets and we must begin our prayers."

"You've told her about me?" Wilfred queried Simon.

"I may have mentioned you a time or two in my letters to her husband, may he rest in peace. Can I help it if he allowed an impertinent woman to read our correspondence?" Simon asked as he helped Wilfred up from the low kist and guided him to the door. "Now do try to stay off that leg for a few days and eat lightly, watered ale and gruel. A bit of chicken or fish if it's not too salty or drowned in rich sauces."

"You are cruel, Simon. How am I to stay warm sleeping alone on these frigid nights with so little food inside me? If I survive, I shall return on Monday for fresh bandages and some more of your widowed sister's wonderful balm and charming company."

Wilfred limped back to his chambers, dreaming of Miriam, sister of Simon ben Isaac. He didn't feel the cold a bit, nor did the snow that soaked his cloak chill him to the bone.

The next morn Wilfred sent word to his nephew by merchant caravan that he could not travel because of the ulcer on his leg compounded by the worsening weather. Winter did seem to come earlier and earlier each year.

When students traveled home for Yuletide, Wilfred remained in his chambers, entertaining the few remaining in Merton College. They mulled wine on the hearth and helped him through the snow every three days to the home of Simon ben Isaac. Four times Miriam dressed his wound, then declared him healed. Wilfred found new ailments, aches, and pains to justify additional trips across town into the Jewish quarter.

The snow grew deeper. Christians and Jews alike ran out of firewood, peat, and sea coal. Many had to borrow money from the Jews to pay inflated prices for fuel to stay warm.

And the snow grew deeper yet.

Still Wilfred beat a daily path to the home of Simon ben Isaac. By Twelfth Night he gave up making excuses. He courted Miriam openly. Her wit, charm, and intelligence enchanted him. They argued politics. She knew history nearly as well as he. Best of all she never doubted that King Arthur existed and that he had died a martyr, believing that the law, justice, and peace could work and that honor, truth, and promises were important.

Neither of them could remember a monarch since who had lived up to those qualities.

Wilfred hesitantly claimed distant kinship to the great king of the past.

" 'Tis only logical that a man as great as you with kin of ancient and honorable lineage should descend from King Arthur. 'Tis more logical that you descend from King Arthur's Merlin, the greatest magician of all time," Miriam countered.

Wilfred blushed. "What if I told you that my family can trace its lineage to both King Arthur and his Merlin?"

"I am happy that you take such pride in your heritage. My mother traces our lineage back to Abraham."

Her big brown eyes met his in shining affection. Wilfred's heart melted anew and his loins were set afire.

The world tilted around him. His eyes found focus in a new dimension. He caught a glimpse of Miriam holding an auburn-haired babe to her breast while three others, also sporting the auburn hair and deep blue eyes of the Kirkenwood family, played at her feet. He knew without question that he had fathered/would father all four of those children within the bounds of wedlock.

Pride and joy swelled within him.

On Shrove Tuesday, as the Christian community feasted on the last of the lard, eggs, and milk before the forty days of Lenten fasting, Wilfred dressed in his finest, and cleanest robe. He washed his hair and trimmed his beard. As usual Simon ben Isaac greeted him at the door. The two old friends exchanged formal greetings then ducked inside.

"Is the world about to end?" Simon asked as he

tweaked Wilfred's curling beard. A few strands of gray had crept into the auburn mass during the winter.

"I bathed. What is so unusual about that?" Wilfred growled.

"Snow still encrusts the verge and ice makes the roads treacherous. No one has extra fuel to heat water for a bath," Simon replied. A bit of mirth tugged the corner of his mouth upward.

"We need to talk, Simon." Wilfred looked around for a place for the two of them to sit. He settled on the low kist, leaving the taller, flat-topped chest for his friend.

"May I take your cloak, Wilfred of Kirkenwood?" Simon remained standing by the door.

"Oh." Wilfred blushed as he handed over the heavy and sodden garment.

"What portends?" Simon asked, settling his skinny bottom upon a pillow atop the chest, the place of honor.

"I . . . um . . . don't know your customs well enough to do aught else, so I've come to ask your permission to marry your widowed sister Miriam," he said all in one breath.

"No." Simon refused to meet his gaze.

"What do you mean 'no'!" Wilfred exploded, half-standing in anger.

"You are not one of us and never can be."

Wilfred settled back into place, prepared to match Simon's arguments with logic. "Miriam can become a Christian. I'll sponsor her baptism."

"Never!" Simon half rose in anger.

"Then I'll ask Miriam directly. Certainly she has a say in the matter," Wilfred's tone turned as icy as the weather.

"Our women are sacred. We take our lineage through the mother. Any children Miriam births will be Jews, even if she becomes a Christian," Simon insisted.

"Miriam!" Wilfred called into the back rooms, still eyeing Simon levelly.

She appeared from behind the curtain to the inner portions of the tall and narrow house. "Must I settle another political argument between you two?" She stood with her hands on her rounded hips, a lovely wisp of dark hair peeking from beneath her wimple. She wore knitted gloves with the fingers cut off to keep her hands warm while she worked with the other women of the household.

Wilfred jumped to his feet and gathered those hands in his own. "Miriam, forgive my bluntness. I have asked your brother for your hand in marriage. He refuses because I am not a Jew. I believe that we can overcome the differences of faith. I love you, Miriam." He bent his head a little, expecting her to reach up and meet him for a kiss, a pledge of their love.

She stayed put and he had to bend further forward to capture her lips in his own. He found her willing enough, meeting him with gentleness if not outright enthusiasm.

"I would be proud to be your wife, Wilfred of Kirkenwood. But I must remain a Jew. I must marry a Jew." She pulled away from him reluctantly.

"There is a way for you to become a Jew, Wilfred," Simon said quietly. "But this is something you must not enter into lightly. This is more than a matter of upbringing and lineage. This is a matter of true faith."

Standing so close to Miriam, holding her hands, seeing her breasts rise with each breath, Wilfred could not think beyond possessing her, body, soul, and mind.

"Teach me what it means to be a Jew," he said. "Teach me so that I might believe."

"Before you can marry, you must attest your faith. You must submit to the extreme ritual of circumcision, to mark you as one of the Chosen," Simon said.

Wilfred turned his head to face his friend, still holding Miriam's hands. His own fingers grew icy and his palm moist. "But . . . but . . . isn't that done only to young children?"

His manhood shrank and he instinctively held his thighs closer together.

"It is Jewish law. Only those circumcised can be Jews."

Wilfred gulped and looked back to Miriam. She lifted her eyes to meet his, troubled and hesitant.

He needed to be with her, protect her, grow old with her, father her children.

He'd seen it in a vision. He would marry her.

"I've never been a good Christian. I think too much

and disagree with the Church at every turn. Teach me to be a Jew."

"There is more. You will lose your place at Merton College. Your family will denounce you. You will be subject to the king's onerous taxes upon us to fund his military campaigns, his mistresses, and his jewels. If he cannot tax us, he will demand we loan him money we no longer have. He has bled us dry. We dare not hope that he will ever repay any of his loans."

"I have no money for him to tax or to loan. He cannot squeeze blood out of a turnip, though he will try. The boneheads at Merton College do not deserve my wisdom. As for my family . . ." He had to swallow deeply and blink back a tear. He didn't know his nephew well, but he trusted the young man to guard the family honors and their heritage well. "My family has little use for me or my piddling talents. They nearly turned their backs upon me when I took myself off to Paris to study."

"You must renounce your 'piddling' talents and never use them again. You might defy the Church by your little magical tricks and experiments with alchemy, but we will not brook such defiance. Should you use your magic again, you will be driven from our community and your marriage to Miriam dissolved. She will be as a widow, your children orphans."

Now Miriam pleaded with him with her eyes and the firm grip on her fingers.

"How did you know about that?" Wilfred asked Simon.

"All of Oxford knows you dabble in alchemy. All of Oxford has seen you light the way through our dark streets with a ball of cold flame in your hands."

" 'Tis a hard thing to give up my magic. But, for Miriam, I will do it. Teach me to be a Jew."

And so his instruction began. They taught him the law. They taught him the Torah and the Talmud. He learned to speak the ancient prayers, he learned to eat the proper foods in the proper combinations. He learned to wear a cap and prayer shawl.

He learned to love Miriam more with each passing day. She tutored him, she held his hand, she loved him in return.

Six weeks later Wilfred of Kirkenwood sat down with his new family to the Passover feast. As the newest member of the family he took the part of the child and asked the questions of the Simon, the eldest. Why is this night special? Why do we drink this wine? Why do we eat bitter herbs? Why do we sing these songs? He knew the answers now, knew the stories, the history, and yet he felt as if he learned them all over again. Tears of joy and beauty filled his eyes.

Then all the family stood, each with a cup of wine and said together, "Next year in Jerusalem!"

Suddenly the room tilted and he saw the temple on the mount, sun baked brick, coarse roof tiles. He felt the sun upon his back and smelled the dust of centuries.

"Wilfred! What ails you?" Miriam clutched his arm and his face.

He looked down upon her worried countenance. Her eyes cleared when he smiled. "Next year we *will* be in Jerusalem," he replied.

"You cannot know this, my friend," Simon said. He too looked worried. "For centuries, all the Jews who have endured exile from our homeland have made this pledge of hope. Rarely do the Chosen return to their homeland. Rarely are we allowed to travel so far."

"I may have renounced my magical powers, but they have not renounced me. I have had a vision. A true vision. Next year we will celebrate the Passover in Jerusalem," he said with authority.

The rest of the family shook their heads and murmured in dismay.

The weather warmed at last. Spring and summer came to England in damp glory. Flowers bloomed, crops sprouted. Wilfred's students ceased coughing.

At the end of term, Wilfred resigned his position at Merton College and moved in with Simon. The day before he was to undergo the painful but essential circumcision he received a letter sealed with heavy red wax and many dangling ribbons. The king himself, Edward Plantagenet, summoned him to court to answer for his treasonous and blasphemous intentions.

Reluctantly, Wilfred made his way to London. Alone. Without the solace of Miriam at his side.

At Windsor Castle, a page showed Wilfred into a private solar where King Edward, called Longshanks, and Lord Griffin of Kirkenwood studied a map of Gascony, where Edward had campaigned last year. Griffin's wolfhound familiar rested by the hearth. She lifted her great head and gave a woof of greeting. Then she settled again, satisfied that her master was safe.

"Our Pendragon wishes you to return to the family fold," Edward said as soon as the page had announced Wilfred and then withdrawn.

"I have no quarrel with my family. 'Tis they who have refused me access to Kirkenwood and the loving embrace of my relatives," Wilfred replied.

The wolfhound opened one eye and seemed to stare at him in doggy mirth.

Wilfred winked back at her. They understood each other.

"If you have no quarrel with the family, why have you rejected us and God to become a Jew?" Griffin shouted. For a man of little more than twenty, he usually carried himself with better authority and dignity. His face purpled with anger and he pounded the map table until it shook. The map scooted free of its restraints and re-rolled with a snap.

The wolfhound lifted her head once more, alert to her master's moods.

"I follow my heart and my faith. The Jews offer me what the rest of England cannot," Wilfred said simply.

"The Jews have refused to loan us necessary funds to pay for our campaign in Gascony or for our forthcoming crusade," Edward said in an icy tone. "We can only presume that you have influenced the entire Jewish community to this decision with the magic inherent in your family."

"There is no more money in the Jewish coffers, Your Highness. We cannot loan what we do not possess."

"The Jews own property they could sell to raise the funds."

"They did that last year and the year before. We now possess little more than the clothes upon our backs and the Synagogues that no Christian will purchase. We have sold our houses and crowd in together until we have no more room to share." Wilfred held firm. "If you had ever repaid any of the loans, then perhaps there would be money to lend you once more."

Edward's face grew as enraged as Griffin's. "How dare you question your anointed monarch!" he shouted.

Griffin and Edward continued to shout and berate Wilfred and all of the Jews in England. They heaped blame upon them for every ill from the homeless outlaws that ranged throughout the country to the terrible winter and poor harvests, to the diseases that had felled many during the bad weather.

Wilfred kept his mouth shut. He could say nothing more without further complicating the situation.

"Will you renounce your Jewish connections and seek penance from the Church?" Edward finally asked.

"No. I have chosen to worship God according to the old and original ways of the Bible."

"Blasphemy!" Griffin declared.

"Then you give us no choice," Edward said proudly. "Every Jew in England, including you, Wilfred of Kirkenwood, has until the first of November to convert to Christianity or face exile from this land."

Wilfred gulped. Never to see England again? He had given everything he was, everything he valued, to become a Jew so that he could marry Miriam. Was she worth it?

A new peace settled on his shoulders. He had gained more than he had given up. More than Miriam. More than faith.

He had gained his rightful place in history and among the community of the Chosen.

"Please reconsider, Your Highness," Wilfred said quietly. "The Jews offer more to England than just loans of money to you and your nobles."

"Our mind is made up. The official pronouncement will follow you to Oxford within the week. You are dismissed."

"Think carefully on this, Your Highness."

"Get out of our sight! Get out of our kingdom!"

"If you do this, Edward Plantagenet, then you are not

worthy to be king." Wilfred's body began to shake as the words spilled out of him. He could not control the pronouncement if he wanted to.

"You deprive England of one of its most valuable resources. You deprive England of doctors and scholars and goldsmiths as well as moneylenders. You deprive England of honor. You are pledged to protect the Jews. Now you break faith with your coronation oaths and the Magna Carta signed by your grandfather John and reaffirmed by your father Henry III."

He had to stop speaking before Edward arrested him for treason. He had to stop.

The words kept rolling out of his mouth with the authority of all of his ancestors combined. All of his ancestors going back to King Arthur and to his Merlin. They spoke through him. They needed his voice and his mind to show England the vision and prophecy of their kind.

"If you do this, Edward Plantagenet, then never again will England have a king worthy of the name Arthur. England will forget and take a long time relearning that law, justice, and peace work; that honor, truth, and promises kept mean something. England will suffer for this heinous act. Your enemies will gain."

"So be it," Griffin echoed, also with the weight of prophecy in his voice. "Never again will the likes of King Arthur rule this land. Never again will a king of England carry that beloved name." He bowed his head sadly.

Wilfred left England along with his bride Miriam, his new brother-in-law Simon, and the rest of the family within days of the Royal Decree. They did, indeed, celebrate the next Passover in Jerusalem.

Never again in over seven hundred years has England had a king named Arthur.

GHOST MISSION

by L. E. Modesitt, Jr.

L. E. Modesitt, Jr., is the author of more than forty novels as well as many short stories and technical and economic articles. His novels have been translated into German, Polish, Dutch, Czech, Russian, Bulgarian, French, and Italian. He has been a lifeguard; a radio disc jockey; a U.S. Navy pilot; a market research analyst; a real estate agent; director of research for a political campaign; legislative assistant and staff director for U.S. congressmen; director of legislation and congressional relations for the U.S. Environmental Protection Agency; a consultant on environmental, regulatory, and communications issues; and a college lecturer. In 1989, to escape nearly twenty years of occupational captivity in Washington, D.C., he moved to New Hampshire where he married a lyric soprano. He and his wife moved to Cedar City, Utah, in 1993, where she directs a college opera program and he continues to create and manage chaos.

AFTER SUNSET ON WEDNESDAY, I found myself standing outside the Sherratt Inn, one hand on the small pack attached to my belt and concealed by the dark gray windbreaker. I took a deep breath, lifting my hand carefully away from the pack. I didn't want to touch it again any sooner than I had to.

The air was cold and still, the acridness of burning coal confined by a winter inversion, but even that smelled wonderful. I'd enjoy it while I could, for all would change, change utterly. I gathered myself together, pushing away the burning that ran along all my nerves and the thought of how little time I had, and stretched my legs, turning toward the Relief Society House. Four blocks later, I could see it, an imposing structure on the south side of the park, almost directly across from the tabernacle. Covering the rededication was the assignment for Thursday, not that it mattered to me, except for the conditioning. Tonight was what counted.

The sky to the west glowed faint orange from the last rays of the sun striking the particulates emitted from the ironworks. The massive power plant in the flats to the north of the ironworks didn't emit anything. In a convoluted but direct sense, that special high-tech power plant, surrounded by more security than the Saint air base farther to the northwest, was why I was in Iron Mission.

When I reached the rear of the Relief Society House, I waited in the shadows on the far side of the back gate, my breath steaming in the chill and still winter air. The dark gray windbreaker and gray slacks let me blend into the indistinctness of late twilight. By moving my head just slightly, I could see the door to the Relief Society kitchen. Before long, the scullery maids would be bringing out the refuse from the evening meal served to the disfavored wives—that was the semi-official term for unpropertied wives who had either lost their beauty or been unable to provide sons and who had been discarded.

The first scullery girl was short and squat. Her eyes darted from side to side. She wasn't the one. I eased farther back into the shadows. After she dumped her load from her basket into the squarish brown Dumpster, she walked hurriedly back along the stone walk to the rear door of the Relief Society Kitchen. There was silence for a long time then, and in the stillness I was far more aware of the nerve-burning sensation, psychosomatic as it was, that nagged at me.

I didn't like the thought of having to enter the servants' quarters to find the scullery girl I needed, but I could . . . and would, if I had to. Intelligence had confirmed she was there, but zombies had no legal rights in

Deseret—not that they had many in the Republic—and the Spazi wasn't about to waste assets to recover an operative with blown cover and a memory they believed worthless—if not lost entirely. The Federal Security Agency believed otherwise, but the FSA had no official jurisdiction outside Columbia.

Finally, the door opened again. But it closed, and no one came out.

I kept waiting. A good fifteen minutes passed before the kitchen door swung wide, and light cascaded on the stone walk. A tall and slender figure carrying a large basket stepped out onto the walk. The door closed. The scullery girl's steps carried her toward the refuse Dumpster. They were the mechanical steps of a zombie. She was the target, and I eased around the brick pillar of the gate.

She lifted the basket and dumped the contents into the open Dumpster.

"Charity?" I said softly, looking up to meet her eyes.

"Yes, sir?" Her voice was flat, or almost so. In the deepening darkness, standing behind the twilight-darkened red stone of the Relief Society House, her brown cap, dark gray ankle-length frock, and grayer jacket made her seem almost invisible.

I couldn't see the color of her eyes, and it was probably better that way.

"I've come to take you to the General Authority, Charity. You're to come with me."

"Sister Barrow told me to come right back."

"You must always obey a brother over a sister. Come with me."

She didn't argue. No female, zombie or otherwise, would have dared to contest a man in Deseret, even one much shorter. Besides, we were headed to one of the General Authorities. Zombies do know when you're telling the truth. That, too, is a terrible beauty.

We walked over to Third South and took it west along the south side of the university—Joseph Smith University—and then up the curving road onto Leigh Hill, wide enough for an ox to turn with a wagon in tow, as were all the main streets in Deseret, although the oxen had long since been replaced by steamers and steam-lorries.

It was close to pitch-dark when we reached the high stone wall on the south side of the estate—and the maintenance gate that was our immediate destination. It took me a good three minutes to open the lock, even with the picks and my training. I gave the hinges liberal doses of the special lubricant before I opened the gate and stepped through the stone archway. It did not squeak. After closing the gate, but not locking it, I led Charity a good ten yards along the gravel path before turning uphill. We stopped in the darkness.

"Stay here. Say nothing." I kept the words to Charity simple and low.

She stood, mute, beside the pinon pine and just forward of the wall between the upper and lower gardens. Her gray garments blended against the dressed stones of the wall.

As I eased along the wall, I knew I wouldn't have much time—just the one night. My borrowed body wouldn't take more, especially if I had to call up full hysterical boost—what once had been thought to be a property just of berserkers—and even a zombie's absence would be noted before long. My palms were damp inside the black leather gloves.

After another twenty yards, I could see the target—a ghost who stood alone in the shadow of a juniper just a few yards downhill and east of the wall. On both sides of that darkness the reflected light of the full moon flooded down. I wouldn't even have noticed the ghost if I hadn't been specifically looking for her. I remained in the shadow of the wall, moving across the frozen grass, knowing that I had left footprints. From what I could tell, no one else had walked the lower garden recently, not since it had frosted, but the prints would either melt with the next day's sun or be covered by the next snowfall.

Absolem had said there was a ghost in the older section of the garden, and one not seen before six months previous. That late June had been when Verial had vanished, not that I'd known it then, leaving but a zombie behind, found sitting on a bench in the Bishop's Park of Iron Mission. That was the official report filed with the

Iron Mission police. Where there was a zombie, there should have been a ghost, but one was never reported.

Everyone in the FSA was hoping that the ghost in the garden was the one I sought. But why had the Saints zombied Verial in the lower garden—if indeed the ghost was Verial? It didn't make sense, unless they thought her ghost would fade into oblivion before being discovered and that no outsider would see her there.

I kept moving, slowly, deliberately, until I finally stood in the patch of shadow closest to that where the ghost hovered, concealed from the mansion uphill and to the west by the upper garden, and by the wall in whose moonlight-created shade I stood. She'd been young when she died. Had she been beautiful? Verial had been, especially to me, but with ghosts, it's hard to tell, because so much of beauty is vitality, and most of that vanishes when the body dies—or when spirit and body are separated.

What was I doing? Certainly, I was trespassing by sneaking around the walled hillside gardens of Heber Cannon, but trespassing would be the least of my sins were I to be discovered on the private grounds of one of the General Authorities of Deseret. My alter ego's cover as a journalist for Republic Press International might be jeopardized, not to mention both our lives, such as mine was. Building that journalistic cover had been difficult enough, especially with the assignments in occupied France. Deseret was nominally neutral, but few foreign reporters were allowed into Deseret, and only those deemed either harmless or helpful in some way.

My alter ego had come the first time to cover the second Salt Palace Concert of Llysette duBois and Daniel Perkins. With her kidnapping and her husband's heroics, no one had ever remembered the small and slightly lisping reporter from West Kansas. So when she'd been asked to sing for the rededication of the renovated Iron Mission Tabernacle before her final Deseret concert in St. George, his visa to cover her tour was accepted without objection.

I eased closer to the ghost, careful to remain in the shadows. My breath steamed, appearing almost more solid than the figure of the ghost. She did not breathe, although her chest seemed to rise and fall under the filmy and bare-shouldered gown that was so unlike anything a woman of Deseret would have worn. I frowned. Was this the right ghost? Verial had been a mistress of disguise, and never would have worn something so inappropriate. At least, not without a good reason.

"Verial?" I whispered.

The reply was much as I had expected, typical of a ghost who'd been surprised and fully aware when killed—or one who'd been zombied.

She turned to me and cocked her head—that was one of the mannerisms in the file, although I'd known it far earlier. Then she spoke, if a faint whisper in one's thoughts could be considered a voice.

First dew that gives the grass its sheen,
then for the frost that coats the green . . .

Had I heard a door creak? Steps on stone? Much as I disliked it, because it shortened the time I had, I concentrated, bringing up full sensory intensity. I had to hold onto myself to keep from staggering. Every nerve tingled with edged flame, and the steps on the stone walk in the upper garden sounded like distant thunder. No one else would have heard them at all.

"Who was the prince who loved you?" I asked, quietly, pressing the question toward the ghost.

The hint of a smile crossed her face before I heard the words in my own thoughts.

My prince had proffered love in words so meet
that seraph birds alone could sing that sweet . . .

That didn't tell me enough. It hinted that the ghost was Verial, because Prince Mykail had fallen for her—before the Cheka had warned him off, if after she had gotten what she had been tasked to obtain. I don't know that she had fallen for him. She'd always kept her feelings to herself. Good agents do. That was why I'd never been a good agent. Now, there was no one other than me available to recover Verial, if it could be done at all.

The FSA only had a handful of agents, and that was a handful more than the Security Act allowed. No one else had been available, not without jeopardizing other priorities. And it didn't hurt that I cared about her. I always had, and that had been my undoing. FSA had nothing to lose. I had everything to lose, one way or another, and little enough to gain—except a final measure of self-respect.

The psych-scientists had said I should try indirect prompts first, but I was running out of time, and I couldn't ignore the two men descending through the upper garden to the gate in the wall to the lower garden.

"Why did you leave physics for the Spazi?" I asked hurriedly.

As humans, rules of law we'll change,
as time and fate shift what we know,
but nature's laws, fixed fermions,
endure unchanged, forever so.

The rhyme made sense, and would have made more sense had I been able to identify the poet—or poetess. Only a handful of ghosts could communicate, and always by rhymed words, usually of a favorite poet. Still, the use of the term fermion was a favorable indication that the ghost I was dealing with was Verial. She had been a brilliant grad student in the physics of materials engineering when she'd been recruited.

The gate from the upper garden creaked as it opened.

"What is the formulaic basis of fossil-fueled MHD?" The question was nonsensical, but the terms weren't and were calculated to get a response.

The enigmatic smile of the ghost vanished. She almost did as well, wavering for a moment in the deep shadows. Then, her intensity redoubled, her features clearer. In one hand was the shawl that had surely covered her shoulders before it had been ripped away, most certainly after she had been zombied.

I was certain now that she was Verial, but I had so little time, in more ways than one.

Two figures—they had to be men—walked unhurriedly through the stone archway to the lower garden.

I eased back along the stone wall as quickly as I could. With each step, the crackling of the frozen grass threatened to engulf me, and with each step, the knives of sound pierced my eardrums. I kept moving, then froze. Three Saint security types waited outside the gate. Not Danites, not police, but security, in the black and brown they wore when they wanted to be noticed.

The footsteps from higher in the garden were louder, thunder drawing ever closer to the ghost by the juniper—and me.

"This way . . ." I whispered to Charity. "Follow me."

She did not move. I took her hand and led her back toward the juniper and the ghost, staying in the shadows.

"Take two steps forward and wait until I speak again." I couldn't tell her to stand behind the ghost, although that was where I wanted her, because zombies cannot perceive ghosts.

Charity took the two steps, standing immobile just behind the ghost.

In turn, the ghost that I hoped was, and wanted to be, Verial glowed brighter.

The two men slowed as they neared the juniper. Verial's sudden brightness almost obscured the zombie, as I had planned.

"She is still there. Nothing has happened." Those words came from the younger and taller man.

"Footsteps," said the older and broader figure. "There in the frost on the grass." His deep voice boomed in my ears, even though I was crouched against the wall, at an angle where the juniper mostly obscured their view of me—hardly enough if they actually were looking.

"More like a child's."

"Or a woman's. I told you there would be an agent using duBois as cover."

"Her husband is with her. He has been the whole time."

"This time, he is a decoy. They want us to watch him."

"Your ghost was still here, Father. She was beautiful."

"She was nothing of the sort. She was brilliant, and slightly attractive. More important, she was a typical Columbian woman—hard and calculating—a perfect spy beneath that persona. She almost got away with it, too . . . because of my own son. She was not *my* ghost. She only wanted you to think that." The snort that followed was deep and rumbled in my ears. Verial had never been anyone's, and Heber was right. She had been hard and calculating. I'd known that. It didn't change anything.

"She was just using me to get to you, Father. I told you that. That was why she was here . . ."

"And you let her?"

"How was I—"

"Enough, Jared . . . Enough. The trap is set. Before long, we'll know."

Heber Cannon was right. The trap was set. In fact, several traps were set . . . and a net. Could I avoid theirs and spring mine?

I eased the projector from inside the windbreaker, easing open the wide film antenna. I made sure the projector was not pointed anywhere near me or toward any energy-reflective surface—and that I was shielded behind the antenna that was both transmitter and collector.

The ghost spoke to them, not to me.

What you did in faithless need,
in time, no one will heed . . .

The irony of those words almost paralyzed me, because they could have applied to Verial when she'd left me to the Cheka.

"Silence, hussy." Heber's words rattled my skull.

I stepped to the side and aimed the projector toward the ghost and Charity. I wasn't sure I wanted it to work, but the conditioning held, and I pressed the activating stud. Energy flared from the projector, returned, and was reprojected, far too fast for anyone to see.

The ghost vanished. Charity's face went from immobile to angry in that microsecond before she moved—not toward Heber, but toward Jared.

I knew the moves she used. Jared didn't. His throat was crushed, and his nose broken in less than a second. He grasped at his throat, flailing.

I had already dropped the projector and was moving

far faster than any man should, especially one so small and slight.

Heber Cannon gaped for a second, then reached for the sidearm he always carried. "You killed him." He looked as though he were about to yell for the security types. Yet he hesitated, still arrogant, his eyes looking at a woman and a man not much larger than a prepubescent boy.

Knowing about the sidearm, I was already moving. My knife was quicker than he was. That was to be expected from an agent under conditioned hysterical boost. For a moment, he looked down, stupidly, at the blood welling out over his waistcoat and overcoat, his mouth moving silently, with only gurgling sounds, unsurprisingly, since I'd slit his throat first, deeply.

"You had a choice, Heber," I said quietly, not that he'd be likely to hold the thought before he died. "You chose to protect a corrupt and evil son." Was I any better? Probably not, but that wasn't the question. It never had been.

I could sense the life leaking out of both of them. Where there had been one ghost by the juniper, now there would be two, both different from the first. The conflict had been quick, and almost silent—quiet enough that the Saint security men still stood by the lower south gate, waiting for a signal from Heber Cannon.

"Jared brought me down here," murmured Verial. "He said he wanted a picture of me in the garden. One that could be made into a portrait. I should have known better."

"Heber was probably watching." I bent and scooped up the projector before rummaging through Heber's waistcoat and jacket pockets. In a moment, I came up with a set of keys.

"Now what?" asked Verial in the lowest of voices, knowing that I would hear.

"We walk up the way they came and out the west gate. Then we'll walk to the safe house. In this case, it's the Republic consulate. The Saints may know that, but they won't violate it for a youth and a woman."

"You have a key to the gate?"

"Heber's keys here will do." I held them up. "We

should go." The keys would be faster than picking the lock—if they were the right ones.

I followed the footprints in the grass back through the gardens until I could see the north gate to the upper garden. Then I took the graveled path to the gate. The third key I tried fit the lock to the outer gate, the one on First South. I locked the gate behind us, then tossed the keys back over the gate.

We walked in the shadow of the wall until we reached Ridge Lane, where we turned south until we got to Third South.

"Do I know you? You seem familiar," she finally said.

I didn't want to answer that question. Not in the slightest. "Do you have the plans? Can you recall what you learned?" I hated to ask, but I wanted to know if what I faced would be for something.

"What are you talking about?"

"You're Verial. The code is absolem green, and the plans are for the proprietary and secret technology to the magnetohydrodynamic power plant here. I wouldn't know one end of an engineering spec from the other, but once the Spazi wrote you off, FSA decided on an experimental effort to reclaim you. Call it a terrible beauty being born." That could have referred to the way I had been used or Verial had been reclaimed—or the theft of the power plant technology.

"I should be grateful?"

I recalled that tone of voice all too well.

"No. You never were. You don't have to tell me. I have no need to know. I just was the tool able to get you back. I wondered if it was worth the cost."

"Don't speak of costs."

"I won't." I kept walking along the shaded side of Third South.

"They'll be glad you succeeded. That's all I'll say."

That was about what I'd expected.

"You never answered my question about whether I should know you."

"I couldn't say, not in a way that would make sense in the present tense."

"Don't mouth rhymes at me. I recall enough that I'd prefer not to hear another line of verse."

I ignored her request and quoted Yeats, in my own fashion.

Being high and solitary and most stern,
Why, what could you have done, being what you are?
Was there another Troy for you to burn?

"Alexander? You're not Alexander."

Again, I misquoted.

"You could have warned me, but I was young,
And we spoke a different tongue."

"You knew the risks. Still . . . how—?"

"Birth-hour and death-hour meet . . .
"I dance on other's deathless feet . . ."

She was silent. What else could she have said?

We walked eastward in the darkness, down Leigh Hill and along Third South, still on the dark side. Behind us, sirens rose. The security types had found bodies, and perhaps ghosts. They would find little else, besides the footprints that looked to be those of a woman and a boy and Heber Cannon's keys beside a gate.

Neither of us said another word until we approached the heavy wrought-iron gates of the small estate on the east side of Iron Mission, set on the north side of Coal Creek. I could see the Republic Marines manning the gatehouse. They were expecting us.

"You wrote and memorized your own poetry, didn't you?" I asked.

"Yes."

"Because you thought they would find you out?"

"No. It was the logical thing to do, whatever might happen. Sommersby knew from my first assignment."

"She would have." I didn't really want to escort her through the gates. I did anyway, after the Marines opened the gates. They closed them behind us.

When she stood at last in the archway of the front door to the Republic consulate, the two guards flanking her, she turned, and all three looked down at me. I handed her the knife and the now-useless projector. The single-use film antenna had destroyed itself in accomplishing its task. "Dispose of them. You know how and why."

She would, but only to protect herself. As always.

"What happens to you now?" she asked.

I just smiled and shook my head.

I left her there, as once she had left me. She had not changed, and tomorrow the man whose body I held so briefly would cover a rededication concert, sore and bruised, but his nerves would not burn. He would doubtless wonder what had happened in the hours that he had lost—and I would become, at last, what lay beyond ghost and zombie.

I walked toward the darkness of oblivion, out of my own nerve-jangled, gong-tormented sea, toward my freedom from what never could have been. In some ways, I pitied Verial—now. I had repaid her in the only way possible. My fingers moved toward the waistpack under the windbreaker.

COIN OF THE REALM

by Fiona Patton

Fiona Patton lives in rural Ontario, Canada, with her partner, a fierce farm Chihuahua, and inumerable cats. She has four novels out with DAW Books: *The Stone Prince, The Painter Knight, The Granite Shield,* and *The Golden Sword*. Her fifth book, entitled *The Silver Lake,* is available from DAW in a hardcover edition. She has twenty-odd short stories published in various DAW/Tekno anthologies including *Sirius: The Dog Star, Assassin Fantastic,* and *Apprentice Fantastic*.

THE CITY OF CERCHICAVA had a festive air in late autumn. The cool air sweeping down from the northern mountains had banished the noxious odors that plagued its markets during the summer months and the rains had rinsed the wide, tree-lined avenues of the wealthy Carmina and Ambrogio districts until they shone. Even the ancient Piero Devanza Necropolis, built at the very heart of the city, sparkled as the sun reflected off the many marble crypts, headstones, and statuary markers that crowded around the huge ducal mausoleum at its center.

In the northeastern merchant section, Coll Svedali crouched behind the toppled gravestone of a prosperous vintner's family, peering down at a pathetically small bundle lying in a shallow trench between the grave and the line of shrubbery that masked the cemetery's outer wall. Wrapped in rough cloth and tied with a length of twine, it was probably the body of a child, laid to rest by a father or a brother who could not afford the exorbitant internment and purification rites the Church demanded of even its poorest citizens. In such a quiet, out-of-the-way place, it might never have been found at all, but last night's rain had undermined the stone the family, come to restore the dignity of their deceased relatives, had discovered the body. Burial ground in the Devanza was at a premium and those who could afford it guarded it jealously. They'd immediately summoned the Watch.

Off to one side, Corporal Uberti of the Lambruschini District Watch coughed nervously. Coll ignored him. Once in the pay of the Cerchicava Death Mages, now their most notorious betrayer, Coll could sense whether the highly lucrative and illegal Necromantic Trade had been involved. If it had, then the entire gravesite would have to be repurified and, notoriously *frugal*, the vintner's family had insisted that Coll be brought in—the five soldi he charged was significantly less than the thirty the Church would demand.

Not surprisingly, the Church took a dim view of Coll's activities and not just because he cost them the price of a purification. Those in the Trade were damned, and those who aided or supported them were tainted by heresy. The Church had even gone so far as to petition Cerchicava's duc to rescind the pardon that had kept Coll from the gallows, but Coll had saved the duc's son from the Death Mages and so Coll was sacrosanct. But if a priest happened on the scene, Corporal Uberti would be considered equally guilty of heresy, and he was not so protected. However, Corporal Uberti would never be in this position—he was guaranteed a legitimate grave in the Devanza's military section—so Coll refused to be rushed, turning his attention to the ground around the body instead.

The makeshift grave had been dug within the last two days; the cloth shroud was still in good condition and although yesterday's rain had begun to flatten the clods of disturbed earth around it, there were no indentations or footprints to suggest it had been dug while it was storming. The wall behind was rough and pitted and faced an area generally deserted at night. It would have been easy to scale unseen, even burdened with a corpse and whatever tool had been used to dig the grave.

The corporal coughed again, more loudly this time, and finally Coll turned to the body. Pulling his knife, he carefully cut the twine and open the makeshift shroud.

As he'd suspected, it was that of a child: a ten-to-twelve-year-old girl dressed in a faded, threadbare tunic, with long, brown hair falling across her thin shoulders. Even in death, her features were gaunt and pinched, and her limbs, although carefully arranged, carried the marks of the poverty and malnutrition she'd suffered in life. A single clay bead threaded onto a piece of hemp around her neck was her only adornment—possibly the only one her family'd even owned. There were no burial herbs or smell of preserving or magical oils, and no obvious signs of foul play.

Holding one hand above her forehead, Coll laid the other against an old scar on his abdomen, a wound taken in the fight against the city's premier Death Mage, and waited for the characteristic tingle that would tell him if a necromantic spell had been used against the child.

There was nothing.

He glanced up.

"She's untainted."

The corporal nodded, visibly relieved. "I'll tell the vintners and Lenzi can come and collect the corpse."

Coll nodded resignedly. Nando Lenzi was the undertaker for Debassio's Heretics Cemetery. Although untainted, the unknown child still had no one to pay for the rites needed to bury her, so she would have to lie in an unprotected grave outside the city walls. It was the way it was for Cerchicava's poor as well as for its heretics and criminals. He couldn't change that any more than she could have.

Carefully rearranging her limbs, Coll made to refit the shroud, then started as a glint of silver suddenly flashed in the sunlight. Reaching down, he pulled a small coin from her hand, then held it up so that the corporal might see the two-headed eagle of Riamo, a small city-state to the west, on its face.

The two men stared at each other for a long moment,

each wondering if they could pretend they hadn't seen the foreign coin that had just elevated the girl's clandestine burial from a crime of trespass to one of politics, before the corporal shook his head in weary resignation.

"The captain won't want her carried through Lambruschini," he said. "She'll have to go San Benedito's. I'll make the report. You examine the body any way you . . ." He glanced away. ". . . have to, and find out who put her there."

"And the coin?"

The corporal backed up a step as if Coll had suggested he rob a church. "You keep it for now," he said hastily. "If the captain wants it, he'll send for it. If not . . ." His expression softened into a sadness that was uncharacteristic in the City Watch. "You might use it to bury her properly."

Coll nodded. "Good enough."

The church of San Benedito in Bergo—the city's poorest housing district—doubled as a morgue when necessary. Laid out on the large table in the nave, her body speckled with the shadows cast by a single work lamp, the dead girl looked even more pathetic than she had in the Devanza. After a preliminary examination that told him nothing new, Coll straightened with a grimace as the young woman working beside him shook her head.

Eighteen-year-old Maria Gervasio had been fighting the necromantic trade almost as long as twenty-one-year-old Coll. Both of them had seen enough death in their short lives to become familiar with its ways, but neither one of them had seen anything quite this puzzling.

"A *silver* coin?" she said wonderingly.

"From Riamo."

"Enough to have her properly interned at San Salvi's. Why would it be buried *with* the body instead of used to bury it?"

"Foreign coins are tightly controlled," Coll hazarded. "Her people would have to explain where it came from to the Church or to the undertaker."

"Do you think it was stolen?"

"Maybe. But a lifter would just go to a changer for a Cerchicavan coin. So would a beggar." He frowned. "For that matter, so would anyone."

"Could it be part of some spellcraft?"

"None that *I* know of." He drummed his fingers against the table in growing agitation. The last time he'd seen a Riamo coin it had been given to him by an assassin named Drey. Dubbed the Huntsman, he'd stalked and murdered three of Cerchicava's nobility over a year ago. If Drey had returned, it was going to take more than a physical examination of a child's corpse to find him. He straightened. "We have to get her to Mona's."

Mona Masaccio was a Death Mage, or had been until age, encroaching infirmary, and Coll had convinced her to return to the skills of her youth when she'd served a medical apprenticeship. Now she aided Coll and Maria in their fight against the Trade, teaching them all she could in exchange for their protection and care in her final years and, although she often grumbled that they'd invaded her warehouse home like a pair of sanctimonious priests, if truth be told, she enjoyed the thought of cheating the Church out of her own damnation. And Coll's.

Bending over the body laid out in the cellar that had once been used for the darkest of necromantic magics, her eyes flashed blue rather than the usual red of a death spell and she grunted in satisfaction.

"You never really lose it," she muttered to herself. "Consumption," she declared over her shoulder. "And, from the state of the body, I'd say two days ago. I could tell for certain if . . ." Her eyes strayed to the line of vials and jars on the shelf behind her, but at Coll's frown, she sniffed disdainfully. "Fine, be delicate." She picked up a scalpel. "There's an unusual heaviness in the belly region. Do you mind if I discover why in the *primitive* way or do you object to *cutting* into corpses now as well?"

Ignoring the pointed reminder of his days as an actual corpse-cutter in the Trade, Coll just waved his hand at her to continue.

A few minutes later she straightened. "She had a meal just before she died," she said with a frown. "And a fine one, too. Finer than she should have been able to afford. Meat, actual lamb, and fresh vegetables with bread and wine to wash it down with. She couldn't have gotten that on her own. No child of her class could have walked alone into a place that serves a meal like that. She was taken in and fed, either to a private home or to an inn."

"But why?" Maria asked.

Mona shrugged. "Sexual favors?"

The younger woman gave a cynical snort. "You don't feed someone for sex, favored or not, you just pay them to duck behind a wall with you."

"You don't feed a servant that well either," the older woman retorted. "Not without dressing her better along with it."

"It doesn't matter why she was fed," Coll interrupted. "It matters why she was buried in an illegal grave with money enough to have her buried legally."

With a haughty glare in his direction, Mona hobbled over to her chair, heaving a deep sigh as she lowered herself down. "Obviously, the person who buried her either didn't have time to change his money for local coin, or didn't want to be identified by the local authorities," she snapped, reaching for the jug of wine beside her chair.

"So why bury her with money at all?" Maria insisted.

Mona gave a cynical snort. "*That* smacks of a sentimental streak." She turned to Coll. "Does this Drey you mentioned fit the bill there?"

Coll glanced over at the child's body, noting both her age and obvious poverty. "Drey and I spent our first six years in the Svedali Innocenti Foundling Home before the authorities destroyed it to expand the Devanza," he answered. "We were the only two to make it on the streets, so yes, I'd say he fit the bill." His expression hardened. "But if he's here, it isn't to feed beggar children, it's to kill someone. Someone important."

"Do we care?" Mona demanded.

"That depends on who it is."

"You mean it depends on if it's your precious duc."

"Yes."

"So, how do we find out if it even is Drey?" Maria interrupted.

Coll held up the Riamo coin. "I have an idea," he said.

Four months ago, Coll had nearly died when he'd ingested an infusion formed by a new combination of prophetic magics and necromantic components. It had interacted with the residual spellcraft in his abdominal injury, changing him in ways even Mona couldn't understand. Together with a retired necromantic scholar pressed into Mona's employ, they'd been mapping out the slowly advancing transformation, testing it in combination with all the traditional spellcrafts, but they were groping in the dark, and Mona was extremely reticent about using any new properties they'd discovered.

Now, she favored him with an egregious frown, but did not interfere as his eyes began to flash an unusual, opalescent white.

Across the city, in the upscale Vinano Tavarnelle Inn on the city's Ardechi River docks, a brown-haired man in the clothes of a foreign merchant raked his cold gaze about the taproom, his pale gray eyes suddenly suspicious.

Someone was looking for him.

Laying a hand against his chest where the rich embroidery of his tunic hid a very special magical component, he frowned as it tingled against his fingertips.

Someone . . . familiar.

Ordering another glass of wine, he leaned back with a thoughtful expression. Known as Domito Preto to the Cerchicavan agents and shippers he dealt with, Drey Orcicci had been back to the city of his birth a dozen times on legitimate business. On any one of those occasions someone seeking him magically would not raise his suspicions. This, however, was not one of those times.

Turning the empty glass between finger and thumb, he frowned deeply. His current mission was time sensitive and the death of the girl he'd hired to keep an eye on the city's foreign docks for him had already put him behind schedule. Her burial in the Devanza had been a sentimental indulgence he should never have allowed himself. However, it was done and at least she'd managed to pass on the information he'd needed before she'd died in his arms.

The server, come to refill his glass, interrupted his reverie, and Drey brought his mind back to the problem at hand. The touch he was feeling was too intimate to be a business acquaintance, priest, or member of the Watch. There was only one man left alive in Cerchicava who knew him that well, and that he should be looking for him now was suspect.

Holding up his glass so that the dark-red wine gleamed like fresh blood in the candlelight, Drey mouthed a single word.

"Coll."

In Mona's cellar, Coll's eyes returned to their natural color.

"I have to see the duc."

"The Huntsman's returned."

The duc Giovanni de Marco had been waging an unrelenting and very bloody war against the Trade ever since its most powerful Death Mage had launched an attack against his nine-year-old son, Lorenzo. Coll had been instrumental in that war from the beginning and, as such, had unrestricted access to the duc, day or night. Now, as he outlined the events of the last few days, the duc's expression grew increasingly grave. When he finished, de Marco turned to stare out the tall, leaded-glass windows of his audience chamber, watching silently as the sun set over the darkening gardens beyond.

"The Trade is the single greatest threat to the people of Cerchicava," he said after a time. "For two years my soldiers and my priests have arrested, tried, and executed hundreds of Death Mages and their minions, and yet I'm told that the necromancers still hold this city in a grip of fear. Is this true?"

Coll considered the question seriously, then gave a cautious half nod. "Not so much as before, My Lord, but, yes."

"Why?"

"People are still hungry?"

"My Captain of the Holy Scourge tells me that it's because foreign mages have moved in to the ensuing void, acting through local intermediaries."

When it looked like he was expecting an answer, Coll shrugged diplomatically. "I don't know about such things, My Lord. I only know what I hear on the streets and that's from people opposed to the Trade, not working for it."

The duc caught him in a penetrating stare, but when Coll met his eyes steadily, he nodded as if coming to a decision.

"In two days' time five of the most powerful of Cerchicava's trading partners on the Ardechi River will meet in this very room to hammer out the final details of an allied offensive against the Necromantic Trade. Three have already arrived, two are due tomorrow. I don't need to tell you how important this meeting will be or how secret it must remain. You know the Huntsman and his methods. You have until the ship *Fortunata* out of Pisario docks tomorrow afternoon to find him."

"He showed up at the Pallazzo de Marco just like you said. The guard took him right in an' he stayed till the big bell rang five, then he left."

Drey's new informant, a ragged boy of eight or nine, held out his hand for payment, but Drey just eyed him coldly.

"He went into Bergo," the boy continued resentfully. "To a warehouse on Via del Masaccio. There was wards on the cellar door. Real *nasty* wards."

Drey handed over a single copper coin. "Who owns the warehouse?"

The boy shrugged. "I dunno Bergo so good, not like I know here. But I know someone who does," he added with a sly smile. "He could tell you all about him if I brought him to you."

Drey handed over another small coin. "Get him."

As the boy darted off, the Huntsman glanced over at the foreign docks, noting the half-dozen merchant ships from Riamo and Montecino. There was still time, he noted; the *Fortunata* was not due until tomorrow. Leaning against a wooden pier, he pulled a clay pipe from his pocket as he waited for the boy's return.

In Mona's cellar, Coll set the Riamo coin in the center of the work table beside a bowl containing a handful of both medical and magery components.

The old woman glanced up from her chair with a frown. "You shouldn't use that magic twice in one day," she admonished. "It's too experimental. You don't know what it could do to you."

"It's effective," Coll replied.

"So are plenty of other spells."

"You mean necromantic spells."

"You think that doesn't have a necromantic element?"

"I know it does, but it doesn't matter. I'm the only one it damns."

"It damns me if you melt your brain into a pool of useless soup before I can be properly interned myself."

"You'll still have Maria. Besides," he added before she could reply. "We have less than a day to find Drey and stop him. We haven't got the time to gather necromantic components even if I was willing to use them. Which I'm not."

"The wound and infusion transformation is tied to death," she continued stubbornly. "The identify spell worked because the coin was found in contact with a corpse. You have no idea whether a spell as complex as the location of a living person will work at all."

Coll glanced over at her, the brown of his eyes already turning a misty white. "The Huntsman deals out death for a living," he said quietly. "It'll work."

At Vinano Tavarnelle, Drey watched a middle-aged man make his surreptitious way across the crowded taproom. Balding, overweight, and nondescript, few would have guessed that in his prime Roberto Ricasoli had been one of the most talented research scholars in the Trade. Pushing his unfinished supper to one side, Drey considered this new development while he waited for the man to approach him.

The boy's contact had plenty to relate about Coll and his new associates on Via del Masaccio. And for an extra pair of coins he'd given him the names and addresses of every person they'd been in contact with over the last year.

Drey shook his head in silent wonder. "You need to exercise more caution, my old friend," he whispered as the now-familiar magical trace feathered across his personal wards. "Or you're going to end up on some necromancer's table. Maybe sooner than you think."

The first name on the list had turned out to be one of Drey's own contacts, Roberto Ricasoli.

He'd sent the boys to fetch him at once, then returned to Vinano Tavarnelle to order supper and plan his next move. If handled correctly, this could put him back on schedule and deal with Coll and whatever ducal interference his fellow foundling had elicited. As Ricasoli sidled up to his table, Drey gestured tersely at the bench across from him and, once the other man was seated, cast his cold gaze across his features. Ricasoli was nervous, sweating, and refused to meet his eyes. As the amulet around his neck gave the faintest of tingles informing him of what he already knew, Drey cocked his head to one side.

"You've been *busy* since our last meeting," he said, noting the other man's guilty start as he emphasized the word.

"N . . . no, not so much," Ricasoli stammered.

Drey's eyes flashed with just a hint of red, and the older man stiffened.

"It's nothing," he hastened. "Nothing that should interfere with our business relationship, that is."

"It's a binding spell," Drey answered in a voice just loud enough to cause the other man to pale and glance about nervously. "And that's very definitely going to effect our *business* relationship. But I was given to understand that there wasn't anyone that powerful still operating in Cerchicava."

"I cannot . . . please . . ." The veins in the older man's neck began to throb dangerously as he struggled to speak around the spell's silence compulsion, and Drey gave a dismissive flick with one hand.

"Calm yourself, old man," he said in disgust. "I'm not here to chase after the competition. If and when I am, that's when you'll have reason to be afraid." He leaned forward, fixing the older man with his pale gaze. "There are ways to break a binding spell, as you well know, but for now you can just warn whoever set it in place not to get in my way."

Ricasoli slumped, visibly relieved, and Drey sat back.

"In the meantime," he continued in a more conversational tone, "I find myself in need of your services. First: I need a week's access to a small mansion on Via Caparo in Ambrogio. The Pallazzo de Maggiore. I'm given to understand the family's in Montecino for the year and the mansion's empty."

The other man nodded eagerly, happy to change the subject. "That can be arranged with no difficulty, of course."

"Next: I require fresh components for a targeting-and-ward-breaking spell to be tied to a physical object. I trust the duc's people haven't arrested every corpse-cutter in the city?"

Ricasoli nearly swooned as he spoke the last word. "Please," he said anxiously. "There are far too many people about."

"Regardless, I need those components by midnight."

"But I don't know if I can manage such an order so quickly," the older man pleaded, swiping at his face with a stained handkerchief. "The duc's men are everywhere, and the Church . . ." he lowered his voice. "The Holy Scourge has spies on every corner. And with so many of our old . . . associates dead . . ."

"Find new *associates*." Drey's eyes glowed dangerously. "There are always people in Cerchicava willing to damn themselves for money. Find someone young and hungry or someone old and desperate, I don't care which. Just have those components delivered by midnight."

The older man nodded in miserable understanding, and Drey shoved a silver Riamo coin across the table with one finger. "That should be enough to get started," he said, then jerked his head in the direction of the door.

Once Ricasoli had scuttled away, Drey returned his

plate to its original position, taking up a piece of bread with a satisfied expression.

"Now, follow the coin, Coll," he whispered. "Follow it all the way to Via Caparo in Ambrogio."

When Coll's eyes cleared again, he turned a dark glance in Mona's direction.

"He was with Ricasoli."

The ex-necromancer's eyes glittered in the lamplight. "Was he now?" she cackled. "Well then, why don't we invite our research scholar over for a nice cup of tea and a little chat? Maria, be a dear and fetch me that vial."

The upper floors of the Pallazzo de Maggiore were shadowy and dark in the hour just before dawn. As Coll entered the large front bedroom overlooking the ducal gardens, he could barely make out the figure crouched by the open window, but as he stepped forward, he heard a faint chuckle.

"I wouldn't come any closer, Coll," the figure warned. "I *am* armed."

"I've no doubt of it." Leaning against the doorjamb, Coll crossed his arms over his chest. "More *Riamo* coins, Drey?" he asked with a intentional sneer. "Sending me another cryptic message about your home base, or did you just get sloppy?"

A faint tracery of crimson mage fire illuminated the walls and Coll saw Drey turn, his crossbow cradled in the crook of one arm.

"Perhaps it was the only coin I had on me," the Huntsman answered conversationally. "I couldn't just leave her lying in the street, now could I? *What* would the priests of the Svedali Innocenti think of me?" He tipped his head to one side. "Did you reinter her?"

Coll nodded. "At the Gervasio Foundling Home's cemetery in Bergo."

"But you didn't use my mysterious coin."

"No; one of my own."

"Then you've come up in the world since we last met. A year ago you couldn't even afford a cheap pair of boots. Is this newfound prosperity because of your duc or your little old Death Mage?"

"Bit of both."

"Glad to hear it. By the way, how'd you leave my old friend, Ricasoli?"

"Alive."

"Did he give you my message?"

"The one about not getting in your way or the one about meeting you at the Pallazzo de Maggiore?"

"Both."

"Yes." Coll stepped forward. "I'm not going to let you harm anyone at the ducal conference, Drey."

The other man lifted the crossbow almost negligently. "Why not?" he asked in a tone that suggested he actually wanted to know the answer. "What do you care about a bunch of soft, overfed potentates from along the Ardechi River?"

"I don't. You could kill all five of them, and I wouldn't shed a tear. As long as you did it outside the walls of Cerchicava. But you're not outside the walls, you're inside them, and I can't trust that your target isn't the duc Giovanni de Marco."

"How're you going to stop me?"

Coll suddenly threw one hand forward. A streak of white light spewed from his fingertips, following the path of a small, green stone, but as they impacted against the other man's wards, Drey pulled the trigger. The quarrel took Coll in the shoulder, throwing him backward and pinning him against the wall.

Drey strode forward, his expression both angry and disappointed.

"You should have known better," he spat as the tracery of white light along his body faded. "A paralyzing spell with a *medical* component. You're either damned or you're not. You're either a Death Mage or you're not. And you can't work necromantic spells if you haven't the stomach to use actual necromantic components."

He made to turn back to the window, then stiffened, his gray eyes widening in shocked surprise, as the white light reformed along his limbs. When they reached his chest and the hidden necromantic amulet, he collapsed.

Very slowly and deliberately, Coll forced himself forward, fighting against both the pain and the spell that pulsed along the quarrel sending waves of fire coursing through his shoulder and down his arm. When he finally pulled himself free, his legs nearly gave out beneath him, but pressing one hand against the entrance wound, fingers wrapped about the shaft, he dragged himself over to Drey.

"No," he panted. "*You* can't work necromantic spells without necromantic components. But *I* can."

He leaned down, his lips almost touching Drey's temple. "I know how to turn a man into a living construct, how to find the last person to handle a corpse just by touching it, and how to combine any spellcraft that I want to." He reached out and ran his fingers along Drey's face, leaving a thick line of blood across his cheek. "And I know, I can *feel*, how to find you, as of right now, just by *thinking* about you." Tucking the original Riamo coin into Drey's fingers, he forced himself to stand. "You're right about one thing, though; the spell's components aren't necromantic so they take a little longer to take effect and they aren't as strong as they might be. This one may wear off before I get back. If it does, go home; to Riamo, Pisario, or wherever home is for you now. Cerchicava and its duc are under *my* protection. Don't make the mistake of assuming that protection is meaningless again."

When he returned with the Ambrogio Watch half an hour later, the room was empty save for a single crossbow quarrel lying by the open window.

"So, he just left, did he?" Mona demanded some hours later after Coll'd finally returned home.

"Seems like," he answered wearily, lowering himself carefully into a chair by the small, wrought-iron stove.

"Just like that, eh? How convenient."

"Do you think it's a feint?" Maria asked, handing Coll a cup of catmint tea before helping him out of his bloodstained jacket and shirt.

Coll raised one hand in a weak shrug. "The ducal conference might not have been his target at all," he allowed. "Or he might have fled when he was discovered. It's hard to say with Drey. He's tricky."

"But not so good a shot as the Huntsman's made out to be," Mona observed dryly as Maria removed the Watch Physician's bandaging with a disapproving scowl. "He's missed your vital organs. Not to mention your head."

Coll smiled painfully. "No, that was deliberate. There was a very advanced targeting spell on the quarrel. It hit the exact spot he was aiming for."

"Why?"

"Again, it's hard to say with Drey. Maybe so the Watch would think he'd left, or maybe because I'm the closest thing to family he has. He does have that sentimental streak, remember?"

"That why you didn't kill him either?"

"Maybe." Coll leaned back as Maria began to bathe the wound with lavender oil, her eyes glowing the deep, jade green of a healing spell.

"At any rate," he continued. "The ducs have come and gone . . . alive. De Marco won. Drey failed. That's good enough for me."

Closed his eyes, he pointedly ignored Mona's skeptical snort.

Far to the west, crouched on the gabled roof of a tannery overlooking the Ardechi docks of Pisario, Drey set a quarrel to his crossbow, watching as, across the river, the city's duc Cosimo Talicozzo, disembarked, chatting amiably with his fellow potentate, Johanni Gagio of Riamo. Old friends and allies, it was expected that Gagio would spend a few days in Pisario before continuing on to his own city, and so Drey had taken a fast ship west, made himself comfortable, and waited.

As he brought his weapon to his shoulder, Gagio's laughter drifted across the water and Drey's gray eyes narrowed in concentration. His master, Riamo's premier Death Mage, had left it up to the Huntsman to decide which of the five ducs attending the Cerchicavan conference would not be returning home. And where to accomplish the deed. Any leader murdered in any foreign state would disrupt Giovanni de Marco's carefully crafted alliance, but now, thanks to Coll Svedali, there was only one possible city and one possible target. As Drey took aim at Johanni Gagio's barrel chest, he stroked the crossbow along the line of white magic on his cheek, sending a mental salute in the direction of his fellow foundling. One day, his master's influence would extend all the way to the largest and most powerful city-state on the Ardechi. On that day, Coll would learn just how absurd his threat had been; as absurd as his so-called protection of Giovanni de Marco, but for now, the Huntsman had other prey and Cerchicava's duc and his self-appointed guardian were safe enough.

But only for now.

As the duc of Riamo crossed in front of his sights, Drey pulled the trigger.

THE SILVER KNIFE

by Michael A. Stackpole

Michael A. Stackpole is an award-winning author, game and computer game designer, and poet whose first novel, *Warrior: En Garde* was published in 1988. Since then, he has written thirty-six other novels, including eight *New York Times* bestselling novels in the *Star Wars*® line, of which *X-wing: Rogue Squadron* and *I, Jedi* are the best known. Mike lives in Arizona and in his spare time spends early mornings at Starbucks, collects toy soldiers and old radio shows, plays indoor soccer, rides his bike, and listens to Irish music in the finer pubs in the Phoenix area. His Web site is www.stormwolf.com.

"FOR THE LOVE OF God, Watson, use the knife. Use the knife, else I will die!"

The lean young man hung by one hand in the doorway of my Montague Place practice, washed in silver by the full moon's light. His right hand gripped the lintel, his left arm hugged his chest tightly. The left side of his torso seemed coated in tar, but there was no mistaking the scent of blood.

Nor could I miss the hiss of air escaping his lung.

I might have stood there forever, in shock at his appearance, in shock at his knowing of the knife, but he collapsed into my arms and bore both of us to the foyer floor. I struggled beneath him, furious that my strength had so faded in the twilight of my life. I shoved him off me, not roughly, but hardly gently. I rolled him onto his back and felt at his neck for a pulse; both fearing and hoping, dearly hoping, he lay dead.

His pulse came strong, and the call of my profession determined how I would act. I quickly closed the door against the London night and its cold, licking tendrils of fog. Stooping, I took him unceremoniously by the ankles and dragged his naked body to my surgery. I would clean the blood later, though the Persian carpet in the hallway would never again be quite the same. Once I had him in the tiled surgery, I made use of the block and tackle arranged to deal with my heavier patients and got him into the table.

Quickly, automatically, as no true conscious thought was possible, I cleaned the area of the wound. Pink bubbles frothed with each labored breath, so I clapped a sponge over the hole and lifted him enough to see if there was an exit wound. I found none, which gave me no choice of action.

I do not know why I did not just reach for the tray of instruments I leave prepared for emergencies. Instead I left him on the table and went to the locked cabinet in corner. I opened it, then opened the false panel. I withdrew the leather satchel, and from it took the linen package. I untied the cord binding it, then unrolled it, revealing the knife.

The silver knife, its edge as sharp now as it had been a generation ago. I needed not test it and resisted the urge to press my thumb to it. That knife, the thirsty knife, always drank and would drink again this night.

I turned back to my patient and was reminded he knew of the knife. How much he knew did not matter, that he knew of it at all meant he could ruin me. He could destroy my life, my reputation, shattering my family. With this knife I could open his throat and take him to pieces. I could pack him up and haul him away, while my neighbors—kindly people, feeling indebted to me for various services—would console me on the loss of another patient.

And I would smile and say, as I always did, "It is in the hands of God."

For the love of God, Watson, use the knife. His words

rang in my ears again. Yes, perhaps this, too, was of God's doing. Curiously feeling the touch of a God I had rejected after what the Great War had done to flesh and bone, I bent to my work. It had been a very long time since I had plied my trade on human flesh, and that of another sex.

I did the work, the bloody work, and did it well. It was ironic—perhaps one of God's jokes—that he had come to me and that I used the silver knife to save him. Fitting even.

For resting next to his heart I found a silver bullet.

My young friend remained comatose for three days, but did not develop a fever. Nor did the wound suppurate, which was a great comfort to me. I was able to transfuse saline into him to prevent dehydration, but there was little else I could do. He truly was in God's hands.

There were things I was able to learn about him. The bullet wound on his chest had two companions, one on his right flank and another through his left thigh. They looked old and given that I imagined him to be David's age—a quarter century, no more—I assumed he'd taken those wounds in France. There were others—several knife scars, and the memorable track of scourging barbed wire. Of the same vintage were bite marks left by dogs—being a doctor of veterinary medicine makes me something of an expert in them. Most were normal—Alsatians I guess—though one had been of prodigious size and had sunk his teeth deep into my patient's right shoulder.

It occurred to me, on the second day, that I had stayed my hand with the knife because he did remind me of David. In fact, he proved to be David's size, so I was able to clothe him in things David would never again use and I had never brought myself to discard. They were clearly of pre-War vintage, but in 1923 they still served. Many people still wore such, as if thus clad they could pretend the War had not happened and their sons still lived.

On the third day, he opened his eyes—brilliant green eyes—and regarded me as I sat there in a chair, slowly letting the silver knife spin between my hands. He opened his mouth to speak, then took water from the tumbler on the side table. He sipped slowly, then licked a crystalline drop from his lower lip.

"Thank you." He nodded at the knife. "Just as it was imagined."

I felt my heart beat faster, but no anger rose in me. "I won't harm you."

"Nor shall I harm you, Doctor." His words came slowly, barely more than whispered, but I could not deny their sincerity. "I am no threat to you."

"But you know about the knife."

"I know many things, Doctor." He winced as he took a deep breath. "Many of them are more important than telling the world you were the Whitechapel murderer."

Those words, spoken matter-of-factly, puckered my flesh. For so many years I had feared hearing them spoken in accusation. Someone surely had to have known, and I had dreaded the day I would be exposed. Then, somehow, when I married, when we raised our children, when my wife died, I had let my role in the horrors of 1888 fade. If I thought of it at all, I thought that after so much time, no one would believe kindly Dr. Jack Watson, friend to animals, could have been the whore-butcher.

And yet, in the back of my mind, I knew that were I accused, the only defense I could have offered would have confirmed a diagnosis of insanity. Perhaps I *was* insane, for the knife was the thing to link me to that time and those events. Had I discarded it, I would have been safe.

My patient regarded me closely, his eyes sharp and intelligent. He sipped more water. "You have already deduced things about me. You know I am a Yank. You have guessed I fought in France. I was captured by the Huns and imprisoned in Villingen. Along with others, I attempted an escape. I was recaptured."

"They used dogs on you."

He nodded. "After the Armistice I came to England." Here his voice faltered for a moment. "I had been diagnosed with shell shock and invalided. A distant cousin heard of my affliction and took me into his Sussex home. He managed to help me heal."

"That explains many things, sir, but not how you happen to be here and so sorely wounded." I frowned. "I should have gone for the police, but . . ."

"You could not because I knew of the knife." Again, a nod, solemn and thoughtful. "That's not the reason I came to you. It is fortunate you did not. That could have brought danger here. It would also mean I am wholly compromised."

It struck me as terribly odd how this young man, wounded almost unto death, could wake in the presence of Jack the Ripper and not be concerned with his immediate peril. He seemed to be looking past it toward something else, with unshakable confidence that I would not murder him to protect myself.

As unlikely as I found that, I also found it intriguing and even seductive. Clearly, in his mind, a greater evil than I existed in the world. I knew there were such, I had seen them, and the Great War had been a concentration of same. I had supposed, had hoped, that all of them had somehow died in that conflagration.

"Doctor, I must ask you to trust me." He threw back the covers and levered himself into a sitting position. "Once again, there are horrors afoot in London. They must be stopped."

I stood quickly, the knife in my right hand. We both glanced at it, then I set it on the side table and took him by the shoulders to steady him. "I shall choose to believe you, and help if I can, but you are in no shape to move right now."

"Which is exactly why I must." He reached up with his right hand and took my shoulder, gripping it far more strongly than I could have imagined possible. "They'll think I'm dead, which means they will be far more open and bold in their actions. Hubris will be their undoing."

"They? Who are they?" I helped him to his feet. "For that matter, sir, who are *you!*"

"My name is Holmes. Farrell Holmes." His eyes tightened. "And those arrayed against us are servants of evil incarnate."

* * *

Lean though he was, Farrell Holmes ate with wolfish delight, devouring everything I put in front of him. He showed a marked preference for meat, which hardly surprised me since his body needed to rebuild itself. He eschewed tea, apologizing for never having acquired the taste for it, and beseeched me to find some coffee. As I had none, I had to venture out and he promised me that I would be reimbursed for all expenses I incurred on his behalf.

I reluctantly quitted my house, but not before returning to the cabinet and its false panel. I withdrew from it the shoulder sheath I had fashioned for my silver knife. The blade hung beneath my left armpit, the hilt at my hip, ready to be drawn and used in an instant. Curiously, feeling its weight once again brushing against my ribs gave me a sense of strength I'd not known in many years—certainly not since the death of my beloved Kathleen.

On my errand I saw a number of acquaintances who asked after me. I reported that all was well, and that I had a guest from America. I told them he had known David during the war and had come for a visit. I wasn't certain how long he would stay, but it was quite pleasant, and they wished me all the joy of my guest.

I obtained the coffee and returned home feeling as good as I had in a long time. That feeling fled when I entered the house and glanced into the parlor. I caught a flash of a tall man with dark hair in David's brown worsted suit and, just for a moment, I, too, succumbed to the illusion that the war had not taken place.

Then Holmes turned and his jade gaze returned me to reality. I set my package down, giving me a moment to recover myself, then crossed to him. "Really, Holmes, you shouldn't be up. It's much too early."

He reached out and braced me with hands on both shoulders. Though it could not be possible, he was stronger than he had been just hours before when I had helped him to the dining room. While I had been gone, he'd traveled up to the first floor, washed, shaved, and dressed himself in David's clothes, and then returned to the parlor. That should have left him exhausted, but I had little doubt he could repeat that trip with me tossed over his shoulder.

"There are a few things to which I must attend, Doctor, but I shall return here by midafternoon."

"I have your coffee."

"I can smell it, thank you." He gave me a smile that was equal parts sincere gratitude and deviltry, pleasing me and exciting me at the same time. "There will be no trouble until the evening, I can warrant that. Since they think I'm dead, we have an advantage."

I nodded. "I've told people you are David's friend from the war."

"I thank you for the loan of his clothes. He won't mind?"

I shook my head, unable to say anything for a moment. "He has no more use for them."

"I'm sorry for your loss." He gripped my shoulders again, firmly. "I'll return as quickly as I can."

"And if there is trouble, you will send word."

"Of course, Doctor Watson, of course."

He did return in the afternoon, a bit later than teatime. I had worried, and had taken the ringing of my bell to be his return twice before he actually made it. The first had been a telegram delivery. The second had been a servant who handed me a sealed ivory envelope. No address had been put on it, but the letters FH had been inscribed in a great and flowing hand. I accepted it as silently as it had been offered, then returned to my kitchen to puzzle out the correct formula for coffee.

My labors produced dubious results, but Holmes proclaimed them quite satisfactory. I gave him the messages whilst I brewed myself some tea from a small store of Darjeeling, for which I had acquired a taste long ago in Nepal. He read the telegram quickly, grunted, and tossed it into the fire.

As he did so I noticed the one thing that had changed about him. On his right hand he wore a ring of gold set with a massive moonstone. "You ventured out to buy a ring?"

"Not buy, recover." He smiled. "I have rooms elsewhere in the city and they were not being watched. This is good for us. I ventured in to recover my ring, watch, and wallet."

He produced the latter and drew out a ten-pound note. "This on my account, Doctor. I shall pay whatever else you deem I owe."

I frowned and waved away the money. "You owe me nothing for what I have done."

"A life for a life, Doctor?"

"You could think of it that way."

"But I don't." He gave me an open smile which Americans produce with maddening ease. "I told you, I am no threat to you, so I still owe you."

"Then repay me by telling me what is going on."

"I will, Doctor, but not quite yet." He opened the ivory envelope and his smile grew wider. "I think you will learn much soon, however."

"How soon?"

"After dinner." He brandished the card as if it were the armistice agreement. "Get dressed, Doctor. Tonight we dine at the Diogenes Club."

I had heard, of course, of the Diogenes Club. It had been long described as a club for those men who were singularly unsuited to the sociable company of their peers. It had once been suggested that Saucy Jack might even be a member, as no one there would take notice of him. By agreement, not a word was spoken in the place save in the Strangers' Room.

Holmes confirmed its peculiar rule still held, and I expected we would be conducted straight there. Instead, we were taken directly to the dining room and led to a table dominated by a man so corpulent that I suspected the elderly man would have weighed more than the steer from which the steak he was devouring had come. In fact, I would have dismissed him at a glance save for his restless gray eyes which took in every detail of his surroundings and companions even while his hands, utensils, and mouth conspired to make his meal vanish.

Once we had been seated, our meals came without our ever having consulted a menu. I had been treated to a beef wellington, which I greatly favored but had not enjoyed since Kathleen's death. Holmes was presented with a steak that, I presumed, had been the twin to the one our host had consumed. He made short work of it, taking his meal at great bites, and likewise took keen notice of his surroundings.

Since this seemed to be the game, I played as well. I noticed little out of the ordinary. The men, whether dining alone or in groups, remained silent by rule; but I sensed they would have done so out of preference. This was not unusual among men of an age in England, who were mourning companions or scions. It struck me that Jack the Ripper might well have been at home here, had it not been for my family saving me from that fate.

If there were anything unusual there, it would have been a pair of men, each dining alone, whom I took to be foreigners. Each had the look of the continent about him. The younger man I decided was German because of the Hidelburg scar over his left cheekbone. The eye-socket above it was covered by a patch, and I assumed he'd lost the eye in the war. The other man had a familiar appearance, and I was certain I'd seen images of him in the *Times.*

An end came to our meal and our host led us to the Strangers' Room. He moved slowly, and I suspected he suffered from a touch of gout. He settled himself into a chair which may have been specifically built to hold his bulk, then gestured for the two of us to draw other chairs up. He patted Holmes on the arm, then turned and gave me a mannerly nod.

"I am pleased you could join us, Doctor. I would have called upon you at home, but I have never had energy, and have less these days. I have had a wire from my brother vouching for you, and Farrell has similarly sung your praises."

I blinked with surprise. "Your brother?"

"Do forgive me, I should have known my colonial cousin would kept you in the dark. I am Mycroft Holmes. You have likely heard of my brother."

I wanted to laugh, for his brother had been the man whose hand I had most expected to fall on my shoulder and call for my surrender. "I am aware of him, yes, sir."

"We both appreciate your aid to young Farrell." He drew a card from his waistcoat pocket and presented it to me. "If I may ever be of service."

"Most kind, sir. Thank you."

Mycroft then looked past Farrell and nodded to the elder of the Europeans. "You saw them in the dining room, of course."

Farrell closed his eyes. "The younger one is the man who shot me."

The elder Holmes pushed his lips out and steepled his fingers. "Count Joachim von Wittenstein, a minor noble from a poor holding. His only accomplishment of public note is having represented Germany in Stockholm in 1912 on the Military Pentathalon team. Your Patton beat him so badly at fencing that their entire team finished out of the medals. You already know he is a very dangerous man."

Farrell winced and rubbed a hand over his left breast. "I do. The other man is Grand Duke Cyril, heir to the Romanov dynasty?"

"Quite. They seem to be concluding their business. Cyril has just given the Count a cipher that will allow him to obtain ten thousand pounds sterling from a broker in Paris."

"Then the exchange will be tonight?"

Mycroft glanced toward the club's bow window and the fog drifting in to mute the streetlights. "The perfect night for it. No one can see but a dozen feet. A night for thieves and scoundrels."

Farrell smiled wolfishly. "I know what needs to be done. If you will excuse me."

My companion stood and a remarkable change came over him. He had previously comported himself as a gentleman, but his gait became loose. His shoulders shifted and I might have thought him intoxicated save for the swagger with which he moved. He bore straight in at the German, and barked at him with an accent I associated with the American South.

"That's you, ain't it? You're Wittenstein."

The German's dark eyes became slits as he turned to face Holmes. "Do I know you, sir?"

"No, sir, you do not, but I know you. You got

whipped by George Patton in the Olympics. Then you bribed a judge to say Colonel Patton missed a target, when his bullet just went through a hole he'd shot in it before. Your kind disgusts me, sir. Excepting your treachery, he'd have won the gold."

Von Wittenstein's face tightened. "Would you demand satisfaction of me, sir?"

Holmes moved in, looking down at the German, their chests an inch apart. "Hell and damnation, I shot enough of you Huns in the war. You couldn't give me satisfaction. You'd run off just like Kaiser Willie did. Just wanted you to know some of us never forget."

"And you, sir, are a fool. I have no time for the likes of you, and it is your good fortune that this is so." The German turned on his heel, but looked back over his right shoulder. "Perhaps we shall meet again, my friend, and you will learn what a serious mistake you have made."

Farrell reached up and tapped his own nose with his index finger. "One of us will."

Through the window I saw the German vanish into the fog, moving away hurriedly. I looked up at Farrell. "Was that wise? We are meant to follow him, are we not, and now he is gone."

"Don't worry. We'll find him." He nodded to our host. "I'll send word."

"You'll be careful."

"More so than the other night." He laughed lightly, then turned to me. "Come on, Doctor Watson, we have work to do."

Even on the nights I had prowled Whitechapel, the fog had not seemed so thick. It smothered us in a gray blanket the moment we left the club. Though I had seen the count run off, once outside I could not even hazard a guess where he had gone. I strained my eyes and ears, but it was no use.

"This way, Doctor, quickly." Holmes headed off down the street, moving briskly, but I managed to keep pace with him.

"How do you know where we're going?"

"Trust me, I do." He grinned at me almost boyishly,

and again I saw a flash of David's face. It made me feel young and the rising excitement of adventure began to burn in my veins.

He raised an eyebrow. "You do have the knife, yes?"

I nodded. It rested against my ribs.

"Good. You might want to draw it." Farrell stopped suddenly and threw off the heavy pea coat he'd worn. With a flick of his wrist, he'd wrapped his left arm from fist to elbow just in time to ward off a blow from a figure hurtling forward out of the mist. The man attacking him brought a cudgel down with a muffled thud, but did no serious damage because of Holmes' adept parry.

Then two things happened that, had I not once been exposed to horrors beyond the ken of normal men, surely would have shattered my psyche. Farrell snarled, his lips peeled back from strong white teeth; his snarl nothing a human throat could produce, only a creature that had been extinct in these isles for over a century. His right fist flashed forward so quickly it would have been blurred on a clear night. He struck his foe a fearsome blow to the sternum. Bones and cartilage snapped as his hand burst into his attacker's chest, then ripped free again clutching a shriveled and dry organ that could only be the thing's heart.

"Your knife, Doctor," he growled at me, "Use it."

Three more forms emerged from the fog and they were well beyond the ordinary. Black of skin, not by heredity, but by dint of putrefaction, hollow of eye because they had none, these things shambled forward in eerie silence. Their leader, whom Farrell had already dispatched, had been more recently resurrected than his fellows, all of whom looked as if they'd lain in a Thames estuary for years. Two of them descended on Farrell, burying him in an avalanche of dead flesh, while the third—a tiny and vicious Lascar by the look of him—reached for me with clawed fingers.

Despite the celebrated evidence of my work with the knife in the past, I am not a combatant. In my youth, in Nepal, a kindly gunnery sergeant had drilled me in the finer points of close-in knife work, but it had been a lark for both of us. Even so, I recalled clearly his admonition that an unarmed man facing a knifeman would not emerge from the fight unscathed, and I proceeded to prove his dictum correct.

The silver knife flashed and sliced through dead flesh with the ease of a spoon serving a pudding. My first cut laid open the Lascar's forearm, and would have made a living foe quail and shriek. I quite would have been victorious with that first cut, but the dead know no pain and are driven by a hatred of the living. The Lascar came for me again in his clumsy way, attempting to grapple and claw me to pieces.

Though I may have one foot in the grave, I am faster than one who has both there. I ducked beneath a swipe, then lunged, driving the silver blade deep into its chest. My thrust found its mark, piercing the thing's heart. I felt a tingle along the blade—though not as strong as I'd felt years ago—then the thing slackened and collapsed as if all its bones had turned to mush.

Beyond it, Farrell crouched, hunched over, surrounded by a trio of rapidly decomposing corpses. He glanced at me over his shoulder, his once-green eyes now golden and burning. His face had become darker, eye-sockets a bit deeper, but his shoulder hid the rest of his face.

"Are you unhurt, Doctor?"

"I will feel the exertion tomorrow, but I am otherwise sound." He nodded and I noticed a sharpness to his ear. "You knew to go for the heart. It's that, or the brain."

"I've read the Van Helsing monograph on the subject, Holmes." I moved toward him, the knife in my right hand.

Farrell shied. "Forgive me, Doctor, but I have an aversion to silver. An allergy, if you will."

"Of course." I nodded toward the bodies. The count set them on us?"

"On whoever was following him. He suspected the Russians of it, I'm sure."

"But how does he control the undead?"

Farrell frowned. "He didn't lose his eye in the war, but after it. Germany's disgrace has led to a revival of some of the elder religions. Like Odin, von Wittenstein traded his eye for arcane knowledge dark and foul."

My stomach tightened. "Knowledge better forgotten."

"We'll have to convince him of that." He rose from

his crouch, raised his face for a moment, then nodded. "Come, Doctor, we must hurry."

The growl had left his voice and he moved with haste. I followed as quickly as I could, and I do not think he slackened his speed much at all. We sped through the fog. He paused a couple of times at intersections, but made changes of course without true hesitation. Finally, we entered an alley where, twelve feet in, lay stairs to some basement apartment.

Holmes stopped me. "I don't know what we'll find there, Doctor. I'll go in first. If you see the girl, free her and get her out of here. That's vital."

"Who are we seeking?"

He frowned, his eyes green again. "Anastasia, Tsarina of Russia. She survived the slaughter of her family and made her way west. The count befriended her, then betrayed her after initiating contacts with the Grand Duke's people. The count will sell her to them."

"Because Germany needs the money to pay reparations."

"So the Russians think. But the count will not turn her over because he can also sell her back to the Bolsheviks." He smiled slowly. "Are you ready, Doctor, to save a piece of the world?"

"Lead on, Holmes."

Holmes descended the steps, which sent him into shadows. This meant I really had no chance to see him change. I thought his diminution came from crouching, but that could not account for the tearing of his jacket's spine seam. He reared back and kicked the stout wooden door over the handle. The jamb splintered as the dead bolt drove back through it, then the jaundiced glow of gaslight illuminated him and what he had become.

A thick black pelt rose through the split seam, matching the tufts on his sharpened ears. His face changed, a muzzle now jutting forward, full of sharpened white teeth. Muscles bunched and bulged, further ripping David's jacket and shirt—the tie he'd worn snapped as the shirt's collar popped loose. A snarl rose from his throat, then he launched himself into the room from whence came a woman's panicked scream.

My cloak fluttering, I descended and entered the chamber. Two more of the German's undead grappled with Farrell, but they spun away with the ruins of his clothes in their hand. With a backhanded slap, he crushed one's skull, then pounced on the other and ripped its chest open.

Von Wittenstein turned from where a slender girl had been bound in a tall, wooden chair. His right hand drew a pistol from a shoulder holster. He paused to aim, his expression painted with contempt. He leveled the weapon at Farrell.

"Farrell, he has a gun!"

My shouted warning would have come too late, save that my companion moved with supernatural reflexes. In an eyeblink he plucked the zombie's head off and flung it at the German. The skull smashed von Wittenstein square in the chest, spoiling his aim. Farrell snarled as the bullet whizzed past his shoulder and then, with a prodigious leap, he tackled his enemy and slapped the pistol from the German's hand.

I ran to the woman and slashed the bonds at her ankles. I turned the chair and began sawing through the thick rope at her wrists. I had to take more care there, for a careless cut would have laid her flesh open. She shielded me from view of the struggle, though it sounded fearsome. I worked as quickly as I could and parted the last strand as she cursed in Russian.

I stood and, for a heartbeat, froze. Holmes could be seen in all his lupine glory, fangs flashing, hands clawed, eyes golden suns burning in a darkly furred face. His ears had flattened back and his growl made my blood run cold. *Allergy to silver, yes, secondary to lunar-lupine influences.* I was in league with a werewolf and while I found that a curious comfort, I was afraid our association would be tragically short-lived.

Von Wittenstein, too, transformed. His body had doubled in mass and grown such that he had to stoop lest his horned head burst through the ceiling. His arms had lengthened and his body had taken on the terrible proportions of the newly discovered mountain gorilla. The resemblance ended there, however, for his flesh had the look and color of a crocodile's hide, and he sported a thick tail which clearly counterbalanced his hugely-muscled torso.

The German flicked a stubby-fingered paw and batted Holmes halfway across the room. The werewolf slammed into the wall and cracked plaster and lath. He rebounded into a crouch, shook his head, then roared a challenge.

I dashed forward, coming at the German from his blind side. The silver knife had proved deadly against zombie and vampire in the past—I suspected its brilliance might be a bane to all creatures touched by the dark arts. I had to take the chance I could plunge it into his flank and find his heart.

Farrell roared again and started forward as a distraction, but somehow the German detected my advance. His tail swept out, catching me over my right hip. I spun away to the left, my knife flying to the right, well beyond any hope of my recovering it. Von Wittenstein stepped toward me and raised a fist to where it knocked dust from the rafter. His blow would easily smash me through the floor.

Blurred black fur and white fang flew through the air and landed on the demon's broad back. Farrell plunged his fangs into the thing's neck. Black blood pulsed from the wound. The German howled in pain, then reared up, smashing Holmes into the ceiling. Boards above cracked and slender beams of light poured down, growing as the demon pounded him again and again against the ceiling.

Farrell took a terrible beating, but clung there fiercely. His fangs opened great gashes. Blood that flew burned as it splattered my flesh. I hoped, I even prayed, that the demon would grow faint with loss of blood, but another blow brought blood, red blood, from Farrell's nostrils and I knew that our valiant battle would soon end.

Then something silver flashed through the air. It sank to the hilt in the demon's pale ivory breast. The staghorn hilt quivered, then the demon crashed to his knees and started to fall forward. Its bulk would have crushed me flat, but, as it fell, it once again resumed von Wittenstein's form. He crashed face-first between my feet, his blood slowly pooling around him.

I regained my feet, casting a glance at Anastasia. She seemed quite pleased with the results of her throw. She gave me a nod, then we both advanced and wrestled Farrell from the German's back. He'd already begun a return to his normal form and the angular cant of broken ribs began to soften beneath his skin.

He glanced up at me, half-growling. "They will be waiting for her outside, Doctor. Take her to safety."

"I can't leave you here."

"I will be fine. I have a remarkable constitution." He pointed at the German. "Don't forget your knife."

I led the girl from the cellar. Outside I found Farrell's coat and wrapped her in it. Not really knowing where I should be going, I retraced our steps toward the Diogenes Club. Halfway there, the Grand Duke appeared with retainers and led Anastasia away, but not before profound thanks had been expressed.

I waited a while in the fog to see if Farrell would find me, but he did not. I went back to Montague Place, returned the silver knife to its hiding place, and put myself to bed. At every little noise I woke, thinking it might be Farrell returning, but he remained away. In fact, I did not see him for a week.

An invitation came for me to dine again at the Diogenes Club. I arrived alone and was brought to the Strangers' Room, where Mycroft and Farrell were awaiting me. Warm greetings passed, then we settled down with Mycroft looking quite pleased.

"Of your part in this affair, Doctor, you can say nothing; but you should know that the highest people in our government are pleased with what you did. You have their thanks." The elder gentleman nodded solemnly. "Likewise, you have the thanks of Russian nobility in exile."

"Really?" I smiled. "I have given it much thought, and I wonder why they would be grateful. She was an imposter."

Mycroft glanced at Farrell, but he shook his head. "I said nothing."

I smiled. "But you knew. Your sense of smell is quite keen. Part of your affliction. This is why you braced the German here, to catch his scent. That's how we followed him through the fog."

The American nodded. "*Touché*, Doctor. In Sussex,

there was a glove found in Whitechapel. It had your scent."

"Doctor, you do not have Farrell's unique talent." Mycroft regarded me with those restless gray eyes. "How did you know?"

"Her English." I settled my hands in my lap. "When she thanked me, her English was broken, but the Romanovs are related to our own royal house. All of them had English tutors and corresponded among themselves in English, and I doubt she was schooled in the art of knife throwing. That girl, though of the right age and bearing, is not Anastasia."

"Quite likely not, but she *is* the hope of the exile community." Mycroft steepled his fingers. "She is, my brother believes, the daughter of a Polish circus knife thrower and his Russian wife. The girl decided to assume Anastasia's identity. She's not the first and won't be the last."

"The Russians will use a fraud to aid them?"

"Perhaps, Doctor, we shall see." The elder Holmes smiled ironically. "Then again, we know that having one's true nature hidden can be a great benefit."

A chill ran down my spine, and I glanced at my hands lying dead in my lap. "A very astute observation, Mr. Holmes."

"The world has changed, Doctor Watson. Despite the best efforts of reactionary forces, there is no turning back." Mycroft's eyes half-lidded. "There is, however, providing direction and momentum to the future's course. Those who are able to do so, must do so, lest the world descend into the darkness of man's basest nature."

I nodded slowly. "A nightmare war fought in the shadows."

"Indeed." Mycroft looked at his American cousin and then me. "A war demanding great courage, keen wit and, yes, Doctor Watson, the sharp edge of a silver knife."

THE END OF SPRING

by Russell Davis

Russell Davis has published numerous short stories and more than a half dozen novels in a variety of genres under several different names. Some of his most recent short fiction has appeared in *Gateways*; *Maiden, Matron, Crone*; and *You Bet Your Planet*. He lives in southern Arizona with his family.

—for Monica, because this is the last one

THE MAN SITTING IN his pickup truck is staring at the ridgeline and thinking about patterns.

He knows, for example, that rain in the high desert is orange curtains draped over mountain silhouettes and unexpected rivers. That the rains come in summer, July and August, when the mesquite is in full bloom and the ocotillo bushes spread their arms wide to catch every drop of moisture in the dry air. They call it the monsoon season, perhaps because the storms come up from the south, on the jet stream from Mexico, and pass over the mountains with a lightning ferocity. The winds get trapped in the valleys, swirling up dust devils, and then the rains break over the land, and life is renewed.

This pattern is usually quite predictable, if not as reliable as the laws of physics. From the colors of the sky to the scents of the plants to the way the winds move across the land like a series of invisible ocean waves, the pattern has been the same for so many years that the man has memorized it. It has become a part of him, he has internalized the land like the legendary King Arthur. He and the land are one.

The man sitting in his pickup truck is staring at the ridgeline and thinking about patterns, and how the patterns of his life, which have, until recently, been as predictable as the weather, are suddenly changing. He is thinking about the way the sky is growing pregnant with thunderheads and how this year, the weather pattern is different.

The monsoon season is early. Very early, as it is just now the middle of April. Everything is changed. The colors, the scents, the wind, each of them is new in a way he has never before experienced. He and the land are unquiet together.

The sky is like ash-coated iron, the mountains stark and gray and foreboding. As though they are as uncomfortable with the change as he is. The clouds shape themselves in bizarre wisps that look like the outstretched wings of demons. The scents are not of blooming mesquite and the sharp tang of ocotillo, but flat, sulfurous, and rusty. And the wind doesn't swirl or wave, but is a ferocious, howling beast that tears at man and sky and ground alike. Even the dust devils lie flat in this wind. His beloved desert has become the very picture of how he imagines the landscapes of hell itself.

The man sitting in his pickup truck is staring at the ridgeline and thinking about patterns, and about Julia. His wife is Julia and at this precise moment she is standing in the kitchen and trying to make dinner while wrangling the children. She is at home and doesn't know he is here. That his pattern has brought him to this place as surely as the jet stream will bring storms.

Thunder rumbles overhead and the clouds boil. It is going to be a crackerjack of a storm and Julia is at home. Making dinner. Maybe meatloaf or stroganoff or spaghetti. He can see her in his mind and his memory as clearly as he can see the storm coming over the mountains.

Julia is probably waiting for him.

The man in his pickup truck is waiting, too. He is

waiting for the moment in the pattern when he is ready to die. He has never been so afraid in his life. He is afraid for her future, afraid for her to be without him. He doesn't want her to leave him, doesn't want her to know that all her complaints over the last few years have been heard and he was paralyzed by fear. Thinking about her, about what she has said, is very hard. It is like someone has scooped out his insides and replaced his organs with strange coals that burn hot and cold and yet leave him feeling hollow and broken.

She says she wants to leave him, that she doesn't love him anymore. She says that it's too late.

The man has tried to tell her that he hears her, that he never meant to hurt her, that he is more sorry than words allow him to express. Images of her life without him dominate his thoughts, plans to get her to change her mind, to know that he loves her and—more than anything in the world—he wants her. He wants to make her feel *something* for him, because she says she is dead inside and that is the worst indictment of all. He has caused her to emotionally wall herself away from the world. He is a writer, a poet of sorts, and knows that this would have broken him.

It is said that people change slowly, if at all. The man doesn't believe this anymore. Her words awakened him from the dreamlike state of the last few years of his life in a single instant. He knows there are no excuses that will appease her, no pleas she will hear. He was accused, tried, convicted, and sentenced, and he didn't even know that court was in session.

The man sitting in his pickup truck is staring at the ridgeline and thinking about patterns, and how some patterns close in on themselves. They come full circle, returning to their place of origin and consuming themselves like snakes swallowing their own outstretched tails. His pattern has been here before, long ago, and that was when he met Julia and she saved him. He thought she had changed his pattern forever, but now he knew that the pattern had not been changed, only subtly shifted, and he had returned to the place he began.

The wind picks up speed and the first stinging pellets

of rain ping off the hood. The man turns up the heater and feels the warm air wash over his face. Next to him, on the seat, is the gun he will use. Beside it, a bottle of sour mash and a package of cigarettes—habits that have hounded him throughout his pattern.

He looks up at the ridgeline, staring, thinking, and waiting.

The man sitting in his pickup truck pulls a drag from his cigarette and watches the rain.

He knows that this current deluge is just the beginning. The real storm won't begin for another few minutes, maybe longer. Through the windshield, the sky has turned an odd green color and when the lightning flickers, clouds casts shadows like horned demons on the mountains. Behind them, the moon is full and the stars are bright, but here in this valley, there is only the growing dark and the storm and his thoughts. He opens the bottle of sour mash and takes a drink—it burns on the way down, but he doesn't mind. It is good to burn.

He thinks for a time about this and how the first girl he fell in love with had red hair like cigarette embers burning in the dark. He'd always had a strange weakness for redheads, but his soul mate had hair like a Greek princess. It was full and ran down her back in curls and whorls, black like a raven's wing in the rain. Her eyes weren't green or blue, but the shadowed brown of a forest in autumn. In fact, he'd always thought of her in association with that time of year, autumn secrets, and was glad that it was the end of spring. It was better somehow.

The man sitting in his pickup truck pulls a drag from his cigarette and watches the rain, and wonders if she'll know. Once, they had been as connected as identical twins, feeling each other's hurts and pleasures and passions with ease. He thinks the connection is still there, shorted out by time and mistakes and circumstances, but she doesn't believe that's true. If she is as closed off as she says, she won't know, she won't feel—and that will be good. He doesn't want to hurt her any more than he already has, but this ending is necessary. He cannot trust himself to live without her—she has been his ballast for too long, and without her, without her heart, he will founder and eventually die anyway. He doesn't want to take anyone else with him, doesn't want his children to see that, to see what he was before she came into his life.

When they'd met, the man was almost gone. He was working hard at drinking himself to an early grave, and he didn't care about that or about anything else. He cared about booze and cigarettes and food once in a while, but that was it. Julia had taught him to care about more than that, how each day was precious, how life could feel when he was happy. She had given him reasons to live, and more reasons with their children, and still more reasons with her love, and somehow, his pattern had caused him to throw it all away. The man had trouble understanding all this, it was like trying to understand the motivations of storms, but the pattern itself was clear enough.

Julia said she was leaving him, that she didn't love him anymore, that she didn't need him anymore. It didn't seem fair because he still needed her, still loved her, and would never have left her in a thousand lifetimes. He had always felt that way, even when he expressed doubt to her, there had been no real doubt in his heart or his mind. His faith in her and in them and in their family had wavered, but never broken.

The writer in him knew that he'd been running on automatic pilot for the last few years, that the words came out but didn't have any heart. His heart had been silent, and all he'd wanted in the world was to scream loud enough to be heard. But no scream could do it, no fight, no nothing—and if he couldn't be heard, then by damn he'd try to be right. And his stubbornness, his willingness to cling to this bit of stupidity had cost him the woman he loved, his children, and the last dregs of passion left in him for anything at all. He was back to sour mash and cigarettes and staring.

The man sitting in his pickup truck pulls a drag from his cigarette and watches the rain, and sees that the storm is coming in harder now. He wonders if Julia will feel it when he dies, but more than anything else, he wonders if she will miss him at all. If the damage is so great that his death will be a relief to her, a kind of freedom from him. They had married young.

He remembers her, shy and gentle and fragile like a tiny bird. And his own amazement that for some inexplicable reason she cared about him. He remembers their first tentative attempts at lovemaking and how clumsy they were with each other. He remembers nights that didn't feel like they would ever end, and that would have been fine with both of them. He remembers her smile and her laugh and the way she would touch him on the arm to get his attention.

The man sitting in his pickup truck pulls a drag from his cigarette and watches the rain. He rolls down the window a crack and flicks the butt out into the weather. He imagines he can hear the hiss as the embers get wet. The man is afraid, more afraid than he's ever been in his life, and he would give anything if she were with him right now. If she would hold his hand and tell him that it was all right, that she loved him and needed him and she believed he could do anything. The man wishes she were here to help him, but he is alone, and she is alone, and that's what she wanted.

The rain is coming down in sheets lit by lightning and the thunder booms over the valley. The man takes another swallow of the sour mash and stares into the storm.

The man sitting in his pickup truck is chain-smoking and drinking steadily and caressing the butt of the pistol when he sees the apparition in the clouds.

At first, he thinks what he sees is his imagination playing tricks on him. The boiling clouds, the thunder and the lightning, the massive storm pulling light in different directions, all causing him to see what isn't there. Then he realizes that the apparition is unmoved by the winds, does not flinch when lightning flashes. It has wings.

"What are you?" he whispers into the dark. He attempts to light another cigarette, and sees that his hands are shaking terribly. He fumbles it, tries again, and somehow manages to get it lit. He takes another swallow of sour mash. This thing is a vision from his worst fever dreams as a child: massive, winged, with a blurred face carved from old granite, and hair the color of the sea. A gigantic sword, the blade flaming, is clenched in its right fist, and a shield marked with a strange emblem is strapped to its left arm. It is staring at him.

"What are you?" he repeats, but his only answer is the howling winds.

The man sitting in his pickup truck is waiting for what happens next.

Strangely, the apparition does not frighten him. At least not badly. Perhaps it is because he came here to die anyway. And in the end, one death is about as good as another. Death is death. The instant these thoughts pass across his mind, he hears a voice.

It is, he knows, the voice of the apparition, though it does not speak aloud. The voice is in his mind. It says, "Death *is* death, and sin *is* sin, but some deaths, like sin, are worse than others." The voice is an odd mix of masculine and feminine, and it rolls through his mind, echoing back and forth as though he were standing in a box canyon.

The man shrugs. If this is all imaginary, he's only killing time until the pattern unfolds completely, the storm is just past, and he can pull the trigger. If not . . . he shrugs again. He has nothing left to lose. "What are you?" he asks again.

"I am an avatar," the voice replies in his mind. "I am the bringer of darkness, the storm warden, the harbinger of dawn and dusk. In one hand I carry death and fire; in the other, I carry protection and shelter. I am called by many names, have many faces, but I only serve one Master."

The man sitting in his pickup truck is waiting for what happens next. "Who do you serve?" he asks.

"I serve Him who created the heavens and the earth, who set the stars in their courses, and brought forth life from the nothingness. I serve Him who you call God."

The man hard swallows, once, and feels his Adam's

apple catch and then release. He finds his voice, but it is a harsh remnant of its former self. "God?" he says. "God. That's good. It's about time He showed up."

"Who are *you* to question the purposes or time of Heaven?"

The question slams into him with the force of a lead bowling ball, making him gasp for air. Just as suddenly the pressure relents. "I . . . I am nobody," the man says. "Without her, without our family, I am only part of who I once was, and not a very good part at that."

"Who are *you* to question the commands of Heaven? You are who God made you."

"I am who *she* made me."

The man sitting in his pickup truck is waiting for what happens next, when the apparition, or angel or avatar or imaginary being raises its sword and points to the sky above the mountains. A burst of flame shoots upward and the clouds part, revealing a blanket of cold stars and the universe beyond. "Watch," the voice commands.

Compelled, the man stares at the sky and watches as scenes from his life begin to play against the backdrop of heaven. It must be, he thinks, like dying.

The man sitting in his pickup truck cannot stop crying.

His daughter being born . . . his sons . . . his wedding day . . .

Making love to Julia and eating pizza in bed . . .

Mistakes small and large . . . words spoken harshly, choices made badly . . . a woman here . . . a forgotten touch there . . .

The man sitting in his pickup truck cannot stop crying, and he tries to turn his head away, but nothing can change the visions filling his sight.

Laughing with friends . . . hunting with his father . . .

Sharing a poem or a story with Julia in the middle of the night because he cannot wait . . .

Times he didn't share his poems or stories and should have . . .

Times he should have upheld her needs first and wouldn't . . .

The man sitting in his pickup truck cannot stop crying,

and all he wants to do is beg Julia's forgiveness, to touch her once more, to let her know that he understands.

Christmas wrapping paper all around her and the kids' joy . . .

Walking hand in hand in the desert and holding her smile in his heart . . .

Forgetting to tell her that she made him proud . . .

Forgetting to tell her that he loved her more than anything . . .

Forgetting to be the kind of man she needed and deserved . . .

The man sitting in his pickup truck cannot stop crying, and now that he sees and understands, now that he *knows*, it's probably too late. He'd give anything to take the time back, anything to kiss her and tell her that now that he's awake, now that he's not lost anymore, that he can do it right, they can do it right.

Remembering small touches or laughter in the dark of their bedroom . . .

Remembering his children's first words, first steps, so many firsts . . .

Remembering the way her eyes sparkled in candlelight . . .

Remembering her sense of humor, so off kilter that even she didn't know when she was making him laugh . . .

Her pain at his mistakes and her patience . . .

Her forgiveness so often granted and now withheld . . .

The man sitting in his pickup truck cannot stop crying, and his voice is barely a whisper. "I did this, didn't I? My mistakes . . . they've been like little deaths for her, and I could have stopped it, should have stopped it, but didn't. How could I have not seen it?"

The sword drops slowly and the storm reappears, though it is almost past now. The apparition is silent, allowing him to take in the depths of his errors, how he had wronged her, his family, God, and even himself.

The rain begins to taper off, and the man knows that it is very nearly time.

The man sitting in his pickup truck inhales, exhales, and dries his eyes on his sleeve.

"What do I do now?" he asks the angel. "What choices are left to me?"

"None," the angel says. "She is beyond you now. You made mistakes, yet God believes in forgiveness and in marriage and in family. Only God can turn her heart back to you."

"Will he?" the man asks. "Will God help us?"

The angel is silent for a long moment, then says, "God helps those who help themselves."

"What if she won't?" the man asks, hearing the sound of despair in his voice. "What if she won't turn her heart back to me?"

"Then you will know something that she, in her bitterness, has forgotten. In her anger at herself and you, in her despair, she has lost sight of God's will, and she is unwilling to bend. Her ears hear, but her heart is hard. She is walking now with the Darkness, and will not turn to face the Light, for she fears being convicted in her heart. God believes in choice, and will not force her."

"I don't deserve her," the man wails, "but I love her. I've seen it. I get it. I understand it all. Why can't she come back to me?"

"Choice," the angel says. "She now chooses to hurt herself, punishing herself for allowing your relationship to come to this pass. She has chosen a dark path for herself, yes, and for her family and you, too. God grieves for her and sends her signs, but she might not hear them, might not see them. She has been hurt greatly, and great hurt blinds us to the Truth."

The man sitting in his pickup truck inhales, exhales, and dries his eyes on his sleeve. "I'm sorry," the man says. "I'm so fucking sorry for everything."

"To be contrite, to know your sins, is to stand on the path to Heaven," the angel says.

"Now what do I do?" the man asks, staring at the cigarettes and the sour mash and the pistol. "What do I do?"

"Pray," the angel says, "then do what *you* choose, for that is also God's will."

And as suddenly as it had appeared, the angel was gone, and the last clouds of the storm were passing overhead.

* * *

The man sitting in his pickup truck is staring at the ridgeline and thinking about patterns.

He knows, for example, that the pattern of his life has led him to this place, this moment, and for the first time ever, he knows that God is real. He knows that God is watching and that He hears prayers. That God can and does work miracles, but only if they're asked for. He wonders if Julia has ever asked for a miracle about them, and thinking that God has not responded, has lost faith.

The man thinks maybe she has. The angel asked him about questioning God's purposes or time. A miracle has come to them, the man knows this, because he suddenly sees so much more than he ever did before, but he thinks maybe it's come too late for Julia and for them and their family. He prays this is not so, prays that she will let God into her heart and find a way to restore them both, but he is still mortal, and still afraid.

The man sitting in his pickup truck is staring at the ridgeline and thinking about patterns, and he picks up the bottle of sour mash and takes one last drink.

The sky is growing lighter in the east, and he watches the end of the pattern begin to unfold.

The man sitting in his pickup truck is staring at the ridgeline and thinking about patterns, and he takes one last drag off the cigarette and tosses it out the window.

The sun is rising now, slowly, and the storm is a fleeting bank of clouds on the horizon. In the distance, the birds have begun their morning songs. For the man, the world is both changed and unchanged. He knows what he wants, what he believes, what he feels so clearly for the first time in years, but what he doesn't know is if any of that matters to her wants, her beliefs and her feelings. Julia was a woman of deep feelings and beliefs, but perhaps in her hurt, she has forgotten them.

The man sitting in his pickup truck is staring at the ridgeline and thinking about patterns, and he picks up the pistol, opens the cylinder, and removes five of the six bullets inside.

A last burst of quiet thunder shudders in the sky, and for a moment, the birds stop singing. The air is still, like a held breath, and even the tiny flowers hidden in rock crevices seem to shrink a little. His world is forever changed by her words, her hurt and her leaving. His world is forever changed by the knowledge that he could have prevented this, and didn't. His world is forever changed by knowing that God has been watching all this time and he failed to yield, failed to kneel. But the birds still sing and the sun still rises. And he still loves her, wants her, cries for her with his whole convicted soul.

He spins the cylinder of the pistol, and clicks it shut.

The man sitting in his pickup truck is staring at the ridgeline and thinking about patterns, and he wonders about Julia. What she feels, what she thinks, what she would say or do differently if she'd seen the angel, too. If she were here right now, with him. If it would make a difference if somehow she could *feel* that he loves her and is sorry and was so caught up in himself that he failed and faltered, but that it's not too late for their mutual salvation.

The man sitting in his pickup truck is staring at the ridgeline and thinking about patterns, and as the sun makes its first, full appearance in the sky, he puts the pistol in his mouth.

He says a prayer to himself, wondering if God or Julia or both will hear him. He hopes so, because she is all he has ever really wanted or needed. Without her, he knows that he is *nothing* and that his words, like his heart, are now empty and hollow and meaningless.

He inhales, exhales, stares at the ridgeline and the chaos of the coming dawn at the end of spring.

The man sitting in his pickup truck is staring at the ridgeline and thinking about patterns, and he knows that his pattern has come full circle, that for better or for worse, it is time to find out if the pattern can ever be changed.

He pulls the trigger.

Author's Note: This story is the final installment of a set of four stories going all the way back to a book called *The UFO Files*. The first one (and the first pro story I ever sold) was "The End of Winter"; the next, "The End of Summer," which appeared in a book titled *Merlin;* the third, "The End of Autumn" was in a book titled *Texas*

Rangers, and now this one. While it was never planned in advance, each story has been in a different genre—SF, fantasy, and western, respectively—and it's nice to end it in a genre that's so new, no one is really even certain what it is yet. If you've read the others, thanks; if you haven't, don't worry about it too much, as they have nothing to do with each other. Probably. Okay, maybe. Well, they might, but I sure didn't plan it that way when I started. —RD

Julie E. Czerneda

Web Shifters

"A great adventure following an engaging character across a divertingly varied series of worlds."—*Locus*

Esen is a shapeshifter, one of the last of an ancient race. Only one Human knows her true nature—but those who suspect are determined to destroy her!

BEHOLDER'S EYE
0-88677-818-2
CHANGING VISION
0-88677-815-8
HIDDEN IN SIGHT
0-7564-0139-9

Also by Julie E. Czerneda:
IN THE COMPANY OF OTHERS
0-88677-999-7
"An exhilarating science fiction thriller"
—*Romantic Times*